IN THE RIFT

MARION ZIMMER BRADLEY

HOLLY LISLE

IN THE RIFT

This is a work of fiction. All the characters and events portrayed in this book are fictional, and any resemblance to real people or incidents is purely coincidental.

A Baen Books Original

Baen Publishing Enterprises
P.O. Box 1403
Riverdale, NY 10471

ISBN: 0-671-87870-0

Cover art by Clyde Caldwell

First printing, April 1998

Distributed by Simon & Schuster
1230 Avenue of the Americas
New York, NY 10020

Library of Congress Cataloging-in-Publication Data

      Bradley, Marion Zimmer.
         In the rift / by Marion Zimmer Bradley & Holly Lisle.
           p.   cm.
         "A Baen books original"—T.p. verso
         ISBN 0-671-87870-0
         I. Lisle, Holly. II. Title.
      PS3552.R228I48   1998   97-49668
      813'.54—dc21   CIP

Typeset by Windhaven Press, Auburn, NH
Printed in the United States of America

To Matt
who knows the price of happiness

Every dream achieved someday demands a reckoning,
just as every choice comes at a price. This is life:
that nothing worth having can ever come easily,
that nothing loved can last forever
without care, attention, and sacrifice.

*T*he last of the search parties had given up looking for her months earlier. When the American woman pedaled her bicycle out of a little-traveled mountain pass in the heart of the Italian Alps, her husband had already received the notice that she was missing and presumed dead, her home town had already mourned, her friends had already paid their last respects. She had lived through a month of days in her absence; the world she'd left behind and finally rejoined had, in that same time, lived through half a year.

She and her guide rode into the town of Bardonecchia, where they caused a sensation. The guide brought with him a mangled corpse which he had strapped to a makeshift travois attached to the frame of his bicycle. The woman carried in her pocket a book. Neither the corpse nor the book were what they appeared to be.

The corpse looked like the body of the woman's best friend, also reported missing, but it was in fact a magical construct created to give the woman on the bicycle an alibi, while her real best friend remained behind in Glenraven, serving as the new Watchmistress for that beleaguered magical realm.

The book appeared to be a common guidebook. The woman knew it had once been the key that permitted her and her friend to enter the realm of Glenraven, but she believed that its magical qualities had died when she left. She kept it with her only because it had sentimental value—it would serve, she thought, as a remembrance of her friend and of the adventure they had experienced in a world of magic and wonder. She knew she would never return to Glenraven and her best friend would never leave, but she knew also that this was the best and happiest outcome either of them could have imagined.

In the center of a brief storm of publicity—a storm that would have been longer had anyone suspected the truth—the woman returned to America, to the little town of Peters in southeastern North Carolina, where she resumed her life and her marriage, had a child, and was happy. She forgot about the book, but in that she had help from the book.

Had it actually lost its magical properties, the book would have ceased

1

to exist in any form. But it had not. It was changed, but it remained a powerful, complex artifact.

Further, it had a desperate mission, but the woman who had served it so well before would not serve again. The book needed to belong to someone else, someone it hadn't found yet.

It altered its appearance so that outwardly it became a copy of a techno-thriller written by an aging actor who had in the writing proven himself incompetent in two professions. Then the book sat on a shelf in the woman's house for nearly two years, until finally she put it into a large box of full of other books she didn't intend to read and took it to a used bookstore. There she traded it in, never suspecting what she had just done.

One

The dead horse lay across Kate Beacham's pinestraw path, hidden from the road out front by the mooncast shadows of the loblolly pines and the heavy overgrowth of the azaleas, rhododendrons, and camellias. The sharp, hard scent of impending frost and the hotmetal stink of blood clogged the air. Kate leaned against the trunk of a pine and clenched her fists, digging her nails into the palms of her hands, fighting back tears. Her breath plumed out in front of her, frozen by the cold night air, the plumes as ragged as her breathing.

Someone had cut letters from magazines and pasted them to a sheet of college-ruled notebook paper and had nailed the note to her horse's forehead. From where she was standing, she could read it clearly.

YOU'RE NEXT

Her tongue slid along the backs of her teeth, tasting blood, feeling the new wobbliness in the front incisors. Her fingers touched her right cheek, probing at fresh swelling over the bone and beneath the eye, feeling the stickiness of scrapes that were beginning to scab over, setting off sharp needles of pain to counterpoint the dull throbbing in her back and ribs and thighs.

She looked at her torn shirt, at the dirt and the blood, at the gaps where the buttons had come off in the fight. She looked down further to her bloodied, scraped right knee that glowed in the moonlight through the new hole in her jeans. Further, to her feet. She still wore one Nike Air cross-trainer. The other had come off when she kicked at one of the attackers; he grabbed her foot, she pulled away, the shoe had stayed with him.

That attack hadn't been random.

She shivered and stared at the black, unwelcoming windows of the tiny house she'd bought, wondering if she dared to go in long enough to pack. Were they waiting in there for her? Were they standing on the other side of the glass, watching her find her horse? Were they laughing?

They'd been waiting in the alley. She owned a saddle shop on the corner of Main Street and Tadweiller, a block from the police department and the county courthouse in one direction and right next to the used bookstore that had once been Baldwell's in the other. Like the other shop owners on the block, she parked in the service alley behind her store. She was working late. The saddle business she did in Peters wouldn't keep a mouse in scraps, much less rent a store and buy a house and feed her and her horse. But like a lot of other successful small business owners, she'd learned how to market to specialty buyers. She had a thriving catalog business and her reputation for high-end custom-made English and Western saddles and tack earned her visits from riders all over the United States and Canada. She even had a customer in Australia.

She'd been doing the finishing touches on a matching western show saddle, bridle, martingale and crupper for a client who barrel-raced: oak leaves and acorns and lots of engraved silver on black leather. It was going to set off the client's dapple-gray half-Arab, half-Quarter-horse; Kate could picture the completed saddle as she worked. She wanted to finish tooling the seat before the leather dried and she'd gotten involved in pebbling between the oak leaves and doing some extra detailing she hadn't actually planned until it started to be beautiful and suddenly it was ten o'clock and Lisa and Paul, her two assistants, had been gone for hours.

Weary but pleased, she let herself out the back way, locked up, and found her car key while she was still standing on the top step. She noticed only peripherally that the light by her back door was burned out and so was the one at the end of the alley. It didn't seem to matter. She lived in Peters, North Carolina, population ten thousand and a few, and though she and everyone else she knew locked their doors and took precautions, it was more because Interstate 95 ran right by the town than because anyone expected trouble from neighbors. Besides, the full moon lit most of the alley and the sky was full of cold-brightened stars, and everything was as quiet as it should have been.

Deep shadows swallowed her car, but she hadn't really thought about that. How many hundreds of times had she left work late? Alone?

How many?

One too many.

Three of them had been waiting for her. They wore pantyhose over their heads, and one of them had a roll of duct tape. They grabbed her, the one with the duct tape wrapped it twice around her head, covering her mouth. "You're going to like this," they kept saying. "You're going to like us, witch." She'd fought, kicking and punching and head-butting, trying as hard as she could to hurt the three of them.

They didn't have weapons with them. No knives. No guns. They'd evidently figured they were three big men and she was one average-sized woman, and they hadn't anticipated the amount of fight she would be able to put up in her own defense. They should have. They certainly would the next time. Not all the blood on her shirt was hers. She'd kicked one in the nose when the three of them tried to pick her up to carry her somewhere. That one had dropped her and when her feet hit the ground she'd launched herself head first into the face of the one who had his arms locked under her armpits and around her chest. She'd heard the crunch of bone and he screamed and swore. She wasn't winning, though. For every blow she got in, they hit her with three, and the more she fought, the madder and meaner they became.

Then, from the shadows where she was fighting for her life, she saw the gray backside of the store at the end of the alley light up. Headlights were coming down the service road from the opposite direction.

"Shit," one of her attackers said, and his friend said, "Later, witch."

They ran, and she stepped out into the light of the headlights, hoping for help.

The car had been a prowl car, and the officer in the black-and-white had put her in his front seat, driven her around while she tried to spot the three men, and finally, when it became clear the three of them had gotten away, had taken her to the emergency room. The ER staff determined that she had a hairline fracture of the right zygomatic arch, which meant—they'd translated when she'd asked—the thugs had broken her right cheekbone, but not badly. She also had numerous abrasions and contusions and a couple of bite marks and a slightly sprained ankle, but she didn't have a head injury or internal bleeding and she wasn't going to die. So she got a prescription for Darvon and a couple of tablets to last her until she could get to a drugstore, and the RN had her swallow one Darvon before she left.

Then she went to the police station and gave her statement and let a female officer take photographs of her injuries.

The police were kind, but they weren't very encouraging. She hadn't recognized any of her attackers. She hadn't gotten good descriptions. She hadn't been able to come up with any surefire identifiers—no tattoos or scars. She described three youngish white men, all between five ten and six one, all between a hundred eighty and two hundred twenty pounds. All three were going to be bruised and scratched, and she was sure one would have a broken nose. Maybe, she said, two.

Worse, she'd lied when they asked her if she knew why anyone might want to hurt her. She wasn't about to admit to the police in a small North Carolina town that she'd been attacked because she was Wiccan—a witch. Freedom of religion might be a constitutionally protected right, but that didn't mean anything in most small Southern towns if the believer belonged to the wrong religion, and Kate knew it. She'd learned the hard way to keep her mouth shut. So what she did know about her attackers—that they were after her because of her religion—the police didn't find out. As a result, they were all very caring but not very helpful.

A different officer took her back to the alley to pick up her car. He watched her get in it, watched her start the car up and check to make sure it would run. Then she waved to him that she was all right, and she backed out and drove home.

Parked in the driveway.

Walked up her walk.

Found her horse.

It was three thirty in the morning, and now she knew that they knew where she lived. She didn't know them, but they knew her, had been waiting for her. In spite of what they'd said when they grabbed her, she had wanted to think what happened to her was just the odds, but her last, futile hope of that died. She'd wanted to believe the attack had been random violence that resulted from her carelessness, from her being in the wrong place at the wrong time, from bad luck. She had wanted to believe that any woman walking down those steps would have had the same thing happen to her, because if it were just random, then it would have been over. She could have put it behind her and gone on with her life.

But this was personal. These men were after her, and they weren't just going to go away.

She didn't let herself cry. She swallowed the tears and felt them blurring across her eyes. She'd raised Rocky from a colt. She'd trained him herself; had ridden him every day; had let him steal apples and carrots from the pockets of her coats; had talked to him and played with him and brushed him and loved him. He was, she supposed, the child she'd never had and probably never would. They'd killed him to hurt her, and they'd succeeded. Standing there staring at Rocky lying across the pinestraw with his eyes open and dull and cloudy, she hurt worse than she had when the thugs had beaten her.

But she wouldn't cry. She wouldn't let them make her cry.

She wouldn't let them make her stupid, either. Carefully, she retraced her steps to her car. She got in, locked her door, and backed out of the pinestraw-covered drive. She drove two miles to the Dairy Mart, used the pay phone to call the sheriff—she lived out in the country, so she was beyond town police jurisdiction—then drove home to await the arrival of help.

A car with two deputies got there twenty minutes later. Both men got out; the one that carried a camera went straight to the horse while the other came over to talk to her. His name was Merritt. He was genial, thirty pounds overweight, in his early fifties. She told him an abbreviated version of what had happened to her at work, then showed him Rocky and the note. The other deputy had finished with the photos of the horse and was working his way around the house by then, checking windows and doors.

Merritt said, "Death threat like this is a serious thing. Maybe they're only trying to scare you, but I wouldn't bet the farm on that."

The other deputy called from the back of the house, "No sign that anyone tried to get in here. Doors and windows are fine."

She turned to Deputy Merritt. "Would you mind coming in with me and making sure they didn't get in? I know it sounds paranoid, especially when everything looks okay out here—but I just want to be sure."

"I'll be happy to." He headed up the walk with her. The other deputy moved slowly down the driveway with his head down—looking for evidence, perhaps—got something out of the county car, and returned to Rocky. "Bobby, you getting that note?"

"I am."

"Fine. I'm going to take this young lady inside and make sure there aren't any surprises waiting for her. Call back to the station when you're done there, and I'll be out in a minute."

The other deputy just nodded.

Kate unlocked the door, but Merritt walked in first. She followed and closed the door behind them.

The house smelled of cinnamon and apples from the pie she'd baked for herself the day before; and of Old English Red Oil, which she used to keep up the antique walnut dining room furniture she'd acquired piece by unmatched piece from various secondhand stores around the state; and of Murphy's Oil Soap. The house was old and still a little run-down, but she'd recently redone the wood floors with a drum sander and stained them herself, and she kept after them. The homey smells didn't make her feel better. They just made her feel that terrible things could happen in the safest of places.

The deputy switched on the light.

The floor in the entryway gleamed. "This is right nice," he said. He peeked through the doorway to his left, into the dining room, and then to the right, into the living room. His hand rested on the butt of his gun. "You wouldn't think from the outside that this place was so pretty inside."

"I haven't had a chance to repaint outside yet," Kate said. "That's my big goal come spring. I've been working on the inside for the last year. I did most of the inside work myself in the evenings and on weekends." She tried to hide her distress in small talk. It didn't help, though.

The deputy opened the coat closet to the right of the entryway and said, "No one in there."

Kate reached in, grabbed the baseball bat she kept leaning against the wall and pulled it out. She worked off her remaining

shoe and kicked it into the closet. The deputy eyed the baseball bat and raised an eyebrow. "That's not bad, but for home
protection I really do recommend a gun. You're a long way out
here, and no matter how fast we come, it ain't going to be fast
enough if you need help right away."

"I have a shotgun," Kate said. "And I shoot once a week."

"What do you have?"

"Mossberg twenty-gauge pump action. I keep it loaded with
slugs."

"That'll do. What do you shoot?"

"Clay birds, mostly. Boy down the road will come over and toss
them for me when he can. When he can't, I toss them myself."

"Damn. You hit any when you do the tossing?"

"Most."

"Damn."

They went into the dining room. Moonlight shone off the polished surface of the oval Colonial drop-leaf table and the arms
and backs of the chairs, turning them silver. The deputy switched
on the light, and the warm dark tones of the wood came alive.
"Your chairs don't match," Merritt said.

"I got them one at a time at yard sales. Got the table the same
way. Refinished everything and did the upholstery on the chair
seats."

"You'd be pretty handy to have around," the deputy said, crouching down to look inside the deep storage area beneath the china
cabinet. "I can't get my old lady to wash the damn dishes without an argument. If I didn't say anything, she'd just live in shit."

He walked around the counter that separated the dining room
from the kitchen and started opening the cabinets. "Have you
seen anything so far that looks out of place?" His flashlight illuminated the dark spaces under the sink, where orderly rows of
cleaning supplies sat waiting for use.

"Not yet," Kate told him.

"God, if it were, you'd sure know it, wouldn't you? Don't think
I ever saw anyone kept a place so neat."

"I live alone. I'm the only person I have to clean up after."

"There's that," he said. He checked the pantry, then the little
downstairs bathroom and the storage area at the back of that.
"We got three young'uns, Sharla and me. Oldest is nineteen now,
youngest is thirteen." He turned from the storage area. "Let's take
a look in your living room, then go upstairs."

He was as thorough in the rest of the house as he had been in the kitchen, and just as chatty. He commented on the afghans she'd crocheted, on the stenciling she'd done around the ceiling and doors in the living room, on her taste in decorating, on the size of the upstairs bathroom. She appreciated the fact that he was taking his time and taking her concerns over hidden intruders seriously, and he was kind and he never crossed the line between casual conversation and nosiness, but by the time he finished checking in her closet, she was looking forward to seeing him go.

He stepped out of her bedroom and walked to the dormer window at the top of the stairs; he looked down at the front yard. "Nobody here but us chickens, young lady. I'm done, and it looks like Bobby's done, too. I don't see him out there; he must be back in the car." He looked over at Kate and smiled. "You going to be all right, then?"

Kate nodded. "I'll be fine."

"We'll call Animal Control about the horse. They can take care of moving it for you unless you got other plans."

She pressed her lips together tightly and inhaled. "No other plans." Tears blurred her vision for an instant, but she blinked them back.

"Then we'll be on our way." He headed down the stairs and Kate followed him.

"Thank you."

"That's what we're here for."

She walked him out. From her doorstep, she could see the other deputy, Bobby, sitting in the driver's seat of their car, talking on the radio. He glanced up when he saw them step outside, and just for an instant he looked into her eyes; then he looked down so that the wide brim of his hat hid his face, but in that instant she'd gotten a clear look at him. He was in his late twenties or early thirties, and he had two black eyes and a tremendously swollen nose. "What happened to him?" she asked.

"Stepped in between a couple of fighting drunks off duty. They quit fighting each other and started fighting him."

Off duty. That meant Merritt might not have been with him when the fight occurred. "When did that happen?"

"Some time yesterday. Last night, I reckon." Merritt gave her a long, level look and said, "He might have been fighting the same bunch of troublemakers tried to hurt you. I'll ask him about it—if he thinks there's any connection, we might be able to look into it a little. It's really city's case unless we can say for sure this incident and that one are connected."

Kate nodded again. When Merritt walked down the path she closed the door behind him and locked the deadbolt and hooked the security chain into place. Then she stood in her entryway shaking, watching through the peephole in the front door as the county car backed down her driveway and moved out onto the road.

The other deputy, Bobby, had done everything he could to keep her from seeing his face. She'd seen it when he was surprised into looking up at her. Maybe he was just embarrassed about the way he looked. She was probably jumping to stupid conclusions. The county was large, and there had to be people besides the ones she'd hit who had black eyes and swollen noses.

But if Bobby was one of the men who attacked her, she couldn't even count on help from the sheriff's department. She wasn't safe anywhere.

She hurried to the stairs; eight up, right turn on the landing, and eight more. When she reached the top landing, she went to the dormer window and looked down, half expecting to see Bobby back in her yard skulking around. But of course he wasn't there. Nothing moved in the yard. No traffic moved on the highway. She was alone.

She went left, into the bathroom she'd remodeled; she stood over the sink and rinsed her face. She stared at herself in the mirror. Her long blond hair was caked with blood. Blue-purple bruises mottled her right cheek and her jaw and built up swollen half-moons beneath both eyes. The sclera of her right eye was bloody. She opened her mouth, checked her teeth, and stuck out her tongue—she could see the deep, bloody marks where her attackers had slammed her bottom lip into her teeth. She opened the medicine cabinet, pulled out some Neosporin with lidocaine, and smeared it onto the cuts on her face. It stung.

She wanted to take a bath, but she wasn't going to undress or do anything that made her as vulnerable as soaking in a tub until she had the shotgun beside her.

She looked in the linen closet again, just to be sure. No one was in it, of course.

She walked across the landing to her bedroom, eased the door open, and went in. She didn't have much furniture in the room; just the bookshelves, a Queen Anne wingback chair in the left corner opposite her, a solid walnut chest of drawers on the far wall, and her bed, a high, elaborately carved spindle bed that had cost her two show saddles in barter. She could see from where she stood that no one was under the bed. She felt ridiculous for even looking.

She walked around the foot of the bed and past the dresser and went into the closet. She slid her hand along the left closet wall until she felt the slight depression of the hidden panel she'd built into the closet when she remodeled. She pressed and the panel door popped out, and she reached in and took out the shotgun. It didn't look like much—Mossberg was a big believer in black plastic. The ribbed pump and the stock were molded of it. She thought of the guns she'd learned to shoot when she was little: the Browning over-and-under shotgun with the hand-checkered stock and engraved silverwork on the breech; the little Remington .22 rifles; the 30.06 pistol that nearly took her arm off the one time her father let her try it. Those had been sporting guns. Her father liked to shoot targets, and occasionally he went hunting for their dinner.

She'd had no such intention when she bought the Mossberg. She'd been suddenly a woman alone in a house a long way from anyone, and when she bought the shotgun, she'd gotten it with only the defense of her home and her life in mind.

The Mossberg held five shells plus one in the chamber, but she didn't leave it that way when she wasn't home. She kept it locked. Now she unlocked the wire breech lock and removed it, grabbed two extra shells from the ammunition shelf, loaded the fifth, pumped it into the chamber, and thumbed the sixth shell into place. With the safety on, she stepped back into her bedroom. She checked her watch. Five A.M.. The sun would come up right around seven. She had two more hours of darkness, and she thought once she got through that, she might be able to crawl into her bed and sleep for a while. She was going to have to call either Lisa or Paul and have one of them open for her. She didn't think she would go in to work that day. But it was still too early to call anyone.

In the meantime, she wanted a bath.

She laid the shotgun across the bed and got some clean underwear and a pair of flannel pajamas with teddy bears on them out of her top right drawer. She took her watch off and dropped it on top of the dresser. When she turned back to pick up the shotgun, she noticed something she'd seen the time she came in with the deputy, but this time she really saw it.

On the nightstand nearest her, between the telephone and the reading lamp, lay a book. It was a Fodor's Guide, a travel book.

Gold with black lettering, a photograph on the lower portion of the glossy paper cover. The photo was gorgeous: a gleaming white fairy-tale castle; a dark-haired, blue-eyed beauty leading a donkey over a cobblestone road that ran through a field of flowers; a blue lake in the background that reflected the mountains that lay behind it. The cover read, *Fodor's Guide to Glenraven: A Complete Guide to the Best Mountain Walks, Castle Tours, and Feasts.*

Kate always had a book or two sitting on that nightstand, so she hadn't really paid attention to that one. But she had never owned a Fodor's Guide. Had never borrowed one. She had never had the urge to be a tourist, to go someplace where she didn't speak the language and didn't look like everyone else and didn't know where things were and didn't understand the customs. She figured she was enough of an outsider anyway; she didn't see where adding to that feeling of alienation would enhance her life experience in any way.

She stared at the book. It was proof that someone had been in her house. But what did its presence mean? It didn't seem like the sort of thing the thugs would have left . . .

Unless they'd used its pages to cut out the letters of the note they'd nailed to Rocky.

Unless they'd left a note for her in it.

Heart pounding an erratic roulade, hands trembling, she picked up the book.

It felt like it was purring. The sensation so startled her that she almost dropped the book, but the vibration died away. She riffled the pages, wondering if the tiny thrill had come from a bomb hidden inside, but the book hadn't been hollowed out. She decided to go through it more slowly. She opened to the first page. For an instant she saw a typical cover page. Then the paper cleared as if someone was erasing it while she watched.

No sooner were the last words gone than new ones appeared.

Hello, Kate. I know the timing is terrible, and that you probably don't feel like dealing with this now, but now is when we're going to have to do it. You need to take me outside, and you need to do it quickly.

She dropped the book and stepped back from it. *Be logical,* she told herself. *You've been through a lot in the last few hours. This could be any of several different, perfectly rational things. You could*

be having an allergic reaction to the Darvon you took. You could be
suffering from some delayed effect of trauma to your head. This could
even have been a hallucination resulting from post-traumatic stress.
If you pick up the book again, it's just going to be a book. It won't
purr, it won't hum, and it won't write little messages to you.

She picked up the book again. This time it didn't hum. So far,
so good.

She opened it to the first page.

> The hell I won't. You're dealing just fine with your
> stress, you aren't injured, and you aren't allergic to
> your medicine, but if you don't get me outside fast,
> you are going to have a mess in your bedroom you'll
> never get clean.

Kate nodded. It would have been nice to have found a rational explanation for the book, but she wasn't willing to insist on
one. She had always prided herself on her ability to take the unexpected in stride. As a Wiccan, she accepted the reality of magic
in the universe—she just hadn't anticipated having it intrude so
blatantly on her. She'd spent much of her life making herself as
self-sufficient as she could, though. She believed she had the tools
she needed to survive just about anything that life threw at her.
Now she was going to find out if she was right.

"On the positive side," she told the book, "if you got here by
magic, then at least the bastards who beat me up didn't leave
you here."

I'll take the good news when I find it, she thought. She held onto
the book, picked up the shotgun, and headed downstairs. She
couldn't imagine why a book would need to go outside, or what
could possibly be urgent about the request, but sometimes survival became a matter of knowing when to shut up and follow
instructions.

Until she saw evidence to the contrary, she was going to assume
this was one of those times.

Two

Rhiana Falin trotted across Allier's Bridge and reined in her mount at the base of an enormous oak. She reached out to rest her hand on the trunk of the tree. "Here," she said.

The rest of the riding party halted. Val Peloral, eldest son of the local Kin lord, shook his head. "Lady Smeachwykke, this place is too far from the current boundaries of your town. If you expand Ruddy Smeachwykke this far, you will eventually more than double the current population within the city walls. You will destroy Hier's Plot and Little Greening and much of the Kin-Hera Triad with these new boundaries."

Rhiana brushed the hair back from her forehead and looked around at the forest. If the Kin negotiator and his associates had any idea how frustrated Rhiana had become, they would end the talks without reaching an agreement, and the Machnan of Ruddy Smeachwykke would continue to live on top of each other, to scrabble a meager living from too-small plots of land, and to resent the Kin who claimed the vast forests all around them.

"Lord Faldan," she said, trying to keep her voice pleasant, "historically, the Kin-Hera Triad was home to the Beling dagreth and to several families of tesbits. The Alfkindir Lord Hier used Hier's Plot as a hunting ground for stags. And a few Kin lived in the cotha in Little Greening." She smiled. "But all three of these pieces of ground have been abandoned for the last fifty years. Both Kin and Kin-hera have moved south into the Faldan Woods or east toward the cothas above Sinon. This portion of the Great Golian Forest is empty and unused."

"But it's ours," Val said.

"We know. We have always respected your claims to the ground. Now we wish to know what we can offer in exchange for it." She leaned forward in her saddle. "We aren't asking to expand to the south or to the east. We aren't asking to move into territory your people occupy. But I ask for my people, and for their children, that we be permitted expansion to the north and west, in exchange for such goods and favors as both our peoples find agreeable."

Val Peloral turned to discuss the matter with his associates: a second Kin man, a dagreth and a warrag. The other man was named Caet something; he was lower Kin, and was probably a companion rather than a fellow negotiator. The warrag was a massive black-furred yellow-eyed male whose leather tool harness bore the embossed crest of the Grallagg clan. The bearish dagreth Rhiana knew socially. His name was Tik and he came into Ruddy Smeachwykke from time to time to visit the market. Such visits weren't unheard of anymore, not since the arrival of the new Watchmistress had given the Kin and the Machnan opportunities to deal as allies instead of enemies. Still, Tik was something of an anomaly; a progressive among the usually backward-thinking Kin-hera. Rhiana considered his presence among the Kinnish representatives a good sign.

She turned to her own colleagues, Bron Egadon, who had been her advisor since the death of her husband earlier in the year, and Tero Sarijann, the architect who had designed the expansion plans for Ruddy Smeachwykke. She raised an eyebrow. Bron nodded slightly; he thought the Kin would deal. Tero, though, just as subtly shook his head; he anticipated no deal. She kept herself from giving any audible or visible response, and returned her attention to the Kinnish party.

Val and his colleagues came to some sort of decision, and all of them looked to Rhiana. "Let's ride back," the Kin lord said.

"You can feed us and we will discuss the concessions we would like in exchange for granting you the land."

"So you'll do it?" Rhiana couldn't hide her smile.

"If you're willing to meet our price."

Rhiana nodded. She didn't dare let the Kin think she'd agree to anything, but she was willing to accept some fairly sweeping concessions in exchange for the land. "With work, we'll find something that will please everyone," she said. She thought that sounded neutral and not like self-abasement or groveling. "By all means, let's return. We've roast suckling pig and wild boar and stag on the groaning board."

They recrossed the Great Ruddy River and rode south and west on Allier's Road, through the deep gloom of the forest. The horses' hooves thudded on the hard-packed earth; the warrag and the dagreth made no sounds at all as they trotted alongside. Rhiana listened to the jingle of the bridles and the pleasant creak of leather saddles, and thought of beginning the expansion of Ruddy Smeachwykke in the next few days, before spring came and brought with it the urgency of tilling and planting and the endless cycle of calving and lambing. She imagined Tero's new streets spreading out to either side of her, replacing the endless darkness of the forest. They would be streets that didn't terminate in walls as the old ones had done, but that looked out over the fields beyond them. She imagined the new houses Tero planned, neat and narrow and double-storied, and the new guild halls and trade centers, like the ones the Watchmistress, Jayjay Bennington, was establishing down south in Zearn and Rikes Gate. She was just wishing for the hundredth time that Haddis had lived to see the changes that were coming to Glenraven when a scream ripped her out of her reverie. She turned in time to see an enormous gray-winged monstrosity pull Caet off his horse's back, rip his head off with a single bite, and swallow it. The monster kept the dead man locked in its claws and lifted with ponderous flapping of its wings for the forest canopy high overhead.

"No!" Tero shrieked.

She twisted around in her saddle and found that another of the monsters had grabbed him.

She looked up and saw the shadowed forms of more of the creatures lurking in the branches high above; some were spreading their wings to drop down on the people below.

"Ride," she shouted, and dug her heels into her horse's flanks. The warrag took the lead with the dagreth at his shoulder. Rhiana and Val rode neck and neck behind them, but Bron lost ground. His horse had been chosen because it could carry Bron's great weight, but it could not carry it quickly.

Why didn't we bring weapons? Rhiana wondered. *We were so eager to show our trust in each other that we left ourselves helpless against anything else that might find us, and now something has.*

Rhiana heard Bron scream once. His scream, like those of Caet and Tero before him, was short and horrible, but quickly silenced. Rhiana glanced at Val and saw that the Kin man was as frightened as she.

She heard one of the monsters bellow from behind them. They fled faster, taking bad risks by galloping on the uneven surface of the dirt road, but putting distance between themselves and the flying nightmares behind. Then an answering bellow erupted from the road ahead. Rhiana sawed on her reins so hard her horse nearly sat down as it skidded to a stop. Rhiana felt herself start to slide over her mount's neck. She tightened her thighs and locked her toes under the horse's belly and gritted her teeth.

She didn't lose her seat. Val made a more graceful stop, and the warrag and dagreth skidded around and took up positions facing in opposite directions, growling and snarling.

"What now?" Val asked.

Rhiana had an answer, but her answer didn't allow time for words. She was busy casting a gate spell. The spell was new to her; she'd learned it a few months ago and had only had two opportunities to use it since. She had to open a path into the spirit plane and locate and hold an anchor at the destination to keep the path in place until the traveler was safely through. The spell required intense concentration, and under the circumstances Rhiana fought for that. She created the gate, then struggled to find an anchor within Smeachwykke Castle. Briefly she latched onto the stone pillar in the central courtyard, but she was having a hard time maintaining her focus.

"There," Val said, and pointed upward.

Rhiana could hear the leathery flap of giant wings. She released the energy she had drawn into herself and a shimmering curtain of light appeared in the center of the road. She urged her horse forward and shouted, "Go!" Kin-hera and riders leapt through together. The monster dove for the gate, so close that Rhiana could smell the stink of it and feel the wind from its wings.

The four survivors raced along the shifting, glowing floor of the tunnel that cut through the spirit world, while around them

the walls billowed and bulged. She'd done a poor job of forming the tunnel. The walls should have been as smooth and slick
as ice, and they should have held steady. Instead they blew like
fabric in a windstorm. Rhiana felt movement behind her and
realized the flier that dove at them had followed them into the
tunnel.

*Maybe we can get out and shut the gate before it comes all the
way through,* she thought, but she didn't believe it. The monster
was too close and too fast.

Rhiana felt a shift and a snap, and realized the tunnel had
broken away from the feeble anchor she'd given it and established
another, stronger anchor on its own. The four of them were going
to come out someplace other than in Smeachwykke Castle. She
didn't care. She urged her horse to greater speed. All she wanted
was to survive.

"Darkness ahead," Tik shouted.

"That's the gate," Rhiana yelled.

Val shouted, "Faster! It almost has us."

The walls shimmered and fluxed, and the dark circle got larger.

Rhiana could smell the monster's breath behind her. She
crouched low over her horse's withers. She didn't need to urge
him forward. The gate was dilating open, but not fast enough.
The warrag leapt through it with the dagreth right behind him.
She felt her mount gather herself for the jump, and she wished
she could know what was on the other side; would she be jumping
off of a cliff or into water? Would she be leaping to certain death?

No time to think. Time only to do—and Rhiana did. She curved
her back, tucked her head low, balanced her weight with her
thighs, and she and the horse rose and sailed through the gate
and out into the darkness beyond.

Three

Kate left the security chain in place and opened the door. The moon had dropped to just above the horizon behind the house, and the sun wouldn't start to rise for another hour or so. In the meantime, the front yard was darker than it had been when she got home.

"The darkest hour is just before dawn," she said, quoting, or perhaps misquoting, a line from a song by The Mamas and The Papas. She'd heard the song recently and had taken the lyrics to heart. She was waiting for sunrise in more than just a literal sense.

She switched on her porch light. The yellow bug light cast a sickly circle that showed her Rocky, still lying across the path, and her little Escort in the drive off to the left. Nothing moved. The rhododendrons and camellias and azaleas hunkered with unnerving solidity beyond the edge of the light.

Kate clicked the shotgun's safety off, closed the door long enough to undo the safety chain, then went out. She opened the book again.

Put me on the ground out in the clearing in the middle of your yard, then back away fast.

Kate wasn't going anywhere. She tossed the book off of the stoop into the middle of the semicircle of grass she called her yard. Then she waited. For perhaps twenty seconds, nothing happened. Then the book began to glow, and above it a tiny sphere of light appeared. That sphere, made up of a rainbow of swirling colors, spun and grew and flattened with frightening speed until in less than a minute a shimmering oval curtain ten feet high and nearly eight feet wide hung in the air inches above the ground.

As soon as the curtain of light stopped growing, a black dot appeared in its center. Then that began to expand, too, eating away at the shimmering oval like a spreading stain. When she saw movement behind the blackness, she realized the black circle was a hole, and that things on the other side of that hole were waiting to come through. She raised the shotgun and sighted along the barrel. She exhaled to steady her aim and concentrated on slowing the beat of her heart.

Then something jumped through and ran for the woods, and another something right behind it, and then two bigger shapes at almost the same time. She heard horses' hooves, then. She didn't shoot. They were running away from her, not toward her.

But then a shriek like sheet metal ripping shredded the early morning hush, and a massive black shape tore its way through the circle of light, flapped, rose, and turned toward her.

It was moving toward the light, she realized.

Kate got just a glimpse of a sharklike maw and beating wings, sighted for the spot between the teeth, and fired, pumped, fired, pumped, fired, pumped, fired, pumped, fired, and jumped from her stoop into the azalea hedge to the right as the thing came slamming down, crashing into her door, crashing *through* her door. A stinking leathery wing flailed down on top of her and thrashed while the monster shrieked and gurgled and tried to rise. The wing slammed her into the front of the house and bounced her head off the wood; points of white light exploded behind her eyes and she sagged to her knees. Above her she heard glass shatter as the leading edge of the monster's wing slammed into the dining room picture window.

Kate dropped to her belly. The bushes gave her a little bit of cover and the wing didn't hit her again. She took stock of her situation. She had one shot left and she needed to make it count.

She clicked the safety on, pumped the shell into the chamber, and crawled beneath the beating wing, out into her yard. When she was safely behind the monster, she saw that she could crawl along its back to reach its head. If the back door hadn't been locked, she could have gone around the house and come at it from the front, but unfortunately, that wasn't an option. She tucked the twenty-gauge under her arm and slid onto the thing's back as if she were trying to ride a horse. She felt the monster shudder at her touch; then it began to roll from side to side to dislodge her, but it couldn't roll far enough to succeed. Its outspread wings, tangled in the shrubbery, prevented that. She kept scooting forward. She could see that it didn't have a neck, and that its huge eyes were placed low on either side of its head to give it a wide field of vision.

One eye rolled up as she inched close. She could hear the monster's jaws snapping open and closed. She wondered if the single shell she had left would be sufficient to kill the thing, even if the shot were well placed. She slid down one side just in front of the shoulder, jammed the shotgun into the thing's eye socket, and pulled the trigger. It shuddered again and a ripple ran through its body. Then it twitched and spasmed, and finally lay still.

For the first time she was actually able to take the time to look at it. Her first impression hadn't been too far from the truth. It still gave her a sharklike impression; it was essentially a gullet on wings. The enormous jaws with their multiple rows of triangular, serrated teeth could have swallowed her whole. The head connected directly to the torpedo-shaped body—the neckless design had worked in her favor. If the thing had been able to turn its head, it would undoubtedly have eaten her. Its pebbled, leathery skin was hot to her touch; it stank of rotten meat and death and filth. It wasn't a bird, but she didn't have the impression that it was a mammal, either. She wondered if perhaps it was some sort of dinosaur. It was unbelievably ugly, the most hideous thing she had ever seen.

She stared at it lying there on her doorstep, thought of Animal Control coming over in a few hours to pick up Rocky, and suddenly she started to laugh. "When they see this thing, they're going to shit," she said, and laughed some more.

She felt stronger than she had all night. The nightmare on her doorstep would have devoured her, but she'd taken care of it. She didn't falter, she didn't fall apart, and she didn't get herself killed. Now she could see the first faint graying of the horizon, as dawn began to make cutwork lace of the winter-bare trees and telephone lines across the road. She'd made it to morning.

She felt tireder than she'd ever been, too, and more in need of a long, hot whirlpool bath. She tucked the shotgun under her arm, clambered back over the monster and walked into the grass to pick up her book.

"You killed it," a man's voice said.

She flicked the safety off and raised the weapon in the direction of the voice before she remembered that she was out of shells.

"Don't kill us," the voice said. "We're friends. The monster was after us, and you saved us."

Kate remembered the shapes that had launched themselves out of the circle of light before the flying horror came tearing through. "Who are you?" she asked, lowering the shotgun slightly. As long as they believed the gun was loaded, they would think twice before attacking her.

A man leading a horse moved toward her out of the shadows. He was tall and slender, with slanted eyes and thick, pale hair. Kate thought something was wrong with the shape of his mouth, but she wasn't sure. A woman, also leading a horse, walked behind him. The woman was barely five feet tall, with black hair and large blue eyes and a frightened look. The man said, "My name is Val. The woman is Rhiana."

Kate lowered the shotgun. "I'm Kate Beacham."

Something hit her between the shoulder blades and knocked her face down to the ground. All her dulled hurts became sharp again; she cried out from the pain.

"Take her inside," the man said. "We'll go in with her. We aren't likely to find another place that will allow us to get out of the light."

Rough, claw-tipped hands grabbed Kate around the waist, turned her around, and picked her up. She got a quick glimpse at a face that made no sense, and then she was hanging over a sloping shoulder and being bounced along while whatever had her carried her to her house. An ugly black dog the size of a Shetland pony followed right behind, watching her with intelligent yellow eyes. The man picked up the shotgun, then led his horse around to the side of the house—evidently he'd found and intended to take advantage of Kate's pasture and shed. The woman knelt and picked up the book that had brought them through from wherever they'd been before. She looked up at Kate, her eyes full of curiosity. Then she shrugged and led her horse to the pasture, following Val.

Four

They'd lowered the blinds, pulled the curtains closed, and turned on her lights. When she got her first clear look at them, Kate wished they'd left her in the dark.

The woman, Rhiana, looked normal enough, but the other three 'people' in her living room were a freak show. Val's long fingers were tipped with retractable claws, and when he smiled, Kate got a good look at a set of canines that would have made a werewolf fall in love. The overall shape of his face was subtly wrong, too. The cheekbones were too high and the chin pointed sharply ahead of strong, square jaws. He had long hair that he'd tucked behind his ears, which Kate could see were small, slightly scoop-shaped, with pointed tips. His long, slanted eyes were pale amber in color. The space between his narrow, sharp nose and the full upper lip seemed excessive. Val was compelling in an exotic, uncomfortable way, but he wasn't handsome.

Next to the last two visitors, though, even he looked normal. The big black dog wasn't a dog at all. Its name was Errga—

25

Kate had picked that up from conversations it had with the bearish thing, whose name was Tik, and with Val and Rhiana. It had settled itself into one of Kate's two armchairs. From this vantage point it watched her, grinning. Its face had a hint of greyhound to it, and more than a touch of wolf, but the high forehead and the intelligence in the lemon-yellow eyes would have told Kate it was nothing that belonged in her world even if she hadn't seen its furry, spiderish hands or heard it speak.

On the floor beside it sat Tik. If Smokey the Bear had shaved himself, worn bright red hair pulled back in a braid and dressed himself in a gaudy silk kimono, he would have approximated Tik, but imperfectly. This creature's bearish nose was the same tan color as the rest of its skin and it had stubby-fingered hands instead of regular paws; its pointed ears sat lower on its head than a bear's would have. But essentially, she thought, it was a bare bear in a party dress.

Kate lay with her feet up on her couch, her head on one of the overstuffed cushions, the blue-green afghan she'd crocheted pulled up to her chin, pretending a calm she didn't feel. She said, "What are you doing here, and what do you want with me?"

Val kept the gun pointed at her. Kate didn't bother letting him know it was no longer loaded. She figured anything she knew that the intruders didn't know could only work in her favor. Val said, "Rhiana is making another gate for us, and as soon as she completes it, we'll go home. The only reason we need you is because neither the warrag nor the dagreth can stand direct sunlight." He nodded at the bearish creature and the doglike one. "We needed to use your home and we didn't have time to ask nicely. The sun was getting ready to rise."

Rhiana looked up from her place in the center of the floor and said, "We aren't going to be going anywhere, Val. Probably not ever."

Val and Tik and Errga all turned and stared at Rhiana. Val bared his teeth and snarled something Kate couldn't quite make out. Then he said, "I hope you're joking."

"I wish I was. We can't go back for several reasons. First, something is blocking my access to the magic in this place. Second, whatever magic there is happens to be so weak I doubt I could form a gate strong enough to get us home. Third, if I could overcome both of those problems, I couldn't take us home because we're outside the boundaries of Glenraven, and the wards are now working against us."

Val shifted his attention completely away from Kate. Kate didn't try anything, because both Errga and Tik were still looking in her direction. She waited, watching while pretending not to watch at all. Sooner or later, she would have the advantage. When she did, she intended to make the most of it.

Val said, "The wards are working against us."

"Yes." Rhiana rose and stretched.

"I don't understand."

"The wards, Val. The barriers that keep the exiles out of Glenraven and protect us from the Machine World. We're on the wrong side of them now. As far as the wards are concerned, we're just four more exiles."

"So we can't go back?" Errga jumped down from his chair in a fluid motion and turned his back on Kate.

Tik rose, too. "We're exiles? You've made us exiles?"

None of them were watching her anymore. Kate pulled her knees up and shifted to her side, ignoring the pain, readying herself to leap.

Both Tik and Errga walked toward Rhiana. Val stayed where he was, holding the shotgun loosely in his right hand with the barrel pointed to the floor.

Ready, Kate thought.

"You *have* to get us home," Val said.

Set . . .

Errga lowered his head and growled. His lips skinned back from his teeth. "I do not wish to die an exile."

Go! Kate launched herself from the couch, crossed to Val in two running steps, grabbed the shotgun from him at the same time that she slammed into the Kin and knocked him to the ground, then jumped over the fallen outworlder and spun around to aim the shotgun at all four of them.

"Move and die," she said.

None of them moved.

Thank God I didn't tell them this thing was empty. They'd seen what it did to the flying monstrosity. They had a lot of respect for what it could do to them. Val raised his head and glared. Rhiana's face showed no expression at all. Tik and Errga slowly sat on their haunches, eyes wary.

"Now," Kate said, backing to the doorway that opened into the front hall, "the rules have changed, and I want to make sure you know them. I don't know what you people are. I don't know where you're from. But you're in my world now, and from now on you're going to do things my way. You can't go back home. That's too bad, and I'm sorry. But I didn't invite you here, and I don't see where you're my problem. I ought to send all of you out into the sunlight . . . just let you take your chances. Is that what you want?"

Errga and Tik shook their heads. Rhiana and Val watched her impassively. Val said, "The sunlight doesn't affect me."

"That's a lie," Errga said. "You aren't Kintari. You're just plain Kin. Maybe the sun won't kill you, but it will hurt you."

And Tik added, "The only one the sun won't bother is the Machnan. Isn't that right, Lady Smeachwykke?"

Rhiana nodded once, simple affirmation. She never took her eyes off Kate, and never said anything.

"Fine," Kate said. "So you don't want to go out in the sun. I don't particularly want to shoot you. Blood is hard to get off of walls, and if you were dead, you'd be hard to explain to the police." She pointed the shotgun at each of them in turn. "But I'll shoot you if I have to. You understand?"

They nodded.

"Back up against the far wall," she said, pointing with her free left hand. "You, Val, and you, Rhiana, sit on the couch. Tik and Errga, sit on the floor in front of them. Keep your hands where I can see them, and don't give me any reason to shoot you, because after what you did to me, I don't need much of a reason at all." They backed and sat. They were as far from the doorway as she could get them, and they couldn't split up and move behind her. She backed along the wall opposite them to the little bay window with the windowseat. Rhiana had dropped the *Fodor's Guide to Glenraven* there, and Kate wanted it. If anything explained what was going on, or what she was supposed to do about it, that would.

With the book in hand, she edged over to the doorway again.

She kept the shotgun leveled at her four visitors, resting it on her right hip with her finger hooked through the trigger. The book was in her left hand; she tucked it against her ribcage and inserted her thumb beneath the cover, never taking her eyes off her company.

Then she lifted the book, holding it so that she could read it and watch them at the same time.

> Nice work. I'm surprised you were able to get control of them so quickly . . . but then I thought you would be right for this job when I met you.

She wondered what it was talking about. Ardent reader though she was, she'd never thought of herself as "meeting" books—and she didn't remember any chance encounters with a *Fodor's Guide to Glenraven*.

> I was at the used bookstore when you stopped by two days ago. I tried to summon you back, but I couldn't make you hear me.

My wards would have protected me from that sort of manipulation, Kate thought.

> No doubt. But when you didn't come back to get me—and since we were running out of time—I used a huge amount of the little raw power I can control and brought myself to you. I'm not going to be much use to anyone for months now, except for offering advice. If I don't overextend myself, I should be able to do that.

What could possibly make a magical book want to follow her home?

> Long story. I'll write it out for you when we aren't in such a hurry.

Were they in a hurry? Why? What job did this book think she could do, and why had it chosen her to do it, and how was she supposed to deal with the creatures in her house, and where in the hell was Glenraven? She had a hundred questions, but the book addressed only one of them.

> You've done a good job of dealing with your visitors so far, but you're going to have to make friends with them. They're here to help you, just as you are here to help them. Though considering how badly they acted after you saved their lives, I wouldn't be surprised if you weren't happy to discover that.

> You'll find an ally in the dagreth, incidentally. He was not in favor of capturing you. He wanted to thank you and ask for your help. The Machnan was neutral.

> All she wanted was to recreate her gate and go home.
> The warrag might be won over to your side if you
> treat him well. You'll have to decide for yourself
> about the warrag and the Kin.

"Which of you is the dagreth?" Kate asked, though she had
an idea. When the bearish creature growled, "I am," her guess
was confirmed. She asked, "Can you read?"

"Of course."

"Then read this, and throw it back to me when you're done."
She tossed the book to him. He caught it with a surprisingly deft
movement. She filed the knowledge of that agility for future use,
then turned her attention to the other three. "While he's reading, I'm going to talk to the rest of you." Kate leaned against
the doorframe and let the barrel of the shotgun dip toward the
floor. "We're supposed to be allies. Apparently you aren't here
by accident, and neither am I. I'm going to be honest with you.
I didn't volunteer for any of this. Nevertheless, the four of you
are sitting in my living room and that monster is out on my front
step, and I'd be a fool to deny the reality of what's happening,
and a bigger fool if I didn't take the necessary steps to deal with
it." She sighed and looked at the four of them. The three who
weren't reading looked back at her, faces impassive.

"Okay. I'm going to tell you where I stand in all of this. Three
men attacked me last night. They were going to do worse than
just beat me up, but a police car on a routine patrol came by
before they had a chance to finish what they started. While I
was at the hospital, they came out here and killed my horse and
left a message nailed to his head telling me that I was going to
be next. If I don't show up at work today—and I am *not* showing up for work today—I think they may come by here. I suspect that one of them might be a sheriff's deputy."

She looked into four pairs of eyes, wondering if what she was
telling them meant anything to them, or if such concepts as hos-
pitals and police cars and sheriff's deputies were so far from anything they had ever experienced that she was wasting her breath.

The dagreth, who had put down the book to listen, said, "Go
on. The book says you are concerned that we may not understand, but that it is translating your concept words into things
we know from Glenraven."

"Oh." It had occurred to Kate that the four spoke awfully good
vernacular English, but she'd had bigger things to worry about.

"Fine. It's just that I haven't had any sleep in . . ." She looked at her watch. It was past seven. " . . . In more than twenty-four hours, and I've been beaten up and those creeps killed Rocky, and then you . . . people . . . showed up out of nowhere and I've had to fight with you, too. Evidently I wasn't supposed to have to fight with you. You were supposed to help me.

"Now I'm exhausted and I hurt and I'm afraid the thugs will come here to kill me. If we're going to be allies, and if I'm going to help you do whatever it is you need to do, you're going to have to protect me while I sleep."

All four of them looked at each other, and the dagreth said, "Here. Catch," and tossed the Fodor's back to her. It landed at her feet and she knelt to pick it up, still keeping her eyes on all four outworlders and her gun visibly at the ready.

The dagreth turned to his three companions and said, "The book brought us here to close the Rift. It says it can tell us how to get back home, but before it will do that, we have to find Callion and the Watchers. They're in this world somewhere. Until we either capture or destroy them, we aren't going to be able to leave. And the book says we won't be able to get to him without her, because she can show us this world's magic, and how to survive here."

When the dagreth fell silent, Val looked up at Kate and said, "I am in charge of all of these save Rhiana, and I am Rhiana's superior by birth. Why didn't you give your book to me to read, instead of to the dagreth, who is least among the Lesser Peoples?"

Kate looked at Val and thought, *I really don't like him.* She said, "I gave the book to Tik because Tik suggested that you ask for my help instead of attacking me. Rhiana didn't care one way or the other, and you and the warrag were in favor of taking what you wanted by force. I preferred Tik's approach."

Val's eyes narrowed. "How did you know that?"

Kate held up the Fodor's and shrugged. "It was right in here. So. Do we have an agreement? You'll watch out for me and I'll help you?"

"You don't know what you're getting into," Rhiana said. It was the first time she'd spoken directly to Kate. "We are being asked to capture one of the preeminent magicians of Glenraven, a vile, cunning murderer with enough magical ability at his command to destroy all of us. And the Watchers we're supposed to find are creatures of the Rift."

"What's the Rift?" Kate asked.

The warrag growled something about ignorance and outsiders, but Rhiana shushed him. "In Glenraven more than a thousand years ago, a Watchmistress named Aidris Akalan used a spell that opened a door between two worlds. The door was much like the gate we came through, but unlike it, this door stayed open. She used the door to bring through creatures who could give her magic that she needed in order to live forever, and she made a pact with them that they could devour the people of Glenraven if they would give her the magic from their victims' souls in return.

"For a thousand years, Aidris stayed in power, driving our world further toward death with every year. The evil she did drained the magic from the world and hope from the people, until a Machnan wizard named Yemus Sarijann brought two heroes from your world into ours to defeat her. Jayjay Bennington and Sophie Cortiss didn't just destroy the Watchmistress, though—they changed Glenraven in fundamental ways."

"Sophie Cortiss . . . and Jayjay Bennington? They're both from Peters," Kate said. "Or *were*, in Jay's case. Sophie's husband is a lawyer. She and Jayjay are the women who went missing over in Italy, but Jay died when she fell off the side of a mountain. Sophie brought her body back. I know Sophie. I used to play softball with Jay, until she was killed."

Rhiana shook her head. "Jayjay Bennington became Glenraven's new Watchmistress."

"I'm telling you, I knew Jay. She pitched for the Peters Library Lions. I was a first baseman. I met her when Craig and I moved here . . ." She caught her breath at the inadvertent mention of Craig, then went on. "We weren't friends precisely, but we were teammates. I went to her funeral. She died."

Rhiana was still shaking her head. "That is what you were intended to think. Sophie returned home bringing a copy of Jay's body. Sophie can never return to Glenraven, but we and our world owe her our existence and our freedom. Still, Jay and Sophie couldn't close the Rift. When Aidris died the Watchers would have had to go back to their own world and the Rift would have closed on its own, but another wizard, one of the First People, whose name is Callion, bound the Watchers to himself. Then he and they vanished. Because the Watchers remain on the wrong side of their gate, the Rift remains open, though it has been quiet."

The warrag said, "It hasn't been quiet. It's been waiting. *Waiting.* That monster on her front door is from the Rift."

Val and Rhiana turned startled faces toward Errga, though Tik sat nodding his head in agreement. "From the Rift?" Val asked.

And Rhiana said, "Are you sure?"

"It stinks of the Rift," the warrag said.

"I smell it, too," Tik said. "The otherworld smell, strong as the smell of wrong about this place, but different. Stink from the Rift world."

Kate didn't like the import-freighted looks Rhiana and Val exchanged. And she didn't like the idea that the Watchers, which Rhiana said had devoured the people of Glenraven for a thousand years, were now somewhere in her world.

She thumbed the book open again.

> That's right. Your stake in this is just as big as theirs. Callion and the Watchers will destroy your world if they aren't stopped, just as they are destroying Glenraven. The three bastards who came after you aren't much of a problem at all by comparison. In fact, I think the Glenraveners and I will be able to solve them shortly.
>
> Meanwhile, get some sleep. You won't be able to do much to help them or yourself until you do.

"I'm still in," Kate said. "Maybe I don't know exactly what I'm getting into, but I'll help you if you'll help me. Will you?"

The dagreth grinned. "I like you," he said. "You can count on me."

Rhiana said, "If I ever want to get home again, I don't have much choice, do I?"

Nothing like a vote of confidence, Kate thought.

The warrag just nodded.

Val smiled. "Of course you can count on me," he said. "We share a common cause. And what could be more important than saving our worlds?"

Five

Fort Lauderdale wasn't the way Callion remembered it, but unlike most things in the universe, it had changed for the better. He stood on the manicured lawn beneath a stand of India dates and Queen palms and looked over the house. It was a typical two-story stucco development home with a heavy, pale orange tile roof; every other house in the planned community was a variation on it. Behind him Callion heard the steady hum of traffic over the main highway out beyond the wall, and the rise and fall of human voices from a soccer field that lay on the other side of a tall hedge.

He turned to the real estate agent and smiled. "How much?"

"The owners are asking two hundred."

"I'd like to move in right away, and I really don't want to waste time dickering. I've already checked prices on comparable houses in the neighborhood, and they're asking too much. If they'll sell immediately, I'll pay one eighty-five in cash. That's the only offer I'll make, and I won't negotiate. If they won't sell for that, I'll find another house just like this one with a different seller who will." He let his smile broaden. "Quite frankly, dear, I intend to be in a house today, and I don't care if you sell it to me or if someone else does."

She nodded. "Let me run inside and call them." She frowned. "The paperwork will take some time, of course."

"I expect that if you want the commission, you'll find a way to expedite that, too."

She raised an eyebrow, started to say something else, then thought better of it. "Let me call and see what they say." She walked across the lawn, avoiding the sagos and the palmettos that poked out beyond the edges of their manicured beds.

When she was gone, Callion looked down at the palmetto bug that had been crawling toward him for the last couple of minutes. He crouched and grabbed it before it could escape, then popped it in his mouth, chewed it slowly, and swallowed, savoring the flavor. He liked palmetto bugs. They were a larger sort of the cockroaches he'd found elsewhere in the United States, and they were everywhere in South Florida.

Munching on the insect caused him to lose the fine focus of his concentration, though. One of his hands began to crumble, reverting to the sand he'd used to form it. He frowned, focused, and reformed the fingers into a perfect representation of human flesh. He'd decided when he went house-hunting that he would have trouble buying anything if the sellers or their agents got a look at him in his true form. Real estate people happily sold their properties to drug dealers and racketeers and pornographers, but they balked when faced with a client who bore a more than passing resemblance to an overdressed badger.

He didn't intend to be refused. He liked Fort Lauderdale for more than its ubiquitous palmetto bugs. It was the sort of place he'd spent three years looking for: it offered pleasant weather in a boomtown atmosphere, with people living right on top of each other and spending as much time as they could ignoring each other in order to preserve the little bits of privacy they could wrest from their busy, overcrowded lives.

He was willing to put up with some inconveniences to gain neighbors with blind spots like that.

The agent came bounding out the door, a big smile on her face. "Let's go do your paperwork," she said.

He smiled back at the agent. Then he smiled at the next door neighbor who was watering his lawn, and he smiled at Fort Lauderdale and then all of South Florida in general.

Almost home, he thought. *Almost home free. Suckers.*

Six

Rhiana walked from the broken window in the dining room to the door that she could not close because the Rift monster blocked it, then back to the window again. What if the men Kate had spoken of had weapons like the one Kate had? What if they came after her with those weapons?

Val and the warrag sat together in the living room, heads together and voices low. Rhiana suspected they were plotting some way to rid themselves of Kate as soon as they could—the longer Rhiana spent with Val, the more she disliked him. She wondered if he might be a member of the Kin Resistance, which fought against the new Watchmistress and the changes she wanted to make in Glenraven.

Tik sprawled on his belly on the living room floor, sleeping. Every so often he snorted and grumbled and shifted position, but he never woke up. That was typical, Rhiana thought. The dagreth were rumored to be the most comfort-loving and sedentary of the Kin-hera. If he found the larder, no doubt he would apply himself to enjoying that the way he was applying himself to getting the most out of his nap.

Leaving me to worry alone.

Kate had handed the book to Tik before she went upstairs. Tik, in turn, had passed it to Rhiana before he took his nap. Rhiana moved away from the partially open front door and the stink of the monster to the window again. She peeked through the curtains in time to see a sort of horseless wagon pull onto the little dirt road that led to the house. She'd been watching as similar horseless vehicles raced past on the smooth stone road out in front, and had been horrified by how quickly they moved. This one— beige with writing on its sides—stopped under the pines, and doors on both sides popped open.

She wondered if these were the killers and debated raising the alarm.

But then two large men got out, walked around to the back, and removed a mechanism she recognized as a variety of hoist on wheels. They wore matching clothing in an ugly shade of light brown and heavy leather work boots with laces and leather gloves, and they didn't carry anything that she could identify as a weapon. She realized they had come to remove the dead horse.

They looked almost like the southwestern Machnan—their features were broad and flat and their skins were deep shades of brown. Their hair was tightly kinked, though, while the southwestern Machnan had hair that curled more loosely. And both of them were much taller. Closer to the height of Kin, as was the woman Kate. As was the new Watchmistress, for that matter. Rhiana wondered briefly if all the people of the Machine World were so tall.

She wondered what the men would do when they saw the Rift monster.

She wondered what she ought to do. She opened the book, hoping for advice.

> You can't pretend no one is home with the front door obviously standing open. But you don't need to have much to do with them. They're here to do a job, and they won't be a danger to you unless you make a mistake dealing with them. When they ask about the Rift beast—and they will ask—tell them you shot it with your shotgun. You won't need to tell either of them any more than that. But you should go outside

and wait. You don't want them to come to the door
and see Tik or Errga or Val. That would be unfortunate.

I'm not from this world, Rhiana thought. *I don't know anything
about this world. My clothes are wrong. My voice will be wrong. I
won't know what to say.*

But the book was right. If people from this world got a good look
at her companions, trouble would ensue. So she took a deep breath
and opened the front door the rest of the way and slipped out of
it. She climbed over the stinking carcass of the Rift monster and
hopped down to the grass on the other side as the men wheeled
the hoist up the path to the horse. She kept the book with her. She
was afraid she wouldn't understand either of the men without it.

It was only when they could see the horse that they could see
the monstrosity on the front step, and both men came to a halt,
mouths hanging open.

"What in the hell is *that?*" the one with the rich brown skin
and black hair asked.

The other, who was lighter brown with graying hair, said, "Sweet
Jesus, Roy."

Both men looked to her.

"Ma'am, what is that thing?" the younger one asked.

The book did a good job of translating for her. The movements
of the men's mouths didn't match the words she heard, but she
had no trouble understanding their meaning.

"I don't know," she said.

"My . . . God . . . that wingspread must be close to thirty feet.
Maybe it's a dinosaur. I read about the Loch Ness monster maybe
being a dinosaur. There are all sorts of places on earth people
haven't been yet—maybe this came from one of those places."

The older man said, "They ain't any places in North Carolina
people ain't been, Roy. I say it's a sign of the latter days."

Roy looked at his colleague and sighed. "You *would,* James. I'll
bet if we called a paleontologist, he could tell us what it was.
And I'll bet a paleontologist would pay good money for the carcass,
too." He looked at Rhiana. "You realize you could probably get
money for this?"

She shook her head. "You came to take it away, didn't you? I
don't want to keep it."

"Well, technically we came to get the horse," Roy said. "But
we sure can't leave that here. We can take it first since it's
blocking your door. Then we can come back and get the horse."

"I don't believe you're telling her that," James said. "We ain't supposed to dispose of demons."

Roy had gone over to the monster and was running his fingers over its side. "Man! This is amazing." He looked up at Rhiana. "What happened, anyway?"

"I shot it," she said.

"Well, yeah." Roy looked impressed. "But I mean, where did it come from? How did it get here? What do you know about it?"

Rhiana shrugged. "It attacked me. I shot it. That's all I know."

He'd moved onto the stoop, where he could see the monster's teeth. When he looked up at her again, she could see respect in his eyes. "You shot this? While it was coming at you? This is the scariest thing I ever saw."

"Me, too," she told him. Then she clambered over the monster's stinking back and stood for an instant in the doorway. "I will leave you to your work." She went into Kate's house and closed the door as far as it would go. Then, heart pounding and pulse racing, she leaned against the cracked wood and waited. At last she heard the hoist in action, and the sound of the Rift beast's carcass dragging along the ground. She peeked around the corner long enough to be sure the men were taking the creature with them and not just moving it. Then she shut the door, studied the mechanisms for a moment, and locked the sliding chain lock. The door was cracked and the frame had been split in places, but both ends of that lock were in solid wood. She thought that if someone attacked it, the door would hold long enough for her and her three associates to find places to hide. That was her only real concern.

But once the men were gone, the hours passed and no one else came to the door. Rhiana started when they returned for the horse, and every time the house broke its silence with some unexplained humming or clanking or shushing; she learned to identify the sound that preceded hot air blowing out of the vents in the walls, and located a huge white metal box that occasionally purred to itself, then fell silent. She found a mechanical contraption that forced a bird out of a little wooden door at regular intervals, and punctuated the bird's arrival with a startling "HOO-hoo! HOO-hoo!" She thought perhaps the device served to mark the passage of the day as the bells in Ruddy Smeachwykke marked the stations of the sun as it marched across the sky. Val and Errga slept, and Tik snuffled and snorted and pawed at the air in some chasing dream, and at last, weary from pacing and worrying, she settled into one of the broad, cushiony, comfortable chairs and slept, too.

Seven

Kate woke with her hand on the shotgun, brought to consciousness by a sharp distant *crack*. She sat up and strained to catch the noise again, but it was not repeated. She turned painfully to one side and studied the gun. For just a moment she couldn't understand why the weapon was in the bed with her. She experienced the confusion she always felt when her sleep had been troubled by nightmares. She'd dreamed of Craig again; dreamed that the two of them were still together and happy—and always, the dream ended with Craig leaving for work on that sunny Thursday morning and not coming back. As always she woke hoping to find that the nightmare would dissolve into a happy reality where Craig still lived and loved her.

As always, she woke alone.

But this time, she woke alone with the shotgun in hand and a throbbing head and an aching body; she hurt worse than she had when she went to sleep. She twisted around in spite of the pain and checked her door. It was closed and locked. She looked

out the southeast-facing windows at the foot of her bed. Through
the partially open slats of the blinds, she could see the length-
ening shadows of late afternoon, and the gold-touched tips of the
trees that caught the light up above the shadow cast by the house.
She'd lost most of her day.

Full memory returned. The men. The horse. The outworlders.

Anger stirred in her belly. She rose and slipped a terrycloth
robe over her pajamas. With the shotgun in hand, she quietly
unlocked her bedroom door and went to the dormer window above
the landing. She peeked down at her front yard. The monster
was gone. So was Rocky.

She wasn't even awake when they took him away. She should
have set an alarm or insisted that one of the Glenraveners come
and wake her. She should have been out there when Animal Control came to take him away. He deserved better. Before she could
stop it, a tear rolled down her cheek. She wiped at it roughly, for-
getting the fractured cheekbone in her fury. The blinding pain
shocked her out of her grief, but transmuted her white-hot anger
into a cold, ugly rage. She wanted to find the men who had hurt
her and killed her horse. She wanted to destroy them.

She thought of the outworlders downstairs—she found herself
hoping they had left while she slept. If they were gone, she
wouldn't have to figure out what to do about them. Time had
tempered her resolve, which had been so clear and urgent before
she slept. Now common sense and pain made her reconsider
helping them. She was no hero; she wasn't the right person to
go charging into a situation she didn't understand against magic
far different and more powerful than anything she could manage, nor the one to do it on the say-so of a ridiculous magical
book. Mere humans had managed to hurt her and would almost
certainly try to hurt her again. How was she supposed to fight
something supernatural?

And why should she?

She stalked back into her bedroom and started tossing clothes
onto her bed: a pair of jeans, clean underwear, socks, shoes, and
her favorite sweatshirt, the one with *New York Rangers, 1994
Stanley Cup Champions* embroidered on the front. She did load
the pocket of her shooting vest full of shells and added that to
the pile.

She didn't owe the universe any favors. Before she slept she'd
been much more amenable to the idea of helping the poor, lost
otherworlders, and much more willing to consider their plight as

something she had a stake in. But what had they done for her? Invade her home? Wreck her door? Add more bruises to her already-battered body? Point her own gun at her, threaten her, keep her prisoner on her own couch? They had done all of those things. And she'd been willing to help them?

Not anymore.

She showered, letting the stinging water pound on her bruises and cuts and bites, letting it remind her of all the things she deserved to be angry about. When she finished showering and dressing and drying her hair, she stood at the top of the stairs holding the shotgun, wondering what she needed to do next. She decided to be practical. She tucked the shotgun against her side and went down to rid herself of her uninvited guests.

The front door was closed and on the chain. Both the door and the door frame were damaged, but when she tried the deadbolt it still worked, and the metal bar she jammed under the door-knob and wedged against the floor would hold, too. She would have to find time to fix both door and frame, but for the time being only someone with an ax would be able to break through the front.

She went looking for the outworlders. None of them were in the living room, where she had expected to find them. She checked the kitchen and the bathroom, then looked outside. She didn't see them anywhere. They had left the back door unlocked, though, and the Fodor's lying on the dining room table.

She wasn't as relieved to find the Glenraveners gone as she would have expected to be. The sharp noise that had wakened her was making her nervous. It had sounded like a tree limb breaking off in an ice storm, or like lightning striking nearby . . . or like a gunshot. She wished she had been awake to hear it.

She locked the kitchen door, feeling edgy and uncertain, then returned to the dining room table and picked the book up. Once again she felt that disconcerting tingle. Throw it out, she thought, but she didn't. Instead, keeping watch over her backyard from the corner of an eye, she opened the book randomly.

> Why don't you feel a little more sorry for yourself? Why don't you dredge up the fact that your family disowned you? Why don't you mull around in misery over Craig's suicide some more? That's always productive. You can use that to excuse yourself from accomplishing anything for days on end. Why don't

you remind yourself of how much you miss your brother and sister, and blame your parents for turning them against you?

"I don't feel sorry for myself," she muttered.

Really? You came down the stairs sulking about how you didn't owe the world anything, didn't you? You lost your family; you lost your lover; you lost your horse; you don't have any friends here; some intolerant creeps beat you up. Your life is shit, so you don't need to care about what happens to your world or someone else's world? Poor girl. Life's been so hard on you.

But all of that's true, she thought.

So what? Are you successful? Are you doing what you want with your life? Do you have food to eat and a place to sleep?

She didn't have to answer. What the book was saying was true and she knew it. She rarely let herself indulge in self-pity. Her parents had turned their backs on her because they refused to accept her choice of religion. She'd known that might happen when she became pagan, yet she had chosen to follow her heart, regardless of the consequences. Craig had been prone to depression long before she met him. The time they lived together had been the happiest she ever knew, but all along she saw that Craig wasn't dealing well with other aspects of his life. He was often moody, his personality could change abruptly, and he frequently considered dying as a remedy to the problems he faced. He refused to accept any help and he refused to discuss his fears even with her. Knowing that, she chose to love him anyway, and to start building a life that included him as an integral part.

After his death, she chose to stay in Peters, in the house they'd acquired together. She knew Peters was a backward, close-minded town; she knew people in it wouldn't accept her if they knew anything about her. She stayed anyway, and now she had to accept the consequences of that choice, as well.

At every step of her life, she'd had the opportunity to make other decisions, and those other decisions would have changed everything.

But I made the best choices I could at the time, she told herself.

> Then stop complaining about the results of those
> choices now. Or else do what you have to do to make
> everyone else happy with you. Sell your house and
> move away from Peters. Give up your religion. Beg
> your parents forgiveness. Be the person other people
> expect you to be instead of the person you choose
> to be.

"No. I won't pretend to be something I'm not ever again."

Someone tried to open the back door, and Kate jumped, grabbed her gun, and turned.

Rhiana stood there, visible through the window, expression grim. Kate kept the gun but went to unlock the door.

Rhiana didn't waste any time on pleasantries. "The warrag heard someone prowling around outside your house," she said. "He and the dagreth went outside to investigate—they are still chasing the vehicle the two men were riding. But now that you are awake, you need to come outside and tell Val and me what they were doing."

Kate tucked the gun into the crook of her arm and followed Rhiana out the door.

Outside, she found cans of spray paint. Someone had written, BURN IN HELL WITCH! and DEVIL LOVER across the front of her house and had painted inverted pentagrams on her car doors. They had started to paint something on the side, but were interrupted, probably, she thought, by the warrag and the dagreth coming out to investigate.

Her gut tightened. Staring at the graffiti, she told Rhiana and Val, "They're harassing me . . . trying to scare me away. They want me to run away." She read the things written on the house to them and added, "The pentagrams are a common symbol associated with witchcraft and magic. Locally, people assume any religion that isn't theirs is some form of devil worship."

"What can you do to stop them?"

"Catch them in the act. Maybe." Kate shrugged and turned away from the vandalism. "Maybe nothing. I can tell the sheriff's department about this, but if the man who did it is a deputy I don't think that will help."

"Your sheriff is corrupt?"

"No. Actually I think the local sheriff is honest. I think he

cares about the people who elected him, and that he does a pretty
good job. But if this is being done by someone who works for
him, that person will be able to follow the investigation and
influence the things that are found and the things that are done.
He could plant false clues or lose real ones, and he'll know exactly
what his fellow deputies will look for. He won't make the same
sorts of mistakes someone who wasn't in law enforcement would
make."

Rhiana said, "So you aren't going to inform the sheriff."

"I am. But I don't think it will help."

They went inside and waited for the warrag and the dagreth
to return. Kate wanted to hear what they had to say about the
two men before she called the sheriff again.

Errga got back first. Tongue lolling out of his mouth, panting
heavily, he let himself in, stood on his hind legs to get himself
a bowl, turned on the tap, and filled it with water.

Kate couldn't help but feel surprised. "I see you've figured
everything out," she said. He panted, nodded, and lapped at the
water, but didn't say anything until the bowl was empty. When
it was, he turned to her and growled, "They got away. That
thing they rode was too quick, and we couldn't follow the scent.
There are too many scents we don't know here. The dagreth
was doing better with the smells, but traffic on your roads is
so fast. . . ." He got another bowl of water, sat it on the floor,
and flopped down beside it. At that moment he looked doggish, and somehow not intimidating. He lowered his head and
lapped again, this time slower. Like a dog, he spattered water
across the floor as he drank. Kate found that endearing, though
she couldn't say why.

When he lifted his head again, Errga said, "Tik should be back
soon. I'm not as fast as he is in a short run, but—" he grinned
broadly "—I can run the legs off of him in the stretch."

When the dagreth arrived, no more than three minutes behind
Errga, he was in a foul mood. "One of those horseless wagons
nearly ran me down," he said. "As if I didn't have the right to
use the road. It howled at me, but I turned and stood my ground
and it swerved." He glared at Kate.

Kate tried to imagine the reaction of the people who had almost
hit the dagreth. "You don't want to run on the roads," she told
him. "Even though you're supposed to be able to ride bicycles
and horses on them, they're really only safe for cars. Besides, no
one around here has ever seen anything like you. If they get a

good look at you, you'll cause an accident." She sighed. "Tomorrow there will probably be something in the paper about a grizzly bear sighted out this way."

He got himself a bowl of water as Errga had done, and growled while he carried the water toward the dining room. He said, "Your world stinks."

"It isn't so bad," Kate said, not liking to find herself on the defensive.

"Maybe not, but it stinks. Those wagons smell like fires in a garbage dump. All the smells I need to smell muddle up and disappear underneath the stench."

Oh, Kate thought. *He meant it literally.* She said, "You'll get used to it after a while."

Neither of them had gotten anything more than a glimpse at the two men, though Kate finally figured out from their description that the two men were riding pillion on a motorcycle. That would be next to useless.

She called the sheriff's department, told them about the vandalism, and that when she went out to investigate, the men had run away. She told the deputy it would be fine if the department wanted to send someone around to take a look the next day. She said she didn't think they would be back.

She hung up and said, "Evidently this is one of the bad Fridays. A friend of mine who worked a beat up in Detroit told me she got the most violent crimes, women in labor and crazies when she had a Friday and a full moon on the first of the month. She called them three-F nights, and she said they were like pulling combat duty." Kate went back to the table and sat heavily. "Our complaint doesn't even come close to a shooting or a stabbing or a rape."

Rhiana said, "It doesn't matter whether they can come tonight or not."

"No?"

"The warrag and the dagreth might not have gotten a good look at the men who were painting your house, but the men got a good look at them. They were terrified. They won't come back tonight."

"Good." Kate hurt, but she hadn't gotten her prescription for Darvon filled, and she didn't want to go anywhere right then. She decided to take two Tylenol and two Advil and hope that her pain would ease off. Rhiana followed her out to the kitchen.

"If you don't have something else you need to do, perhaps you could show me how you make magic work here. I've tried everything I know, and I've come to the conclusion that I'm wasting my time."

Kate got her medicine and took a caffeine-free Diet Coke from the fridge. She popped the top and tossed the pills down two at a time. When they were down, she said, "Sure. We might as well. We need to get that figured out as soon as we can; I know you want to get home. And I can't go outside and paint tonight, anyway."

Rhiana was watching her, the expression on her face curious.

Kate said, "What do you want to ask me?"

The other woman blushed. "Why did you think I wanted to ask . . . ? I didn't want to . . . I was only curious. I'm sorry."

"Don't apologize. If you have a question, ask. You aren't going to hurt my feelings."

Rhiana nodded thoughtfully. "I was just wondering . . . are you afraid?"

Kate laughed. "God, yes. Of course I am."

Rhiana still looked curious. "But you don't act frightened. You shot that monster, and you know the men want to hurt you, but you haven't run away, and . . ." Rhiana shrugged. "I only wondered because you are alone. And for women alone, things are sometimes very hard."

"They are. I'm not alone by choice. The man I loved . . . died . . . and I don't have any choice now but to keep on going."

"Yes," Rhiana said. "I'm the same. My husband was killed in battle. For the last year and a half I've been without him."

Kate was surprised. It was hard to imagine the self-possessed, cool Rhiana as someone's wife. "It's hard, isn't it?"

"Very. I have my husband's advisors and they are some help, but all the concerns of Ruddy Smeachwykke descended upon my shoulders when he died. The taxes, the debates, the law. Some of the townsfolk thought I couldn't sit in judgment or determine a fair tariff or oversee marriages or bless the crops," she said, her voice dropping low. "They looked at me and decided I was young and a woman and alone, and they tried to appoint a successor for me."

"You run a town?" Kate asked.

Rhiana smiled slightly. "I *am* Lady Smeachwykke. And I kept them from appointing their damned replacement, too. I tested for an Adjudicator Without Title, which I added to being Adjudicator With Title, and I became a Juris." Her smile grew smug.

"Few people even qualify to begin study, and most study for years before testing. I looked like quite a genius when I tested, I tell you. What the testing board didn't know was that before Haddis died—Haddis was my husband's name—I spent years looking up precedents for him, and I frequently wrote his opinions for the Canons. So I knew my way through the Precepts and Canons of Law."

"So you're a lawyer."

"I'm a Juris. One of three Machnan Jurisa in all of Glenraven, and the only woman. People come before me and tell me their problems, and I determine the solutions. When I earned that honor, it became hard for the men who wanted to replace me to convince anyone that I wasn't capable of running Ruddy Smeachwykke."

"And you do magic."

"That's part of being a Juris. Being able to cast a truth spell and make it stick." She pointed to the Coke and said, "May I try one of those, or would you rather I didn't?"

"You're welcome to them anytime you want." Kate got Rhiana the Coke and showed her how to open the top.

"You look like you really enjoy these." She took a sip and immediately made an awful face. She took another tentative sip, wrinkled her nose, and looked at Kate.

Kate said, "They're an acquired taste."

"So is self-flagellation." Rhiana took one more tiny sip, shook her head, and put the can down on the counter. "But I've never seen the point."

"We'll find something that you like, then." Kate had a hard time not laughing at the faces the other woman was making.

"Ale," Rhiana told her, not hesitating. "Smoky red wines. Cider. Spring water."

"We'll find something."

Rhiana looked toward the living room, where the Kin and Kinhera had gone, and said, "Do you miss your husband?"

"We weren't married yet, but yes . . . I miss him. I loved him very much."

"Did you?" Rhiana was still looking away from Kate. "I wonder what that would be like. I never loved Haddis. We were good friends. We rode and hawked and hunted together. We laughed at each other's jokes, and we were partners, but the question of love never occurred to either of us. He had his mistresses for that. I had the children."

She turned and looked at Kate. "Ours was an arranged marriage. He was twenty years my senior, and his first wife and his son, his only child, died in the Plagues. So he arranged with my father to marry me."

"You have children?"

"Three. A daughter and two sons. Both of my sons are interning. One is at Sarijann Castle with Torrin Sarijann. The other is with Bekka Shaita, Lady Dinnos. My daughter is learning keep management and magic at home."

Kate looked at Rhiana. She looked the same age as Kate, but she had three children who were old enough to be learning jobs. "How old are they?" she asked.

"Thirteen, twelve, and ten." Rhiana said, "I married at fourteen, and had the first boy when I was still sixteen."

"You were so young," Kate whispered before she realized the comment might be rude.

Rhiana didn't take offense. "Yes. But after the Plagues, so many people were dead that any woman who was of age married and started having children immediately."

I was feeling sorry for myself, Kate thought. *I think I'll remember not to do that anymore.*

Eight

Rhiana didn't want to think about how much she missed her children. She didn't want to think about the fact that surely they had to believe she was dead. Perhaps Ty was back from Rikes Gate already, sitting down with the advisors and trying to figure out how to take over the work he was not completely prepared to shoulder. He was a sensible boy, and she thought he would do well in her stead, but she wanted to go home. She wanted to tell him that everything was fine, that she was alive and safe, that his world hadn't fallen apart.

The only way she could tell him that was if she found her way home.

She looked at Kate and said, "Perhaps we could get to work."

"The magic?"

"It's what I need to understand most desperately. Everything else can wait at least a while."

Kate nodded. She gathered a few things from her kitchen pantry, and switched out the lights as she led the way to her dining room

table. "I don't know how useful you'll find this," she said, putting candles and an incense burner down on the table.

Rhiana shrugged. "I don't know either. But I have to find some
way of working with the local magic if I ever hope to create a
gate that will take us home."

"My way of working with magic may be completely useless
to you. I can't create doors between worlds. I can't change
weather or throw bolts of energy from my fingertips, and quite
honestly, I don't know that anyone on Earth could. Magic to
me has always been indirect, nothing more than a slow nudging to encourage things to go in the direction in which I want
them to go."

Rhiana thought magic of that sort would be useless. When she
cast a spell she wanted immediate results, and Kate was telling
her immediate results were impossible. "Slow nudging isn't going
to get us a gate," she said.

"No. But if I show you what I know, maybe you can see some
way to use it and change it into what you need."

Rhiana nodded. That sounded reasonable.

"Okay. Watch me." Kate closed her eyes and began breathing
slowly and rhythmically.

Rhiana watched her, leaving herself open to feel the flow of
energy around the two of them. She recognized Kate's first actions
as grounding and centering herself, and her next as creating a
warded sphere within which the two of them would work. Both
of these actions were the same ones Rhiana would have taken,
though Kate's approach was different than Rhiana's would have
been. However, the warded sphere startled her. As soon as Kate
cast it, it billowed around the two of them, fierce and strong and
blue-white to her mind's eye but invisible to her physical ones.
In that simple sphere, Rhiana felt more magic than she had felt
up to that moment in the whole of the Machine World. Kate
had not touched the lines of power that coursed across the surface of her world, yet now those lines of power were drawn toward
her as iron filings were drawn to a magnet.

Rhiana struggled to find Kate's power source. The planet's weak
surface power now curled around her in a weak green nimbus,
but she didn't use any of it. She didn't need it; that brilliant hot
power surged through her and around the two of them, almost
blindingly brilliant to Rhiana's magical senses. Then Kate opened
her eyes. "I know that doesn't look like much, but what I've done
is—" she started to say, but Rhiana interrupted her.

"Where did you find your power?"

Kate looked puzzled.

"Earth, air, fire, water?" Rhiana tried to clarify her question.

"The four magical elements?" Kate shook her head. "None of those. I use them very little, really."

"Then from which well do you draw?"

Kate shrugged. "It's a little vague, really. I know a lot of pagans call on a god or goddess, but I've never really thought about the universe's power in that way. I believe there is a creative force, a guiding force, perhaps, that gave all of us our start. I draw from that."

Rhiana made a strangled little sound and closed her eyes. She considered her own world. Glenraven's magic ran on the surface where anyone who knew how to touch it could use it. But the source of Glenraven's magic, the entity Rhiana had always thought of as the real Glenraven, kept distant and untouchable, speaking only through its chosen Watchmistress or Watchmaster. Kate was speaking of tapping directly into that power. In fact, it was evident to Rhiana that she had successfully done so. The human woman, in an act Rhiana considered unthinkable hubris, was treating a deity like her own personal well.

Yet with this blinding force at her fingertips, she could only nudge events, without any certainty of the results she would get?

Maybe there were complications Rhiana couldn't see yet. She opened her eyes and looked at the human. "Now what?"

"Now we perform a spell. I think I'll renew the wards on the house. That needs to be done anyway." Kate did a few things with her candles, said some words, stood inside the sphere she'd created and faced the four compass points. During all of this, Rhiana saw that nothing was happening. The magic curled and surged around her, unchanged. Then Kate said, "Once I've formed the spell, I set it over the house." She closed her eyes again, and once again Rhiana felt awe at the amount of power that was suddenly in Kate's grasp. Enormous sheets of energy flung themselves outward, wrapping the house in blankets of crackling power so brilliant to Rhiana's second sight that she grasped instinctively at the weaker earth magic and pulled it in around herself as a buffer and a shield. Oddly, as soon as Kate's wards settled into the structure of the house, they effectively disappeared. Rhiana, eyes closed, was able to locate the power nestled within the wall nearest her, but the wards would give no warning of their presence to even the most talented wizard who was looking for telltales of magic.

Rhiana had never seen such superb wards, and she had never seen wards cast in such an irrational, bungling manner. The wards did not exist until Kate conjured them in her mind—what she had called her spellcasting was nothing but a diversion from the real magic this world had to offer.

Kate opened her eyes, shrugged, and smiled. "It isn't much, I suppose. Not compared to the sorts of magic you're used to. I've never had any problem with people breaking into my home, though. I could credit the wards . . . but I might just be lucky."

Rhiana considered that abrupt, unexpected, coiled power that had leapt out of nowhere and wrapped itself around the house, and she considered the woman who stood before her looking down at her, almost apologetically, and she shook her head.

"If I had that much power to work with, I could fly," she said. Her voice came out sounding curt, but she didn't care.

Kate's eyes widened. "All what power? I have never seen a single tangible result of my magic. There are some events in my life that I think I've influenced, but quite honestly, they were events I could have influenced by my behavior, too. And perhaps I did."

"Can't you see the power you summon up when you cast your house wards? Or when you create the circle in which you work? Can't you see that your magic is coming from your source, wherever that is, and not from the little ritual things you do. When you lit your candles and recited your poetry and drew your symbols in the air with your finger, you weren't doing anything. But both times when you closed your eyes and reached, you reached right into the heart of something stronger than anything I've ever seen before."

"What do you mean, see?"

"The circle you cast . . . the wards you threw. Can't you see them?"

"Of course not."

"I don't mean with your physical eyes. But with your inner eye . . . with your second sight . . . can't you see them with that?"

"No. I can . . . well, I can visualize them. I imagined them there, after all, and the picture I created when I imagined them . . . when I close my eyes I can see that. Or I can imagine it with my eyes open, of course."

"No. When you close your eyes, you should be able to see the

sphere you cast around us as a brilliant blue-white light. Even
if you aren't thinking about the energy you've called up, you should
be able to see it as clearly with your eyes closed as you see this
room when you have them open. With your eyes closed, you
should be able to walk around the perimeter of your circle, never
straying once from the edge . . ." She frowned, thoughtful. "But
you can't, can you? Not at all. When you close your eyes, nothing
is there but darkness."

Kate nodded. "That's right."

"What happens when you touch your wards?"

"Nothing."

"Nothing? Nothing at all?"

"Nothing. I know they're there—or at least I tell myself I know
they're there, but I don't feel anything."

Rhiana raised her fingers to the blue-white curve of power that
arced over her head and down behind her back. The deep, heady
thrill of the magic reverberated against her fingertips as if she
had touched the strings of an instrument another musician had
just played. The purity and fierce strength of the magic Kate had
cast was heartbreakingly beautiful.

And Kate was in essence blind and deaf to what she had done—
more blind and deaf than the bell-ringer Kadurr had been deaf
to her own Songs of Lost Souls, for she felt the vibrations of her
bells in the soles of her feet, in her breastbone and her gut, in
the palms of her hands and the bones of her face. Kate felt nothing. Nothing at all, and yet, magic-blind, she had found a source
of power deeper and richer than anything Rhiana had ever
touched.

"You can see what I've done, can't you?" Kate asked.

"Yes."

"And it's real, isn't it?"

"Yes. Real and powerful."

"Can you teach me how to see it?"

"No." Rhiana looked at the human woman. "Could you teach
a blind woman how to see, or teach a deaf woman how to hear?"

"No. But I could find ways to show that woman how to com-
pensate for the sense she didn't have."

"Hold your hand up and lift it until you touch the circle you've
created. When your hand touches the circle, stop."

Kate raised a hand and lifted it slowly, falteringly, and Rhiana
could tell she felt nothing. Her hand rose, stopped, rose, stopped,
rose right through the leading edge of the sphere without fal-

tering even slightly, rose until her fingertips were completely through, stopped, rose incrementally and stopped a final time. "There?"

Rhiana wanted to weep. "No," she said softly. "Lower." She felt helpless, watching Kate lower her hand again, face scrunched with concentration, trying so hard to feel the magic. The sight was as sad to her as if she had been watching a blind child trying to make his eyes function by sheer willpower. "Right there," she told Kate, as the other woman began to move past the sphere she had created.

"You really feel something there?"

"Yes."

"I don't."

"I know."

They stood looking at each other, and Rhiana said, "This is the problem. You cannot tell me how to find the power source you've used, because whatever sense you have used to locate it, I obviously don't have. I cannot feel anything in this world of yours that could be the source of such tremendous power. I can't show you how to use the power, because you can neither see nor feel it."

"What about telling me the spells you use, and letting me try them."

"Spells? The things you did with words and your hands and the lighting of the incense?"

"Yes."

Rhiana shook her head. "Pointless. Those things didn't even work for you. You did something in your head that worked, but if you don't know what it was, you can't tell me how to do it. And I don't use spells of the sort you mean. I . . ." She sighed. "I'm not sure how to put into words what I do. I shift the energies I use directly, shaping and forming them, directing them by sight and feel. I could *show* you if you could see, but you can't see. I could guide your hands and mind if you could feel. But *telling* you would be worse than useless."

Kate pulled out her chair and settled into it. "You're saying no matter what we do, we will not be able to get magic to work for us. That we won't be able to create your gate."

"Yes. I suppose I am."

"I don't accept that. We're missing something. The book insisted that we needed each other, and that what we had to do, we could only do together."

"The book says. That *book* says. Hah. That book dragged us here and trapped us, and I have the feeling that the only thing that is ever going to get us home is our own hard work. If there is any way to get home." Rhiana pulled out her own chair and sat, too. She closed her eyes and felt the flow of power from the sphere. She tried to imagine the effect of bursting through wards set by someone magically blind, and wondered if they would do too little or too much or nothing at all. She tried to sense the source of power Kate had used, and all the while her frustration grew. Did the damned book know Kate was a magical cripple? Did it know that out of all the people on this planet, it had drawn Rhiana to someone who couldn't teach her what she needed to know and couldn't do what needed to be done? Didn't it care that it had marooned her and three other Glenraveners? Didn't it—

"Perhaps," Kate said, "I could draw up the energy and pass it on to you."

—matter that Rhiana had a home and friends and that she was responsible for the people of Ruddy Smeachwykke and . . .

Something of what Kate said penetrated her self-pity. Rhiana opened her eyes. "What did you say?"

"I said, perhaps I could draw up the energy and pass it on to you."

Rhiana sat forward and rested her arms on the table. "Could you do that? Never mind. Silly of me to ask—you don't know whether you could do it or not. You've been taking everything you do on faith."

"Not precisely. I keep a mirror book. I record what I've done, and write down any results that might be applicable. I've seen enough success to be fairly certain I was doing something."

"Trust me—that's essentially doing it on faith." Rhiana wondered if she would have had the patience to stick with something she couldn't see and couldn't feel, trying to control it blindly, keeping a book in which she wrote down what she had done and while she waited to see if her actions had any effects. She doubted she would have.

"Why don't we try your idea," she said. "See if you can draw up magical energy from wherever you're getting it, and pass it to me."

Kate nodded. She closed her eyes and inhaled, then exhaled, then inhaled again. Rhythmic breathing, that expression of intense concentration, silence except for the ticking and whirring of various devices in the house.

Again she saw the other woman fill herself with magic. The air grew bright around her and Rhiana reminded herself that Kate saw and felt nothing of the radiant nimbus that suffused the air around them.

Kate opened her eyes and looked at Rhiana.

Without warning, magic wrapped itself in a tight cocoon around Rhiana, shattering the frail shield she'd drawn up around herself and assaulting her senses. She panicked and flailed out at it instead of absorbing it the way she would have absorbed the magic from a natural ley line; this was the worst possible thing she could have done. The energy arced and ignited into a fireball that enveloped everything in a roar of thunder and a searing flash of light.

Nine

Kate didn't have time to react. Out of nowhere, out of nothing, Rhiana disappeared in a firebomb, and the searing blue-white flames exploded outward and enveloped Kate, the table and the chairs they sat on, the ground beneath their feet, the air they breathed. Kate threw her hands over her face as a shock wave hit her. She felt herself lift into the air; a thunderous explosion deafened her and she pulled herself into a little ball and screamed and wrapped her arms over her ears and squeezed her eyes shut and—*Shit! Shit! Shit! I don't want to die! I don't want to die!*—tried to breathe, flew for what felt like a thousand years, tumbled weightless and frantically tried to protect herself as her weight came back and her body slammed into something hard and icy wind flayed her skin and the thunder pounded her and battered her and drove through her brain like nails and the fire burned beneath her eyelids and pain ate her and chewed her up and spat her out and left her washed up in a huddled ball in utter silence and total darkness alone and lost and freezing cold.

She lay on her side, knees drawn up to her chest. She opened her eyes and saw only blackness. She could hear nothing. She could feel, but all she felt was pain. Her every joint screamed, her head pounded, and she was cold. Cold. *What sort of fire burned and left you cold?* she wondered. She wasn't just cold; she was freezing. Freezing in silence and darkness. Maybe she was dead. Maybe she was lost in some bitter Nordic hell.

Or maybe not. Better to think she was still alive. She might have a chance to stay that way if she acted on that assumption.

Her pains began to sort themselves out, and she discovered that some were worse than others. Something hard dug into her ribs, and she rolled to one side enough that she could reach it with one hand and move it. It was a rock. She was lying in sand.

Sand?

Blind, deaf, lying in sand. Cold. Cold.

She rubbed her arms and discovered her sleeves were gone. She touched her legs, her belly, her breasts, her back. She was naked. She'd been fully dressed an instant before. Her skin was intact, but every bit of her clothing was gone. Shoes, socks, underwear. Her favorite Rangers sweatshirt.

Dammit! Her favorite Rangers sweatshirt!

Blind, deaf, *naked*, lying in sand, and getting angry.

The lying-in-sand part she could fix. She rolled her knees under her and sat up and slammed her head into something so hard white light flashed along the backs of her eyeballs and she howled and fell forward again holding her head. Rocked back and forth, swearing a blue streak, clutching her head, feeling the lump rise.

"Kate?"

The voice belonged to Rhiana.

Kate groaned and turned toward the sound. "What?"

"You aren't dead?"

"Unfortunately not."

"Where are we?"

Kate snarled, "I don't know. We blew up and everything went black. Why are you asking me?"

"I'm so cold," Rhiana said. "And all my clothes are gone."

"Mine, too." Kate opened her eyes again. The darkness began to recede from the very center of her field of vision, and gradually she realized a circle of light lay above her and a few feet away. "But I can see now," she whispered.

Rhiana said, "My vision is coming back, too."

"Are you hurt?"

"I hurt, but I don't think I'm injured."

"Except for hitting my head on whatever is right above me, I think I'm okay, too. Don't sit up," Kate warned.

"I won't. Do you think we should crawl toward the light?"

"I don't think so. Not until we have some idea what happened to us and where we are. Has anything like this ever happened to you?"

"No. You?"

Kate's short laugh this time sounded harsh to her own ears. "No. But I could say the same thing about everything these last two days."

Kate rolled cautiously onto her belly. Her eyes were adjusting to the darkness, and she began to make out a geometric pattern of pillars standing blacker in the darkness. They were extraordinarily low pillars—the ceiling couldn't be more than three feet above her head, and she tried to imagine who would build such a place. Sand floor with rocks left lying around, broad squat pillars, areas of total blackness to her right and left.

To her left, something began to roar. She jumped, fearing the worst. Then she smelled oil.

And suddenly she knew where she was. She began to laugh. She'd been under her house half a dozen times to manually light her furnace during the year when she couldn't afford to have anyone come in to service it. Now she was under her house again.

"Crawl toward the light," she said. "Keep your head down, though, and watch your knees. There's all sorts of junk down here."

"You know where we are?"

"Oh, yeah."

They reached the circle of light. The light came through a hole in her floor easily six feet in diameter, that cut through wood flooring and subfloor and support beams and part of the air duct so smoothly the edges of the cuts looked polished. Kate crawled out first, and found the remains of her chairs and a small sliver of one side of the table that had evidently been just outside of the circle she had cast. Except for the furniture fragments, there was no mess. Nothing shattered. Nothing disturbed. The explosion hadn't even left dust.

Kate crawled up out of the hole into her dining room and stared down at what had once been a beautifully refinished old hardwood floor. Rhiana crawled out beside her and looked, too. "Perhaps we shouldn't do that again," she said.

"You might be right." Kate shook her head slowly. Two chairs had survived the blast intact. They were the two Kate had kept against the wall on either side of the picture window. The others all looked like they'd been bait in a shark feeding frenzy. Dammit. Her floor—hours of back-breaking labor, stripping and drum-sanding and staining and varnishing. Her table. Her chairs. She'd gone to so much trouble finding them. Had worked for weeks on her days off, turning them into beautiful hand-rubbed tung-oil-finished artworks. She'd been so proud of them when she was done. But the work on the furniture and the floor had been more than simple work. The floors and the furniture had been some of the ways she dealt with her pain after Craig's death. Work and more work; the conscious and deliberate avoidance of anything alluringly self-destructive; the constant reminder to make something good and something beautiful of her time; the utter adamant refusal to let herself give in to her despair.

And nights when she fell exhausted into bed and passed into undreaming sleep, and mornings when she woke to darkness and the alarm clock's steady bleating, she knew the bleakness in her soul and felt the call of the abyss into which Craig had flung himself, and she spurred herself harder. She could think back to those days and the only moments of silent reflection she recalled were the ones when she rode Rocky through the pine woods. And Rocky was gone, too. She wondered if everything she still cared about was fated for destruction.

Then she stood straighter. How easy, how very easy, to fall into self-pity. Her *world* was fated for destruction if she didn't find a way to stop it, and in the face of that, things could not be allowed to matter. So her floor was damaged. She would repair it. So her table and chairs were gone. She would replace them. And Rocky was gone. She would miss him. And that was all she would, could, allow herself to feel.

She turned to Rhiana. "I have some clothes in the dryer. Why don't we get dressed and then see if we can figure out what went wrong."

"Is it safe to come out there?" Val called from the living room.

Both women shouted at the same time, "NO!" and hurried to the downstairs bathroom to find clothes and get dressed.

When they returned to the kitchen, Kate got the *Fodor's Guide to Glenraven*. She came back out, got a good look at her guest, and barely kept herself from laughing. Kate guessed Rhiana couldn't have weighed more than ninety pounds, and she might have been five feet tall if she rose up on her toes a bit. Kate was five ten and weighed one-forty. Rhiana looked like a starving waif dressed in a pair of her jeans with the legs rolled up four times and a belt pulled to the tightest notch to hold them up and a T-shirt that hung down past her knees. The two of them settled onto the barstools at the bar that separated the kitchen from the dining room and Kate opened the guide.

"What did we do wrong?" Kate asked.

> You have the right idea, but you're drawing too much power when you get ready to pass it to Rhiana. When you tap your source, I felt you visualize the tides of an ocean, the crashing surf, the unstoppable forces of the sea. Think smaller. Try visualizing a slow, steady stream from a water tap. Maybe just a thread of water. Maybe just a faucet dripping occasionally.

Rhiana snorted. "That won't do much." Then, sounding annoyed, she asked the book, "Why didn't you tell us that Kate was magic-blind and that I wouldn't be able to touch the source of magic in this world?"

> I did not know she was magic-blind, nor did I know that you would be unable to locate her source of power. I had never seen either of you work; you seem to assume that I know you better than I do. You assume a prescience on my part that, sadly, does not exist. I can follow the individual threads of some events through the weft and warp of reality, seeing where they go in and where they go out, but I can no more see the steps that form the greater pattern of the weave than you can. The "how" of any specific event is as much a mystery to me as it is to you.

Kate stared down at the words and frowned. The comparison of weaving with reality wasn't new to her, but the comment about seeing the greater pattern of the weave . . . that left her puzzled.

> The pattern is this . . . I foresee that by bringing the five of you together and informing you of the danger to your worlds and the fabric of reality, you may

be able to alter what is an otherwise unstoppable fall to destruction for Glenraven and Earth. The steps that will create that pattern . . . I do not know those. If the knowledge were mine to give, I would share it. It is not.

Rhiana gave Kate a look of purest disbelief. "So the book is going to tell us what we need to accomplish, but we have to figure out how to do it? What good is that?"

Until I brought you together, you didn't know there was a problem.

Kate said, "And I preferred it that way."
Rhiana laughed. Kate realized it was the first time she had seen any sign of humor from the woman at all. "As did I," she agreed.

Ignorance is rarely bliss. Ignorance is cancer untreated and growing.

"We were joking," Kate muttered. "Nobody was seriously suggesting that we would be better off letting our worlds die." She turned to Rhiana, her hand resting on the page, and said, "I guess we ought to get back to work. We need to find a way to do magic together without atomizing things." She caught a flicker from the book, and turned to stare at the page again.

Before you go, here is the pattern you must weave. You must locate Callion and the Watchers, go to them, find out what they have been doing in this world since they arrived in the Machine World, and nullify any damage they have done. You must create a gate back to Glenraven and take Callion and the Watchers through it. Then you must return them to the Rift and force Callion to release the Watchers back to their own world and when they are gone, you must force him to close the Rift. Finally, you must make some provision that will prevent him from reopening the Rift.

"Oh, is that all?" Rhiana said.
Kate glanced at her sidelong. She could see the faintest hint

of a smile at the corners of her mouth. More evidence of a sense of humor. Kate said, "We ought to be able to take care of that by tomorrow, don't you think?"

"But of course. I suspect we could do it tonight if we cared to, though I don't want to work that hard."

And even though nothing about the situation was funny, both of them began to laugh hysterically.

Five hours later, after two more large explosions, perhaps thirty small explosions, and the accidental summoning of a spirit from the spaces between the worlds, with both Kate and Rhiana dressed only in brown Glad lawn bags with holes punched through for their heads and arms so that they wouldn't vaporize any more of Kate's rapidly dwindling wardrobe, Kate successfully passed to Rhiana a flow of magic small enough that Rhiana could transform it without destroying anything. Rhiana created a sunflower, which she made to grow up out of the hole in the center of the dining room floor. The plant burst out of the ground and unfurled rapidly; Kate thought the process looked like stop-motion photography and found the fact that it was real delightful.

Still, she would have preferred Rhiana to materialize some new Wrangler jeans to replace the ones all their experimentation had destroyed.

They sat on the edge of the dining room hole with their bare legs dangling down into the cold darkness of the crawl space. Both of them were sweaty and filthy. Their ropy hair stuck to their foreheads and the backs of their necks, and the plastic bags they wore clung to their skin. They cheered softly when the sunflower bloomed.

"Enough for tonight," Kate said.

Rhiana looked over at her, eyes heavy-lidded. "Enough for the rest of my life. I'm exhausted."

"I know. I've never done anything so wearing."

"Do you know the worst part of this?" Rhiana asked.

Kate didn't, but didn't know that she wanted to, either. "No."

"When we wake, after we've practiced with small energies until we're sure we can use them accurately, we have to start increasing power again."

"What? No."

"Oh, yes." Rhiana let herself sag forward until her torso rested on her thighs and her arms draped down into the crawl space. "That I've learned to catch your sort of magic doesn't mean I can catch enough of it to blast a gate from here to Glenraven. So tomorrow it shall be more explosions and more flashing lights and more flames and booms and crashes and more of these stinking sticky hot bags. . . ." She sighed heavily. "And we don't even know where the bastard is, or where to start looking for him."

"We'll find him," Kate said. "We're going to succeed, Rhiana."

"We shall at least die trying."

Ten

Callion tapped his finger on the desk and stared out the window, holding the phone pressed to one ear.

"*Sun-Sentinel*," an efficient female voice said.

"Classifieds, please."

"One moment."

The voice that came on the line a moment later was also female. "*Sun-Sentinel* classifieds, Shelby Barnott speaking. How may I help you?"

"I'd like to place two advertisements," Callion said. "Can you write them down, please?"

"Certainly."

"The first must read: 'Career opportunity: The successful candidate will be an intelligent, well-educated single female between the ages of 18 and 30 who is willing to move to advance her career, and who is a voracious reader. Should enjoy SF/F and occult literature and have a working knowledge of magic. Starting salary can range from $40,000 to $70,000 dollars per annum, commensurate with education and ability. Job includes company house and company car and all benefits. Apply in writing, describing yourself, your interests, and your qualifications, and give a contact number.' "

He gave her the address of the post office box he'd rented.

"Wow," she said. "I'd love to have a job like that. I'd be perfect."

"You're welcome to apply," he said. "In writing."

She said nothing for half a beat. Then she said, "And your second advertisement."

"Identical, except that all references to a female must be changed to a male. And the address is different." He gave her the second post office box number, then insisted that she read both ads back to him.

"Anything special you would like to do with these? We can outline with a black box, use a larger typeface—"

He made a face over the phone. The female candidate he was looking for would read the small print. The other, though . . .

"On the ad for the male candidate, give me a fourteen-point sans-serif typeface, with the first two words in bold print. I'd like a one-point solid border around the ad, and if you can arrange to narrow the ad to less than a column in width so that I can get a bit of additional white space all the way around it, I'd like that, too."

He heard her clicking away at the keyboard. After a moment, she said, "Done. And the same treatment for the other ad?"

"No. Nothing special for it at all. I've discovered that women read the small print, while men frequently need to be thumped over the head."

She laughed. "I always thought the same thing."

He made another face at the phone. He wondered if the woman to whom he was speaking was capable of independent thought.

"How long do you want to run it?"

"Six weeks to start with."

A silence. Then an uncertain, "Six *weeks?*"

"The company has more than one opening to fill, and suitable candidates are extremely difficult to locate. I imagine the ad will run considerably longer than six weeks."

"Right. I have you down for six weeks." She went over the details of each ad for him, then said, "How would you like to pay?"

"Will my gold card suffice?"

"Of course."

He gave her the number and expiration date and his name. "Can you have them in tomorrow's paper?"

"Yes."

"I'll look for them."

They hung up and he dialed another number.

"Rickman, Rickman, Slater, Stern and Brodski."

"Is this Elaine?"

"Yes, it is. To whom am I speaking."

"This is Callion Aregeni, dear."

"Mr. Aregeni! How good to hear from you. Have you gotten settled?"

"I have indeed. South Florida is lovely, and seems to be good for my health. Is Daniel in?"

She laughed. "For you, always. Hold on, please, and I'll connect you."

A moment later, Daniel Stern came on the phone. "Callion? I'd begun to worry. How are you feeling?"

Callion managed to inject the faintest hint of the sickroom into his voice, and a touch of forced cheer. "I can't complain. I thought I'd see how my little project was turning out."

"You're a saint, Callion. A regular saint. Three more of the girls delivered since I last heard from you. Janni Tucker, a boy; Elonia McSavity, a girl; and Sharon French, another boy. Mothers and babies all healthy, no complications. The trust funds are set up and the checks are going out like clockwork."

"So that's eighty-seven babies total."

"It is indeed."

"And all of them and their mothers are provided for completely—educational opportunities, housing, transportation. I don't want them living like paupers, Dan. These are some bright young women and they'll have some bright children. I want them to have opportunities they wouldn't have had without me."

"Absolutely, Cal. Everything is taken care of."

"Excellent." Callion leaned back in his chair and templed his fingers so that the heavy digging claws arced to meet in two smooth semicircles. He sighed heavily. "I'm not dead yet, Daniel, and I think I'm doing something worthwhile. I'll have a few more deserving young ladies to put on the program before my time runs out. South Florida seems to be agreeing with me. Perhaps my heart will hold out for another year. It's a lot to hope for, but . . . well, I can always hope, can't I?"

"I'll hope with you, Cal. The world needs more people like you, people who get involved on a personal level—people who aren't afraid to step in and do something."

"It'll get them," Callion said with a little chuckle. "If you and I succeed with these girls and their children, the world will have them."

When he and Daniel hung up, Callion hopped down from his chair and walked to the mirror at the corner of the room. He smiled at himself and admired the sleekness of his striped fur, the sharpness of his muzzle, the brightness of his black-button eyes.

He said to the absent Daniel, "More people like me. Isn't that a lovely idea?"

Eleven

The phone went off beside her left ear like the detonation of a bomb, and Kate's hand whipped out from under the covers and jerked the receiver to her ear before she was even fully awake. "Yeah, uh . . . hello," she muttered, squinting at her clock. She felt like she'd only been asleep for minutes, but sunlight no longer poured into her bedroom. So it was afternoon. Three, the clock said. Plus a few minutes.

She hadn't had enough sleep. She'd slept from four A.M. until a little before eight. Then the sheriff had come by—in person, this time—and once he left, she went grocery shopping and picked up her prescriptions and called her insurance agent and checked with Lisa to see how things were going at her shop. She managed to get back into bed at noon.

She was expecting a return call from her insurance agent, with whom she had both her homeowner's policy and her car insurance. The agent, Janey Callahan, had already been out to get pictures and said she would let Kate know what the settlements were going to be on the door damage and the graffiti, and when she could take her car in to the shop. Kate was hoping she'd get good news.

"Hello," she said a little louder, starting to wake up, thinking that maybe she hadn't answered clearly enough to be intelligible.

She didn't hear anything, but the line was open. Maybe Janey had switched to another line, she thought. Or maybe not. Her heart beat faster.

"Janey? Hello?"

"You know those words on your house?" a familiar, frightening voice said. "We're going to carve them into your ass. Bitch."

Before she could even think of how to respond, a soft click broke the connection. She slammed the phone down, flung herself onto her back, and stared at the ceiling.

They weren't going to go away.

She got up and showered, feeling filthy even after she scrubbed herself. Her body ached and her bruises looked horrible, and the water hurt like hell. She swallowed the giant antibiotic tablets and took a Darvon, then studied the bite marks, noticing the beginnings of redness around the wounds that indicated infection.

Damn them. They weren't going to go away. They would keep calling. Keep sneaking up on her. Keep escalating. Sooner or later, one of four things would happen. The police would catch them. They would chase her off. They would kill her. Or she would kill them.

Dressed, tense, queasy from lack of sleep and fear, she went down the stairs to find Val pacing from the kitchen into what was left of the dining room and back. He'd already eaten; she could see the mess he'd left.

He studied her as she walked into the room. "You had some success last night."

She didn't really feel like talking. "Some."

"You don't sound excited."

"I'm not." She wasn't going to say anything else, but then she thought that maybe talking about what she and Rhiana were doing would help her get her mind off the things that frightened her. She shrugged and gave him a halfhearted smile. "We finally managed to keep from blowing ourselves up. That doesn't mean the work went well."

He watched her. He stood all the way across the kitchen near the back door with his back to the counter, coiled, tight, his spine unnaturally straight. In the dim light, his pale eyes looked vividly yellow, lemon-yellow. He brushed his hair back from his forehead. She had seen his hair before, of course, but now she noticed that it was both thick and fine, and that it was perfectly straight. It fell forward again, covering the points of his ears, hiding some of the wrongness of his exotically beautiful face. "You doubt that we'll leave here, don't you? You don't think you can do the magic."

Kate sensed both fear and anger underlying the question. She sat down on one of the barstools, so that the bar lay between the two of them and the expanse of the kitchen with it. "I have no way of even venturing an educated guess. I know nothing about the sort of magic Rhiana does. She's learned a great deal about what I can do. We'll work together, we'll learn everything we can, and we'll do whatever we're able to do."

"That isn't much reassurance." The anger in his voice became more overt.

Kate didn't want to sound curt. She tried to imagine how she would feel if she found herself trapped in a world other than her own, a world where none of her kind existed . . . a world she'd ended up in accidentally, and because of someone else's mistake or someone else's scheming. She nodded. "I understand, but that's the best I can offer."

Val looked away from her, nodded stiffly. His face changed, then changed again. She could see that he wanted to speak, but he didn't. The lines of his body altered subtly, fluidly. When he looked at her again, it wasn't as if he had gotten his anger under control, but as if he had never been angry. The totality of the shift unsettled her. He watched her in silence, and she broke first.

"What?"

He said, "I'm sure I'll find a way to make a life for myself here. At least I'll have plenty of potential mates."

Of all the things he might have said, Kate could never have anticipated that one. "What? You *will?*"

He stared off into space, showing no sign of having heard her question, giving no indication that he realized he'd shocked her. He murmured, "Resign myself to living in this stinking hole . . . find some isolated wilderness . . . take a woman as a breeder—"

Kate interrupted him. "Wait a minute!" Her protest was loud enough to cut through his self-absorption. "I thought you and Rhiana and Tik and Errga were the only Glenraveners in this world."

He cocked his head at an angle and gave her a long, searching look. "We are," he said, and his voice was emotionless. "What point are you trying to make?"

"You said you could find a mate here."

"I said breeder, but except for matters of emotional involvement, you are essentially correct."

"Breeder . . ." She shook her head and frowned. "How. Do you have some way of bringing one of your women through from Glenraven?"

"No. Of course not. Any road traveled in one direction can be traveled as easily in the other. If I could bring a Kin here, I could go there."

Kate said, "Then what the hell are you talking about?"

But he wasn't listening to her. His gaze was locked on something far away, something that only he could see. "In fact . . ." Both his voice and his expression became thoughtful. "In fact, you could be my breeder." The flat dispassionate timber of his voice and the way he began to stare at her made her skin crawl.

Kate laughed, trying to defuse the situation. The laughter sounded hollow and nervous and stupid, and she stopped herself. "I'm not Kin. I'm human."

"Yes. But humans are the progeny of the outcasts of Glenraven." The Kin was watching her intently now. "Since the first gate was formed, Glenraveners who were no longer welcome in Glenraven were made to leave. Aregen, Kin, Kin-hera, Machnan: they were all thrown through the gate into this world. Here—" He wrinkled his nose, and paused. "Here they mated with each other, and the result was a mix of all the bloods. Your people. Mongrels. Humans."

"That's ludicrous," Kate said. "Genetically, there's no way such divergent species could cross and have fertile young. It isn't even possible to cross a horse with a donkey and get something that can bear young, and those two species are closely related. Yet you believe that you and a Machnan or a warrag or an dagreth could have children and they would look like me? And be able to have children of their own?" She decided he thought she was gullible, or perhaps just stupid. "You expect *me* to believe that?"

"I don't expect you to believe anything. I only tell you the truth. What you think of it concerns you alone. Or perhaps you and me, if you became my breeder."

"I'm not going to be your breeder." *You pig,* she thought. *You creep. You asshole.*

He walked over to the other side of the bar and leaned down to rest his elbows on the counter top. Leaning forward like that, his face was no more than two feet from hers. She leaned back on the barstool to put distance between them, but she didn't want to show her fear openly. She stayed seated.

Val said, "For all our external differences, the Aregen, the Kin, and the Kin-hera, including the Machnan, are the same inside." He smiled an oily smile. "Which means that you are the same, too."

"Right." Kate looked him steadily in the eye and crossed her arms over her chest. "How can that be?"

"The Aregen created the Kin, and the Kin created the Kin-hera. This is not fairy tale. It is fact. The Aregen didn't create the Kin out of the air. They took those of their own children who displeased them, altered their bodies into the form of the Kin, and made them servants. When the Kin won their freedom from the Aregen, they took with them the magic that helped them conquer their parent-masters and the magic that allowed them to create. So the Kin changed their out-of-favor children into the Kin-hera. The Machnan finally fought their way to freedom, but they have not yet attempted to create a slave race. Perhaps they've learned what my people didn't know or refused to see—that slaves do not remain downtrodden forever. That is irrelevant, though. What is relevant is that the Aregen, the Kin, the Kin-hera, and the Machnan share the same blood."

"So you're all really human, are you?"

"No. But you and I would be cross-fertile. Our children would *look* human. If the Kin histories have the details right, and I have every reason to believe that they do, deeper characteristics, such as length of life and magical aptitude, would hold true, though. If you and I had a child, it would look like you, but would live longer. Perhaps not as long as a full-blooded Kin, but much longer than a human. It would have some of my other strengths, too. Improved stamina. Increased intelligence—"

"I think you flatter yourself," Kate said coldly. "In any case, I'm not remotely interested in becoming your breeder. I'll help you get back to your home if I can. And I'll be glad to see you go."

"She's much politer than I would have been if you had approached me with such an indecent proposal." Rhiana moved from the shadows in the entryway into the dining room, skirting the hole in the floor and the sunflower, and coming over to sit beside Kate at the bar. "He didn't tell you about the Kin and their *eyran*, did he?"

"I didn't take his proposal seriously," Kate said. She kept reminding herself that she had to remain on good terms with all of the Glenraveners. More than her own feelings were at stake. She tried to smooth over the incident. "I understand that he's afraid he won't ever get home again. I know he's under pressure. As you are. As I am. And I know all of you are alone here—that there probably isn't anyone else in the world who's like you. . . ."

"Don't make excuses for him," Rhiana said, glaring at Val. "You don't know what he is. You don't know how treacherous his sort is, or what liars they all are, or how manipulative they can be. They haven't been seducing and impregnating the young girls in *your* world for thousands of years, lying to them and manipulating them and playing on their trust, using the magic in their voices to break down their resistance." Rhiana's face tightened into a mask of fury. "You don't know what bastards they are, Kate."

Val's eyes narrowed. "And you do, dear Rhiana? By personal experience, perhaps? Futtered a Kin lordling in some enchanted glade and came away with a mongrel brat, I expect."

Rhiana was on her feet and snarling when Kate slammed the flat of her hand on the counter and shouted, "That's enough, dammit!"

Val and Rhiana turned to stare at her, both of them looking as angry with her as they had looked with each other an instant before.

"You don't tell me that's enough," Val said at the same time that Rhiana said, "Lady Smeachwykke doesn't take orders from a mongrel."

Kate stood up and said, "I don't give a good goddamn who you are or what you think you ought to have to take, or how you think you deserve to be treated. I don't care who you were before you got here, or what you think of each other, or what you think of me for that matter. We have a job to do and we need each other to do it. And if you ever want to get home you need me. So shut up, both of you." She felt like punching both of them in the face. *Tired,* she thought. *I'm too tired. I'm too scared. I have too many other things to worry about.*

Not the least of which is the survival of my world.

Rhiana and Kate worked themselves as near to exhaustion as they dared. Kate thought they showed some improvement in their teamwork—Rhiana said she was learning how to handle the magical energy Kate sent her, while Kate believed she was developing a feel for controlling the amount of energy she drew and passed on.

She'd come up with a new way of handling the energy. She thought her solution was a silly one, but it seemed to be working. She had to give up on the water metaphor she had always used before to visualize magic. It was too slippery and fluid, too impossible to quantify. Instead, she ended up visualizing a large black Bakelite rheostat that she could set anywhere from zero to ten. She gave herself a hundred submarks between the zero and the one. And she and Rhiana successfully moved from the point zero five mark to the point three five mark before they wore out. At the point, though, where they had two explosions inside of Kate's circle, both of them decided they'd done enough for one night and called quits to the experimenting.

Rhiana went out to clean the stables and feed and exercise the horses, something Val had taken care of the night before. Errga went with her, saying that he thought someone ought to stay with her in case the thugs showed up again.

Tik and Val ventured into the kitchen to get something to eat.

It was only eleven thirty. Kate settled in on the couch and turned on the television. She switched to ESPN2 to pick up the hockey scores and highlights. Barry Melrose was going on about the Buffalo Sabers, who weren't even going to make the playoffs—again—and how the rest of the league needed to be afraid of them, saying how he liked them because they were a hitting team.

"Come on, Barry," she told the television set. "Your career average was under .500 and you had Gretzky playing for you. If you knew what you were talking about, you'd still be coaching." She wished he would wash his hair, too, but that was only a minor quibble compared to the fact that every time he opened his mouth, nonsense poured out of it.

She saw clips from the Rangers, who took out the Flyers with a gorgeous goal by Adam Graves and two from Messier, one of which five-holed Hextall from the blue line through a wall of legs and sticks. The final score was three-nothing, with the Flyers held to eighteen shots total and Eric Lindros to a mere two. Richter had another shut-out to add to his record, and the Rangers inched closer to finishing the regular season with better than a hundred points. It was a great game—as much as Kate loved the Rangers, that was how much she couldn't stand the Flyers.

She yawned her way through wins by the Ducks and the Stars,

then gloated when a vastly improved Islanders team humiliated the Penguins seven to one. Kate couldn't stand the Penguins, either. But it wouldn't have mattered if that score had been reversed. The Rangers beat the Flyers and for one brief, perfect moment, all was right with the world.

She switched off the television, thinking she could go to bed at a normal hour and get up in the morning in time to enjoy some daylight, but as she was heading out of the living room, Val stopped her.

"Wait a moment, will you?" he said.

She stopped just inside the archway and crossed her arms over her chest. "Look," she said, "I'm willing to take the circumstances under consideration, but that doesn't mean I want to be your friend. And I certainly don't want to be your mistress. So while we're still on speaking terms with each other, and while we can still work together, why don't you leave well enough alone?"

"I just wanted to say I was sorry." He stood well back from her, not crowding her. "I tried to make you uncomfortable and I tried embarrassing you and I shouldn't have done that."

"No." She shoved her hands into the pockets of her jeans and studied him. His expression looked sincere enough. "You shouldn't have. But I said I was willing to consider the circumstances. And I don't hold grudges."

He nodded and waited, watching her intently.

She waited, too, not saying anything.

At last he sighed. "But you still don't want to be friends."

"I don't know you well enough to want to be your friend, and what I do know hasn't made me desperate to know more."

"I suppose I can understand that." He backed away to let her pass. "But I hope that I'll find a way to win your friendship. You're attractive, Kate, and attractive in more than your appearance. I believe you would be a good friend."

She gave him a tight-lipped smile. "That's kind of you. Thank you." Then, before he had a chance to say anything else, she brushed past him and went, not upstairs as she had intended, but through the dining room and into the kitchen. Behind her, she heard him let himself out the front door.

She hadn't meant to charge into the kitchen, but once she was in, she couldn't retreat. Tik was there, and he waved her over to his side. He sat with his back against one of the counters, his legs stuck out at forty-five-degree angles and his heavy forelimbs resting across his round belly. His kimono wore the battle scars of a war fought against ketchup, mustard, and relish. Fought and lost, Kate thought.

"A word with you, if I may," he said. His voice reminded her of water racing over boulders, a current pounding through dangerous rapids. When he spoke, she saw the clear green of summer river water tumbling over a falls, backlit by the setting sun, and the froth of brown-white foam that flecked the river edges and collected in thick spirals in the eddies. Minnows and crawfish. Bare feet dangling into the water, the mud oozing up between her toes feeling like cold silk. The scent of pine trees and freshly mown grass, picnic tables, and someone barbecuing hot dogs. The bow of an aluminum canoe slicing through the sun-flecked currents, the J-swept arc of a paddle, the flash and sparkle of droplets flung away as she lifted the paddle, swung it forward, dug into the river, and the muscles of her shoulders and back burned pleasurably . . .

Kate shook her head to chase away the startling flow of impressions and said, "Of course."

He smiled. The smile pulled back and curled up at the corners, an amiable smile. His brown eyes were as deep and soulful as a Springer Spaniel's, she thought, and he had the same busy eyebrows, sliding up and down his forehead independently of each other, constantly in motion. Red-brown eyebrows thick as caterpillars. Silly eyebrows for such serious eyes.

"I like you," he said. "You're brave and sensible and competent, and you don't scare easily."

"Thanks." She waited. The compliment was a warmup for what he really wanted to say; she could feel something big waiting behind the trivialities.

He chuffed and stared down at his thick-fingered hands with their dark, heavy claws. "As competent as you are, though, you need to promise me you'll be careful about . . . things. People. Don't take chances. Don't be too . . . trusting."

Kate crouched beside him. "What are you talking about, Tik."

He ducked his head down further and chuffed again. Then he sighed and looked up at her from under the funny eyebrows.

"I'm not going to be angry with you," she said. "Tell me what you're thinking."

"Val has been my friend most of my life," Tik said. "A good friend, Kate. I would give my life for him . . . perhaps he would give his life for me, too, in spite of the differences in our station. I owe him many things."

"But . . ."

He nodded. "Quite right. But. But he has a flaw. He is charming and romantic, and women in droves have fallen for his
charms. He's brave and intelligent and he tells good stories and
better jokes." Tik looked down at his hands again, and rolled
his shoulders forward in a bearish shrug. "But he is not an
honorable man, Kate. He uses people when he finds it convenient to do so."

"You think he would find it convenient to use me?"

"I know he would," the dagreth said. "He comes to me for
advice, though once he's heard me out, he rarely takes the advice
I give. He asked me how I thought he could get you to do what
he wanted. I suggested that he didn't need to manipulate you;
that you had as much reason as we did to find the Traitor and
help us get home."

"But he wasn't satisfied with that." Kate glanced over her shoulder to be sure that Val wasn't standing there, even though she
knew Tik wouldn't have said what he was saying if there was a
chance his friend could hear.

"No. I suspect him of dark motives. He's suffered at the hands
of his father, and he has great ambitions that the elder Peloral,
Lord Faldan, will squelch until he is too weak to do so. Val's father
is a miserable power-mongering martinet, but Val errs by being
too like him in some ways instead of too unlike him."

"What does he intend to do?"

"I don't know," Tik said. "I cannot imagine. But I know Val
is hungry for the power his father has been waving in front of
his face his entire life, and I think he sees you as the weak link
in the chain leading to that power."

"According to the book, all five of us have to work together
if we are to beat out Callion."

"I'm not saying you should refuse to work with him." Tik rested
one enormous hand on her shoulder so lightly it could have been
a butterfly settling there for a brief rest. "You must work with
him . . . with all of us. You are the glue that will keep the rest
of us together. Just . . ." He looked so sad, sitting there contem-
plating the failings of his friend. "Just don't trust him."

Kate nodded slowly. "Thank you. I know telling me this wasn't
easy."

"No."

"But I needed to know."

She rose and smiled at him, and he returned a wan half-smile
before he looked down at his hands again.

"You did what was best for all of us. For your world and mine."
She wanted to make him feel better, but he wasn't going to. He'd
been forced to say things about a lifelong friend that he obviously
would rather have never said. All her reassurances and words of
intended comfort weren't going to mean anything to him right
then. So she patted him lightly on his shoulder and said, "I'll
see you tomorrow, Tik. If you're going to be up, you can watch
the television. Just don't let the sound get too loud."

"I'll see you tomorrow," he said.

He was still staring at his hands when she turned the corner
to go up to bed.

Twelve

Rhiana dug her fingers tighter into the padded grip on her right side and closed her eyes so tightly they hurt.

Beside her, Kate said, "Relax. We aren't going fast."

"Yes we are." Rhiana had no confidence in the slender belt that clipped over her lap and across her shoulder. She had no confidence in Kate's insistence that the horseless carriage was safe. She had no confidence, in fact, in anything except her own senses, and her senses insisted she was mere instants away from sudden, total annihilation.

"I've never had an accident," Kate said. "I've never even had a ticket."

"Just get me out of this thing."

"We're almost there."

"Really?" Rhiana opened her eyes in time to see them racing headon toward a huge devouring metal monster, and she slapped her hands over her eyes and shrieked and drew herself into a compact ball on the seat. But the screams of tortured metal and the crash of shattering glass never came, nor did the flames and the pain that Rhiana expected. Instead, she felt the car slow down. Then she felt it stop.

She put her hands down and squinted through one eye. They weren't moving. Neither were most of the other metal monsters that covered the vast stone field.

"This is Wal-Mart," Kate said. "It's the only place in town where I'll be able to afford an entire wardrobe for you plus replacement clothes for me."

From the outside, the building looked comparable in size to Smeachwykke Castle, though Smeachwykke was considerably taller. Inside, though, Rhiana had another shock. No walls divided the space into rooms. It was one great pillared hall, and what it lacked in grace or elegance or the delicacy of detail it made up for with brightness and color. Rhiana stopped inside the bank of glass doors and stared.

"Welcome to Wal-Mart," an old man said to her and offered her a four-wheeled push-wagon contraption. She looked at him, not certain what she was supposed to do with it, and Kate reached in front of her, took the wagon, and said, "Come on. We have a lot of shopping to do."

Rhiana followed Kate into a forest of clothing hung on racks. Displays stuck to boards and on life-sized dolls showed the clothing as it was supposed to look. Barbarous. Graceless. Blocky. The fabrics didn't drape, the colors clashed, the pieces weren't fitted. She turned one garment inside-out and studied the stitch-work. It was very regular, but coarse. She could see raw fabric edges instead of the neatly matched interfacings and contrast-colored silk linings she found inside her own garments.

Rhiana pointed out the flaws she'd found and said, "The seamstresses in your world do a dreadful job," she said.

Kate looked down at her, the expression on her face exasperated. "Look, Rhiana. In this world, hand-stitching belongs to couture fashion, and a single garment of that sort of quality would cost us as much money as I make in a month. This stuff is stitched by machine. For what it is, it isn't too bad."

Rhiana considered that for a moment. In Glenraven her clothing was expensive, too; it took her seamstresses enormous amounts of effort and time to create, and bore little resemblance to the clothes worn by commoners. Some Glenraveners would not make in a lifetime the amount of money that would it would cost them to have a gown or embroidered silk shirt like the many she owned.

She looked again at the clothing, realizing that it was the Machine World equivalent in affordability to the very cheapest clothing worn by the lower classes. Suddenly, seen in that light, she realized how extraordinary it was. The dyes were bright, the seams solid, the fabrics new instead of used; unpatched, unworn, the finely woven cloth had nothing in common with the coarse homespun materials in dreary browns and grays and dull blues that made up the Glenraven commoners' wardrobes.

She said, "How many outfits did you have . . . before we exploded them, of course?"

Kate looked surprised. She thought about it for a moment, then shrugged. "I don't know."

"You had more than four, I know, because we exploded that many and you and I still had clothing to wear."

"God, Rhiana, I have dozens."

"Still?"

"Of course."

Rhiana nodded. "How many pairs of shoes do you have?"

Kate laughed. "Two pairs of work boots, a good pair of Western riding boots, a good pair of English riding boots, two pairs of cross-trainers—though I did have three until recently—two or three pairs of old running shoes, probably five pairs of high heels, a couple pairs of slip-ons, some sandals, a pair of brown penny loafers, four pairs of Keds in rainbow colors . . ."

"You aren't rich, are you?"

"I get by," Kate said, "and I'm doing better this year than I've ever done before, but I'm not rich."

"I had a single pair of riding boots," Rhiana said thoughtfully, "and three pairs of indoor shoes—a night pair, a day pair, and a dancing pair. The majority of people in my world have only one pair of shoes. Perhaps two sets of clothing, not including their celebration clothing, which they will wear when they marry, at each holy day and festival, and when they are buried." She stared down the aisles where women ambled, pushing their wagons ahead of them, dropping clothing into the baskets as if this were something they did every day.

"These other people here aren't rich, are they?"

"Probably not. This isn't the sort of place where rich people shop, at least not most of the time."

"Compared to the people in my world, they're rich."

Kate laughed. "You won't convince them of that. People in this part of the world have one of the highest standards of living anywhere. But most of them don't appreciate it because it's so common. People don't value the things that anyone can have, no matter how valuable those things truly are." She was quiet for a moment, and the look in her eyes darkened to somberness. "That's one of the terribly stupid things about humans, I suppose."

"You aren't talking about buying clothing now."

"No. I'm not. I'm talking about every good thing that I had in my life that I took for granted until it was gone."

"Then humans and Machnan are no different in that way. I, too, have failed to appreciate the good things in my life until I lost them. If I did not love my husband, still I cared very much for him. And my children . . . and my friends . . . and my city . . . and my world . . ." Rhiana sighed. "But life moves forward, and so must we."

Kate seemed to be far away, her eyes focused on something beyond the reach of the moment and all it held. But she turned to Rhiana and said, "Quite right. And to move forward, we must have clothes."

They shopped, and Rhiana tried on outfits and discovered the numbering system that indicated sizes in the machine-made clothes. They found shoes and pants and shirts and bizarre undergarments and all manner of personal hygiene products and did not stop until their wagon, which Kate told her was a shopping cart, was full.

"Now we have to go to my saddle shop," Kate said as they loaded the last bags into the back of Kate's carriage, which she called her "car."

"You are a merchant?"

"Sort of. I'm more of a craftsman, actually, though I sell my own goods." Kate walked to the side and unlocked and opened Rhiana's door for her.

Rhiana climbed into the car and strapped herself in, closed her eyes, and wished she were able to draw up magic from Kate's source on her own. She would have wrapped it around herself, or perhaps around the vehicle, and perhaps even the space around the vehicle, so that anything that came within range would explode.

It was, she decided, probably just as well that she couldn't use the magic of Kate's world without Kate.

"I'll show you what I make. Maybe when you go back to your world, you'd like to take one of my saddles with you. I'm sure we'll figure out some way of trading . . ."

Rhiana, with her eyes tightly shut and both hands gripping the armrest, said, "Fine."

Rhiana liked the shop, enjoyed her tour, and liked meeting both Lisa and Paul. She listened while Kate gave both of them instructions, touched the finished saddles, admired the silverwork and the lovely engraved leathers, and imagined herself owning a saddle and bridle like those she saw.

"So, what do you think?" Kate asked as they walked out the back door to the place where she'd left the car.

"They're lovely saddles. I've never seen leatherwork like that. Painted leather, and embroidered leather, yes, but never carved leather."

Kate opened the door on Rhiana's side and started to go around to her own. "Technically, it's embossed," she said and then a hard, hairy arm grabbed Rhiana and a man with something over his face grabbed Kate and a third man, who also had his face covered, said, "Throw them into the van and tie them up and let's get out of here."

Rhiana saw Kate go limp. She didn't scream, she didn't fight. She tossed her car keys down the alley, and seemed to give up. Then Rhiana realized Kate was drawing up magical energy. Lots of it. The shield billowed out blue-white and powerful, nearly blinding to Rhiana's second sight.

The man who'd grabbed Rhiana dragged her toward his big, boxy car, but Rhiana had her eyes closed, watching the movement of magic up from Kate's source in a river, a torrent, an uncontrollable tidal surge. Kate diverted the whole nightmarish river to her, and Rhiana tried to catch it.

This time the explosion vaporized not just their clothes but their attackers' clothing and the back portion of the men's cavernous vehicle, a deep circle of the alley road, and part of a huge wooden pole that began to topple forward, dragging wires with it. The roar of the blast and the blinding flash of light stunned everyone within Kate's circle for the duration of a heartbeat and another; Rhiana found it hard to believe neither the light nor the sound carried beyond the magical wards. But no one stepped out into the alley to investigate the noise. No one threw open back doors to shops, or peeked around corners.

The men screamed and fled; Kate yelled, "Get in the car," and while she ran down the alley for her key ring, Rhiana climbed into the vehicle and watched broken wires snaking across the ground with light dancing from their ragged edges. Her second sight saw nothing when she studied those wires—they looked like something magical to her eyes, but they were not.

Kate jumped in the car and inserted the key in the lock. She unlocked the monster that made the machine run, and it growled to life. "Grab us some clothes out of the back—just shirts. I don't want to get stopped for indecent exposure, but I don't want those bastards to get away again, either."

"Those were the men who beat you?"

"Unless I'm more unpopular than I thought, those were the ones."

Rhiana handed her a shirt and pulled on one herself, and a pair of pants, and one pair of the soft, cloth-topped shoes. As soon as Kate pulled a shirt over her head, she backed the car and stared down the road in the direction their attackers had fled.

They couldn't follow. The hole in the road was too deep. It would have swallowed Kate's car.

"Shit. We'll have to go the other way." Kate backed again, turned, and sped out of the alley in the opposite direction. She tore around the block and Rhiana discovered that she hadn't been joking when she said before that they weren't going very fast. Now they were going very fast and Rhiana wanted to be anywhere else. Anywhere.

Except with the three men.

"What are you going to do when you catch them?" Rhiana asked. Anything to get her mind off of the fact that they were going to die any instant.

Kate and her car roared around a corner, barely missing a brick wall, and raced back into the alley from the other end. Rhiana could see no sign of the men.

"I'm going to make them wish they'd never met me."

"How?"

"I don't know how!" Kate snapped. "I'll think of that when I catch them."

"They'll realize quickly that we didn't hurt them," Rhiana said. "They'll realize all we did was humiliate them and destroy their carriage. And we don't know how to damage them with magic; how to inflict pain or make their skin ooze with sores or how to cause their lungs to burn or their eyeballs to explode."

Kate looked over at her, an odd expression on her face, and for an instant Rhiana wondered if she'd said something wrong. She decided, however, that Kate was only realizing the precariousness of their attempt to find the three ruffians. She said, "If we could do any of those things, I would say we should keep searching for them. But we cannot. If you find them, you will have to hurt them with your hands or your carria—your *car*, and I don't know how you're going to do that."

Kate slowed down. She drove through the alley looking into the little side corridors that ran between some of the buildings. Rhiana looked, too, because looking was better than thinking about Kate driving, and better than thinking about figuring out a way to fight off the men who had attacked her. She couldn't see them, nor could she see any sign of how they might have escaped.

When Kate reached the hole their magic had blown in the alley, she backed, turned, and drove out onto the main street.

"You still want to find them?"

"No." Kate's brows furrowed over her eyes and her lips thinned to a hard, angry line.

"Then what are you going to do?"

"I'm going to go home."

"Perhaps we could work on a way to destroy them with magic—"

"No."

Rhiana studied the woman beside her. She heard anger in Kate's voice, and she couldn't understand why Kate would direct anger at her. "You don't want to hurt them?"

"I want to kill them," Kate said. Her voice seethed with bitterness. "But I won't unless I have no choice. And as for using magic to destroy them . . . or to hurt them . . ." She exhaled sharply and glanced at Rhiana long enough for Rhiana to see the dark anger in her eyes. "Only a fool would ever consider using magic as a weapon of attack."

"Why?"

"Have you ever heard of the Threefold Law? It says that anything we do, whether good or evil, comes back to us threefold."

"I've heard that said, but never stated as a law—and I've certainly never considered it as fact or as something immutable. Offensive magic comprises a major part of the curriculum for wizards, and while they use destructive spells cautiously, they do use them. Had I done more with my magical studies, I have no doubt that I would have learned destructive spells."

"Perhaps you would have. And perhaps you would have used them, and maybe you wouldn't have seen how your spells came back at you." Kate steered the car roughly, going hard around turns, jamming her foot against the floor pedals that made the vehicle stop and start. Rhiana once again thought that the little

cloth belt that held her to her cushioned seat was poor protection against the danger of Kate's driving. "But I think your spells
would have come back at you. Not right away, perhaps. Not soon,
even. But I truly believe that the shit people throw up in the
air falls down on their heads again. I think if you set out to harm
someone, you may succeed, but the harm you do will find its way
back to you many times over, and your own evil will bite you
worse than it ever bit your enemies."

Rhiana recognized Kate's house only as they pulled into the
driveway. Relieved that their journey was over and that she would
probably live to greet the morrow, she leaned back in the seat
and breathed slowly. "What you say cannot be proven either true
or false. I have, I admit, seen some things that would seem to
show you were right, but I've seen as many that would seem to
show you were wrong. And I have to tell you, Kate—if I had a
magic that would permit me to destroy those three bastards before
they could come at me again, I would take it and damn the consequences."

Kate nodded. She brought the car to a halt, pulled up on the
stick that rested between the two front seats, and when it clicked
loudly, turned the key again. "I understand how you feel. And
perhaps I am wrong, and the Threefold Law is a matter of faith,
not fact. It doesn't matter. As long as we're working together and
you are depending on me to supply you with raw magical energy,
we will not attempt to harm or destroy any living thing with our
spellcraft."

Rhiana shrugged. "I don't imagine that I can change your mind.
I would if I could; your stubborn insistence on fighting fair could
be the ruin of us. But I have to count on you to help me get
back to Glenraven, and I won't do anything that will destroy my
chances of seeing home."

Kate got out of the car and locked the door behind her. She
went to the back and lifted the hatch, then pulled out bags and
handed them to Rhiana. "Good is a stronger force than evil, and
fighting fair is part of keeping yourself on the side of goodness.
Refusing to become destructive is another part. I think only if
we keep that in mind will we ever get you home."

Thirteen

Val studied the little paper squares intently. The pictures on the shiny sides of them were obviously of Kate when she was younger; he saw her as a child, holding a string of fish in one hand and a fishing rod in the other. She was grinning, and he could see that her baby teeth had come out and her adult teeth were just beginning to push through. An invisible wind tousled her hair and her eyes sparkled. In another picture of her done when she was older, she stood on the shore of a great body of water, the bottoms of her breeches rolled up to mid-calf and her striped shirt plastered tight against her torso by the same wind that whipped her hair behind her like a banner. She was a young woman in that picture, a maiden fair of form and full of grace, if he cared to quote the poets and the bards. But a maiden holding another, larger fish, and this one by the tail—and grinning as she pointed to the fish's toothy, gaping mouth and displayed its triangular dorsal fin and lean, predator's body.

She was a maiden with a penchant for picking up monsters,

he thought. Another picture, this one of a younger child hold-ing a huge crawfish. And two of her with an enormous snake draped around her shoulders. And one of her bareback astride a brown-and-white spotted horse. A series of her hanging out of various trees.

Laughing, always laughing.

And then pictures of her with boys and girls older and younger than her, all with the same facial features, all with the same golden hair and pale, freckled skin. Her brothers and sisters, he thought. He discovered a large picture in the bottom of the box—in this one, the girls all wore emerald green dresses, the boys wore dark gray long pants and coats of an ugly shape, and dangling bits of cloth at their throats. They dressed in the same manner as the two adults; Val guessed these had to be Kate's parents. He stud-ied the faces, seeing that she had her father's smile, her mother's eyes.

He put the paper pictures back into their box and slid it onto the stack of boxes like it. He wished he could read the words Kate had written on the outsides; surely all of these miniature artworks would tell him something that he needed to know, if he could only understand why she'd grouped them the way she had. All they could tell him so far was that even as a child she hadn't been afraid of much, and that someone had spent enor-mous amounts of money to record her every triumph over the world of things that slithered and swam and bit.

He thought of the painters who had toiled to put their works onto the tiny squares and wondered why they did so many paint-ings, why they painted so small—and why Kate had so little reverence for the efforts of the artists that she hid their work away in brown boxes. They hadn't spent a great deal of time emphasizing her perfections and hiding her flaws. Perhaps that was why she hid the works. Artists in his own world never did portraits where their subjects looked like they'd been through a windstorm.

He pulled out another box, remembering where in the stack he found it, and carefully lifted the lid off of it. More faces stared back at him. This time Val found Kate much as he knew her . . . except she was not alone. These pictures were more formal, more con-cerned with appearances of beauty. And they didn't feature any animals, either living or dead. To him they were more comprehen-sible. He found a picture of Kate seated in a red velvet chair, while a man stood behind her, staring forward. Kate's hair was a pale cascade that flowed to her shoulders and curled under—worn soft and loose, as young maidens wore their hair before they braided it and put it up and became women. But Kate was a woman in the picture, and even though she smiled, he could see a sadness in her eyes that he had never seen in the stacks of pictures made of her when she was younger. He looked more closely at the picture. The man who stood behind her smiled, too, but in his eyes Val could see the ragged edges of despair, carefully disguised but not sufficiently well-hidden. Her lover, Val thought. The one who had killed himself. Yes. He could see the emptiness in the dead stranger's eyes that would some day bring him to annihilate himself.

He wondered at the skill of the artist—in Glenraven an artist was considered skilled who did not make the nose too large or set the eyes too close or give his subject's face the sort of leering expression that would make later generations believe their old ancestor was a sot or a lecher or a debaucher. No artist he knew could capture in such a tiny space such a wealth of detail, render it so finely, and add in a measure of the soul, too.

Each world has its own varieties of magic, he thought.

He put the pictures away and delved further into the closet. Behind clothes and more clothes, he discovered a panel in the wood, and he pressed it; his people loved puzzle boxes and intricate, hidden doorways and tricky locks. He was disappointed when the door popped open immediately, but less so when he realized he had found what he'd been looking for—the cache where she kept her weapon and, if he guessed correctly, a store of the missiles she'd used to blow such impressive holes in the Rift monster's body.

He lifted out the weapon and studied it, trying to discern from touch the function of the cold metal levers and switches. He didn't disturb anything—he had a healthy respect for what the weapon might do to him if he mishandled it. He studied the blue-coated wire that ran into one portion of the center of the weapon and looped out another part, and realized that when he had seen the weapon before, that dangling bit had not been there.

Closer inspection proved it to be a lock, one no doubt intended to prevent use of the weapon by anyone who might accidentally come across it. Someone such as himself, for instance.

He frowned. How inconvenient—she had reason not to trust her houseguests, of course, but to distrust them in such a way that she not only hid her weapon but locked it . . .

He slipped the weapon back onto its rack and stared at it. He would have to discover where she kept the key, and somehow he would have to find out how to shoot the gun. He needed to do it without arousing her suspicions, because if she doubted the best intentions of any member of their little party, she might not be so inclined to help them track down Callion and find a way home.

Through the closed closet door he heard the slamming of other doors outside. He recognized the sounds as coming from Kate's carriage, and he swore softly and shoved the hidden panel back into place. She was back sooner than he'd anticipated. He didn't dare let her catch him digging through her room; she'd locked her bedroom door before she left and he certainly did not wish to have her find out that he was capable of going through that lock as if it didn't even exist. Nor did he want her to know that he'd been spying on her.

He made sure everything in her closet was as he had found it. Then he hurried out, this time not admiring the elegant simplicity of her furnishings or her choices of colors and fabrics. He found her an interesting woman, but did not think he would be as intrigued by her if she refused to help him get back to his home and the little battle he had been so near winning—at least, he had been before Rhiana and her poorly-cast spell had trapped him in this exile's hell.

He carefully turned the knob, all the while listening to the sounds from downstairs. He had not yet heard Kate or Rhiana come into the house. He still had a moment; he could get downstairs before she found him out.

He pushed Kate's lock back in and stepped onto the landing.

The dagreth sat by the door waiting, a cold smile curling the corners of his muzzle. "Caught you," he said.

Val didn't bother trying to create an expression of innocence or surprise; he looked at the Kin-hera and said, "I'm taking care of the things I have to take care of."

"Right. In her room."

"You don't know what's at stake. You don't know how much lies at risk for you . . . for me . . . for all of us."

"You're talking about Glenraven business, and she doesn't have any part of that. You're trying to use her, Val. You're trying to take advantage of whatever magics you can find here to play with politics back home, and you could end up destroying her as easily as falling down stairs." The dagreth's eyes glowed coldly in the dim light, and Val saw his old companion for the first time as someone formidable, even dangerous.

"I won't hurt her. That wouldn't help me, would it?"

The dagreth wasn't mollified. "I've seen your singlemindedness before. I've seen you stop at nothing if you thought it would bring you the reward you were after." Downstairs, the kitchen door opened and Val could hear Kate and Rhiana talking at once, their voices lacking the happiness and lightness he'd heard in them when the women left.

"I'll tell her," the dagreth said.

"Don't. You'll destroy everything."

"Maybe the everything I'd destroy would be for the good. You're moving into places you don't belong, old friend. You're meddling with people you have no business touching. If you do it again, I'll tell her and ruin your game outright."

Downstairs, he heard the warrag delay them. Val said, "This is about lives, Tik. This is about taking advantage of an opportunity to make Glenraven over the way we want it to be."

The dagreth shook his head slowly and said, "This is about the betrayal of a trust. You have my warning. Ignore it at your own peril."

The giant Kin-hera turned and padded down the stairs. At the middle landing, he said, "Val will be down shortly. He's finishing up his bath. I thought to wait for him, but he's taking much too long."

Val moved himself to the bathroom and made the necessary cleaning-up noises, and thought about Tik and his threat. Tik could destroy him, and out of a sense of misplaced loyalty or friendship to the woman Kate, he might choose to do it.

How could Val neutralize the threat without hurting his old friend?

As he went downstairs to join everyone else, he thought perhaps he couldn't.

Fourteen

Two days after her shopping trip with Rhiana, Kate was feeling better about everything. Val and the warrag had learned to use the stove and proved to be talented cooks, even if they did lean heavily to meat dishes. They'd also repaired the dining room floor, using Kate's power tools and some Old World skills she'd never seen. She no longer had an icy draft blowing up from the crawl space, and once they finished sanding and staining, she'd have a beautiful parquet circle in the center of the old boards that looked not only intentional but even classy. Meanwhile, Tik had taken to patrolling the perimeter of the property at night, which meant Kate slept sounder. However, the three thugs seemed to have given up on their harassment of her; Kate thought the magical explosion was probably responsible for that.

Better yet, spring was finally in the North Carolina air, and the azaleas were beginning to bloom, the birds were coming back, and the temperatures had soared into the sixties during the day and the forties and fifties at night. At that moment, with the sun just below the trees and the cool breezes blowing through the open windows, Kate could have thought she lived in a perfect time and a perfect place.

If it hadn't been for trying to solve her guests' problems, life would have been almost idyllic. Life, however, was far from idyllic.

"It won't work," Rhiana said. She sat cross-legged on the living room floor, shaking her head and looking frustrated.

"If we can't find Callion, we can't get you home."

"I know that, Kate. But trying to use the book as a divining tool won't work, because the book doesn't know where he is. And not all the spells in the world can make it know what it doesn't know."

"If we had his scent, we could send a bloodhound after him."

"Yes," Rhiana said. "And if we knew his phone number, we could call him and ask him where he lived."

Rhiana's sarcasm had gotten thicker and sharper as the days wore on without any real breakthroughs. "I'm glad you've become so experienced with the phone . . ." Kate stopped. "Wait a minute. There's a CD-ROM disk that has personal phone numbers on it. Lisa has a copy—she was telling me back before all of this started how she'd found an old friend of hers through it. I can call her and have her do a search for me."

"I was joking."

"That's okay. It doesn't matter. You might have something. Let me just call her—"

Outside, she heard a roar. She froze, and Rhiana said, "That's Tik."

The kitchen door opened and slammed. "Val and Errga went after him. Rhiana, go ahead. I'm going to get my gun; I'll be out in a minute." She raced up the stairs and into her room, threw on her shooting vest with the pockets already full of shells, and pulled the gun out of its hiding place. The key that unlocked the chamber lock was on her housekey ring; she got it, took out the lock, and made sure the shotgun was fully loaded.

Down the stairs and outside, running as hard as she dared, worrying that one of the creeps who was after her had hurt Tik . . .

She spotted the warrag first, crouched down behind the old cast-iron tub that served as a watering trough. She heard a shot, but no cries or screams. Maybe none of her people were hurt; or maybe one or some of them were dead. She ran crouched over and tried to keep cover between herself and the barn while she crossed the backyard to the trough. When she reached it, she ducked down beside the warrag and asked, "Where are they?"

He pointed with his nose toward the open door. "Tik has them treed. Look along the first crossbeam," he said, "to the point where the support beam angles into the roof. See that shadow?"

She did. It was a shadow with arms and legs, and it was tucked tightly onto that beam. "And the other two?"

"Can't see them anymore, but they were up on beams, too. They have weapons like yours, but smaller."

Kate nodded. "I figured they'd have guns if they came after me again. Is Tik all right?"

"He's fine. He saw them skulking around in your shrubs and gave the alarm. Evidently scared them. Soon as they heard his roar, they ran for the barn. He's over there, making sure they don't get away." The warrag inclined its head to the right. Kate followed the direction of the gesture and found herself staring at the dagreth, whom she hadn't seen before, even though she'd looked right at him a couple of times. He crouched in a stand of dogwoods underplanted with rhododendrons, and he managed near-invisibility. "Once they climbed into the rafters, they got braver. They started shooting." The warrag stretched the corners of his mouth back in a grin and added, "Tik wanted to burn your barn down, but he couldn't find fire, and the trick he uses to make it didn't work here."

"Is there a chance any of them could have escaped out the back?"

"Rhiana and Val went back there. They won't get away unless you want them to."

Kate wished she had a rifle. She estimated her distance at forty yards from the barn. A shotgun was a weapon designed to spread a broad pattern of shot over a short distance, or to throw a slug a slightly longer distance. Even the best of shotguns weren't designed for sniping, however, and nobody would mistake her Mossberg for a high-end weapon. She didn't dare get in close enough to be sure of her aim, either. From that distance, she would make an equally good target for their handguns. And if one of them was a deputy, she had to at least assume he would be proficient with his weapon.

But she thought the dagreth's idea had been a good one. Burn them out. Or at least threaten to burn them out. She left the safety on and sighted down the barrel at the one man she could see. "I want you to go into my kitchen and get a box of matches. Pull the drawer on the right of the silverware drawer open and you'll see a red-and-blue box with a coarse-textured black stripe that runs along two of the sides. Bring that box to me. We're going to give Tik his fire."

The warrag made a soft barking noise that she realized was a laugh. "I'll be back as soon as I can." He slipped away from the trough and skulked under the board fence and across the backyard. Kate noted out of the corner of her eye that he moved the way she had seen coyotes move in nature documentaries, with a slinking sort of grace that seemed shifty and sneaky at the same time. The men in the barn had evidently been watching him, too, for as he stood on his hind legs and let himself into the house, the first man started to drop from the rafter. Kate thumbed the safety off and placed a shot to the right of him, knowing it would drop before it reached him, but also knowing that the sound of a shotgun striking anything nearby would give the three men a reason to sit still and wait for her to make the next move. She pumped another shell into the chamber and pulled an extra out of her vest pocket and loaded that. "Stay right where you are," she yelled.

The man's feet went back up on the rafter, and Kate noted with satisfaction that he scooted himself into a tighter, more compact mass on the beam.

"You can't shoot us," one of them shouted.

"Sure I can. It would be self-defense. All three of you came looking for me, and you brought your guns. You killed my horse and left a death threat; that's on file with the sheriff's department. You've attacked me twice. You've been making threatening phone calls."

"For you to kill us in self-defense, you're going to have to prove you didn't have any other choice," the same voice yelled. "If you have us pinned out here, you sure as hell aren't going to be able to do that."

"That's okay. I'll take my chances with a jury. As an old friend of mine once said, 'I'd rather be tried by twelve than carried by six.'"

The only sound from the barn was silence.

Kate heard her kitchen door open, and a moment later the warrag rejoined her. He'd carried the box of matches in a pouch in his leather harness; he sat beside her and pulled it out. "This?" he asked.

She nodded.

"I had a hard time being sure it was the right thing," he said.

"I don't see colors the way your sort does; my eyes are designed for darkness rather than daylight."

"I'm sorry. If I'd known that, I would have found another way to describe them." She took the big box of kitchen matches from him and opened it. "You know how these work?"

He huffed. "They have some sort of fire spell on them, I imagine."

She grinned at him. "Not quite, but they're pretty convenient even without magic." She squinted toward the barn. "How well can you see the men now?" The last touches of gold had vanished from the treetops. In the west, Kate could still see touches of pink behind the silhouetted branches, but day was done and twilight was giving over rapidly to true night.

"The near one I can see perfectly." The warrag craned his neck around the edge of the tub and said, "From this angle, I can see a foot of one of the other two, but to see all three of them I'd have to stand in front of the door."

"I wish you could see all of them from here. I want to get them out of there, and I don't want any of us to get killed while we roust them. It would help if I knew where they were, but I suppose it isn't essential. They haven't gotten out."

"No. They haven't. And they won't—not now. Night favors night creatures. All of us save the Machnan will see them better in this light than in the other."

"Good." Kate leaned forward and thought. "I need you to take a torch to Tik, and another to Rhiana and one to Val. Can you gather some sticks for me?"

"You're going to burn your barn?"

"I hope not," Kate said. "But if that's what it takes to get those three to leave me alone, I'll do it."

The warrag nodded and grinned at her. In the swiftly gathering darkness, she could see little but the gleam of his teeth. "I would, too," he said. "I don't think Val or Rhiana will like losing their horses, but those rotten skulkers of yours shot at the two of them. I expect they'll understand."

Kate had forgotten about the Glenraveners' horses in her barn. "Gods, I hope I don't have to burn them out."

"If you do, don't let anyone take the carcasses away. I don't mind a bit of horsemeat now and again." The warrag chuckled when Kate glared at him. Evidently he could see quite well in the dark, because he said, "You need not glower at me. I'll find your sticks and take them for you, and while I'm about it, I'll tell the other three what you want them to do, but I won't stop liking horsemeat because you don't think it's polite." Over the past few days, he and Kate had discussed low-meat diets and healthy eating, and he thought, quite bluntly, that it was the stupidest thing he'd ever heard. And he refused to believe any civilized people would limit themselves to cattle, sheep, and chickens and pass up such delicacies as dog, cat, and horse.

Kate ignored the jibe. She told him what to tell the other three, then showed him how to strike the matches and gave the box back to him. He went off in the darkness, and she waited. When, long moments later, he returned to her side, he said, "The bastards have started working their way to the back of the barn. I think all three of them hope to escape that way, but Tik and the Peloral and Her Ladyship are right up against the sides of the building, near the doors, as you requested."

"Then give them whatever signal you told them you would give."

The warrag tipped his head back and howled. He might have looked doggish, but there was nothing of the domestic canine in that howl. His wordless song rang with the ache of a million years of loneliness, with yearning and hunger and a shivery supernatural quaver that brought the hair straight up on Kate's arms and the back of her neck and sent a shock of superstitious dread straight to the depths of her belly.

When he stopped, Kate saw the flickering of a match around the corner from the front door and one beside the back. She waited until the little sticks had caught, then shouted, "They have torches now, and that barn is full of hay. If you want to get out of there alive, drop your guns."

One of them yelled back, "You can't touch us. Your horses are in here."

"They aren't my horses. I'll cook them as fast as I'll cook you, and anything else in there, too."

"I don't believe you."

"I don't care," Kate said. "You have to the count of five to do what I tell you, and then you won't have any choices at all. One . . . two . . . three . . ."

One of them started to yell something at her, but she shouted him down: "Four . . ."

At both doors, the Glenraveners moved the torches into full view.

Kate heard three thuds.

"None of them dropped guns." The warrag crouched behind the tub, watching around the corner. "They each dropped a shoe."

"Fine." She squinted toward the outline of the barn, black against a sea of stars, wishing she had the warrag's eyesight. She shouted, "My friend here saw the shoes drop. I'm running out of patience with the three of you. Drop the guns or we'll torch the barn. You won't get another chance. This time you'll drop your weapons or you'll die."

She heard three sharper thuds. "Those were the guns," the warrag reported.

"I'm glad to hear it." She shouted toward the barn, "If any one of you is carrying anything besides a gun, drop that, too. My friends and I will search you, and if we find anything we might even mistake for a weapon, you'll regret it for the rest of your very short lives."

A few other items clattered to the floor. "Another gun," the warrag said. "*Two* more guns. A knife." He growled. "I should rip their throats out and eat them."

"The creeps are probably poisonous," Kate said.

The warrag glanced at her. In the darkness she could see his head turn in her direction, but she couldn't even guess at the expression on his face. Then he laughed. "Yes. Very probably." He paused, then added, "They've stopped dropping things."

She told the warrag, "Stay and watch them. If they move, tell them not to. I'm going to get closer. When I'm in position, you move up."

"Go ahead."

She ran toward the barn, keeping herself out of a direct line with the door in case one of the three had kept a gun in spite of her instructions. When she got to the wall, she reached a hand around the doorframe to the switch box and turned on the main light. Two bare hundred-watt bulbs set in white porcelain sockets threw out a brilliant wall of light and drew sudden sharp shadows that cast all three men into clear relief. Kate flicked her safety off and slipped around the corner, bringing her shotgun up as she did. She moved her aim slowly between the three men.

"I've spent enough time shooting this thing that I can drop all three of you before the first one gets a gun out, provided any of you were stupid enough to keep one. Now . . ." She shouted, "Tik. Errga. Val. Rhiana. Put out your fires and come in here. I'm going to need some help." She smiled up at the three men. "Any of you shitheads care to tell me why you felt you needed to beat me up and kill my horse and come looking for me with guns?"

They glared down at her but said nothing. Rhiana and Val came into the barn through the back door, and the warrag and the dagreth trotted in through the front.

"Satan's demons," one of the men muttered.

"That's an insult, isn't it?" Val asked. He snarled up at the three men, showing his elongated canines to their best advantage.

"Yes," Kate said. "Kick their guns out of the way, please. Don't pick them up or try shooting them. Until I've shown you how to handle firearms, I'd rather you didn't do anything that creative. There's more to shooting a handgun than pointing and pulling the trigger—at least if you want to hit what you're shooting." She didn't take her eyes off of the three men or lower the barrel of the shotgun. "Besides, I want to make sure the fingerprints on them are nice and clear for the police."

The Glenraveners carefully kicked the weapons to the wall behind Kate.

Kate recognized two of the men for sure, and thought the third looked familiar. The first was the deputy, Bobby. She felt oddly gratified to discover that she'd been right. The second was a man who had come into her shop a few times, asking if she would like to attend his church. He'd also stopped by her house on two occasions, inviting her once to a church picnic and another time to a membership drive. He'd seemed nice enough, but she hadn't been interested in his invitations, and had, of course, turned him down every time. The third man . . . well, she couldn't place him. All three of them bore fading bruises and healing scars from their fight. She discovered that she was quite pleased with herself, seeing the amount of damage she'd done.

"Good," she said. "Now, assholes, one at a time and not before I tell you to, I'm going to have you climb down from your rafters and lie facedown on the floor with your hands on the backs of your necks and your fingers laced together. When you reach the floor, don't bend over before I tell you to—not even to pick up your shoes—don't try to run, and hope to God you don't trip and fall because if any of those things happen, I'm going to splatter your innards all over the walls of my barn." She smiled up at them, then said to the Glenraveners, "And if they should get stupid enough to try to rush me all together, you will kill and eat them, won't you?"

The warrag laughed. "If you like, I'll eat them now."

"No. Not now. Just if they rush me."

The dagreth said, "I'm hungry. I haven't had dinner yet. I'd be happy to eat them for you."

"Well, maybe you'll get lucky and they'll get stupid." Kate broadened her smile at her attackers. "Good. So. Do we all understand our rules of engagement here?"

Three heads nodded. The men weren't looking at her when they responded; they seemed unable to quit staring at the Glenraveners. But they were listening.

"How nice. Then you're first, Bobby. Down you come."

The deputy started shimmying down the straight brace from the rafter.

The churchman told her, "The Bible says, *Thou shalt not suffer a witch to live*."

Kate didn't take her eyes off of the deputy. "Quite so, Mr. Smeed. Sneally."

"Snead," he said.

"Snead. Fine. I read that verse in the King James version when I was a kid. However, I believe that biblical scholars have several options in translating the word they've chosen to translate as 'witch,' all of them equally valid. Their arbitrary choice of the word 'witch' is just that . . . an arbitrary translation choice."

The deputy landed on the floor and Kate said, "Show him where we want him to lie down, Errga. Rhiana, get the rope hanging on that peg and you and Val tie him up. Tightly, so that he can't move, but not so tightly that you cut off the blood flow to his hands. We wouldn't want to hurt him."

She turned her attention directly to Snead. "But that's in the Old Testament, and if you're a Christian, then you must believe that Christ took the judgment of humankind upon himself when he died, so that my beliefs would then become a matter between me and him and therefore none of your business. In any case, Christian or not, the Constitution, which guarantees freedom of religion, absolutely forbids murder. And whether you are a right-wing fundamentalist asshole murdering doctors who perform abortions, or a left-wing tree-hugging asshole killing the lumberjacks who are cutting down virgin forest, or any other sort of asshole who feels justified killing a human being over a difference of ideology, you would still be in violation of the law of the land." She stared up at him, her anger boiling inside of her. "And you would still be an asshole."

She glanced down at the floor, where the deputy lay facedown, his arms tightly bound behind his back and his ankles and knees tied together. She took a deep, steadying breath. "Nice job, guys," she said. "Keep an eye on him while I bring the next one down."

"Then by your rationale, if you kill us," Snead said, "you'll be committing murder."

Her rage had banked itself down into a slow-burning fury that she thought would never leave her again. "No. If I kill you, I'll be committing self-defense. The Constitution encourages self-defense. Defending yourself is a part of taking responsibility for your own life, and because I am a responsible human being and a good citizen, if you ever attack me again I will destroy you so totally that the police forensics specialists will have to suck you up with a shop vac and haul you to the morgue in a hundred Zip-Loc bags." She kept her eyes on him, but nodded toward the bound deputy near her feet. "You're next, Snead. Down you come and stop five feet away from him."

When Snead was tied, she looked at the third man. "I've been trying to come up with a connection, but I can't. Who are you? I swear you look familiar, but I don't know why."

The third man didn't say anything. Kate shrugged. "Have it your way. I'll figure it out sooner or later."

When he was tied beside the other two men, she went through all of their pockets, pulling out wallets. She told the Glenraveners, "Please wait here and watch these three. I'm going to the house to call the police. When you see flashing blue lights, move toward the back door. We'll come down the path and all of you but Rhiana will need to hide. Rhiana, I'll explain how you and I caught them and you tied them up while I covered them with the gun. Is that all right with you?"

"Of course," she said.

Kate squatted and looked into the faces of the three thugs. "Gentlemen, I am going to turn you in. If you don't tell the policemen who come here the truth about what you were doing here tonight and what you've been doing to me, or if you make the very stupid mistake of mentioning anyone here who might not be exactly human, my friends will come to visit you in jail. Walls and doors and locks don't slow them down at all. They can go anywhere they want, any time they want to, and no one will see them unless they want to be seen. Do you understand?"

From their horrified expressions, Kate decided they probably did.

She removed the drivers' licenses from each wallet, then lay the wallets, other contents untouched, in front of the men. "You saw me remove your licenses. I want to be sure you know I didn't take anything else. Do you have any question about this?"

With difficulty, each man shook his head.

"Good." She stood and looked at the licenses.

Robert C. Sumner, age twenty-seven. With a dreadful picture of Bobby looking like a Hitler youth.

Ogden P. Snead III, age thirty, wearing a black suit, a white shirt, and a black tie for his license photograph.

And Warren B. Plonkett, age twenty-four.

Warren B. Plonkett, she thought. Warren B. Plonkett . . .

Suddenly she could see the man coming in to ask her for a job, mentioning that he knew her from a mutual friend, Liz Baylor, who lived on the outskirts of Peters and who had a nursery and a side business supplying herbs to pagans.

"I'll be damned," she muttered. "Warren B. Plonkett. I refused to hire you, didn't I? You were trying to sleaze your way into the position I eventually gave Lisa. You wanted me to hire you because you knew what I was, as you put it—as if that made any damn difference in what kind of an employee you would be. You didn't know anything about horses, had never done any leatherwork, and thought I would give you a job because I was scared of you. And naturally I didn't hire you. You little creep. You're the one who stirred these two up." She looked down at the back of Warren's head lying so close to her feet, and for just an instant she had an irrational urge to kick it until it bounced. She didn't, though.

Instead she went to the house and called the police and the sheriff's department. They were fascinated by what she had to tell them, and once they arrived, even more fascinated when all three men, including the deputy, were willing—even eager—to give full confessions.

Fifteen

"Come in. I'm Ariani Callion." Callion, disguised in the form of a statuesque blonde, showed the job applicant in. The man who'd come to interview, Callion knew from his application letter, was Jeremy Bridges, and as far as Callion could tell, he fit Callion's needs perfectly. But there might be inconvenient details that would prove him to be, on closer examination, an unfortunate choice.

So Callion showed the young man in to his office and let him pick a chair on the far side of the desk. Callion settled into his chair, steepled his fingers, and in a rich contralto voice that he intentionally made as sexy as he could, said, "From your letter, you sound ideal. You're a reader, and your familiarity with the fields of SF and fantasy is extraordinary. I was impressed by the fact that you're knowledgeable about mainstream fiction and mysteries, too. You presented yourself well on paper."

Jeremy waited for just a second to see if Callion was going to say anything else, then said, "Um . . . thank you. Your ad certainly caught my attention, and I fit the qualifications . . .

but I was wondering what the job was. The ad didn't make that clear."

"Intentionally. I would rather not be swamped by unqualified applicants. Curiosity is one of the finest of characteristics in a human being, and surprisingly hard to come by anymore. But I consider curiosity essential in an applicant. When I'm sure you meet my needs, I'll tell you about the job." Callion cleared his throat and shifted so that Jeremy got a good look at his cleavage. "You didn't mention how your family would feel about your traveling for extended periods of time, or picking up and moving abruptly."

Jeremy looked down at his hands for a moment, inhaled slowly, and looked up to meet Callion's eyes. "I don't actually have a family," he said. "My mother died when I was pretty young and my father and I haven't . . . haven't spoken in years. I'm an only child."

"I see. Will you want moving expenses for your own wife and children?"

He laughed, but the laughter was devoid of humor. "I *had* a girlfriend, but she decided she would rather chase after men with money. I certainly don't have a wife or children."

Callion nodded. "Then you would be able to move at a moment's notice."

"Hell, I could move today," Jeremy said. The bitterness in his voice came through clearly.

"I see."

"I'm sorry, Ms. Callion. That was rude and unprofessional of me. Events in my life have been difficult lately, and I've experienced a certain amount of anger regarding them. But I'm over that, and my past won't affect my job performance for you."

Callion smiled. "That's fine. I would expect you to show some emotion when things have gone badly for you." He sighed. "You said you could move today, but I assume you'll actually have a number of financial obligations you will have to straighten out before you could really be ready to move?"

"Not really. I'll have to pay my final month's rent on my apartment and give notice, but if you hire a packer to move your people, I wouldn't have to stay there to take care of that. I don't own anything really valuable, anyway. Just my books. And I'd have to shut off my phone and my electric and my water, but again, that's something that would take about an hour."

"Excellent." Callion said, "Well, if you're interested, I'll be happy to show you the work you'll be doing with us, and tell you about the company, the benefits, the perks . . ." He stood. "Are you interested?"

"Well, I think so. But first, I'd like to know, from my qualifications, what my starting salary would be. That's pretty important."

Callion took out a sheet of paper and wrote for a moment. "You have a Bachelor's degree and are working on your Master's, you have an excellent grasp of the necessary material, by all appearances your IQ is exceptionally high—you wouldn't happen to know what it is, by any chance?"

"My IQ? One forty-eight."

"Yes, I thought so. That makes it even more imperative that I convince you to work for me. "I can start you at sixty-two five."

"Um . . . sixty-two five what? Dollars per day?"

"Oh, no. Sixty-two thousand five hundred dollars per year. If you already had your Master's I could go higher, but since we'll be covering the cost of your education from here on out, I'm afraid that's the top dollar I'm authorized to offer."

Callion watched him. Jeremy was trying hard not to appear stunned, but he wasn't fooling either of them. He'd never thought he could earn so much money, and his greed was going to put him right where Callion wanted him.

"That . . . sounds very good, actually," Jeremy said. "Certainly reasonable."

"Excellent. Then can I show you what you'll be doing?"

This time Jeremy stood. "By all means. Lead on."

Callion took him to the center of the house, to a room that had been a family room before Callion converted it. Now it had no windows, only the one door, and thick, soundproofed walls. Callion stepped in first, waiting until Jeremy was inside, and closed the door behind them. They stood in utter darkness for a moment, and in silence until Jeremy said, "What is this?"

"Patience. This takes a second."

Softly glowing points of golden light began to whirl up out of the center of the floor. They rose upward, drifting into a beautiful cloud of spinning fire, a slow-moving tornado of fireflies. "Oh," Jeremy whispered. "I've never seen anything so beautiful. What is it? Some sort of special effect?"

"They have a handful of different names. They've been called will-o'-the-wisps. Firedrakes. Watchers. I have always known them as Devourers. They are Rift creatures, predators of an interesting variety. Very rare. They have some amazing abilities."

"Predators?"

The firefly cloud spun itself out into the shape of a face, and a thousand whispering voices speaking in almost-synchronized phrases said:

we await
    we await
your bidding (bidding) have
    have you brought us
    brought us
something tasty wonderful
    something good

Jeremy wasn't amused. "If this is a joke," he said, "I find it in terrible taste."

"No joke at all," Callion said. "I require a lifetime commitment from my employees."

"Just forget it." Jeremy turned and tried the door, but of course it didn't open.

The lights swarmed forward, first a thin stream of them that spiraled around him and settled on his skin, burrowing in and illuminating him from the inside as they went. After the first few lights found their way into his flesh, the rest followed, flowing over him and moving through him. He began to swell and scream simultaneously, and he begged very nicely for Callion to have mercy, to not hurt him, to get the things off of him.

Callion watched, pleased. The Devourers obliterated Jeremy, leaving not even bones or hair to show where he had once been. Callion could have siphoned magic off of them had he chosen to, but Callion had no need for the soul-magic of the dead.

"Another bright breeder vanished," he said quietly, watching the last of the Devourers clean up stray spatters of blood from around the room. "The collective IQ of my enemies drops just a bit more, my own options expand, and someone else who might be able to figure out what I'm doing ceases to exist." He glanced at the Devourers. "And I keep you little monsters fed a bit longer, eh?"

He pressed his palm to the door, which opened instantly for him. He spent a little time making himself look like Jeremy. Then he drove Jeremy's car back to his apartment. He stopped by the manager's office and paid cash for Jeremy's rent for the next two months, then visited the utility companies and turned off Jeremy's phone, water, and electric. By the time anyone thought to start looking for Jeremy, they wouldn't have anywhere to look.

Sixteen

Kate looked at her clock. Seven twenty-five A.M., which was a reasonable time to be up and working, except that she hadn't gone to bed until three. She tried closing her eyes, but she could tell pretty quickly that doing so was pointless; four hours of sleep plus change and she was up for the day.

She yawned and sat up. Rhiana was asleep on the floor beside her bed—Kate had decided Rhiana would feel better sharing a room with her than with Val and Tik and Errga. The arrangement had a second advantage, too; both of them could keep the daylight hours they preferred.

Rhiana sat up.

"Go back to sleep. I didn't mean to wake you," Kate told her.

"I didn't sleep very well, either." Rhiana stretched and brushed the hair out of her face. "Too much excitement."

"I know."

"At least they'll be imprisoned now."

"Don't count on it." Kate got up and went to her closet to

find something to wear. "Our court system won't lock them up, even though they confessed. They'll be out on bail pending trial."

"Out?" Kate couldn't see Rhiana's face, but the depth of disbelief she put into that one word told Kate how she felt anyway.

"Yes, out. Over the years our court system has become geared toward protecting criminals instead of the innocent. Well, some sorts of criminals, anyway. The system has fallen apart to the point that people don't really expect justice anymore." She found a comfortable old pair of jeans and another Rangers sweatshirt. She felt confident enough about the magical work she and Rhiana were doing that she decided to wear it; if the two of them accidentally blew it to oblivion, she'd have a duck. The Rangers were playing that night, though, and she felt the need to support her team. As they neared the playoffs, they were falling in the standings. She thought their struggles were a last taste of the legacy of Neil Smith and Colin Campbell, who'd traded their youth and their future in the 1995–1996 season for a bunch of aging goons.

She'd wanted to see Messier win another Stanley Cup before he retired. The old consolation, "Maybe next year," sounded more and more unlikely. It needed to be this year.

Hence the sweatshirt. She couldn't think of anything else she could do. Well . . . maybe she could light a few red, white, and blue candles. She laughed at that thought, took her clothes, and went to take a shower.

Rhiana was sitting at the top of the steps waiting for her when she came out. "We never called Lisa to see if she could find a number for Callion," she said.

Kate thumped herself on the forehead with the palm of her hand. "I forgot."

"Too many things going on."

"We shouldn't have had the pizza party last night after the police left."

"Everyone liked the pizza, Kate. I liked it."

"Well, the celebration was fun, but the pizza was mediocre. You haven't lived until you've tasted New York pizza. That was just chain stuff."

"Chain stuff?"

"Pizza parlors all over the country prepackage . . . never mind. It wasn't real pizza. Trust me. Anyway, after all of that, I forgot I intended to call Lisa."

"Can you call her now?"

Kate nodded and jogged down the steps. She could hear a

symphony of snores rolling out of the living room; Val, Tik, and Errga had decided beer was the best part of a pizza party and had overindulged. "I can call her in about five minutes. She won't answer the phone until eight-thirty, when the mail-order part of the store opens."

"I'll be down soon, then. You can tell me what you found."

Kate heard Rhiana close the bathroom door, and heard the pipes begin to rattle as the shower hissed on. She watched the clock, and as soon as she could, she called her store.

"Saddlecraft South, this is Lisa. How may I help you today?"

"It's Kate."

"God, Kate . . . I read in this morning's paper that the police captured the three men who attacked you last night."

"Yeah, but that isn't what I called you about. You know that phone number CD-ROM you have?"

"Sure."

"Could you look up a name for me?"

"Of course."

"It's Callion. I guess it would be C-A-L-L-I-O-N, but check for other spellings, too."

"Do you have a first name?"

Kate thought about that for a moment. "Check it as both a first and a last name. Can you do that?"

"Sure. I'll just run two searches, one with the first field open, and one with the second field open. You'll probably end up with a lot of wrong names and addresses, though."

"I can't help that. When can you check?"

"Is there a rush?"

"If you ever want me back there carrying my share of the workload, there's a rush."

"Paul's here now. We aren't busy yet—he could cover for me and I could go home."

"Great. Do that, then, and call me with the results." She considered. "Um, if you have too many, just print them off and I'll stop by and pick up the sheet. And Lisa . . ."

"Yeah?"

"Thanks."

After spending endless hours trying to think of a magical solution to finding Callion, if it were this easy, she was going to feel like an idiot. And wouldn't that be the way; the outsider who never saw a phone until seven days ago being the one to figure out that angle.

Kate poured herself a bowl of Fruit & Fibre, the kind with the peach chunks in it, dumped in skim milk that was squeezing too close to the expiration date for comfort, and sat at the bar to eat and meditate. She'd finished off the first bowl and started into a second when Rhiana joined her.

"Did fortune smile?"

"It hasn't even grinned yet," Kate said.

"I see." Rhiana eyed Kate's cereal and milk, wrinkled her nose, and got out sausages, cheddar cheese, and bread for herself. Kate had discovered that none of the Glenraveners considered cereal to be fit food for humans, thinking of it instead as something appropriate for cattle and horses, and they didn't like skim milk, either. They didn't ask her to supply them with the food they preferred without compensation, though; Val and Tik had some gold which they gave her when it became apparent that they weren't going to be going home immediately. Because of that, she didn't begrudge them their insistence on meat with every meal. She didn't expect to get rich from her guests' small hoard, though. She had no idea how she was going to dispose of circulated gold coins with some sort of Glenraven crest on one side and the head of a woman with fangs on the obverse, and edged with writing from no known language on Earth. She supposed she'd find a way. Someone ought to be intrigued by them.

"She will tell you when she finds something?" Rhiana asked.

The sausages smelled wonderful. Kate glanced down at the soggy flakes floating in her pale milk and sniffed wistfully. *Bad for the heart*, she thought. *Bad for the arteries, bad for the hips, bad for my health in general. Sausages . . . made with the stuff left over after all the parts people are willing to eat are gone.* She'd seen hog jowls and pigs feet and fatback and tripe in the local Winn Dixie. If people were willing to eat that, she didn't want to consider the bits that went into the making of sausages.

Her rationalization did nothing; the wondrous odor of sizzling sausages made her stomach growl, and she ate her last few spoonfuls of cereal sullenly, wishing that someone, somewhere, would find a way to make sausages into a health food.

The phone rang.

"Yeah?"

"Kate? You all right?"

"Of course. I'm just lusting after pork products."

"Winn Dixie had bacon on sale yesterday—really good price, too."

"Great. Just what I didn't need to hear."

"You still doing the low-fat thing, huh?" She laughed. "I got your numbers."

Kate grabbed the pad of paper and the pen she kept by the phone and said, "Okay. Go ahead."

"There aren't many. David and Rick Callion in Montana . . ."

"Probably not who I want, but give me the numbers. Did you get street addresses, too?"

"Of course." She read both sets of numbers and addresses off and Kate wrote them down.

"P. D. Callion in Rochester, New York . . ."

Kate got that one, too.

"Eight Callions in and around the Tennessee-Kentucky border . . ."

"Okay . . ." Kate scribbled name after name, wondering if any of this could be leading anywhere.

"And one Callion used as a first name. Callion Aregeni, in Abilene, Texas."

Kate wrote that one down, too. "No others?"

"If there are, they're unlisted."

"Thanks, Lisa. You might have saved me a whole lot of time."

"No problem."

When she hung up the phone, she showed the list to Rhiana. "Any of these look likely?"

Rhiana stared at the words, then looked at Kate. "I can't read that."

Kate felt stupid. She'd known before that the Glenraveners couldn't read English. She realized that they didn't actually speak English. But because they could read the same text she could read in the *Fodor's Guide to Glenraven*, it was easy to forget that what they were seeing and what she saw were two different things. "Sorry," she muttered, and read the names aloud.

When she read the last one, Rhiana got excited. "That one. It has to be that one."

"You're sure?"

"Of course I'm sure. Callion Aregeni means 'Callion the Aregen.' It couldn't be anyone else."

"Then we have him. He lives at 5236 Camino Lindo in Abilene, Texas. All we have to do is drive there and . . . well, do whatever we're going to do."

"How soon can we leave?"

"I'll call the operator to double-check the number, and then we can figure out how we're going to get the five of us down there and what we're going to do when we arrive."

"You're wonderful to help us, Kate," Rhiana said.

Kate shrugged. "My life has felt hollow for a while. Doing this, I feel like I matter again."

She dialed the area code for Abilene, then 555-1212 for directory assistance. When the operator came on, Kate said, "Callion Aregeni, please."

"One moment."

Kate waited for the automated voice telling her the number, but the operator came back. "I'm sorry, but we don't have a listing for that name."

Kate spelled it for her.

"I'm sorry. No listing."

"You don't see him at 5236 Camino Lindo?"

"I'm really sorry. I don't."

"Do you have any sort of a new listing? Maybe something that says his number has been changed, that gives a new number?"

"I have a notice here that his phone has been disconnected. I don't have any notation of a new number."

Kate sighed. "Oh. Well, that's it, then. Thank you."

"Thank you for using AT&T," the woman said. And as an afterthought, "Good luck."

Kate hung up the phone and sat staring at the number. "Shit," she said, with feeling.

Rhiana sat watching her. "He isn't there."

"No. He's moved."

"Then we are where we were before. We know he's someplace on this planet, and we know nothing more than that."

"No." Kate had no intention of giving up that easily. "No. We know where he was. Exactly where. Somehow, we should be able to connect where he was to where he is. The real estate office that sold his house might be the best place to start."

"I'm sorry. I don't know what you're talking about."

Kate smiled. "It doesn't matter. I have a couple of ideas that might give us Callion's new address. I'll try them. If we get lucky, we don't have to find a magic spell to take us to him." She shrugged. "While I'm trying my ideas, though, why don't you see if you can come up with an angle or two on that spell. Just a couple of things we could try in case the things I'm doing don't pan out."

Rhiana stood for a moment with a blank expression on her face. Then she said, "Yes. I believe the book had difficulty translating for you that time. It took a while for its words to catch up to your voice. But I understand now." She gave Kate a wan smile. "I will do my best on the spell, but I will also do a little medi-tation that you will be lucky in your search."

Kate lifted what was left of her glass of orange juice and said, "To luck, for all of us."

Rhiana lifted her own glass of beer and echoed, "To luck."

Seventeen

Kate said, "Thank you, Mrs. Pederman. Thank you so much for helping me."

"When you see Mr. Aregeni, tell him I hope he's feeling better."

"I will. I promise." When she hung up the phone, Kate sagged against the countertop and rested her head in her hands.

"This time?" Val asked.

"Yes. One more real estate agency, though, and I would have just given up, I think." Kate's shoulders ached and her neck throbbed and she had a headache. She didn't even know how many Abilene real estate agencies she'd called between Friday morning and Saturday morning, but it didn't matter anymore. She had the next piece of the puzzle in locating Callion. She forced herself to sit up, and dug her fingertips into the muscles of her shoulders and neck. "I don't have a street address, but I have a city. The lady who sold his house said he mentioned to her that he was moving to Fort Lauderdale for his health."

"Fort Lauderdale? Is that near or far?" Rhiana asked.

"It's far, but it could be a whole lot further. If we get on 95 and drive steadily at the speed limit, we can be there in about twelve hours."

"That isn't long. Once we get there, how will we find him, though?"

Kate said, "We can probably find him from here. His last number wasn't unlisted. There's a good chance this one won't be, either." She dialed directory assistance again, and this time asked for the phone number and street address for Callion Aregeni. In less than a minute, she had both.

The Glenraveners cheered. Kate felt like cheering, too. Then, however, Rhiana brought up one other difficulty. "How can all five of us travel in your vehicle. We won't all fit in it."

For a moment, Kate wanted to beat her head on the countertop. But something from the events of the past week finally connected, and Kate grinned. "No. We won't, but it doesn't matter. I have to have my car repainted, and the insurance will cover some of the cost for a rental car while that's being done. I'll do that today, and rent a van, and we'll use that to drive to Florida while the car is in the shop."

By the time she'd finished setting that up, she hoped she would never see another telephone. But Jack's Automotive Detailers could take her Escort in that day, someone from Budget Rent-A-Car would pick her up from Jack's, and even though she couldn't get a van with tinted windows, she could get a van . . . and her insurance would cover all but eight dollars per day of the expense, at least until her car was finished, which the manager at Jack's said would probably be on Tuesday.

That might be enough time to get down to Fort Lauderdale, find Callion's hiding place, do what they had to do, and get back. Of course, keeping in mind that she didn't even know how they were going to do what they had to do, she didn't think she would bet the ranch on that. She decided when she went in to pay to make sure that she gave the rental place enough money to cover against any eventuality.

She turned to Rhiana. "You want to come with me? We can pick up the van and buy a few things we'll need for the trip."

Eighteen

The phone rang and Callion picked it up.

"I'm a friend from . . . back home," the voice on the other end of the line said. The voice was male, and deep, and spoke one of the Kinnish dialects with an accent Callion couldn't quite place.

"As far as I know, I don't have any friends back home."

"You'd be surprised. There are a lot of us who don't want to see a human Watchmistress. Quite a lot. For some assistance and a few concessions, I could take you into the heart of the new rebellion. More than a few Glenraveners are ready to see you as Master of the Watch."

Callion leaned back in his desk chair and rested his feet on the desktop. "I'm listening."

"I don't have time to talk. But a small force of hunters has picked up your trail; they're on their way to force you and the Watchers to return to Glenraven. Maybe that won't be such a bad thing; I'm traveling with them, and will continue to interfere

with their actions as I have been all along." Silence for an instant, then, "Damn. I'll have to call you back. This phone isn't
secure."

Callion was intrigued. "By all means, do call back. I'll be eager
to hear what else you have to say."

The line went dead in his hand.

Interesting, Callion thought. *Extremely interesting*. His divina-
tions had indicated a coming break in the pattern of his days,
something that could either lift him to the power and position
he desired or else destroy him utterly. Now the past had caught
up with him in the form of a stranger from Glenraven, but that
stranger was an ally, not an enemy. Callion had cast a spell while
listening to the caller to discern the presence of any duplicity;
he had been pleased to discover that the caller was not an enemy
trying to win his trust in order to betray him. In the stranger's
voice he found no perfidy.

So events shaped themselves in his favor. He smiled. He had
planned for many eventualities, he had expected violence and
bloodshed and mayhem in his quest to regain Glenraven and force
it to bow to him, but in all of his planning and preparing, he
had not anticipated allies.

Nineteen

Rhiana tossed her small bag into the back of the rental van and stood while Kate showed her how to shut the doors and secure them. Val and Tik already had bench seats behind the main one, and Errga slept curled with his nose under his tail on the floor in the cargo area to the very back. Twilight was bringing a storm with it; Rhiana could smell it in the sharpening scents of earth and dust and feel it in the dampness on her cheeks and the backs of her hands. The leaves on the shrubs rattled and the new growth on the trees overhead softened the clacking of the branches to a whisper. The edge of every storm brought Rhiana a sense of heightened anticipation, a knotting of the gut, a feeling of *almost . . . almost . . . almost . . .* that twisted tighter and tighter the closer it approached. At that moment, her skin tingled and she felt slightly breathless, but also tense. Edgy. *Almost . . . almost . . . almost . . .* hummed in the back of her mind and she could not decide if the thing that had almost reached her should give her cause for joy or terror.

123

When the doors were closed, Kate took two rolled strips of paper out of a shoulder bag she carried and handed one to Rhiana. "Hold this just a sec, will you?"

She peeled backing off of the other strip, then stuck the strip onto the back window of the van. She smoothed it out carefully, and Rhiana could see that the strip was covered with writing.

"Hand me the other one now."

Kate copied the procedure with the second sheet of paper, then stood back to study the effect.

"What are they?"

"Camouflage," Kate said.

"Oh. Are they written spells? Words of power?"

"Sort of. They're bumper stickers."

"What do they say?" Rhiana wished the spell that allowed her to understand the local spoken language would allow her to read, too.

"That one says, 'Even the lousiest lover, properly treated, makes a great drumskin—Old Hoos Proverb.' And the other one says, 'Cats with hands were a bad idea.'"

Rhiana struggled to understand. Poor lovers probably could be skinned and tanned and turned into drumskins, but she didn't think human skin would be durable enough to make a long-lasting drumskin . . . nor had she realized that Kate or her people would treat their unwanted lovers in quite that manner. She had gotten the impression that they were slightly more civilized. As for cats with hands, they probably were a bad idea, but since there weren't any cats with hands . . .

Kate had been watching her face. "They're supposed to be funny," she said. "Craig got them at a science fiction convention we went to in High Point a few years ago. He never got around to putting them on his car, and I've had them in my closet ever since."

"You said they were camouflage."

"Trust me."

Rhiana nodded. The knot in her belly twisted tighter, the anticipation of coming events grew more fierce, and she shivered slightly.

Kate went around to the side door and slid it open. "Okay, guys," she said. "Time for some makeup."

She sat on the seat beside Val, squirted a dab of pale cream onto a sponge, and patted it along Val's forehead, across his nose and cheeks and along his jaw. "Don't have any beard, do you?"

"True men don't have hair on their faces," he said. He was

offended. "Only Kin-hera . . . and Machnan . . . and humans." He said the word "humans" like he was spitting something bad-tasting out of his mouth.

Kate didn't seem upset. "Yeah? Well true men don't wear makeup on their faces, if you want to know the truth, but you're going to have to." She dabbed a slightly darker brown cream onto one finger and dabbed under his eyes and along the sides of his nose with it. She moved back, tipped her head to one side, then muttered, "Not yet." She opened a little case, removed a fuzzy round white pad, rubbed it over what Rhiana recognized as some form of face powder, and began patting it all over Val's face. Finally, when Rhiana could see little sparkles of the powder from where she stood, Kate said, "That'll do."

She moved back to Tik's seat and repeated the process.

"What are you doing?" Rhiana finally asked. "Trying to make them look human?"

"Nope. Trying to make them look fake. Let's go."

"But aren't you going to give them some way to hide themselves?"

"Won't need to."

Rhiana couldn't believe what she was hearing. "But people will see them."

"You bet they will." Kate climbed into the driver's seat, closed her door, and fastened her seat belt.

Rhiana got into her own seat, locked the door as Kate had shown her, and struggled with her own belt. The mechanism for this one was different than the one in Kate's car, and she had to work with it for a moment.

Kate, meanwhile, turned around in her seat and told Val and Tik, "If either of you see anyone staring at the two of you, just smile and wave. Okay?"

"Smile and wave?"

"That's right. Let's see it."

Val smiled without showing his teeth . . . a tightly stretched, uncomfortable smile that Rhiana thought made him look like a corpse laid out in its coffin.

"Show some teeth, Val," Kate said. "A big smile. Like you mean it. Like you're having fun, you're happy, you like all the attention."

Val's smile got a little larger, but no more sincere.

Kate shrugged. "You'll get the hang of it. And Tik, don't let your tongue hang out like that. Try not to move it much, okay.

A little, but not much. Don't lick your nose or anything while people are looking, please?"

"Why not?"

Kate sighed. "Because we're going to pretend that you two are wearing costumes. An entire subculture of Americans go to gatherings called science fiction conventions, where they dress up in costumes and discuss books and movies that pertain to their culture. Craig liked to go to them, and I went to some with him. That's where I learned that you can look any way you want if you just smile and wave when people stare."

Errga sat up and looked over the backseat. "What about me?"

"Unfortunately, dogs can't talk even at science fiction conventions. We can explain away your hands as your doggie costume, but I'm afraid you're still going to limit your conversations to 'woof, woof' when anyone might overhear you. We'll have Val or Rhiana or Tik walk you on a leash. I'll pick up a collar on the way so that we can let you out at rest stops. You can cock your hind leg to pee on bushes and take a dump in the grass."

"In *front* of people?!" The warrag sounded horrified.

Rhiana thought, *Poor Errga. A member of the most private species of all the Kin-hera, and Kate wants to make him empty his bladder in public.* She said, "Perhaps we can let Errga out by the side of the road near the woods from time to time. That way he can do what he needs to do behind shrubs and he won't have to embarrass himself."

Kate glanced at her, then looked back at Errga. "Or we can do it Rhiana's way, if you would prefer."

"I *would* prefer," Errga said.

"It won't be that big a deal. We'll be traveling in the darkness, so probably no one is going to notice you guys anyway."

Kate started the van and pulled out of her drive.

"You're sure the horses will be all right?" Rhiana asked.

"Lisa said she would take care of them. She will."

Almost . . . almost . . . almost . . .

Something coming, something about to happen, something ready to change to become something else—trouble, danger, disaster, death. A hard, hot flash inside her head, the sharp bitter current of twisted magic, something wrong, wrong, *wrong*, so wrong Rhiana could taste it. The road rolled by at her side and she leaned against the car door and watched it race by underneath her, trying to hide the fact that suddenly fear so completely consumed her she was about to be sick.

She closed her eyes, pretending to try to sleep while Kate turned on Machine World music that sounded like madmen being tortured with thumbscrews and branding irons to the accompaniment of crashing cars. She didn't sleep; instead, tentatively, she felt around with magical senses for the disturbance she'd felt.

Whatever it had been, it hid itself away when she started looking for it. Trouble, she thought. Evil, trouble, riding in on the storm-front like a banshee. That one sharp stab of magic had been too quick for her to discern distance or direction or even form. She had gotten from it only the quick, certain impression that it meant her harm, and then it vanished into nothingness.

The first drops of rain splatted against the windshield to the accompaniment of the first low, rolling boom of thunder. Rhiana forced herself to breathe slowly and deeply with the monotonous regularity of a sleeper. The splatterings got louder and came faster, as the rain came down harder.

"Wow," Kate said, and Rhiana could tell by the flash of light that glowed through her eyelids that lightning had struck close by. Thunder crashed in its wake, no longer the delayed, rolling booming of a distant storm but the immediate shouting fury found only in the heart of one. Rhiana opened her eyes and sat up.

Metal arms slid in quick, rhythmic arcs across the windscreen, pushing water out of their way. Twin cones of light stabbed into the sheeting rain, illuminating very little, and that poorly. Rhiana realized the van moved forward slowly; Kate squinted through the gloom, frowning.

"We're going to have to pull over until this lets up a little," she said. "My windshield wipers aren't keeping up with this downpour and I don't want to get rear-ended by someone whose are."

"No. Of course not," Rhiana said. She didn't understand exactly what Kate was talking about, but it sounded serious.

Under a bridge, Kate pulled the van to a halt. She left the vehicle running and the headlights on. Rhiana realized they were on a double road, with two lanes of the smooth black surface separated by a wide strip of grass from two more just like them. She recalled Glenraven's tiny riding paths and the dirt roads so narrow that wagons could only pass each other at wide spots, and wondered what sort of people humans were to create such mammoth thoroughfares . . . or to need them.

Giant vehicles with huge wheeled boxes attached to the back rolled slowly by them, and small cars, and vehicles of every imaginable shape and size in between. Rhiana felt like a silly child, but she stared out at the slowly passing traffic until the rain lightened somewhat and Kate decided she could drive in it again.

When they started forward, Rhiana felt another flare of malignant magic. There and gone. As if someone were testing her. Even though this time she thought she was ready, she still could tell nothing more than that the wizard intended her harm, and that he or she was more powerful than Rhiana herself. Otherwise, she would have been able to discern a direction, a purpose, *something* about the wizard other than his existence.

Twenty

At just after midnight, Kate pulled into the parking lot of a Waffle House in Jacksonville and rested her forehead against the steering wheel and closed her eyes. She couldn't hold out any longer. She needed to go to the bathroom and she needed to get away from the unending questions on this intercultural, interspecies road trip from hell. She didn't want to think anymore about why people built their houses out of wood, or what made neon lights work, or why citizens who didn't have children, or who had them but didn't send them to schools, had to pay the same school taxes as those who had, or how a free-enterprise system was different than a feudal one. She didn't want to try to explain the executive, legislative, and judicial branches of government to people who thought one person could embody all three branches and be all things to all people. She didn't, quite honestly, want to think about anything but stuffing her face with a fried steak and some delicious, terribly unhealthy hashed potatoes slathered in melted cheese and chili and tomatoes, and probably even a sugary

129

nondiet soda and a slab of apple pie the size of Montana. *Unhealthy,* she thought. *Give me something that will block my arteries right this minute and drop me dead on the floor of the restaurant so I don't have to listen to that goddamn bear-boy tell me again why things in Glenraven are so much better than things here.*

Sanctimonious did not even begin to describe . . .

She sat up and forced herself to smile. She turned in her seat, the fake smile pasted to her face, and took a deep breath. "Okay, folks. Remember. They're costumes. Rhiana and I made them, and you can't let anybody touch them because if someone touches them, it might destroy the makeup or the tiny little motors that make all the pieces work. And you're wearing them because you have to have your pictures taken tomorrow . . ." *And if any of you asks me how a camera works again, so help me, I'll murder you.* " . . . and it takes *hours* to get all the stuff on. Got it?"

Dagreth and Kin nodded. The warrag cleared his throat. "What about me?"

Kate's fake smile slipped. "You just *went* half an hour ago."

"I wasn't talking about that," the warrag snarled. "I meant what about food?"

"Dogs can't go into the restaurant, and there's no way in hell I could pass you off as a human in a costume, so you're going to have to stay in here and wait. I'll bring you back a couple of steaks. You want a drink?"

"Do they have beer?"

It was Kate's turn to snarl. "No, they don't, and if they did you couldn't have one. Nobody is drinking on this trip. If we get stopped for some reason, I'm going to have enough of a time explaining the three of you without having to explain why the inside of the van smells like a keg party."

They all looked at her as if she'd metamorphosed into Ghengis Khan and told them she'd come to burn down their village, rape their women, and steal their gold. *I don't care,* she told herself. *I don't care what they think of me; I don't care if they like me; I don't care about anything but getting this over with and getting back home to my life.*

"One more thing," she said. "Boys . . . when you go in to the restroom to pee, *lock the door.* Don't—DO NOT—forget to do this. There are only so many things I can pass of as being part of a funny costume." She picked her purse off of the floorboard and added. "And remember, just smile. Be polite.

You're just like everybody else in the restaurant, except that you're hot and you're itchy because you've been in costume for hours."

No more stalling.

She opened her door and got out. She waited as they followed her. She tried to look like a woman who could turn people into creatures from another world—she tried to look confident and proud of her handiwork and just the slightest bit pleased by the stir she knew she was going to cause. She had admired the costumes she'd seen at conventions; they were some of what she'd liked best, in fact.

I made them, she told herself. *I have to believe or no one else will believe. Underneath the latex and foam and makeup, they're people just like me. I made these freaking pains in the ass.*

She decided maybe she shouldn't think about it too much after all. She was getting cranky.

She went first, Rhiana followed, and the Kin and the dagreth brought up the rear. The warrag flopped on the Kin's seat and pressed his nose to the window and managed to make it clear that he felt put out about being left behind.

"Be good," she turned and told him through the glass, "and I'll bring you something tasty."

"Woof," he said, and sounded nothing like a dog when he said it. Smartass.

Inside the restaurant, long-haul truckers lined the row of stools, slurping down black coffee and joking with the waitresses. A family of five crowded into one of the booths, the teenage children sullen, the younger one chattering endlessly. The father, like the truckers, sucked down coffee like he feared he'd never taste it again. A young couple sat in the next booth over, murmuring to each other over the table and holding hands.

No one paid any real attention when Kate and Rhiana walked in. Val and Tik right behind them were another story. The two waitresses' eyes got big when Val smiled at them, and bigger when the dagreth ducked through the door, shifting his shoulders sideways so that he could get in.

"Sweet Jesus," one of them whispered, and when she did one of the truckers turned around. A couple of the others glanced over at their shoulders. Eyes narrowed as the room full of strangers sized up Kate and her touring freak show, and in spite of the smiles that the dagreth and the Kin were passing around, it began to look to Kate like she'd made a miscalculation.

Then the scrawny teenage boy in the booth said, "Oh, man, what *great* costumes! Dad, look, they had costumes like that at ConVolution—you remember I told you about them—" And the father looked over and said, "Yeah, Marty, I see the goddamned costumes, but people who would wear them at this time of the night to go to a goddamned Waffle House are goddamned morons, and besides, if you've seen one fucking costume, you've seen 'em all. Eat your food so we can get going."

And just like that, the truckers turned back to their coffee and the waitresses lost the wide-eyed looks and the customers pretended that the world around them held no surprises, that they could find a rational explanation for every inexplicable event in their lives if only they looked hard enough or far enough, or found someone who had already done the looking and who could tell them all the answers.

People were blind, and they were blind not because they couldn't see, but because they *wouldn't*. In this instance, they were blind because they chose to believe the words of a skinny, daydreaming kid instead of the senses that tried to alert them.

Sad and scary, but it sure worked in Kate's favor.

Marty, she thought, *if your dad wouldn't deck me, I'd kiss you.*

The Waffle House visit went well after that. The waitress who had their booth was charming and cheerful and fascinated by the costumes and the work that went into making the "appliances"— the noses and ears and teeth and hands and other things that couldn't be hidden by clothing. Kate remembered sitting through two rather long convention panels on making such appliances by people who did it for a living. She bullshitted about plaster casts and carving with dental tools to get the small detailing and about having to put in each hair and whisker by hand, and when she couldn't think of anything else to say without revealing her abysmal ignorance of the actual magic of costuming, she yawned with completely unfeigned exhaustion, and the waitress refilled her coffee and left her alone.

Both Val and Tik ordered twice as much as they intended to eat, and Kate asked for a doggie bag. Doggie bag in hand and a couple of friendly "bye's" later, they were out in the parking lot.

Kate's knees went weak when, as they were walking back to the van, a highway patrolman pulled into the lot. He'd probably been stopping for a cup of coffee, but when he saw the four of them, he cruised slowly past the glassed-in storefront, probably looking for trouble. He didn't see it, but that didn't stop him from pulling to a stop next to the four of them and rolling down his window.

Kate anticipated disaster. She smiled, though, and walked toward his car. "Hi."

"Good morning. You folks headed somewhere?"

"Orlando," Kate said. "Professional costumers' guild meeting and a pitch for some work for Disney."

He nodded and looked at the dagreth and the warrag. "They look pretty convincing."

"They'll look better after I've had time to go over all the appliance edges. Some of them are starting to work loose. It takes almost eight hours to apply the full makeup, though, so it's easier for us to do all the major things beforehand and then simply do touch-ups on site. At least it makes more sense when I can't get off from my regular job until early Saturday."

He evidently decided they were harmless, because he smiled a little and glance toward the Waffle House. "You have any trouble?"

"Not really. We get some funny looks, but people are pretty understanding."

"I'm glad to hear it." He nodded again. "Well, have a safe trip," he told her. He put his car into gear, pulled it into a parking space next to the van, got out, and walked toward the restaurant.

Kate ushered everyone into the van, then collapsed into the driver's seat. "This is going to make me nuts."

"He was another of your sheriffs, wasn't he?"

"Florida State Highway Patrol. We're not really in his jurisdiction here, I don't think, but if we'd been doing anything we weren't supposed to be, he would have nailed us."

"Nailed . . ."

Kate said, "Never mind." She pulled out of the parking lot and back onto Interstate 95, thinking that she had another six hours of driving to do, but she didn't have six more hours of darkness and she didn't have six more hours of stamina.

Tik started in on the restaurant. "In Glenraven, you would never find an inn as bare and bleak as that," he said. "No wine, no comforts, no tables, no song—"

Kate refused to put up with any more. "There are evidently all sorts of things you would never find in Glenraven, but that doesn't mean I want a list of them. In fact, I don't want to hear another word about your world or your forests or your people.

You're here now, and I can't help that. I'm sorry for you that you can't get back home. I'm doing everything I can to help you. But in the meantime, just shut up about it, okay?"

All four of them gave her the stricken "she's Ghengis Khan" look again.

Wearily, she tried to soften her sharp words. "This is my home," she said. "This is my world. I'm sorry that you don't like it; I'm doing my best to get you back to your own home. But I love my world. I love my country. I love the stupid little restaurants and the cheap, tacky stores and the towns and cities and the big empty spaces in between. I love the roads. I love the people. They're people who have been kind to all of you; who have mostly been kind to me. None of them attacked you because you looked different. None of them tried to hurt you. Some of the people in my country are stupid or mean or ignorant, but not most of them."

Val shook his head, and his expression was one of disgust. "You can say that after those three men hurt you—after they tried to kill you?"

"I can say it because it's true. Most people are good people."

Rhiana turned sideways in her seat and looked at Kate. "That's wishful thinking. Most people are never tried—they never decide whether to be good people or bad because nothing in their life ever pushes them toward disaster. People aren't good just because they haven't done anything bad, anything hurtful. Most people's lives never rise above mediocrity and passive acceptance because they never have to." Her face, in the pale glow of the dashboard lights, was ghostly green, eerie, lighted from beneath so that the shadows flowed upward and accented all the wrong parts of her features. "I know about people and their capacity for good and evil, because I've lived in a world where a woman of concentrated evil beat us down and sucked the life out of us for a thousand years. I've seen damned few heroes rise out of that despair to fight against the evil. I've seen many more people who willingly embraced the evil and made it their own, a part of their lives. They hurt others willingly; they destroyed lives and futures because they could, because the system supported their behavior and no one would stand up against them. But neither the heroes or the villains made up the majority. The most common people of all were the ones who pretended that they didn't see anything. They pretended nothing was wrong, that if they refused to see the evil being done all around them, it wouldn't touch them. By pretending they saw nothing, they made the evil possible."

Kate didn't want to think the majority of people would choose evil or blind ignorance if confronted with a situation that required heroism. She wanted to think that heroes were all around her, that they weren't really rare or special, that if something terrible happened, she would jump in to help and everyone around would be beside her getting involved, trying to make the bad thing better.

Kitty Genovese, her mind whispered. She recalled reading of Kitty Genovese, the young woman murdered slowly in front of a crowd of people who could have come to her rescue. Those people chose to refuse involvement or personal risk; instead, they listened to Kitty scream, waiting for her to die without doing anything. Anything.

Her mind grew louder in its anger, and more insistent. *Think of Germany in the era of Hitler. Of Italy and Mussolini. Think of the Holocaust. For every Anne Frank hidden in a secret room, how many people found no one who would try to save them? Remember the genocides of African tribes by other African tribes, and Cambodian regimes wiping out their own people and Serbian and Croatian killing off each other even though they were neighbors and had been all their lives. Don't forget land grabs and religious wars, Torquemada and Cortez and the American West, inquisitions and political liars and graft and vice and Tammany Hall and organized crime.*

What do you have to hold up against that? Mother Teresa? Miep Gies? If people are basically good, why are almost all the examples bad?

Kate didn't want to consider the direction her thoughts were taking. Her optimistic nature wanted to insist that her neighbors would do for her what she would do for any of them. She wanted to believe that the little town of Peters would rally around her and support her against its own sons, the men who had attacked her, in spite of the fact that they didn't approve of her religion and probably not of anyone who followed it. She wanted to believe that the businesses she'd dealt with would treat her as a human being instead of as an account, that her friends would never say anything to hurt her, that her enemies could be made to see that their persecution of her was wrong.

She used to fervently hang on to her belief in the Tooth Fairy, too, in spite of all evidence to the contrary.

Maybe it was time to grow up. Maybe it was time to admit that the people worth knowing and caring about were rare. That she wasn't going to meet them every day. Maybe it was time to quit expecting the best of everyone she met; time to stop thinking that if she treated people well, they would treat her well in return; time to quit assuming that if things went wrong, she would be the first person in line to try to make them right again, and that everyone around her would join her in making them right. She was alone. Her own family had turned their backs on her, and would never have anything to do with her again unless she said the things they wanted her to say and did the things they wanted her to do. Her own family. *Better face it*, she told herself. *You're in this alone, and the only person you'd better look out for is yourself.*

She glanced over at Rhiana and looked into the rearview mirror at Tik and Val and Errga. Maybe she *should* embrace that level of cynicism . . . but she wouldn't. She believed that individuals could make change happen. She believed that people were worth effort and care and that the meaning of life was never a matter of getting by without getting bruised, but a matter of living by convictions and holding on to honor and taking stands when stands mattered, regardless of the cost.

Life is more than covering your own ass, she thought. Too many people hadn't discovered that, but Kate had. Her life had meaning. Had purpose. If she lived by her convictions, she would, perhaps, gradually uncover the pattern of that purpose. Even if she didn't, she would certainly leave the world a slightly better place than she'd found it.

Twenty-one

"Outskirts of Fort Lauderdale," Kate said. "This is where we find a place to rest."

Errga closed his eyes and breathed in the machine scent of the place. He tried to imagine himself trapped in this world forever; no deep forests rich with the moist, musky scent of humus, the sharp green odors of growing plants, the hot blood-and-flesh scents of animals. No hot, flat plains waving with tall grasses, full of prey to be caught and crunched and savored. Here there were only the endless ribbons of highways rolling through the remains of what once must have been great stands of trees, and the houses and guild houses and vehicles that filled the air with their fuel scents. When Kate pulled off the highway into the city, he raised up and looked out the window, and discovered the place they had reached sprawled beyond all imagining. Houses squatted beside houses as far as his eyes could see—all of them low and set back on broad roads—and he sensed, from scent and sound, that they spread further in all directions than he could walk in an hour. Perhaps further even than he could run in that time. He flattened himself on the floorboards and closed his eyes tightly and growled. Eyes closed, he could feel the mass of humanity weighing in on all sides of him.

He shivered and huddled, hoping this would not be the place they came to rest.

"I'm going to have to get a map of Fort Lauderdale before I can find Callion's home," Kate said. "And I'm too tired to do anything like that right now. There should be a Holiday Inn around here. The sign said left. I think Holiday Inns allow pets."

Morning waited close by, the knife-sharp edge of dawn crawling just below the horizon. Errga's skin tingled and crawled, warning of its approach.

Kate pulled off the road into another of those enormous flat paved places and pulled the van under an awning. "Hold tight," she told them, picking up her bag. "I'll get us two rooms and be right back out." She ran into the glass-fronted building. A few doors down from the lobby, a man threw travel bags into the back of his car, while his mate and two young children stood on the walkway and watched him. One of the children looked into the van and began jumping up and down, pointing its finger and pulling on the hem of its mother's tunic.

Errga ducked beneath the window. Rhiana said, "Everyone smile and wave now."

"I hate this," Tik said. "It would be easier if we ate the children."

Val said, "What sort of place is this, where no one thinks anything of us if we wave at them? This is insane!"

Rhiana sighed. "The worst thing is knowing that if we don't succeed in capturing the Aregen, we'll never see home again."

"See home again! That will never happen anyway." Bitterness seeped through Val's voice, scathingly sharp. "Kate is a lovely woman, and I'm sure she would be a delight in bed, but you don't actually expect her to succeed against an Aregen and his Rift-slaves, do you?"

"I expect *us* to succeed," Rhiana said. "The five of us."

"Those same Rift-slaves kept Aidris Akalan alive and in power for more than a thousand years, against the combined efforts of the finest wizards of Glenraven—"

Rhiana said, "No they didn't. They and an enormous army of Aidris's loyalists protected her against a few scattered rebels and the occasional wizard who tired of her restrictions or fell out of her good graces. The majority of the people of Glenraven never fought against her. She preyed on the weakest and bribed the more powerful, so until the wizard Yemus brought Jayjay Bennington and Sophie Cortiss into Glenraven, her power never got a real test."

Errga wrinkled his nose and showed tooth at that—the Machnan adored their hero Yemus as much as some of the Kin wizards and Kin loyalists loathed him. Rhiana sounded like a mouthpiece for her kind right then; willing to forget that her war against Aidris Akalan was not the first; willing to ignore the masses of the Kin-hera who rose against Aidris and died in the Water-Pot Rebellion, and the brief, bloody Women's War. The Allies' War wasn't unique in Glenraven's history—except that it had succeeded.

His lips curled back further and the hair on the back of his neck rose. He didn't like being beholden to the humans and the Machnan; his people had fought in the war, but many of them had fought on the wrong side. The Machnan were long to remember mistakes like that.

The van door opened and Kate jumped in. "Rooms are ready. I wanted to get connecting rooms—I thought that might make things easier. But they didn't have any until just a second ago."

She pulled the van around to the side of the inn, then ushered everyone out. "Val, this is the key for your room. Errga, Tik, you'll be sharing with Val. Rhiana and I are going to split a room." She handed keys to Tik and Rhiana, then turned to Errga. "You'll have to go out with one of the others every time, so I didn't get a key for you." She slung her bag over her shoulder, opened the back of the van, and said, "Let's hurry."

People were popping out of rooms on all sides, throwing bags into vehicles—they stopped to stare.

Kate muttered, "Smile and wave . . . smile and wave . . ." and Errga, sick to death of hearing her repeat that, was tempted to comply, himself. He didn't, though. He couldn't imagine how the humans would react if they realized the creatures in their midst weren't humans in funny disguises . . . but he knew he didn't want to find out. So he trotted at Val's heel, and when Val unlocked the door to their room, slipped inside.

He smelled something fascinating in the brief instant that he crossed the parking lot from the van to the room, though. Something wondrous and ancient, primal, alluring, compelling—something he knew viscerally though he had never gotten a whiff of it before. He determined that he would find the source of that scent. He would discover it and claim it, whatever it was. Steal it if he had to, but have it at any cost.

Twenty-two

Kate woke up muddled. She felt like she'd been on a ship all night, a ship that constantly rolled forward and back and from side to side—a ship that fought its way through the turbid waters of a restless sea. She rubbed her eyes and tried to clear her head. The room was too dark, and she could see a single slit of brilliant white light coming from entirely the wrong direction through utterly opaque curtains. Ah, she thought, as realization dawned. *Hotel.*

All her life she had hated waking in unfamiliar places. Always those times brought back the memory of waking in her grandmother's house when she was ten, with her grandmother sitting in the kitchen waiting for the phone to ring. Lying in that darkened Florida hotel room, Kate could still smell her grandmother's coffee percolating on the stove; hear the clock down the hall; see the light through the half-opened door, hear the phone ring, and hear her grandmother pick it up before the first ring had even died away; the soft bubbling of the coffee and the creaks of the old house and her grandmother's voice, roughened with fear, asking "How is he?" and the silence that seemed to stretch forever, forever; then the sound of her grandmother crying. Soft sobs, and between the sobs, "I'll get her up and dressed. No. No. I won't tell her. I'll wait until you're here."

Her grandmother didn't need to tell her, though. Kate knew Jackie was dead. Jack, her brother, twenty-one months older than she was, funny and handsome and smart and athletic, who had gone swimming with some of his friends and who had told her she couldn't come because she was a girl. He and his friends had raced away on their bicycles, laughing, while she stood in the yard, furious at not being included when she could do anything he could do as well as he could do it . . . and most things . . . better.

And he had never come back.

All her life, she'd thought, *If I had been there, I could have saved him. If I had been with him, he would still be alive.* Lying in the Florida hotel room with people who didn't even belong in her world, she still thought, *If I had been there I could have saved him. I would have.*

In some ways she would never grow up, never leave behind the ten-year-old sister who thought she should have been the one who died. She still felt the absence of her brother as an aching, hollow pain that nothing and no one could ever take away.

But at that moment, in that place, she put her pain away, as she eventually had to put it away every time it came to her. She got up, showered and dried her hair, and put on enough makeup to cover the last remnants of the bruises on her face. In spite of a yellow-green bruise across her cheek, she almost looked like herself again.

She turned on CNN while Rhiana headed into the bathroom for her shower. Kate preferred CNN to introspection when she caught herself heading down her well-worn path to guilt. How much easier to watch the unending squabbles between Syria and Libya and Israel; to listen to the latest president lying about the budget, drug wars, foreign policy, and the state of the union in order to get reelected; to see demonstrations of inhumanity and irresponsibility and utter stupidity that had no impact on her, that would never touch her existence, that meant, in the narrow circle of her single short existence, nothing. How much easier than sitting in the darkness and listening to the ghost of her grandmother sobbing over the ghost of Jack.

However, Kate realized nothing the smiling anchors said had passed between the impermeable wall of her memories to touch her awareness, and she reached for the remote to turn off the television. As she did, she heard a thud in the bathroom. She clicked off the TV set and waited.

Silence.

More silence.

And then a faint, muffled groan.

She ran to the door and knocked. "Rhiana?"

No answer. She hadn't locked the door; Kate shoved it open and found Rhiana sprawled across the floor, halfway dressed, rolled into a little ball on the tile with her hands covering her face. She bled from her forehead. She made no noise.

Kate crouched beside her and said, "Rhiana? Rhiana? Can you hear me?"

"Be quiet," Rhiana whispered. "For the sake of the gods, Kate, I'm fine."

"What happened?" Not sure why she was doing it, Kate kept her voice low.

Rhiana sat up. "I slipped on some water on the floor." She pressed her fingers to her lips and shook her head a little—her motions obviously meant *This isn't what happened*, but from whom did she think she was hiding the truth? Sound didn't carry from room to room—

Someone knocked on the connecting doors.

Rhiana scowled and got up; Kate thought she looked pale, and while the place on her forehead wasn't bleeding heavily, it sent a steady trickle down the side of her face.

"I'll get it," Kate said, and opened her half of the connecting doors.

Val stood there, his expression concerned. "I heard Rhiana cry out," he said. "I was sleeping, but the noise woke me."

Kate had barely been able to hear Rhiana while sitting a few feet away. She wondered if his hearing could be that much more acute. She said, "She slipped on a wet patch in the bathroom, but she's fine."

"You're sure?" He looked concerned, even compassionate. Kate wanted to reassure him, but Rhiana's strange behavior made her suspicious of him. Suspicion was stupid—from the other room he couldn't have done anything to hurt Rhiana, but . . .

"I'm fine," Rhiana told him. She came out of the bathroom with her hair wrapped in a towel. The towel, certainly not accidentally, covered the little cut. "I fell because I was careless. No damage done."

He nodded. "If you're sure—"

"I'm sure." She smiled that same cold, polite smile she always used with him, the smile that said, *I'll be polite because I am that sort of person, but keep your distance.* "Thank you for your concern. Are Tik and Errga awake, also?"

"None of us were awake. The sound of your fall woke me—"

"Yes," she said. "I can imagine how it could have done that. Well . . . thank you. I'll see you this evening."

She made a move toward the door as if to close it, but Val stopped her. "Is anything the matter?"

"Nothing except that I'm extremely hungry. When I'm hungry, I become unpleasant." The tight-lipped smile again. "As I'm sure you've noticed. But Kate and I are going out to get ourselves something to eat. We'll be back shortly."

This was the first Kate had heard about going to get something to eat, but she played along. "We won't be long at all," she said. "If you want, I can bring you back something."

Val thought about it. "Sausages," he said. "And maybe one of those giant egg things you made with all the meat and things in it."

"An omelet? That might not travel too well."

"Sausages and something else, then."

The dagreth wandered to the door, and Rhiana's smile for him was, as always, more genuine. "Hello, Tik."

"Lady," he said with a nod of his massive head. "The sound of people discussing food woke me. Did I hear rightly, or was I just having a particularly appropriate dream?"

"We're going to get breakfast," Kate said. "We'll have to get it from one of the all-day-breakfast places, which are more expensive than someplace like McDonalds."

"I'd like more of those cinnamon biscuits," the dagreth said. "With lots of the gooey white icing."

"Those were Hardee's biscuits. I don't think we'll be able to find a Hardee's in South Florida," Kate said, feeling that she was going to end up vetoing everyone's breakfast fantasy wish list. "I have an idea. Rhiana and I will go out and get something we think you'll like." She crouched a little and leaned to one side to peek through the open door. She could see Errga sitting behind and to one side of Tik, his body stiff with irritation. "Is that all right with you, Errga?"

"I would have said so, if Tik the Rump hadn't wedged himself in front of me," he growled.

Rhiana said, "Tik the Rump was hungrier than you, warrag."

"Tik the Rump will be my breakfast, and we'll see who's hungrier," the warrag grumbled.

Kate finally got the door between the rooms closed.

Again Rhiana put her finger to her lips. "I have to braid my hair. It will only take a moment. Then we can get everyone something to eat."

Kate got her keys and her purse and the Fodor's guidebook, then waited.

When they left, she glanced curiously at Rhiana, but the other woman shook her head once and almost jogged to the passenger side of the van.

Only when they had pulled out of the parking lot and driven down the busy street through three intersections did Rhiana begin to talk.

"One of them is a traitor," she said.

Kate took a right turn at random, then a left, then a right. In the distance, she saw an International House of Pancakes and headed for that. "A traitor. What does that have to do with you slipping on a wet spot in the bathroom?"

"I didn't slip, of course. I'm certainly neither so clumsy nor so careless. One of them can use magic, though, because I felt it this morning, aimed at me. I think I discovered what was going on only because I was awake when usually I am asleep; otherwise, this spell-renewal wouldn't have had any effect on me."

"Spell-renewal?" Kate wondered if Rhiana's fall had perhaps made her paranoid. Maybe she was delusional. Maybe she had a slight concussion. Rhiana had been adamant about the fact that none of the other three—not the Kin nor the dagreth nor the warrag—had any sort of magical ability at all. She had insisted that she could tell this, that she and Kate were going to be the only hope for the four stranded travelers because the other three could contribute nothing.

Now she insisted that one of them had some facility with magic, and further, that one of them was using it against her.

Kate studied the Glenravener out of the corner of her eye, then zipped between two New Jersey snowbirds in their Cadillac and a Canadian family in a Mercedes Benz and pulled out of traffic into the IHOP parking lot. She got a space at the far corner of the lot and turned off the ignition. "We can get breakfast here, or we can sit in the van and you can tell me what you're talking about."

"You think I'm making this up."

"Not necessarily. I think it's a big turnaround from your absolute certainty that none of your three friends could use magic. And I haven't seen behavior in any one of them that would indicate to me that he's a traitor."

Rhiana didn't look distressed by Kate's doubt. "Nor have I. But as I was brushing my hair, a hard wave of magic hit me; it surrounded me and for an instant I couldn't breathe, I couldn't move, I couldn't think—I felt like a horse was standing on my chest. I fell then, but I couldn't make a sound. Only when the magic passed was I able to make any noise."

"Sounds like you had a heart attack to me," Kate said.

"Heart attack . . ." Rhiana looked thoughtful. "I understand what you mean, but this is not like that. I could *see* the magic."

"But I thought you said Glenraveners wouldn't be able to use the magic of this world unassisted . . . that my source was too distant or too odd or something."

Rhiana sighed. "I thought that was true. I really did." She turned sideways in her seat and rested her hands on her knees and leaned forward, intent on what she had to say. "But this is *why* I haven't been able to use the sources of magic that I could see. Whoever has done this has blocked me from using them."

Kate opened her door and pointed toward the restaurant. "I don't know about you, but I'm starving."

Rhiana nodded and got out of the van.

As they walked across the parking lot, Kate said, "What does it matter, Rhiana? We found a way to work around the block. I feed magic to you, you use it, and we accomplish what we need to accomplish."

"It matters because for someone to hide magic from me so completely that I can see no trace of it, he has to be a major wizard. He would have to be almost on a level with the master wizards of Glenraven. They're frightening. I studied with one for a while, before my duties to Ruddy Smeachwykke began to take too much of my time. He could do terrifying things."

"Terrifying?"

"He could dissolve stone with the snap of his fingers. He could cause saplings to grow to the size of centuries-old behemoths in the span of a day. He could create illusions so real you not only heard them breathe, but felt their breath against your skin."

"That's terrifying."

"Yes. And those were the things he did to amuse me. What he could have done when he was angry I don't care to think about."

Kate opened the door and let Rhiana go in ahead of her.

"Two?" the woman by the *Please Wait to be Seated* sign asked.

"Two."

"Smoking or non?"

Kate said, "Non," and they followed her back to a tiny table next to two others just like it.

"Enjoy your meal," the hostess said, and gave them menus, then headed back to her post.

Kate said, "The pigs in blankets are excellent. So are the harvest pancakes." She didn't open her own menu. She sat thinking about wizards out of fairy-tale worlds who could use magic for awesome and evil purposes. It would have made for an amusing dinnertime daydream had it not threatened to affect her personally.

The waitress came to the table. A slender black woman with one gold tooth and a smile that would have been just as bright without it, she said, "I'm Jeanette. I'll be your server today. Would you like some coffee?"

"Please," Kate said, "and a glass of orange juice."

Rhiana shook her head vigorously. "Water, please. With ice in it. Do they have wine or beer?" she asked Kate.

Jeanette looked startled by the question. "No," Kate said to Rhiana, and to Jeanette, with an apologetic smile, "She's from Europe."

"Oh." Jeanette nodded as if that explained everything, and nodded off.

"Europe?"

"Europeans have a reputation in the United States for drinking wine or beer with all their meals. It's a gross generalization, but telling our waitress that's where you come from will keep her from wondering about you."

"I see. So in general, drinking wine or beer with breakfast food is frowned upon?" Rhiana studied the pictures on her menu.

"In general," Kate said. "I imagine Ben Franklin started the prejudice against it. Anyway, supposing one of our companions is a—"

Jeanette returned with coffee and juice and water. "You ladies ready to order yet?"

"Pigs in blankets and some hash browns," Kate said.

Rhiana gave Kate a puzzled look, then nodded, folded up her menu, and handed it to the waitress. "The same for me."

"I'll get that right out to you. Isn't this just a gorgeous day?" Jeanette asked.

Both women agreed that it was.

"She's very friendly," Rhiana said when she was gone.

"We'll leave her a nice tip. Now." Kate leaned forward and lowered her voice. She didn't suppose any of the people in the surrounding booths gave a damn about her and what she was saying, but she didn't want any of them staring at her, either. "Supposing one of our companions is a wizard, what can we do about it? The last week or so has been difficult enough for me. I'd rather not wrap up your visit by having my flesh melted off my bones or something like that."

"That would be unfortunate," Rhiana agreed. Kate saw the corners of her mouth twitch into a brief smile.

"Yes. If this . . ." she whispered " . . . wizard . . . is still putting a spell on you, even after he knows we can work together, then he must have planned a way to eliminate us as a threat."

"Yes. I imagine he intends to kill or disable one or the other of us."

"Why doesn't he just go back to Glenraven?"

"Perhaps he can't. Perhaps he wants to meet Callion first. Perhaps . . ." Rhiana shrugged. "I don't know. I don't want to think about it any more right now. I just want to eat and pretend that everything is fine and that my life makes sense."

Kate sympathized with that. She pulled the Fodor's out of her bag and opened it up. "I want to see if it can tell us anything about the traitor," she said.

She looked at the title page. The letters seemed a little fuzzy—they looked almost as they might have if they'd been printed on porous paper that had allowed the ink to wick. Kate squinted at the page, wondered if perhaps humidity could affect the print, and flipped to the next page, and then to subsequent pages. The print continued to have that fuzzy-edged look, and worse, for a moment it would begin to run in toward the center of the page, spiraling slightly as it did so, as if the page had become a sink and the print was water flowing down its drain.

"Something is wrong," she said softly.

Rhiana held out her hand, and Kate passed the book to her.

Rhiana glanced at it, closed her eyes, then opened them again.

She handed the book back, frowning. "Worse than wrong. It's try-ing to tell us something, but it can't."

"Why not?"

"It's been spelled, too. The spell is different than the one on me, both more complicated and subtler. This spell is *proof* that the person who spelled the book—and me—is a brilliant wizard. Worse, I think, is this. It tells us that whoever the traitor is, he knows we know he exists, and he's determined to do what he can to hide his identity."

"The book knows who the traitor is, doesn't it?"

Rhiana shrugged. "Probably, but we can't be certain, and even if we were certain, knowing wouldn't help us. The book is mute—perhaps for just a while, or perhaps for good. It can't tell us any-thing."

"It was going to tell us how to get you back to Glenraven." Kate stared down at the guidebook, at the blurring, streaking, spiraling print that struggled to tell Kate something she needed to know, but now could not.

Twenty-three

Rhiana worried about the book. And she worried that her limited magical abilities would keep her from ever seeing her world again, and that the traitorous Glenravener would conspire to kill her if she discovered who he was. But she also worried about the Kin, because she had been discovering gradually and in little ways that she liked Val much too much.

She kept herself distant from him. She was intentionally rude. She didn't want him to think she was one of the silly Machnan girls he had doubtless deflowered in the moss-green dew-gemmed glades of the forest. She didn't want him to think about her at all, in truth, because the love of a Kin and a Machnan could never amount to anything but pain and despair.

And this morning he'd been first to the door, first to claim her fall had wakened him from his sleep, first to feign concern, when probably he had cast the spell that had sent her sprawling. He no more had wizard's eyes than Tik or Errga, but that meant nothing. When she looked at herself in the mirror, she didn't see a flinty

149

glare or amoral ferocity, yet she was in a minor way a wizard. Harch, the wizard who'd trained her, looked as merry as the first birds of spring and as open as sunshine. The wizard Yemus looked like a traveling poet . . . or would if he laced his shirt with ribbons and wore his hair longer. His languorous dark eyes and sensuous lips sent the women of the various village courts into paroxysms of lust; had he been *anything* but a wizard, bastard babes with his dark eyes and knowing smile would have been popping from the meadows like dandelions. Naturally, as he was what he was, he would have found a mate easier had he been a sot.

So that the Kin didn't have wizardly eyes or wizardly ways meant nought. He could be the secret wizard as well as either warrag or dagreth.

She wouldn't believe it of him unless she were forced to.

Kate finished her pigs in blankets and sat waiting for Rhiana. "I'll hurry."

"Don't." Kate smiled. "We have things to do, but none that won't wait for breakfast."

Rhiana nodded, tried to smile, cut another bite of the griddle-cake-covered sausage, picked it up, put it down, and sighed. She looked at tall, fair-haired Kate, whose loveliness became more apparent with every day, as the bruises vanished and the cuts healed. Kate could have been Kinnish, save for her teeth and ears; if the origins of humans were true, then Kate looked to have Kinnish bloodlines. She wasn't short and dark and Machnan-scrawny. And in Glenraven, with the Watchmistress human and her mate and *eyra* Kin, no one would think to torment Kate or Val if they became *eyran*.

"What do you think of Val?" she blurted.

Kate looked startled. "Why? You think he's your traitor?"

"No. Of course not. Well, he could be, I suppose. I wasn't . . . I didn't . . ." She felt her cheeks flush hot. "I simply wanted your opinion."

Kate leaned her elbows on the table and rested her chin in her cupped hands. "I haven't thought of him much at all, if you want the truth. He stayed in my house, he ate my food, he drank my beer, he helped me catch those lunatics who were after me. As did the rest of you. I appreciate what he did, and I intend to get him back home." She frowned and looked away; her eyes moved down and rightward. "What do I *think* of him?" She looked up at Rhiana and smiled. "He annoys the hell out of me on long trips."

"He seems to be . . . attracted to you."

"No. Sorry. I haven't felt any sparks." Kate leaned closer and lowered her voice. "So if you were wondering if the coast was clear, it is. I wish you luck."

Mortified, Rhiana said, "Oh, no! Not me. Machnan and Kin cannot mate!"

"I thought you and Val said that it's all one big, happy family anyway. That a warrag and a dagreth could breed and have fertile offspring."

"They *could*," Rhiana said. "Physically. But . . . gods' blessings!" She stared at Kate, wonderingly. "But how could you understand? I'm being absurd. In your world, only humans exist. So what could you know of mating restrictions or taboos? You could choose any other human being on your planet as your bondmate and no one would utter a word of reproof."

"Ah . . ." Kate started slowly shaking her head, and Rhiana saw chagrin in the small smile. "Ah. *Now* I understand."

"You do?"

"The various cultures of my world have their taboos, too. Some cultures demand that blacks don't marry whites, that Orientals don't marry any but other Orientals; some religions don't marry outside their faith; men don't marry men nor women marry women—"

Rhiana's mind reeled. She interrupted. "Skin color? Religion? What sort of nonsense is that? And as for the *rosalle*, if they cannot love each other, who are they permitted to love?"

"*Rosalle?*"

"The men who love men. The women who love women."

"Our term is *homosexual*. I wonder why it didn't translate."

Rhiana heard the word as *tondara*, which meant something entirely different than *rosalle*. She said, "A *tondara* is someone with a problem. Someone not normal. Someone with a form of sickness. At least that is what I hear when you say the word. But *rosalle* is just men who love men, and women who love women, without the taint of sickness. What is your word for that?"

Kate smiled sadly. "We don't have a word for that. Every word we have carries some stigma. And as for who the . . . *rosalle* . . . are supposed to love, I suppose if the predominant culture had its way, they would love no one, and would be unloved. Or they'd pretend to be straight, marry someone of the opposite sex, and make themselves and their partners miserable."

"That's insane. But your cultures would see nothing wrong with human and Kin, or human and dagreth, or Kin and Machnan."

Kate laughed abruptly. "No. No. That would be an abomination, too."

Rhiana nodded. "I suppose I can be glad to know that pig-headed stupidity and ignorance are not confined to my world alone."

"No. They aren't. One of my favorite cartoonists, Scott Adams, says that everyone is an idiot some of the time. I think he's right."

"I think he is, too. The gods all know I've been an idiot more than once." Rhiana resolved to finish her breakfast. She felt better, though she didn't know why. She'd resolved nothing. She had no answers. She could not deny, though, that her mood was lighter.

But she wondered one thing. "When you say *cartoonist*, I hear two words, 'oracle' and 'jester.' But these words seem to have nothing in common. So what is a *cartoonist*?"

Kate began to laugh.

Twenty-four

The Devourers spun in restless spirals; ebbed and flowed from one side of the room to the other like waves on the sea; flattened themselves into a single brilliant circle of light on the floor then exploded outward in uncountable streaking shards. They flashed red and green and yellow and blue and gold and white, dimmed to a lusterless ashy gray, rebounded to greater brilliance, deeper colors. In their movements lay pattern and art, dexterity, deep and untouchable emotion, and some purpose, but not obvious cause.

Callion watched them anxiously. If he'd had a barometer for their mood he would have said it was falling fast; he felt in them a storm of unspeakable dimensions and unfathomable passion. They refused to speak, refused to answer any questions, refused to carry out any of the little tasks he had for them—they would not slip through the phone wires to steal from a Swiss bank account the frozen assets of a Miami drug dealer, though Callion had gone to enormous difficulty to locate the proper account and divine the way in; they would not slip next door to devour the loud, obnoxious adolescent son who lived there before the rest of the family returned home; they would not cooperate with him in any fashion, even though they had done similar tricks for him on previous occasions. He'd never seen them act as they were acting. He thought, after three years of working with them, that he understood them—and now that he discovered he didn't, he felt twinges of fear.

They formed two amorphous light blobs and shot toward each other from opposite ends of the room; when they met in the middle they collided silently but with a perfect pantomime of violence. Fragments made up of dozens of the tiny lights showered like shrapnel around the room, shattering further when they encountered resistance.

"Stop," Callion said. He put magic behind the command, and the appearance of calm confidence.

They dropped to a foot above the floor and began racing in circles, forming a whirlpool that sucked the center lights down into its depths and spat them out and across the room in all directions. When they rose, the swirling whirlpool seemed to drag them in again.

The whirlpool spun faster. Callion began to feel dizzy watching it. He again commanded them to stop, but again they didn't listen.

He tried to feel what they were feeling; he tried to find by feel some disturbance in the Rift, some tearing in the small, permanent gate he'd dragged through with him from Glenraven— anything that might have agitated them or frightened them or seduced them—but their world kept its secrets from him, as it always had, and they remained a mystery.

He watched them a while longer, wondering what he ought to do. They weren't threatening him. In fact, he didn't think anything they could do would directly threaten him. They weren't causing problems elsewhere. They weren't making demands.

He decided while he could walk away without losing too much face, he would be well to take the opportunity. He turned, stepped out of the room, and quietly closed the door behind himself.

Twenty-five

After she took breakfast back to the locally unpresentable part of the Glenraven contingent, Kate took Rhiana to the Barnes and Noble superstore in Plantation to buy a couple of maps. While she found them, Rhiana, wandered around the inside of the store, stunned, picking up books, staring at them wistfully, and putting them back.

She came up to Kate just as Kate decided on the two maps she wanted and said, "The man who owns these books must be richer than the gods and mad as a stag in mash. He has more books than exist in all of Glenraven, and four and five, sometimes ten, sometimes twenty copies of each of them."

"It's a book *store*," Kate said. "Not a library. They keep multiple copies of the same book on the shelves to sell."

"We could buy them?"

"They rather hope we will."

"I own two books," Rhiana said. "Well, one is a common book—I keep my accounts in that, and things I've done, and sometimes sketches of the things that I see. The other, though, is a real book. "It's the story of Gerowyn of Tenads and how he fought monsters and Kintari and the vast Kinnish hordes to win Tenads for the Machnan. It's a very exciting story." She picked up one of the books on the shelf nearest her, opened it carefully, and said, "The scribe who did it made it much prettier than this book, too. The cover is fine leather and the pages are covered with gold leaf and red and blue and yellow and green and brown inks, and all of the borders are filled. Not like this book. This is so plain."

Kate smiled. "The difference is this book and a hundred thousand like it rolled off of presses in just a couple of days. And in the length of time it took your bookbinders and scribes to turn out the few books they make every year, book publishers in America turn out millions of copies of thousands upon thousands of books." She pointed to the inside cover and said, "They're cheap, too. How many hours would a commoner have to work to earn enough money to buy a book?"

Rhiana looked puzzled. "Commoners don't buy books. How could they afford the jewels on the covers? How could they take care of something so valuable in their little houses? And you asked how many hours they would have to work . . ." She frowned. "I don't think the field workers could make enough money in their lives to buy one. Some of the merchants do well. I know of one in Ruddy Smeachwykke who employs his own scribe to copy texts he borrows from friends, and once a year hires a binder to bind his newest book. He has six or seven now—but he is terrifically rich, and wasteful."

"The people in this country who are paid the very least make enough money in an hour or two to buy a paperback book. They can buy hardback books with four or five hours of work. And many of them do."

"You're lying."

Kate laughed. "I'm not lying."

They bought the maps. Left. Drove around Fort Lauderdale trying to locate the house, which was on Silver Palm Boulevard. Rhiana sat with her nose pressed to the glass, staring at the foreign vegetation: palm trees and palmettos and enormous ficuses and strangler figs and bougainvillea. Occasionally she'd exclaim over some spectacular specimen, but for the most part she sat quiet and wide-eyed, leaving Kate to her own thoughts.

Kate got lost in them. The pulse of Fort Lauderdale captivated her. She hadn't had a chance to notice it before; she'd been in the hotel room and worried about her odd companions, and she hadn't had the chance to think. But watching the road, moving in and out of traffic, she began to drift. She began to feel a hunger that she hadn't felt in years. She tried to examine it, but it was elusive. She breathed the air, admired the clear brilliant blue skies, thought about the huge bookstore, about the libraries she'd passed, about the people she saw. And she thought about Peters, which couldn't even support a single tiny bookstore because hardly anyone in the town read. The Barnes and Noble superstore had been *busy*; people squeezing past each other in the aisles, crouching to browse, discussing books with each other, looking over the shoulders of strangers to say, "I read that. It was terrific." She compared it to the one real bookstore Peters had boasted, for a while. Amos W. Baldwell, Bookseller, had been an excellent store for the six months it had lasted. Tons of books and a knowledgeable bookseller who'd been enthusiastic about his stock. The only thing the place had lacked had been a base of readers to support it. Kate didn't know if it was fair to use a bookstore as a metaphor for a town, but when she thought of Peters, she thought of the bleach-blonde Dancercized country-club wives standing in the children's section trying to pick out books for their children and smugly confiding to each other that they hadn't had time to read a book in years.

Institutionalized ignorance. Their entire attitude rankled—"We know nothing and we're proud of it." The Peters Chamber of Commerce put out town brochures that said, Peters: The Best Things Are the Things That Stay the Same. The town worshipped its high school football team and its band, admired the fact that the same families had owned the majority of the town since before the Civil War, congratulated itself on its southern hospitality while despising anyone whose grandparents and parents hadn't been born there.

And Amos W. Baldwell, Bookseller, bought by an enterprising young couple when the original owner gave up and left town, was belly up within a few months.

Kate had felt the walls closing in, then. She could see no horizon in Peters. The town had no windows to the outside world, no doors. It neither welcomed nor inquired. But because it had been Craig's town, and because she'd wanted to keep something of him, no matter how distant from the reality of who he'd been, she'd stayed. In that bloodless, dusty, drybone atmosphere, she had accommodated herself to the verities of small-town life; she'd gone to library meetings and looked into the Jaycees; she'd attended events and pretended contentment.

Driving west on Sunrise Boulevard through one of the smaller cities that made up the outer ranges of Fort Lauderdale, she felt herself dropped into the center of a world with a pulse, and its pulse made her own heart beat faster. This place where a new idea was not met with raised crosses and gasps of "spawn of Satan"; where people by-God bought books and read them and discussed them in the aisles of bookstores that were redolent of the rich scents of coffee and paper; where, standing quietly, the rustle of turning pages sounded like wind through the leaves of a forest of trees—this place lived. Breathed.

Kate breathed with it.

Suddenly she realized the road to her left had been Southwest 136 Avenue, where she'd needed to turn. She drove up to the Sawgrass Expressway, realized she would have to pay a toll if she used it to turn around, pulled off into the median and looped into the eastbound lane. Not the most legal of turns, but she was running short of quarters. She rechecked the map, turned right on 136, then left into a beautiful walled neighborhood. She needed a few minutes to locate Silver Palm Boulevard, and a few more to drive the ellipse it comprised, checking house numbers.

But as she swung left and headed west, she found Callion. His house, a sprawling two-story neo-Spanish hacienda, sat not too far back from the road but nearly hidden by the luxuriant, beautifully landscaped jungle growth. Birds of paradise graced bougainvillea-covered white stucco walls, sago palms and palmettos formed islands between a smooth curve of well-tended lawn, and the palms that graced the wrought-iron gate at the front entry gave way to flanking ficuses the size of ancient oaks. The brown-red of hand-baked roof tiles accentuated the predominantly green-and-white motif.

Kate hadn't expected Callion to live in a house like that. She wondered if she had the wrong place.

Rhiana's reaction set her straight. She said, "Kate, get out of here fast. There's something in there—something that's almost ready to explode . . ." The Glenravener went pale and shut her eyes.

Kate didn't stop to ask questions. She accelerated, turned right at her first opportunity, and right again on Sunrise Boulevard.

As she waited to pull out behind a line of traffic, she saw a huge mall complex across the boulevard. The signs that led to it were shaped like alligators. Her annoyance at those tacky signs, juxtaposed against her fear that whatever was going to explode would do so before she could get out of the neighborhood, struck her as at least bizarre and possibly insane.

When they were well away from Callion's area, Kate asked Rhiana, "What did you feel?"

Rhiana sat on the seat with her head hanging down, with her hands clenched in her lap and her eyes squeezed tightly shut. She looked like a child trying to convince herself that the monster wasn't under the bed while at the same time believing that it was. She whispered, "I don't know. Magic . . . angry and hungry . . . a predator pacing in a circle . . . trying to find an opening in the cage it's in . . . trying to break through the bars to the prey that it feels moving all around it, just out of its reach. It has a secret . . . it has a need that drives it to madness . . . but I don't know what it is."

"Callion?"

"No."

"The Watchers?"

"Maybe."

"Can we do something to stop it?"

"Not yet. It feels . . ." She exhaled sharply, frustration evident in every line of her body as her eyes came open and she turned to Kate. "We can't reach it inside of its cage. The trickles of magic I felt, the movement . . . they were only a part. Like light through a crack in a roof. A single pinhole, but the light that came through was so bright it illuminated the room. Terrible. Evil. Everything I could throw at this thing, it would devour. Some magic will keep it in its place, but not the magic I know." She fell silent; looked down at her hands, suddenly still as a wax figure, still as a corpse, as death.

Kate tried to imagine that caged predator. She couldn't get a feel for the sort of thing it was. None of the Glenraveners knew; none of them had been present when Callion took them from the woman who had been Watchmistress of Glenraven before this new woman, Jayjay Bennington. Kate thought of softball, of the Peters Library Lions. Kicked herself back on track.

This monster in Callion's house was a danger that wasn't going to respond to the spells she and Rhiana had practiced. It wasn't going to shrivel into a little ball and die. It paced. It hungered. It had secrets.

She wondered what secrets monsters might keep.

Twenty-six

too close
pressure
hunger and bursting, pain, time closing time almost on them
on us time to move to feed to grow
press here, press there, move faster
the walls the walls the walls the master's walls too tight
too hard a shell that doesn't give doesn't stretch doesn't
fit
must break
must
      break
move faster
thin walls, movement wears them thinner, time growing near,
need
need
      need
            need

rivers of blood flesh warm blood hot skin and bone
and hair and fear and pain running howling screaming
weeping begging meat with bodies legs that run arms that
flail bones that crack and twist and crunch full of moist-
ness full of meat

the gifts the prey outside everywhere wander unhunted
unknowing weak and slow and stupid shell-less, just outside
the cage

contract

feel the pain pulse hotter, feel the power build

expand

the hunger comes the pain hot white pain maddening pain
torture the master tortures it tortures the cage tortures and
they we I

contract

expand

contract

and the walls thin

blood outside the cage blood so thick so hot we will drink
the night to whiteness and the blood will run surge pour
streams rivers oceans

something moves outside the walls

something dangerous

something hurtful cold hot whitelight wrapped in blood and
flesh and bone but bad to eat bad dangerous searching

feeling

them us me

and then it moves away

knew it found them us me but not yet it will come for us
it is hunting us but not yet not now

time they we I have time to move to stretch to fill

    spin

          faster

               and the walls

thin

expand

    contract

        expand

and now the cage bulges

    bulges

and they we I

contract
        contract
            contract
let the pain the hunger the madness build and build and build
and wait, pull in tighter, harder, closer, small be small and angry
hotwhite angrymad bloodhungry small
expand

free

hunt

Twenty-seven

Val and Tik and Errga sat staring at the television when Kate and Rhiana came in, their expressions glassy and stunned.

"This is happening right now," Val said. He didn't look at them; his face never turned from the bright, flickering picture.

Kate heard screaming over the voice of an on-the-spot reporter, who was saying something about people running out carrying bodies.

Tik, his back shoved against the wall, his legs splayed, said, "This is worse than anything I've ever seen."

"What's happened? An airplane crash? A car accident? Did someone try to shoot the president?" Kate moved to the space between the double beds where she could see the screen better and tried to make sense of the images she saw.

By the time she got a look, the camera was leaving the outdoor screaming and hysteria behind. She could hear the sound of a siren in the background, or maybe a lot of sirens, but the reporter and his cameraman were moving past the huddled knots of weeping people who clung to each other and cried out to God in a dozen languages.

The reporter was no longer doing a standup. He was doing a walk-and-talk, a sort of stunned running monologue of what he found. He went through the doors and the picture on the television set did an excellent job of rendering the red of blood and gray-white blur of a young woman's body sprawled just inside, lost in the boneless grace of death. "There aren't any more people leaving the mall; I'm going to see if . . . I can find out what happened in here . . . what . . . I'm going to see if there are any survivors still trapped inside."

He'd come in through a side door. Kate got a quick glimpse of a Target sign and the red-and-white bull's-eye logo—then the camera panned left, down a side aisle. Three black boys in bright clothing lay unmoving. Silent. The store was silent. If there were survivors inside, Kate would have expected to hear some sounds. The cliché "silent as a tomb" took on fresh meaning.

"Again," a voice-over said, "we're looking live at the inside of the Sawgrass Mills Outlet Mall in West Broward County, where just moments ago people poured out of the building's many exits, screaming 'the lights, the lights.' Back to you, John."

John, the reporter, was breathing hard, stopping from time to time to stare at a particularly gruesome death tableau. "Thanks, Bill. I can't see any sign of an explosion. Nothing in the store seems to . . . to be out of place . . . except the . . . ah . . . the bodies. Not too many bodies, really, considering that at this time of the day this place is usually wall to wall."

The camera panned to the right. A brown-skinned woman in Bermuda shorts and sandals leaned against some shelves, her eyes wide and unblinking, her mouth open. Blood ran from her eyes, from her nose, from her mouth, from her ears. Her hands lay palm-upward at her sides, fingers curling gracefully, her last gesture one of helplessness, of incomprehension, of "why me?"

"Hello," the reporter shouted. "Can anyone hear me?"

Only silence greeted his response.

"I hear police cars beginning to arrive. I'll try and cover them, too, but . . . this is unbelievable, this is just unbelievable . . . I can't hear anyone in here."

The reporter was looking at the camera as he reached the main aisle. For once, Kate saw a man reporting news who didn't seem to be getting a vicarious thrill out of the whole experience. He looked scared. He started to turn, to point out the direction he was going to explore, when halfway through his turn, he froze.

"Ohmigod. Ohmigod. Ohmigod." His voice dropped to a whisper. "Those poor people."

The camera panned right from the reporter, showing a thickening trail of corpses. Where the ones Kate had seen to that point looked like they had died where they'd fallen, this new angle revealed a level of violence an order of magnitude above what she'd seen before. Bodies no longer sprawled facedown in the aisles. Now they draped over aisles and piled into drifts and dunes against the shelving and formed a hill against the back wall. There had to be hundreds of people piled in that mound. Hundreds. The camera hung on that image far longer than Kate could bear; she heard the reporter retching off-camera but not out of mike range.

She couldn't believe the local news people were running the film live.

John came back on camera. He looked only slightly more alive than the corpses. "Things might be better in toward the center of the mall," he said. "I might have come in at the worst place. We'll look for survivors there." He turned left, and the scene switched to the news anchor at his desk.

"That film is being taken live at Sawgrass Mills Mall. We still have no reports of what might have caused this terrible tragedy. Survivors outside the building report seeing what they variously describe as 'a tornado of light,' 'millions of fireflies,' and 'something that looked like fireworks, but without the sound.' None report any explosions. Some, however, say they heard voices and faces in the light. To our military reporters, the hallucinatory nature of some of these descriptions suggest the release of some sort of gas, either accidentally or intentionally—"

Kate switched the channel. Another station was interviewing survivors.

She switched again, not certain what she was looking for.

Switch. A movie.

Switch. A game show.

A rerun.

A woman, her hair blowing and the sound of traffic from her side, standing in amongst a stand of palms, on a well-manicured median, in front of a row of large triangles of green-painted metal. Behind her, police cars, their lights flashing, blocked both entrance and egress to the place where she stood.

The camera backed off as she gestured toward her right, the camera's left, toward the mall that lay behind her. Kate wasn't listening to what she had to say. She was studying those huge green triangles.

The metal alligator head that made up the beginning of the sign came into view.

Sawgrass Mills Mall. She'd already known, but this was confirmation. The predator, whatever it was, had broken free.

"That's part of what we're after," she said softly. "The thing that did that, killed all those people—that's part of what we're hunting."

"No," Val said.

"Yes. Rhiana felt it in Callion's house and trying to get out right when we found the place. It must have escaped not too long after we left the neighborhood."

Tik took the remote control and flipped the channel back to Bill and John and the interior exploration of the mall. John and his cameraman were going through a cavernous food court. The lighted signs gave the scene a carnival look at odds with the toppled tables and bodies flung in all directions. Kate could only hear the reporter's running commentary, the questions from the anchor back at the station, and once, the sound of a police officer leaning against a wall being sick.

"Don't watch this," she said, but Rhiana, who'd said nothing until then, shook her head and said, "Don't turn it off. Not yet."

Kate looked over at her. Pale, sweating, her eyes huge in her small face, Rhiana still gave the impression that she was in control of herself and the situation.

Kate said, "Why not?"

"No closure."

"What?"

"No closure. Whatever I felt hasn't finished."

"It's still in there?"

"I don't know." Rhiana closed her eyes, and her body stiffened as she concentrated. Her knuckles and lips went white. Her breathing slowed.

"The death cloud is so thick . . . like dense fog. White fog. A fog made of light. There's light . . . so much light I . . . I can't make out clear details. Because the predator is light, too." She frowned, squinting her eyes tighter. "No. This won't do." She opened her eyes and looked at Kate. "We're too far away, and trying to connect to the site by looking at the TV picture isn't working. I don't know for sure what to expect. The feeling is not knowledge. It's intuition."

"We'll watch." Kate glanced at the screen, then turned away. "No. You watch. I have to go to the bathroom."

She didn't even have time to get up. The reporter and the cameraman behind him went around a corner. She could see a new line of shops, a claustrophobic, low-ceilinged interior, and in the middle of the corridor, down where it turned again, something huge and glowing.

The newsmen moved closer.

Details. Arms and legs and heads, bodies glowing deep ruby red, swelling, turning translucent so that first the muscles and then the bones were outlined in black against the balloon-like skin, and then light burning white-hot through the rifts, the bodies deflating, the skin melting into a puddle, the light moving down a layer, into and through the next bodies.

An enormous pile of corpses, but the pile grew smaller as she stared.

The cameraman had started backing away. The reporter said, "Oh, shit, Lenny, we need to get out of here, man. Now."

Then the light changed. It lifted away from the bodies like mist rising off warm water in the cool night air; like fog rolling down a mountain; like a storm cloud grown enormous that wore its lightning on the outside—a storm cloud that knew anger and hunger and hatred, a storm cloud that, pulsing and flickering and burning, hunted and knew that it hunted. For an instant Kate could see it building momentum. Then reporter and cameraman turned and fled and the light was lost behind them, but not lost far enough.

They screamed. Light clouded the bouncing lens of the camera, firefly twinkles so beautiful she could not look away, and more deadly because they were so beautiful. She heard the first words from the cameraman, no longer nameless. Lenny. His name was Lenny.

"No! Back!"

He was Lenny, who had mistaken his invisibility from the viewers for true invisibility, who thought that journalistic privilege was a fact and not a convenient fiction, who had followed too long.

"God, no!"

Still faceless to the camera, Lenny—dying the way he had lived. And John . . . John, who had words before, had none now.

His screams tore from his throat in short, terrible bursts, and when they died away, did so suddenly. The camera on Lenny's shoulder swung around as Lenny spun and toppled, showing John sprawled on the tiled mall floor; then it spun further, taking in the rest of the corridor in its slow-motion skid that was like an aerial ballet: looping crazily, hitting the ground, sliding forward, coming to rest on its side.

Pointed at the feeding mound.

And the animate light, the golden hell-cloud, descended like rain onto the bodies it had left.

The anchor's voice, hoarse. "Jesus, we let that go out on the air. Oh, Jesus."

And the scene snapped for just an instant to black.

Twenty-eight

When Callion's phone rang, he almost didn't pick it up. But on the fifteenth ring, he grabbed the handset.

"What?"

"What happened?" the stranger's voice demanded.

"It's four o'clock in the morning. What do you mean, what happened?"

"The Watchers. They made the national news. More than three thousand people presumed dead, though no one will ever have a body count because your monsters only left bodies until they could go back to eat them. By now, there won't be anything but a few blood smears on the wall, will there?"

"You're . . ."

"I'm your friend from Glenraven."

Callion sighed, relieved. "Of course. Why are you calling?"

"You chose a bad time to take your monsters on a hunting trip. My group is about ready to come for you. They found your house today; evidently you live right across the street from the site of the unfortunate accident."

170

"That's right."

"I need to know what we're going to do when my people come after you. I need a plan."

The timing couldn't have been worse. Callion needed to get the Devourers back and contained in something stronger—something that would hold them. He didn't need them going off on any wild forays on their own again. He certainly didn't need them causing panics. But he had a problem. They weren't back yet. His control spells should bring them back, but he still didn't know what had gotten into them to begin with. They were out there somewhere, and he couldn't find them. He didn't know if they were at the mall, or if they'd gone elsewhere—a gate into one of the Alternates . . . back to the Rift . . . or to another city here in the Machine World . . .

But he said, "This is our plan. I've decided I want to go back to Glenraven. I want your friends to take me in . . . as a prisoner. I want them to take me before the Watchmistress, so that she can try me. When she and the rest of the important people in this new government are assembled, you'll kill the Watchmistress and release the Devourers. They'll destroy the most effective of our opposition. When we've eliminated them, we'll put the Devourers into the Rift and seal it." He forced his voice to sound cheerful and optimistic. "And then you and I will settle in to make Glenraven the sort of place we want to live in."

The traitor laughed. "Very good. Then you'll only put up a token resistance when they come for you?"

"Yes. I'll make it look good, of course. What weapons do they have?"

"The wizards have some magic, but I can nullify it. The human is magic-blind, but can draw power from a source I can't identify and can't reach. It's something big and powerful, totally outside of my experience. The Machnan can't find it either, though, and the human can't actually use it. She's learned to pass this power over to the Machnan. Meanwhile, I've been blocking the Machnan from using the obvious sources; she thinks something makes it impossible for her to use those sources. From what I can tell, almost all human-based magic is entirely defensive. They have a . . . um . . . a shotgun—"

"That could be bad."

"I'll make sure it doesn't work. I've been doing some research on weapons as I've been able; I think I've figured out a way to disable the thing."

"Good. Then you make sure the gun doesn't work. As long as I know they're coming, I feel I can handle their magic, no matter how odd it is. And if you're right and it is defensive, the only thing I'll have to do is figure out a way to make them look like they beat me on their own, without my help."

"What about the Watchers . . . I mean the Devourers?"

"They'll be contained when you arrive. I would have had to do this anyway, after they got away from me today. They need a lesson in discipline."

"Rhiana said when she and Kate found your house, she felt them trying to escape."

Callion frowned. The two wizards must have been outside of his door when the damned Devourers had started their silent pyrotechnics.

"Yes," he said. "They became quite agitated earlier today. Very odd. I'm still not entirely certain what came over them. They communicate only when they choose and in the manner they choose. While sometimes they are quite . . . talkative . . . and sometimes they are demanding, they have never been particularly cooperative." He sighed. "And they say nothing about themselves at all. Nothing. They never have. Perhaps they sought a mate. Perhaps they intended to spawn. Perhaps some shift of the planets or some phase of the moon drove them to temporary madness. I have no way of knowing. I'm left thinking perhaps I haven't been feeding them enough."

The traitor laughed. "If that's the case, then I think they made up for it."

"Yes. My intent is to ensure that they don't make up for it again in the coming days. I want them dependent on me for their meals. Anything else could make them more dangerous than they already are."

The traitor was quiet for a moment. "Now there's a wonderful thought," he said at last, softly.

Twenty-nine

For Kate, Monday morning followed hard on the heels of a restless, nightmare-ridden night. The lost dead cried out to her, begging her to avenge them, while in the center of darkness a cloud of brilliant many-hued lights followed the direction of the faceless Aregen she hunted. And always she could feel eyes watching her and hear the whispers of a voice she knew but couldn't place, saying, "We'll kill her soon. Soon."

She showered quickly and woke Rhiana, who had been lost in nightmares of her own. "Up," she said. "I need to get out of here for a while. The walls feel like they're starting to close in on me."

Rhiana didn't argue.

They left without telling the other three they were going—just blew out the door and down to the van as quickly as they could.

"What's bothering you?" Rhiana asked.

"A problem occurred to me while I was having nightmares," she said. "And we are going to drive until we find someplace private and we are going to work this out."

"What problem?"

Traffic already crowded the main thoroughfares. Kate passed a fender-bender in an intersection, moved around it, turned off on a side road, and saw a park up ahead. "Great. Someplace where we can talk and where no one will bother us." She pulled in and jumped out of the van. The parking lot was long, the park large, with four soccer fields in a quad over to one side, and a playground, and palm trees that waved their grassy fronds beneath a white-blue sky and light so pure and intense it seemed to have both weight and form. The park was empty. She and Rhiana picked out a picnic table well away from the parking lot and nestled beneath several large trees of a variety Kate didn't recognize.

Settled on the picnic table, she said, "This is the problem. As long as the traitor knows that neither you nor I can do anything magically without each other, he can stop both of us by interfering with just one of us. We have to figure out a way for one of us to do something alone. I don't even think it matters which one. But if whoever it is thinks that he can stop both of us by stopping one of us—"

Rhiana held up a hand. "I can see what you're getting at. Mostly, you're right. We have to have something we can do alone, and it has to be something none of the three others know about. But it can't be just one of us. *Both* of us have to have something."

"Both? I thought just as a diversionary measure, or—"

"But what if the one the traitor stops or blocks is the one who had the second trick?"

"Right." Kate said, "This is so much more serious than I thought it was going to be, Rhiana. I don't think I considered that I could die when all of this started."

"I don't think you did. I think you were looking at the magic and feeling amazed at what you could do."

Kate cringed inwardly at that. She'd been thinking the same thing, but she hadn't realized anyone else might have noticed. "Seeing what the Watchers did yesterday . . ."

"Now you're wondering how we can hope to go up against something that can do that."

"Yes."

"So am I."

"But we can't leave them here."

"No. They were killing Glenraven. You have many more people here than we have in my world, but your people have no protection. They have no magic, and I don't think anything but magic can stop the Watchers." Rhiana's eyes shifted so that she was looking suddenly past Kate's shoulder.

Kate turned and watched several young men get out of a car at the other end of the park.

"So we need to come up with some form of attack each of us can do alone, and we need to find a spell that will eliminate the Watchers as a threat to us." Kate felt nervous; she'd heard about packs of young men in big cities and how dangerous they were. She'd read the crime statistics about Miami and South Florida and she wondered if these were some of those young men. "And I think we ought to go somewhere else to finish our talk," she said.

Rhiana had already stood. "Yes."

"You have a bad feeling?"

"Only of being outnumbered."

"That's bad enough." Kate swung her legs over the picnic table and rose. She walked back to the car, keeping an eye on the men from out of the corner of an eye. They were watching her and Rhiana. They didn't seem to be doing anything else. She kept hoping she would see them get skateboards out of their car, or a radio, or something. But they just stood there watching.

She didn't let herself walk faster; Rhiana matched her pace. Rhiana looked perfectly unafraid and somewhat predatory.

The young men were saying something to each other. Two of them began walking across the park, toward the table where Kate and Rhiana had sat. Two more still stood by their car and watched. The rest were getting something out of the battered old Taurus station wagon. She wondered if they were getting drugs. Weapons. Maybe something worse. Kate's mouth went dry. There were, she guessed, eight or nine of them. Too many to fight off, too many to outrun. The car wasn't all that far away, but she wished she and Rhiana had picked a closer table instead of choosing the one that had the deepest shade. Had they done so, they could have been in the car and gone already.

"They're still watching us," Rhiana said.

"If we have to, we use the magic—the explosion."

"Yes. I'm ready."

"Me too."

One of the young men who had been staring at them suddenly shouted, "Hey, you!" Neither Rhiana nor Kate looked at him. He yelled again. "Hey! I saw your bumper stickers. I read those books, too!"

His friends came bumping out from the other side of their car
with an enormous cooler and a grill, and two cases of Pepsi, and
a soccer ball. Both boys who'd been staring ran over to help with
the stuff. They started hauling it across the deep, heavy carpet
of grass.

I read those books, too.

Kate felt like an idiot. She waved, the boy waved back, and
then she and Rhiana reached the van.

Inside, with the doors locked, Rhiana asked, "Do you think they
would have hurt us?"

"No."

"Nor do I. I feel foolish, but at the same time, after what happened to us when we were leaving your saddle shop, I think we
did the right thing."

Kate nodded. "It's very pleasant to think the world is a safe place
and people are friendly, but it isn't, and sometimes they aren't. The
easiest way someone can get close to you to hurt you is to act
friendly. The second easiest way is to act like someone who needs
help. Most people want to be kind, they want to feel good, and
so they become victims of those who use their better instincts."

"It's the same in Glenraven," Rhiana admitted. "Thieves and
murderers don't lurk by the side of the road and come rushing
out to waylay travelers. They sit in the inns and tell stories around
the fire so that they can find out who has money and where they
might be heading. Then they say, 'Well, I'm going that way, too,
and won't we be safer if we go together?' And sometimes they're
just who they seem to be, and sometimes soldiers will find the
bodies of missing travelers after a few days, robbed of everything,
stripped and hidden in the deep forest. Sometimes," she said softly,
"they never find them at all."

Kate pulled out of the parking lot. For a long while, driving
beneath the amazing Florida sun, beneath tiled houses of a dozen
pastel colors that all managed to look, in the brilliant light, like
different hues of white, she was silent. Rhiana seemed content
to look out the window. But they couldn't just keep riding and
looking. They had to come to rest somewhere. They had to figure out what they were going to do. At last she said, "You said
it was hopeless teaching me magic."

"If you can't see it, you can't use it."

"So if we each have to have some additional defense besides
our magic, mine is going to have to be something nonmagical."

"Yes."

"Why can't yours be, as well?"

"What are you considering?"

"Two handguns. One for me, one for you. I'll get both of them in my name, since I have identification. Florida gun laws are sensible. Georgia gun laws are easier, but we can have them quickly enough. That will be protection. We'll find a shooting range and show you how to shoot. And then we'll—"

"No." Rhiana frowned. "You have faith in your guns, and having seen what one did to the Rift monster, I can understand why. If you can do it quickly, get one for yourself. But as for me, I will have to find my own answer. And I'll find that answer when I answer another question. Who is the traitor and why is he betraying us?"

"What if you can't find out?"

Rhiana sighed. "I'll do the best I can. If I can't find out, I'll try to create something that will be effective against all three of them." She leaned back in the seat and closed her eyes. "*And Callion . . . and* the Watchers . . ."

"We're doomed, aren't we? Whether we come up with backup plans or not?"

"I think so."

Kate stopped by a gun shop and filled out an application to get a .9mm semiautomatic pistol. She left a number where she could be reached and said she'd stop back in a couple of days if she didn't hear anything. It seemed like a futile gesture, but she didn't know what else to do.

When she and Rhiana got back to the hotel, she could still hear snores from the other room. She decided to call Lisa to see how things were going.

When Lisa heard her voice, her polite telephone voice went icy. "I guess I can understand now why you ran," she said.

Kate frowned at the phone. "Lisa? What's wrong?"

"Wrong? That's an interesting question. Do you want to know about before or after picketers threw a brick through the display window?"

"Picketers?"

"They had a permit. They've been out here since before we opened. Paul and I had to cross a line to get in. They had all these signs that said DON'T SUPPORT SATANIC BUSINESSES and STAND UP FOR OUR TOWN—things like that. And they shouted at us. Screamed awful things. How we were going to go to hell for working in this place. . . . Awful things," she repeated.

Kate sat on the edge of the bed. She felt her face getting hot. For a moment she became queasy; that changed briefly to lightheadedness, and she realized she'd forgotten to breathe. She forced herself to draw air into her lungs, then let it out slowly.

"Why were people picketing my store?"

"The men the sheriff's department arrested out at your house before you left gave a statement to Madilee Marson at the *Trib*."

Kate laughed. "People paid attention to something they read in the *Tribulation?*"

Lisa didn't seem to find anything funny in that, though. "Madilee looked into the records of the three men who were arrested, and did this article on them. Snead is a deacon at his church and a member of the Christian Men's Business Association, and he and his church led a driver that raised over a hundred thousand dollars for the medical bills on little Jessie Lockabee when she had to have a liver transplant up in Chapel Hill. Deputy Sumner saved Jody MacNeally from drowning last summer and has done all these civic things. She also told about how Warren Plonkett came to you for a job, and you refused to hire him because he was a Christian." Her voice grew a little colder, a little more distant.

"That's bullshit, Lisa. I didn't hire him because he didn't know anything about the job and because he thought he could intimidate me into giving it to him. I hired you instead. You were qualified. Did I ask you about your religion? Did I say anything about religion at *all* when I hired you?"

"No."

"Did you tell Madilee Marson that?"

Lisa ignored the question. Instead, she said, "And the paper did a write-up about Craig, too. About all the things he did in Peters, and how everyone liked him, and about how he killed himself after he started living with you."

"Is the paper suggesting I caused his death?" Kate asked. She felt sicker by the minute, but also angrier.

"Of course not." Lisa sounded indignant—but not about the obvious bias the *Peters Tribune* had used to slant its articles. Indignant, instead, that Kate dared to question the integrity of the town's paper. "The paper located your family, too."

Lisa's heart sank. "Oh?"

"Your family said they didn't ever want to hear your name again. That you had turned your back on God and them, and that as far as they were concerned, you weren't their daughter anymore."

"That sounds like my family, all right."

"Your parents confirmed that you practiced witchcraft."

"Did they?" Kate felt like she was standing on the edge of a cliff, and the cliff was not stone, but dirt, and beneath her feet, the dirt was beginning to crumble.

"Paul and I closed up the shop, and we've been working on the things that are in here and answering the out-of-state eight-hundred line, but I only stayed because I didn't want to have eggs and tomatoes thrown at me again."

"What do you mean?"

"I wanted to hear it from you, first, but I figure after what Madilee put in the paper, there probably isn't much you can say."

"So if the paper says it, it must be true?"

"You know if they print something that isn't true, they can be sued for . . . slander? Libel?"

"I think it's libel if it's in print," Kate said. She felt surreal, answering that question.

"Right. But I thought I would give you a chance first, to tell me your side of the story."

"How decent of you."

Lisa caught the sarcasm in her voice. "You're damned right it is. It sounds to me like the *Trib* has you dead to rights."

"I'm not a Satan worshipper, Lisa."

"Then why did your family say you were?"

"They didn't. They said I practiced witchcraft."

"And . . . ?"

"They aren't the same."

"They are as far as I'm concerned. You a witch?"

Kate thought, *I could fire her. I should fire her. Except then I'd have to pay her unemployment, and I don't think right now I want to be that generous.* She said, "In case you didn't realize this, I'll tell you that freedom of religion is guaranteed in the United States of America, and my religion is no more your business than yours is mine."

"Are . . . you . . . a witch?"

If I tell her I am, I don't think I'll have to fire her. She'll probably quit on her own. Of course, then she can go to the Tribulation and tell Madilee Marson I confessed. If I fire her, of course, I will have done it because she was a Christian or whatever she is, and not because she's turned out to be a judgmental bitch. "I'm Wiccan," she said. "Pagan."

"I QUIT!" Lisa shrieked. "Do you hear me? I quit! And if you want your horses fed, you can do it yourself!"

She slammed down the phone.

Kate was so angry she shook.

She dialed again. The phone rang eight times before someone picked up.

"Beacham's Saddle Shop." The voice was Paul's, and he sounded out of breath.

"This is Kate."

"Thought it might be. Lisa just slammed out the back door, screaming about witches and quitting and how I could burn with you if I didn't leave."

"Right."

"I got the store key from her before she ran out . . . and the key to your place, too. I guess I can take care of the horses for you while you're gone."

He still sounded sane. She was relieved by that. But she wasn't really surprised. She and Paul had worked together for almost five years. He just lived so far away from her place, taking care of those horses would be a real inconvenience for him. She said, "I can't begin to tell you how much I'd appreciate it. But I will pay you extra for it."

"Kate . . ." His voice sounded funny. Not cold the way Lisa's had, but sort of . . . embarrassed, perhaps . . . or ashamed. "You don't need to pay me anything to do it."

"That's fine. I'll pay you what I was paying Lisa, plus something for the aggravation—"

"What I mean is, I'll watch the horses for you, but I don't want to come into the store again. And I think I'm going to have to quit, too. I was thinking today about setting the answering machine to say that Beacham's was temporarily closed, but I wanted to talk to you about it first."

"Did you say 'quit'?"

"Yeah." She heard chagrin in his voice, and apology . . . but also a certain determination not to be talked out of his decision.

"Why?"

"Because I have a wife and a kid and a mortgage on our trailer, and car payments. I can't afford to move out of Peters, I have to live in this town . . . and I'm not in a position to make any noble gestures or take any unpopular stands."

"What are you talking about?"

"When that article came out, I did a little checking myself, just like Madilee Marson. I looked into Ogden Snead and Bobby Sumner and Warren Plonkett. They're all members of the same church. Well, it calls itself a church, but it's a nasty little radical organization that doesn't have much to do with religion at all, as far as I can tell. It's called the Christian Brotherhood of Purified Souls, and I think the word 'Christian' is tacked on there just to get them a tax-exempt status. These people don't believe in brotherhood or tolerance or love or anything real Christians believe in. They're a paramilitary hate organization with an ugly definition for what it takes to be purified, and some very cultlike practices—regular members have to sell all their belongings and give the money to the Brotherhood; they go through a long, arduous indoctrination period, and bad things have been known to happen to the members who, once in, try to get out."

Kate felt her pulse begin fluttering in her wrists. She closed her eyes and leaned back on the bed and told herself that it didn't matter what group the men had belonged to—that they'd been arrested and they wouldn't bother her anymore.

"How did a deputy get into this group?" she asked. "I would think the sheriff's department would be picky about the sorts of things its members could belong to."

"You would think so, but the CBPS has been careful to keep its charities public and its causes popular. The medical funds drive for that baby was only one of their activities. They also contribute to the Sheriff's Department and the Police Auxiliary, and if their members have a professional standing—like the deputy, for instance—they relax some of their entrance requirements. They would like to get some of their members on the local school board and into local offices."

"How did you find out about them?"

"I knew someone who was—briefly—a member. She almost didn't get out, and she's moved away from Peters to be safe. She didn't want to talk about them, but once I'd made the connection between Snead's 'church' and that mess she got into, I insisted."

"If they're trying to get their members elected, they aren't going to do anything to you. That would be bad press."

"Would it?" His laugh had no sound of humor in it. "Bad press like they're getting now?"

Kate had no answer to that. She stared at the phone. "Can you just go in to work and keep things running for me until I come back? Even just the mail order part of the business? That would be all I really needed. You wouldn't have to work on the saddles. Just take phone calls and discuss orders and things like that."

"Kate . . ." He cleared his throat. "You and I have been friends for years. I knew about your religion, and I didn't care. But if I keep working for you now, it could cost Sandy her job. It could cause Tim problems at school. The people Sandy works with gave her a hard time today." He sighed. "And you don't know what it's like, watching people marching in front of the store chanting and shouting. As for the one who threw the brick through the window, nobody saw that happen. Nobody knows who the people throwing eggs and tomatoes were, either. Nobody saw anything."

"I see."

"I don't think you do. These people think they're on a mission from God. The picketers weren't from the Brotherhood. They were just townspeople. People you and I know. They think you're a danger to their children and their town."

"Can't you tell them I'm not? Can't you say something good about me?"

"I can't let my family get sucked into this, Kate. Maybe it will die down. Maybe once you get back, you can tell everyone your side of the story. You picked a bad time to leave, you know? You look like you're the one who did something wrong, and you're afraid of anyone finding out."

"I wasn't running away. I have . . . I'm dealing with a serious problem for a friend down here, and it just can't wait."

"Like I said, I'll take care of the horses for you. Give me your number so that I can get in touch with you if something changes."

She gave him her number. She wanted to scream. She wanted to go back in time to the point before the men beat her up, so that she could do something—anything—to change this downward spiral her life was taking. She'd thought of both Lisa and Paul as friends as well as employees, but she'd evidently been mistaken. Friends weren't people who would say they couldn't help her out because they had their families to think about, were they? Who would let people think she was a devil-worshipper, a lunatic ready to sacrifice babies or drink blood or mutilate household pets rather than say a word in her favor. Friends didn't quit in a screaming fit.

Well, maybe they did. Maybe she didn't know any more about

friends than she'd known about families. She'd already found out that families were people who would tell a reporter they didn't consider her family anymore, who turned their backs on her and decided she was out of their lives, who, when she had been in desperate need of help, had told her she'd have to believe the way they wanted her to believe before they would consider her one of them again.

So maybe friends and family were two sides of the same worthless coin.

She lay back on the bed and closed her eyes, and felt tears of shame and humiliation and anger beginning to slip from the corners of her eyes. She deserved better, she thought. She deserved better friends, better family. She deserved to have loved a man who loved her enough to live. Or maybe all she deserved was to get away from them. Maybe her real reward was to be free of her cold, self-righteous family and false friends and self-absorbed lover.

Maybe that was true, but it didn't feel true. The truth she felt was that she wanted her family to love her. She wanted her friends to stand by her. And she wanted Craig back.

Thirty

Rhiana recounted the last of the tale to Tik, Errga, and Val, and said, "Now she's lying in there, not crying any longer, still as midnight and cold as stone. She won't talk to me, she won't look at me. She's thinking or she's gone and I can't tell which. But before she went all silent, she said, "Why should I help them? Who are they to me, that I should fight or die for them?"

Errga had sat through her recounting with his head lowered, his eyes half-closed, his ears swiveled sideways, so that he seemed to be listening to many things, all far away. But when she finished, he looked up at her, his yellow-gold eyes wide, reflective, and he said, "We don't know her. She is older than any of us in her way, and deeper."

Tik growled guttural agreement and said, "How could her friends treat her that way? How?"

Val was silent longest. The others turned to look at him when he sighed. He murmured:

184

"Do not assume her, neither heart nor soul.
She is not ours—perhaps is not her own—
she's ancient far beyond imagining
and from strange lands and distant waters grown.
Born once of pain and purified by loss
and scarred by grief and tempered now by fire;
she is a blade of metal purged of dross
and wielded by naught but her own desire.
Do not assume her; her way is not ours.
Hers is a path with homes in heaven and hell,
and she will do as she must do. But still . . .
remember that gods forge their weapons well."

Rhiana sat watching him after he had finished, startled. "What does it mean?"

"It means what it means."

That was the Kinnish way—to declare some ancient bit of poetry and refuse all comment afterward. Rhiana didn't trust poetry; numbers said what they meant, and things were what they were, and poetry turned people into swords and winds and dying fires on cold cliffs and left the listener to wonder after their actual fate. "Your moldy old poem doesn't mean what it means," she said. "Kate isn't a weapon of the gods and she is only twenty-seven years old. I'm older than she is."

Val smiled slowly, that amused smile that so irritated her. "Years mean nothing. Times change lives, and suffering molds souls, and the very young can be older than the very old. She is ancient. And she isn't who she thinks she is, nor who we think she is, either. And my poem is neither moldy or old. I just made it up."

Rhiana ignored him. "I'm afraid that because of what's happened to her, she won't help us. I don't think she cares anymore what happens to her world. And if she doesn't care about her own world or her own people, what will make her care about ours?"

"If you were Kate," Val asked, "would you care about us? Or if four of Kate's people burst through a gate into the courtyard of your castle, pursued by monsters and begging for your help, would you leave your home and your work and risk your life to help them? Even if some ludicrous book told you it was what you were supposed to do?"

Rhiana thought about that. "No," she said at last. "I would have said, 'Find someone else. I have things I have to do here.'" She'd never really paused to consider how extraordinary Kate's behavior had been. Was. She'd only thought, This is what we need, and a stranger had supplied it for her.

She looked from Val to Tik to Errga, wondering which two of them would give her advice she could trust, and which of them would lie. She said, "What should we do?"

Val said, "For the moment, nothing. She must help us of her own choice or else not. We cannot urge her or lure her or trick her, much as we might wish to."

Tik nodded agreement, looking with some surprise at Val as he did so. "Quite right. We have to wait."

The warrag didn't answer. He had lowered his head again, and now, with his muzzle resting across his forelegs, flexed the short, curling fingers of his hands and watched the claws move in and out of their thick pads.

"Errga? What about you?" Rhiana asked.

"I suppose if it were only me, I would try to win her to our cause. Perhaps I would suggest that she could live in Glenraven, that she would find friends there better than those who abandoned her here." He chuffed. "I say that is what I might do, but if I were the one who had suffered her affronts, I would not take kindly to cajolery nor to bribes, no matter how kindly offered or well meant."

"Then you agree with them?"

"Yes."

Rhiana thought, *If all offer the same advice, are all three traitors in league with each other? How could that be? Or are none traitors, and has some other wizard found us and spelled me? Yet how could that be? Or thirdly, could the good of all of us, traitor and faithful alike, still for a while lie along the same road? And if that is the case, then where will our roads begin to branch, and the traitor try to lead us onto his path?*

Val stood. "Lady Smeachwykke . . . darkness has fallen, and I find myself with a deep desire to walk on the broad smooth pathways of this lovely city and explore some of the wonders in it. Would you do me the honor of gracing the walk with your presence?"

Tik gave Val what Rhiana could only describe as a warning look. Errga made no response of any sort.

I could go back to the room with Kate, but at the moment that's like sitting up with a corpse on the night before burial. And I would rather not. If Val is the traitor and he intends to hurt me, I can at least feel the magic start to build before he can attack. I still have my blade.

She could feel the dagger in its sheath, tucked along the small of her back with the short blade fitted into the back of her jeans and the handle riding up along her lower spine. She smiled at him and said, "In truth, I would be glad to see some of this place."

"We'll return," Val said to his two roommates.

"I may be here or not when you return," Errga said. "Last night I followed my nose to a great swamp, all full of birds and beasts and armored monsters as long as Kate's van. I was of a mind to hunt tonight. Kate brings in her share of fine food, but tonight while the moon is waning to darkness, I would like the taste of blood."

Tik laughed. "I may stay and watch the television and drink the rest of the beer. Or I may return to the great salt lake and watch the waves roll onto the sandy shore. In all my life I've never smelled a place like that lake. It calls to my blood and makes me think of the world as it must have been when it was very young."

Rhiana stopped and glanced from the warrag to the dagreth to the Kin. "But if all of us leave, who will be here with Kate?"

"Does Kate need someone to stay with her?" Errga asked. "She seems capable of guarding herself."

Val shook his head slowly. "Rhiana is thinking that Kate, without one of us here to stop her, might come to the conclusion that she owes us nothing and leave us stranded here. Isn't it?"

"I did think that."

"So did I," Val said. "And without Kate, we have no magic and no chance of going home. But we can't make her help us, so we had best let her feel that we trust her to be by herself when she might have reason to wish to be."

So Rhiana and Val stepped out into the night. Val kept his face averted from the few people they passed, and where there were many pale gold and white-blue lights raised high on poles, he kept to the shadows. They walked along the broad sidewalks, moving away from the busiest roads and the heaviest traffic. After a while, the cool air carried little of the scent of machines; instead it was rich with the sweetness of night-blooming flowers, scents Rhiana had never smelled before.

"I walked this way last night," Val said, "and when I smelled the air, I thought of you."

"Did you?" Rhiana didn't know what to say to that, or what

to think of it. It was a line like the poem he'd produced from
the air earlier; a line that forced her to think of him in ways
she didn't trust or quite understand.

They walked further, past a straight lane of still, deep water
that ran at right angles to their path. Rhiana felt life and movement within the water, an ancient danger best avoided. It lurked
well away from their path, but she didn't linger to admire the
sheen of the reflected lights in the glassy surface. She hurried
her steps.

"What?" Val asked.

"Something is there. Some animal, old and fierce and dangerous.
I can feel it."

"I can't."

"It doesn't want us, but it could."

They walked yet further, turning down side roads so that they
strolled beside huge many-storied castles that bloomed with light,
and lovely houses planted all around with flowers and trees and
grasses, and Rhiana wondered what it could be like to live in
such a world.

"If she left us here . . ." she started, but stopped. The words
were too frightening to say.

"Then we would go on." Val took her hand. "You would have
the easiest time. I could, perhaps, find a way to fit in here, though
I'm not certain how. Tik and Errga would have things worst. They
couldn't live in towns or this great city; they would have to go
to the wild place that Errga found, and live there almost as animals." His voice softened. "But for you and me, perhaps it would
make things easier."

She looked up at him, trying to fathom the intent beneath the
meat of his words. "How so?"

"Easier, fair Rhiana. Or can it be that you don't feel the same
tug I feel? Is it true that Machnan cannot truly desire Kin? I heard
all my life that Kin could not truly desire Machnan, but I've found
the lie in that tale, and perhaps the lie beyond the lie, too, that
maybe Kin and Machnan could be *eyran* to each other, so that
the magic of twinned souls might not be—as Kin have said it
is—reserved for the First People alone."

Rhiana's steps faltered. She had felt the pull of him, had felt
it as she felt the tug of the moon, the pull of the sun. But now
he claimed to feel such things, and she was forced to wonder why.
He'd given her no sign. Well, she had given him no sign either,
being instead cold and distant and unlikable so that he would

never suspect how she felt. So that he would never suspect the shamefulness of her half-suppressed longings.

Yet she'd told Kate people in her world were guilty of pig-headed stupidity and ignorance. She knew as well as Val did that the physical differences between the two of them were merely external. The differences in upbringing and beliefs and society ran far deeper than that. Perhaps that was what Val meant when he said things would be easier for the two of them if they were trapped in this new world. If she never had to see censure in the eyes of her people, she would have no reason to doubt her attraction to Val. If he didn't have to face public mockery among the Kin of his *straba*, he would be free to love her as he chose.

If they went back, he would have to face such mockery, though. She would face worse. Her people would shun her, refusing to speak her name, refusing to see her if she showed her face in the streets. They would hold a proxy funeral for her, and when it was done, she would be as one dead to them. Were she a peasant girl, they would kill her in truth—the coffin would hold no straw woman, but a real one. And if a child were born before her shame was uncovered, the child would be killed with her.

The Watchmistress was *eyra* to a Kin, but she was human. No other humans lived in Glenraven, and after Jayjay had saved Glenraven, who would deny the Watchmistress love or happiness? No one. Besides, everyone knew humans were the children of the outcasts, and that in their blood ran the blood of Kin, Machnan, Aregen, and Kin-hera. So Rhiana couldn't look at the Watchmistress as an example upon which to base her own life.

Val said, "Fear stops so many of us from following our hearts," and she agreed. "The balladeers sing of dying for love, but few would choose to do it."

He touched her cheek lightly with one fingertip and she felt the heat of his hand, the hardness of his calloused skin. "Few indeed. But here and now we hunger for each other, and tomorrow we may die with love or without it, but certainly not for it."

"The second year of formal mourning for Lord Smeachwykke has passed," she said softly. "I am free to choose a consort . . . and a few young men have come calling. Those who think they would like to be elevated to the post of Lord Smeachwykke, with his lands and titles." Her voice grated when she said it. "Those third and fourth sons of other lords, who have no hope of title on their own."

"I could never be a Machnan lord, nor do I wish your title

or your coffers or your land. In fact, I believe you were pursuing *my* land." He laughed when he said it, and she laughed, too.

"Then perhaps I ought to be attempting to seduce you, to get you to promise me more land in exchange for a few brief moments of pleasure. I have heard that such things are sometimes done."

"I've heard the same," he said, "but I suspect the men and women who do them don't tell the intended victim that's what they had in mind."

She clucked her tongue. "Then I'm failed as a seductress."

His voice grew suddenly low and rough, and he murmured, "Not failed at all. You have enchanted me."

"Would you kiss me?" she asked.

"Would you have me kiss you?"

Rhiana moved closer to him, close enough that she could feel the heat of his body drawing her like a magnet—close enough that the sweet scents of the night faded beneath his own warm, softly musky scent. She looked up at his face, dappled by the shadows of leaves thrown by one of those tall, bright streetlights. She placed both hands flat against his chest, her hands level with her chin when she did it, and pushed him backward lightly, into the deeper shadows. "I would," she said.

He leaned down, full lips parted, the dagger points of his eyeteeth visible for just an instant before he pulled her closer and she shut her eyes. He kissed her gently, letting his hands slide down her back, and she felt the tiny points of his claws kneading in and out, in and out, as if he were a very large cat, his claws pressing through her clothes and against her skin but never hurting her. She locked her fingers behind his head and pulled him harder against her, tasting his lips with her tongue, reveling in his scent and the smooth skin of his cheeks and the silk of his hair under her fingers.

She had been alone so long. So very long. And he was so beautiful.

Thirty-one

Tuesday morning, the Devourers came home sated, full of blood and power, torpid and heavy and dull, and Callion caught them up in a stronger cage and locked them away in the room in the center of the house. No matter how he tried, he could find nothing about them to tell him what had come over them; he saw no change in them except their slowness after their massive feeding in the mall across the street. Their numbers remained the same, and the amount of power he felt in them, as well as their size and colors and character. He'd considered the possibility that they had been spawning, or in season in some fashion—the thought frightened him, but he faced up to it. If they had been, however, they'd done whatever they did without leaving him any the wiser.

He worried at their behavior as he closed up the room. He couldn't spend a great deal of time thinking about it right then, but he found himself hoping that their brush with madness had a cause he could figure out and correct.

He wore a human guise—the face and body of a handsome man in his late forties, with thick hair already silvering, with bright blue eyes and a deep, even tan—and he checked its details as he moved from the Devourers' chamber up the stairs to his office. He had difficulty sometimes keeping the skin texture correct. In most instances the mere appearance of correctness was sufficient, but for today's interview, he needed to be sure his flesh *felt* human, too. Any slight grittiness or sandiness could lose him his prey.

He finished setting up the office—pamphlets and the policy handbook and all the legal paperwork; transfer of ownership on the house he'd chosen for the next one; the little kits for doing blood tests and a pregnancy test; the checkbook and the company credit card already made out in her name. He rehearsed his lines again, in character. He'd done the real thing so many times already he thought he probably didn't need rehearsal, but a slip would lose him this one, and her letter and his background check had proven her to be one of the best of his finds so far. He tugged on the white lab jacket and tucked the stethoscope into one of the roomy pockets. From tan suede Hush Puppies to neatly pressed khakis to the blue-gray polo shirt that complimented both his eyes and his hair, he was the perfect image of the doctor. The embroidered name on his jacket, Dr. C. Lytton-Smythe, just beneath the neat little Aregeni Foundation logo, added what he considered the perfect touch.

He was still admiring himself in the mirror when the doorbell rang. He trotted into the upstairs hall, swung on one hand around the newel post, loped down the stairs, and arrived at the front door grinning, looking rakishly disheveled and only slightly out of breath.

"Was upstairs," he said with a little laugh at his breathlessness, and she laughed, too. He held out a hand, concentrating on keeping the skin texture just right, and said, "I'm Dr. Constantine Lytton-Smythe. And you must be Angelina Calerni." He looked over his shoulder, back into the empty house, and shouted, "Darcy, I got the door. You needn't." Then he turned to her and said, "My housekeeper has a touch of arthritis and it's giving her a terrible time today."

Angelina Calerni looked even better in person than she did on paper. Twenty-three years old, she had the sparkling black eyes and olive complexion that testified to her Mediterranean descent, and the perfect skin and sound body that promised excellent health. When she smiled, her teeth were just crooked enough that he knew she hadn't needed braces, beautifully cared for and without any signs of early wear or decay. She was neither too slender nor too heavy, and her wrists and ankles tapered delicately. She had a good strong nose and a long, slender neck. Her hair, midnight-black with a gleam of blue, curled around her face where it had escaped from the heavy braid that hung straight to her waist.

She took his hand firmly and shook it. "Delighted to meet you, Dr. Lytton-Smythe. I can't believe how close you live to the mall. Weren't you scared?"

"I wasn't even home until after it happened . . . but I was scared when I heard about it. And call me Smitty, please, Angelina."

She laughed again. "From talking on the phone to Mr. Aregeni, I assumed you'd be British, but you haven't any accent at all. And please call me Angie."

"Angie it is. Come in," he told her. "We'll go to my office for the final interview, if that's all right with you." He headed into the house and she followed him, completely trusting. He said, "I have a dual citizenship; both of my parents were British citizens, though I was born in the United States. When my parents split up, my father went back to Stratford-on-Avon, and my mother and I stayed here."

"My parents divorced, too."

"I noticed that in your bio. Both of them still living and in excellent health to the best of your knowledge?" He led her into the office and pointed out the seats facing his desk. He settled himself in his leather chair, letting his desk provide the barrier that would assure Angelina Calerni of his professionalism and honorable intentions.

"They're both fine. I don't see my father. My mother and I remain close."

He leaned back in his chair and crossed one ankle across his other thigh. "I know Mr. Aregeni discussed your education and reading habits with you, and your interests. And I know he told you that with your intelligence and wit, your sense of humor and your interest in so many things, he desperately wanted to hire you if you passed the physical examination."

She nodded. "He was a delightful old man to talk to."

"He's a wonderful employer, too. Did he mention to you, though, that he's dying?"

"Oh, no!" Her luminous eyes expressed a real and sudden sorrow. "He didn't say anything like that at all."

"He's known for quite a while. He moved to Florida for his health, but I'm afraid his condition has deteriorated beyond the point where even constant warm weather and high humidity will ease his suffering. He would have been here today to meet you, but he is currently in Switzerland receiving treatments from a specialist there. He may not survive this trip."

"Oh . . . I'm so sorry." She considered that for a moment. "But if he's dying, he's hardly going to want to hire someone now."

"On the contrary, now, especially, he wants to be sure that his dream lives on. And it can only live on if he—and once he's gone, his employees—can continue to find brilliant young people to make it happen."

Angie leaned forward. "What is his dream, Dr.— I mean, Smitty? We discussed everything in the world but that."

"I'll get to it. I have to do this the way he wants it to be done, and if you don't pass the physical, I can't hire you and there's no need for you to know."

"The physical is—"

"A urinalysis and a complete blood workup, a drug screen, a pregnancy test, a systems examination including a gynecological exam, an electrocardiogram to be sure your heart is healthy at rest, a cardiac stress test to be sure it stays healthy when you aren't—"

She held up a hand. "In other words, this is going to take a while."

"Yes. These are the permission forms for the exam." He shoved a clipboard across the desk to her. "If, after you've read through them, you decide you want to have them, I'll call my nurse and she'll be here in just a few moments. The value of the medical workup is several thousands of dollars, which we absorb." She was already skimming down the stack of forms, signing her name at the bottom of each one. "You'll note that we, as a private foundation, do not make information on you available to anyone for any reason, unless you are unwise enough to commit a crime." He chuckled. "If our records are subpoenaed, we will comply, of course. In no other way will anyone ever find out anything about you from us."

"Good," she said. "Go ahead and call your nurse." She glanced up at him for a moment, and the corners of her mouth curled up in a mischievous smile. "I didn't come this far to change my mind now."

He nodded, picked up his phone, and pressed 3 on the auto-dial.

When his nurse, a woman named Laramie Dodds, picked up the phone, he said, "Laramie, I have a physical for you." She said she needed ten minutes. He conveyed this information to Angie when he hung up, and she nodded but didn't say anything. She still sat bent over the forms, reading and signing.

Callion had tried, initially, to create a nurse for himself out of sand, but he found out that real nurses were willing to hire out for moderate sums of money, that they knew how to act in a manner his future employees found reassuring, and that they did an enormous amount of work he didn't want to bother with. Further, he found that, like lawyers, they considered the privacy of their clients a professional obligation. He hired several for each of his Aregeni Foundation locations, and had been more than pleased with his results.

He and Angie spent the next three hours in testing. By the time Angie finished the stress test, a coordination test, a memory test, a visualizations skills test, and two tests to check her latent magical potential and her magical aptitude, Laramie had the majority of the lab work done and waiting on his desk. Angie showered and changed back into her own clothes, and Callion studied the results.

He was smiling when she came back into the office and settled into the chair across the desk. "You're blue ribbon all the way," he said. "We're missing a few tests that require a couple of days, but none of those are critical. They're all just baselines."

Laramie Dodds leaned into the office and said, "I'm leaving now unless you have anything else."

"Thanks, no. I'll let you get back to Taversham."

Angie sat quietly until the door closed behind Dodds, then said, "So I'm employable."

"You're damn near perfect," he said, his smile growing broader. "Between your interview and your tests, you qualify to join us at our very top starting salary."

"Seventy thousand dollars a year?" Her voice squeaked just a little when she said it.

"Not including the company car, company housing, and benefits. Full medical and full dental with no deductible and no upper limit, full continuing education, paid travel, paid moves, company day-care and paid private school education for your children, and on and on." He laughed out loud at the expression on her face. "Oh. And company housing comes with a fully-equipped gym, an indoor heated pool, and access to such amenities as ice rinks, horseback riding, mountain climbing, beaches . . ." He shrugged. "Mr. Aregeni tries to keep his employees happy."

"Holy cow," she whispered. She took a deep breath, then said, "I almost hate to ask this, but . . . what am I supposed to do for seventy thousand dollars a year, plus perks?"

He handed her another form on a clipboard, leaned forward and rested his elbows on his knees, looked at her seriously, then said, "We want to hire you, Angie, but we need a guarantee that you won't discuss anything you've found out about the Aregeni Foundation with anyone, under any circumstances. This is a nondisclosure statement that discusses the legal ramifications should you ever discuss the top-secret business of the foundation with anyone, either as our employee or not."

She shrugged, read the form, and signed it.

"Good." He put it with her growing pile of paperwork. Then he leaned back and pointed at the heavy three-ring binder on top of his desk, and waved it toward her. It floated off of the desktop and into her lap. Her eyes got round, but she didn't shriek or panic.

Instead, she looked at him with a glowing smile.

"We're raising wizards," he said. "Not even our lawyers know the actual form and function of our business. The lawyers believe we are a philanthropic organization formed to give homes and futures to unwed mothers and their children." He smiled. "We are nothing that dull or that mundane."

She watched him, a hawk-still intensity in the dark eyes. "I've known of very few genuinely stupid lawyers, Dr. Lytton-Smythe. If they think you're running homes for unwed mothers, then I'm willing to bet that what you're doing at least looks like that on the surface."

"Good girl," he said. "It does indeed. We are not just training up a generation of talented young women. We are breeding children with magic in mind. I'm one of the first children born of the program, back when Mr. Aregeni started his foundation. That was more than forty years ago. I have a great deal of talent, but the children who are being born today, with genetically enhanced magical abilities, are astonishing. If you join the Aregeni Foundation, you will have to have a child to maintain your salary past the first year. Your salary will increase by fifty percent with every subsequent child."

"I have the feeling that I won't get to pick my husband, if this is a selective breeding operation."

"You won't have a husband. We acquire sperm for our sperm

banks from proven wizards. There aren't many, but more now than there were a few years ago." He kept himself professional and cool as he discussed the details with her. If he ever lost them, this was where he did it. "We artificially inseminate, and maintain very careful prenatal and postnatal care of mothers and infants. Once the babies are born, the mothers have complete say in how involved they are in their upbringing. We have some women who have a child every other year—which is our absolute maximum, incidentally—leave the babies with our nannies, and spend the majority of their time in universities or skiing in our facility in Gstaad. We have other mothers who spend all the time that their children aren't in school with them."

She nodded, looked down at her hands, studied them thoughtfully. Her eyes met his with a directness that surprised him. "And if I had one child and never had another, my value to the Aregeni Foundation would seem to deteriorate almost to nothing."

"Remember, Angie, our women aren't just breeders of babies. They're trained to be wizards in their own right. While few of them have the potential of their offspring, because they weren't selectively bred, none of them join us if they aren't at least trainable to a degree will make them full-fledged wizards."

"But having the babies is the job."

"It's what we're paying for. However, you might be interested to know that out of a current population of one-hundred seventy-nine young women in the active phase of the program, we have some very successful artists in the foundation, one famous rock musician, published authors including one who regularly hits the *Times* list, geneticists who have expanded into our R and D program, and a number of other professionals in challenging fields. The work that they do outside belongs solely to them, as does any additional money they earn. If you have something that you want to do or want to be, you can get the education you need to achieve your goals through us. You can get the time you need. You will have no worries."

Angie smiled sadly. "No worries. What an odd thought." She glanced through the handbook, looking at the full-color photos of the company housing complexes in Colorado, California, Arizona, and Oregon in the United States and worldwide in Italy, Austria, and England, and the plans for similar complexes in Australia, Finland, and Costa Rica. "I would move to one of these places?"

"For the first three years, we prefer our employees to move

someplace they haven't lived before. We feel this gives them an opportunity to experience new things and to break out of any ruts they might have developed—"

"And of course it eliminates any strong ties they might have maintained by remaining near their homes." She sighed again. "As for your list of impressive achievements, I rather imagine the percentage of achievers is low compared to your general population. On the order of ten percent, perhaps?"

Eight point five, he thought, but he didn't say anything.

She continued. "They don't have to work for anything, so most of them won't. They'll have their babies, make their money, and let the system take care of them. They've found a way to whore with benefits and without the mess or bother of sex with strangers—how much neater could anything be? And I imagine since the babies are the real interest of the foundation, you have some way of hanging on to them if the mothers decide they want out."

He began figuring out how to get rid of her. He'd been certain she would take the deal—the ones who came so far had already screened themselves out by answering the ad and talking to him in his Mr. Aregeni guise . . . and they always took the deal. But he'd always known if one of them turned him down, he'd have to kill her.

The question was, how?

But when he said, "Then you won't be joining the foundation," preparatory to getting her out of his office so that he could come up with a death for her that wouldn't be linked to him through the nurse, her mother, or any other inconvenient connection, she said, "Don't be ridiculous. Of course I'll take the deal. I'm not stupid. I have things I want to do with my life that I can only do with money. And I'm sure when your mothers aren't in the process of having your babies for you, you make sure they have excellent birth control measures available to them, so that I won't be joining a nunnery and giving up on men forever. Right?"

He nodded.

"If I get a choice of assignments, I'd like to go to Tucson. I hear the area has excellent art colonies and marvelous light."

"It does," he said. "And I'm not certain, but I believe the Tucson community, which is named Arawah, has an opening."

When she was gone, he leaned against the wall and let the human seeming crumble to the floor around him. She'd seen more than he ever intended. Most of the young women didn't ask so many questions or push so hard, taking risks of offending their golden goose. Most of them had been happy to just sign on the dotted line, content to move to a life of ambitionless ease. Angie had been correct—the young women were, by definition, brilliant, but almost none of them took the opportunities available to them to further educations, to travel, to create. The defining characteristic of women who were willing to make a living by selling their bodies in any form was laziness, and these clever young women were as lazy as the whores and the society wives who had chosen the same "career path." Almost all of them settled into bovine lassitude and let their minds rot because they could.

Angie might be one of the ones who succeeded in spite of the system. She probably wouldn't, though. She'd proved she could be bought, so she would probably coast. If she turned out to be one of the few who challenged herself, she might also be one of the few young women who, once in the Aregeni Foundation, decided they wanted to leave. No one left the Aregeni Foundation. Callion didn't intend to let one of his young wizards slip through his fingers. If she turned out to be too much trouble, Callion hoped that at least he could get a child or two out of her before she had to be eliminated. She truly was the most perfect candidate he'd ever found.

Thirty-two

At ten-thirty on Wednesday morning, Kate found a friendly widow who was disposing of her late husband's collections—including his gun collection—and who was only too happy to sell her a nice Glock .9mm semiautomatic pistol, two spare clips, a shoulder holster, and six cases of ammunition for a remarkably low price.

Kate spent the rest of her morning and some of her afternoon at an indoor shooting range, running through ammo and getting familiar with the weapon.

She didn't bother to ask herself why she was helping the Glenraveners. She no longer could satisfy herself that she was doing it for logical reasons. Logic declared that she remove herself from South Florida as quickly as possible, go home, put her house on the market, and move to a place far from the coming troubles. And far from Peters. She didn't owe the rest of the world anything. She didn't owe humanity anything. That was the voice of logic, and she kept wishing that it would speak up, kept thinking that it ought to carry more weight with her than it did.

The voice she *did* listen to was the one that said she had spent her entire life taking for granted the luxuries of civilization. She had been permitted to choose her own occupation, and the one she had chosen dealt in luxuries, not necessities. In her world, no one actually needed a hand-tooled silver-trimmed Western show saddle. Not one life depended on what she did. Not one human being would have been adversely affected if she had ceased to work. Yet she not only found work—she thrived. She had been able to buy herself a home; she owned her car; she never went to bed hungry; she did not toil in life-threatening conditions for wages that could never set her free. She worked hard, but she worked at something she loved. She spent her hours surrounded by the rich scents of leather and wood, feeling beautiful patterns rising up beneath her fingertips, watching her hands creating artifacts other people admired and valued. She got frequent calls and letters from her customers, telling her that they had won this or that show riding on a Silverado Premium, that they had gone on a month-long ride on a Mountaineer or a Suede Daisy and that they and their mounts traveled in comfort, that their daughter or son or wife or husband had been thrilled by the gift of an English Huntsman or Stonybrook.

She wanted at that moment to go back to her life among the leather and the steel. She wanted the comfortable sounds and smells, the feel of handstitching with heavy, waxed thread, the sense of timelessness and kinship with the craftsmen who had gone before her. She wanted the sunlight slanting long across her worktable, while she fit and shaped leather across a saddle tree and stopped from time to time to watch the dust motes dance like the smoke from a spirit fire.

She knew that she might never feel any of those things again. But no one else could fight against Callion and the terrifying Watchers; no one else could stop the evil that had already arrived. Maybe she couldn't either, but she knew that she was the only one who had a chance.

Every dream achieved someday demanded a reckoning, just as every choice came at a price. That was life: that nothing worth having could ever come easily, that nothing loved would last forever without care, attention, and sacrifice. Her dream—to work for herself, creating beautiful things—now demanded its reckoning. And if the price it asked of her was high, so too were the rewards she had already received, and the rewards she might hope to receive again.

She knew all of that. So she did what she had to do. She would continue to do what she had to do, until she won or she died.

Something else kept her going, too. A twenty-eight-year-old friend of hers, a boy with whom she'd gone to high school, ran into a burning building on his way home from work. He pulled out two children who were trapped in an upstairs bedroom. They weren't his children. He had only seen their faces in the window, he didn't know their parents—who had died in the fire— he knew nothing except that at that moment no one could do what he could do. He told her afterwards, lying in a burn unit bed with second- and third-degree burns on his face and hands and legs, "I was scared. I think the only people who aren't afraid some of the time, maybe even most of the time, are crazy. But cowards are the people who let fear make them quit."

Heroes, she decided, were the people who didn't. She promised herself after she left his hospital room that she would never let fear make her quit. Never.

By the time she got back to the hotel room, with the Glock concealed in her purse—counter to Florida gun law, since she didn't have a carry-concealed permit—Rhiana was awake. She'd waved Kate off early in the morning, saying something about having just gotten to bed.

Kate wondered where she'd been and what she'd been doing, but didn't ask. After all, like Kate, Rhiana had secrets she had to keep, at least until the two of them managed to uncover the traitor in their midst and somehow render his treachery impotent.

"I'm glad you're back," Rhiana said. "I'm ready to go out with you for a little while. I think we're almost ready to take on Callion."

Kate raised an eyebrow, but said, "Then you want to take another look at the location?"

"Exactly."

Rhiana wanted to do nothing of the sort. In the car, she said, "I need several lengths of rope, salt water, a glass globe about so big—" she curled her index finger and thumb to describe a circle an inch and a half or two inches in diameter "—and quicksilver."

"Does the globe have to be entirely of glass?"

"No. It only has to break when I throw it, and keep in the water and quicksilver."

Quicksilver, Kate thought, had always been another name for

mercury. Mercury was fairly easy to come by in small amounts, but if Rhiana needed a lot, she wasn't sure what she could do. "How much quicksilver do you need?"

"Just a drop."

Kate drove them to a Publix, and took Rhiana inside. She went straight to the baby-needs aisle and pointed out the tiny jars of baby food. "Would those do?"

Rhiana grinned. "They would be perfect. Maybe I could even make more than one."

Kate shrugged. "They're cheap. We can buy a dozen or two if you would like."

"Yes."

She bought an equal number of old-fashioned glass thermometers. And because the Glenravener told her the jars would be dangerous when they were completed, and would have to be carried in something that would protect them from breaking, Kate bought a little cooler and, from a K-Mart, a roll of bubble wrap and twenty yards of yellow nylon sportsman's rope, a hunting knife, and a cigarette lighter. Then she told Rhiana, "Now we go to the beach. There are easier ways to get salt water, but I think water from the ocean might give your spells a little extra 'zing.'"

Kate wished she'd brought Rhiana to the beach earlier. The Glenravener got out of the car and gaped at the ocean, and suddenly, with the brilliant smile of a child confronted by a puppy on her birthday, said, "It's real." After a minute of silent, happy, contemplation, Rhiana said, "As Glenraven lost its magic and its people, its borders moved inward, toward the core of our world—we have stories of vast bodies of salt water, but no one has seen them or been able to reach them for more than a thousand years. I never imagined there could be this much water. But as Glenraven gets stronger and healthier, her borders will expand. Maybe I'll get to see the Infinite Lakes before I die." Then she shook her head. "Assuming I live to get home." She straightened her shoulders and this time her smile was rueful. "Let's get to work."

Kate and Rhiana dumped the contents of the baby food jars into a trash can at the edge of the public access area, then wandered down to the coarse sand at the water's edge. A few tourists moved along the white sand or skated past on in-line skates; an old couple walked barefoot through the surf, holding hands and staring out to sea. The white prow of a cruise liner sat at the horizon, seemingly frozen in time, while smaller ships crawled up into view or sailed down out of sight constantly. Plovers ran just beyond the water's edge, darting after waves; overhead, gulls cried.

"There's power here," Rhiana said. "The sea is bright with magic."

"Then this water will work?"

"Better than I could have imagined."

They squatted at the edge of the ocean and rinsed the jars out. Rhiana then filled each one to the top with seawater and lined the dozen jars up behind her. When she finished, she said, "Now the quicksilver."

Kate produced the thermometers and handed them to Rhiana. "Break them in half and let the mercury drop into the water. By the way, you know that stuff is poisonous, don't you?"

Rhiana arced an eyebrow. "Of course. It can cause sickness if it even touches the skin."

"I just wanted to be sure you knew."

Rhiana nodded. "I'll need you to draw up magic and hold it, then pass it to me when I tell you to."

Kate nodded. "How much energy will you need?"

"Power? As much as you can draw."

"You're sure?"

"Yes."

"And we aren't going to end up sitting in a hole in the sand with no clothes on, are we?"

Rhiana laughed. "I won't explode us."

"Good." Kate closed her eyes and felt the rhythm of the tide. She smelled the sea air and breathed in slowly, visualizing the shifting currents of the Atlantic Ocean, moving air in and out of her lungs in time to the crashing of the surf. She forged the link between herself and the source of her magic, this time not doing anything to dampen the power that she imagined flowing into her. She pictured all of it perfectly—but as always, with her eyes closed she saw nothing. No light. No magic. She could imagine feeling it, but she couldn't feel it. It didn't touch any of her outer senses.

"I'm ready," Rhiana said. Her voice, soft anyway, almost disappeared into the sounds of the wind and the surf, the passing cars, the dopplered laughter of passing strangers.

Kate built the path between the two of them and imagined the magic moving. Imagined it. Visualized it. Felt nothing.

"Stop, please," Rhiana said.

Kate opened her eyes and saw only a baby food jar with

seawater and a drop of mercury in it. "Well," she said. "That doesn't look like anything."

"It won't look like anything, either. Until I smash it on the floor. I separated part of the spell into the salt water, part into the quicksilver, and triggered the spell to the breaking of glass. When the glass breaks, though, all of the energy you drew, which is forced into the quicksilver, will escape into the salt water and release the explosive spirits of the salt. And while it looks frightening and makes a lot of noise, it should also create such a disturbance in the magical fabric of the area that no one will be able to do any sort of magic at all."

Kate remembered something about the element sodium being explosive when combined with water, and wondered if what Rhiana had done through magic was create the equivalent of a sodium bomb with a magical twist in the middle. If the baby food jars were going to be actual bombs, they could be physically as well as magically dangerous to both sides—flying glass would explode in all directions, not just in the direction of Rhiana's intended target.

They spelled the other eleven jars. Then they wrapped each one in bubble wrap and eased them into the cooler.

"Do you need to try one . . . I mean, just to make sure it works?" Kate asked.

"As much as I would like to, I don't dare." Rhiana frowned. "The flash should be visible to anyone magically sighted within this city. It might be brighter than that. It would probably alert Callion. It would almost certainly warn our traitor. And for at least a while after it goes off, I'll have some difficulty working magic. I can't risk any of that."

"So you're going into battle with a weapon you've never tried."

"I'm doing what I have to do."

Kate nodded and looked at the little red-and-white Igloo cooler. "I know how that feels. God. I know exactly how that feels."

They did the rope next. Rhiana said she wanted spelled bindings to tie and hold Callion and the traitor. So Rhiana cut the rope into five-foot lengths, folded them in half, tied a square knot halfway between the fold and the ends to form a loop, and then spliced the cut ends together to form another loop. When it was finished, it looked like Rhiana was trying to create handcuffs . . . except she hadn't given herself any way to control the size of the cuffs, or to tighten or loosen them. Kate couldn't see how the rope would serve any purpose at all.

"Make one of these," she said, and while Kate tied one, she finished the other two.

"Now," Rhiana said, "give me as much magic as you did when we were spelling the jars."

Puzzled, Kate complied. Rhiana held one of the rope bindings and closed her eyes tightly. When Kate passed the energy to her, she murmured, "K-Mart, K-Mart, K-Mart," until the rope began to glow.

"What in the world are you doing?" Kate asked.

"You heard the release word, right? The name of the store where we got this rope?"

"K-Mart," Kate said.

"Yes. Put this around your wrists."

Kate slipped the yellow rope loops around her wrists. No sooner were both her hands through the loops than the rope shrank until it fit snugly against her skin. It didn't bind or chafe. She thought she would try to get free until she realized that her hands weren't moving. Her arms wouldn't obey her, either. She could feel perfectly, but suddenly her arms acted like they belonged to someone else.

"K-Mart," Rhiana said. The loops expanded to their original size.

"I'm impressed."

"They should hold even Callion," Rhiana said. "In order to undo them, he would have to unravel my spell all the way back to your magic source, and since I can't even figure out what your magic source is, I don't think that will happen."

"Then we're done."

"Except for capturing Callion and the Watchers, yes."

Kate wasn't ready to think about that. She knew she would have to face it, but until she did, she wanted as much blissful unawareness as she could manage. She forced the coming confrontation from her mind; she let the steady pounding of the surf and the slow progress of the waves as they crept toward her on the incoming tide lull her into a state of peaceful relaxation.

Rhiana dug her fingers through the sand and watched a line of pelicans flying just above the water. From time to time one of the birds would drop out of line and plummet beneath the surface of the water, to emerge an instant later with its bulging gullet full of fish. "My people have a saying: 'Some good is born of every evil.' Have you ever heard that?"

"Of course. There are dozens of such sayings. 'Every cloud has

a silver lining' is probably the most common among my people."
She glanced at the other woman. "Why? Have you found your
little bit of good?"

Rhiana smiled at Kate, her face suddenly illuminated by a
warmth and a joy Kate had never seen there before. "Oh, yes,"
she said. "For the first time in my life, I know what love feels
like." She hugged herself and stared out at the sparkling waves.
"And as I have come to know this, I have also come to know
who the traitor isn't."

Thirty-three

Callion felt his enemies moving; they stood out against the bleak landscape of South Florida's magical currents like balefires on a moonless night. The Aregen thought of Angie, already impregnated and on her way to Arizona, and of the other women who carried his children or who had already given birth to them. He'd had enough time to accomplish in this world what he needed to accomplish. More than a hundred young half-Aregen infants would begin growing up in an atmosphere as rarefied, privileged, and secure as Callion's considerable talents could design. They would be kept safe while he returned to his world and took over. They would be ready when he came back to get them: taught to accept the existence of other worlds, given good educations and brought up to believe in their own superiority, they would be ready to step into the power vacuum he intended to create in Glenraven.

He had to consider his work in the Machine World temporarily finished. Now it was time to look toward going home.

Unlike the Glenravener exiles whose offspring populated the Machine World, Callion wasn't trapped there. He could have returned to Glenraven through a gate of his own making at any time. The problem for him wasn't in the trip, but in the destination. Once he arrived, he knew he would either have to hide himself away—and hidden away he could not affect those people he needed to affect—or he could present himself and deal with the consequences. Because he had made an enemy of the current Watchmistress, he could expect that she would hunt him down with the enormous resources at her disposal and destroy him, and as much as he wanted to imagine some other outcome, he could find none he could believe in.

However, through the unknown traitor a perfect disguise presented itself. He could go into Glenraven as a helpless prisoner, captured by the world's heroes, taken before the Watchmistress and her council of cronies. With the aid of the traitor, he could then destroy the heroes, the Watchmistress and the council. And when he was finished, he could destroy the traitor. No one liked traitors, not even those who employed them.

Callion wondered what he might do to make his captivity more comfortable and less strenuous. He settled into his office chair and stared out at the late-afternoon sun that shimmered off the palm leaves. He was going to miss the Machine World. He would miss the giant palmetto bugs and peanut butter and television and electricity. Maybe once all of this was over, he would erect a permanent gate between the two worlds and take over the Machine World as well. Maybe. In the meantime, he needed to tie up the last of his loose ends.

He called Rickman, Rickman, Slater, Stern and Brodski.

When he got past the secretary, he found Daniel Stern as happy to hear from him as always.

"I have another young woman to put on our roll," he said. "The papers went out to you today."

"That's wonderful. Wonderful. I'll set up the trust for her and her child as soon as they arrive."

"Thank you. That isn't why I called, however."

"It isn't?" Stern's voice carried a hint of concern.

"Unfortunately, no. This young woman will be the last I can help." Callion coughed, imitating the rheumy rattle of a man near death. "Primarily, I wanted to say good-bye."

"Oh, no . . ."

"I've been told by my specialists that I have only days to live.

I had the option of entering a hospital, but of course if I went in they would expect to use all their machines on me, and I can't accept that. I'm an old man and I'm dying, and I think I'd rather do it with a little grace."

"I understand. I've often thought I would prefer to go at home, too."

"I'm not *going*, Dan. I'm *dying*. I hate those namby-pamby little euphemisms. I'm not going to pass on or slip away or leave." He coughed again, making it sound like the end of everything when he did. "I'm just . . . going . . . to die."

"I know. I simply wish you weren't. In my entire life I have never had the privilege of working with someone as compassionate and caring, or as determined to help his fellow humans as you. So please forgive me if I try to pretend that what's coming is only a temporary loss, and not a permanent one."

Callion gave his lawyer a wheezy chuckle. "Ah, Daniel, at least I know I'll be missed. I don't think anyone, in the end, can hope for more than that."

"I promise you'll be missed."

"Go ahead and set everything in motion to run without me, will you? I want to know before I'm gone that the things that mean so much to me will continue."

"Consider it done."

Callion hung up the phone grinning. That was him . . . the finest human being his lawyer had ever known. Which only said something about the quality of human beings his lawyer knew.

But if his lawyer had poor taste in heroes, he was excellent with trusts and funds and the business of doing business; Callion didn't worry about the future of his many children. When he came back to collect them, he would find them well cared for, well educated, and ready for the next phase of his plan.

He wondered what Daniel Stern would think of him if he knew that Callion intended to kidnap his female offspring away from their mothers, take them into Glenraven, and mate with all of them. He figured that one out of every two of those children ought to be nearly pure Aregen. He thought he would cull out the females who weren't, and most of the males. He wondered if he could encourage his nephew Hultif, one of the few Aregen still surviving in Glenraven, to breed with some of the females. Callion had to kill Hultif eventually—the ill-begotten back-stabber had turned on him in Glenraven; otherwise Callion would have already been in charge. But Callion had done a little reading on genetic diversity, and he thought he ought to have some. Hultif could contribute that much to his uncle's cause before he died.

Thirty-four

Kate sat down on the edge of her bed and picked up the *Fodor's Guide to Glenraven*. She hadn't looked at it since she and Rhiana had discovered that it no longer worked.

"What are you doing?" Rhiana asked. She folded her clothing and shoved it into a little nylon suitcase Kate had loaned her; all of them were getting ready to check out of the hotel. They wouldn't need the rooms for another day. They would either be on their way back to Glenraven, or they would be dead.

"Hoping." Kate ran her fingers along the edge of the book, noticing that she couldn't feel any tingle in her hands when she touched it. She wondered if it was dead, or if the spell could be removed if she and Rhiana just knew what they were doing. She decided that it couldn't be entirely dead—had it been, she and Rhiana could no longer have talked to each other.

She finally decided that she might know more if she opened it. At random, she opened the book near the middle. The print was gone. She riffled through the pages, confronted by nothing but white. She looked up to find Rhiana watching her. She shook her head slowly.

"I feared things would not have changed," Rhiana said.

"They have, though. Now they're worse." Kate turned the book around and held it up so that Rhiana could see.

"Then we'll have no help finding our way back to Glenraven."

"Doesn't look like it."

Rhiana turned back to her packing. Kate put the book into her backpack, rose, and stuffed her own belongings into her other suitcase. The actions seemed futile.

She opened the door between the two rooms, and Errga, Tik, and Val came over. Since Val and Tik had only the clothes they'd worn from Glenraven, and Errga didn't have any clothes at all, none of the three of them were bothered by the inconvenience of packing.

"I'm going to miss room service," Tik said.

Val laughed. "I won't. I was afraid every time someone came to the door that he would see you or get a clear look at me; I'll be delighted to get back to a world where we aren't the only ones who look like us."

"I'll be most pleased to get back to my mate and my cubs," Errga said. "I don't belong here."

"Nor do I," Tik agreed, "but I'll dream of some of the wonders of this world for the rest of my life. I can imagine myself in a house with fireless heat. And telephones would make my work in Glenraven so much simpler. And I can see myself driving a car between cities and *cothas*," he said.

Actually, Kate could imagine that. Tik . . . hunting, picking up babes . . . the Gary Larson cartoon of the two bears sitting in a rusted-out car abandoned in the woods flashed through her mind, and before she could stop herself, she muttered, "You'd be the bear from hell." None of them heard her.

The three males couldn't have heard an army marching in; they were laughing and joking with each other, all three of them in high spirits. She wanted to tell them to be serious, that they were going to face Callion and that they were probably going to die. But maybe they couldn't deal with fear any other way. Maybe she ought to laugh and joke with them . . . except she couldn't think of anything funny to say.

I'm twenty-seven. I'll be twenty-eight in June. Two more months. I really hope I get to be twenty-eight.

Rhiana stood on the bed and waved her arms. "Listen, all of

you. Before we go, we need to agree on how we are going to attack. There are five of us. There's one of him, plus the Watchers. We can perhaps surround him, but not them."

Tik said, "The Watchers can be contained only by magic. Physical weapons won't do anything against them, but they will against Callion."

Kate nodded. "Rhiana and I planned to go after the Watchers together while the three of you took on Callion."

"One of us needs to have the shotgun," Val said.

Kate saw Rhiana glance at him quickly, then look away. "Who should have it?"

Kate said, "It's made for human hands to operate. That would make Val the logical choice."

Val shook his head. "It would seem to, but I can move more quietly through small spaces than Tik, and could come around from behind. Errga is well armed with teeth and claws, and is the fastest of the three of us. If we can get to Callion before he can create a spell, he'll be forced to use physical weapons like the three of us—and our physical weapons will be better." Val gave Rhiana a little smile and flexed his fingertips, unsheathing long, knife-pointed claws from the fleshy pads. "To me, that makes Tik the logical choice to carry the shotgun."

Tik nodded. "Well-reasoned, old friend. I suggest that the two of you allow the three of us to go through the doors first. We are less likely to alert the wizard of our presence if he senses none of your magic. The house will have two doors on the ground floor, right?"

Kate nodded. "Fire codes require that all dwellings have at least two exits."

"Then I suggest the warrag and I go through one door and the Kin goes through the other, and that we go through the house as quickly as we can, locating and subduing Callion. And that the two of you follow immediately behind us and use whatever spell you'll cast to stop the Watchers. When they cannot attack us, come help us with Callion."

The warrag said, "You should follow us through the door and let the Kin come in from the other side. He can move making no sound at all; should we need more surprise than simply breaking down the door and rushing through, he can provide it."

"What about locks?" Kate asked. "I'm assuming that Callion will have both doors locked. Tik, I'm guessing that you could go through a barred steel door with just a shove, but if Val has to break down his door to get through it, it won't matter much that he can move quietly afterward."

The Kin grinned at her, showing all of his teeth. "You don't know about the Kin, fair Kate. The lock does not exist that we cannot seduce into letting go of its secrets. Callion's door will open for me."

The dagreth nodded. "It's true," he said. "Val can charm the coldest metal."

"Or the coldest heart," the warrag said.

Rhiana flushed and glanced at Val again. Val had the grace to blush.

"Then we need to be on our way," Kate said. She hoped to provide a distraction.

The sun was just setting when they hurried out of the hotel and into the van. Rhiana scrambled into the front seat, buckled herself in, and rested her feet in front of the cooler; Tik, Val, and Errga jumped into the back. Kate, who had already paid for their stay, climbed into the driver's seat, feeling her stomach beginning to knot with dread.

One of them was a traitor.

One of them.

Which one?

And the other four headed into battle, not knowing which of their comrades could turn on them. Or would. Kate wondered if the traitor would attack before they caught Callion, or after . . . or at all. If she only knew what he hoped to accomplish, she would be able to prepare herself. As it was, she felt the .9mm nestled in the waistband of her jeans, hidden by her baggy T-shirt, and she hoped that her defenses and Rhiana's would be enough to counter anything they would face.

Thirty-five

Callion felt the weight of daylight roll off his shoulders when the sun dropped below the horizon. He disliked daylight, and intensely disliked the brightness of the Florida sun, but for that moment, on that day, the unwelcome weight could have lingered a bit longer. Something told him they were coming for him.

He couldn't feel them. They were too careful to allow their magic to show. They would keep it carefully hidden until they needed it—but he had some idea of their abilities. He'd felt the two women working together, and the power they moved had been impressive. Not overwhelming, and certainly not anything he couldn't handle, but they weren't the average three-spell wonders, either.

He didn't know how they would come for him, but he thought he could get himself captured with the least trouble if he made it easy for them to surprise him. The first thing he had to do was contain the Devourers.

They'd been torpid in their room since their huge feeding. Even

216

now, two days later, they didn't flicker or flit; instead they glowed a dull, constant red-gold, and when they moved at all, they flowed like cold oil a finger's breadth above the floor. He'd decided to contain them in something with a stopper, and in a moment of whimsy had purchased a tall, slender ceramic decanter from one of the local knickknack vendors. The decanter looked to him like the genie lamp from his favorite television show, *I Dream of Jeannie*. He liked the show so much that, after viewing one particularly amusing episode, he'd turned himself into a replica of Barbara Eden and transported around the house by blinking and bobbing his head over folded arms. It had been great fun, if a little silly.

The decanter had that same external silliness. He'd done work on the inside of it, however, soaking it in a decoction of hemlock and belladonna and pouring hot wax in to keep the poisons fixed to the inside surface. He'd cast heavy spells on the whole thing, too, so that he didn't think the Devourers would be able to break free for several weeks. He didn't think anything could hold them indefinitely, but he didn't need to hold them indefinitely. He had as many uses for them in Glenraven as he'd had in the Machine World.

He went into their room. They were sprawled in a serpentine rope of diamond light, almost perfectly unmoving. He squatted by them with the decanter closed and sealed.

He sprinkled a mixture of herbs on them, or rather, *through* them, watching the lights change from red-gold to anemic white as the powders fell through them to the floor. He murmured a trancing chant, then watched as they followed the line he described with his left hand, a smooth arc that rose from the floor and curved back down to the stopper in the decanter. He watched them flow upward, move through the curve, and slide down. At the last possible instant he removed the stopper, and the Devourers flowed into the container, packing themselves in as they went. As the decanter filled, the pale light grew brighter, and by the time the last of them had flowed into the bottle, the outside surface shimmered with tiny sparkles of that same pale light. He squatted, holding the decanter, and murmured a keeping spell, all the while rubbing the outside with a tiny herbal broom.

When he finished, the outside of the decanter looked almost normal. Every once in a while, a tiny trail of lights would start from the bottom and float slowly upward, bubbles of light rising through thick and fluid air. Callion thought it was very beautiful.

He carried the decanter up to his desk and sat it on a corner. Then he returned downstairs, where he unlocked both the front and the back doors. He left his porch lights and motion sensor lights turned off—he didn't want any of his neighbors growing concerned and calling the police. That could be messy, and he wanted things tidy.

Then he went upstairs, settled himself at his desk in his office with the light on, so that his location would be painfully obvious, no matter how stupid his attackers were.

He tried a number of surrender lines. "Fancy meeting you here," and "What's a nice girl like you doing in a place like this?" and "What's up, Doc?"

But he decided at last on something a little less funny, but a bit more traditional. When they came bursting through his door, he would wake up from a sound sleep in his comfortable leather office chair and say, "Don't hurt me. I'll go quietly."

Thirty-six

They drove by the house twice. Kate pointed out the light in the upstairs window. Rhiana said, "I can feel him in there. He's not doing much of anything. Nothing magical. He seems to be . . . resting . . . drowsing . . ."

"Then maybe we'll be able to catch him completely unawares."

"Maybe," Tik said. "But maybe he can sense us the same way she can sense him." He nodded at Rhiana. "Maybe he knows all about us already. Maybe he's just pretending to rest and it's all a trap."

Kate thought, knowing what she knew about the traitor in their midst, that was at least as likely as the possibility that they were going to successfully sneak up on him. In fact, she found the fact that the lower half of his house was dark both inside and out an ominous sign. What sort of surprise did he have waiting for them.

She said as much.

Val said, "We'll stick to our plan. The four of you in through

219

the front door, me in through the back. You rush the stairs, I'll keep hidden and see if I can find another way to get at him."

"Don't assume he doesn't know we're here," Kate said. "Don't assume that he won't have the Watchers waiting just inside the door to swallow all of us."

"I'll be ready for anything," Errga said.

Val seemed less sure. "I hope I will."

Tik sighed heavily and flipped his braid back from his shoulder. "We aren't going to be any more ready than we are right now, no matter how many times we drive around the block. We need to go in." He looked at Kate. "I never knew any humans before, but if you're an example of a human, I think we're lucky Glenraven has a human Watchmistress. You'll be our luck."

Val touched Rhiana's shoulder and said, "Be careful, please. Don't let anything happen to you."

Errga said, "We can be sentimental here, or we can be sentimental when we get home to our families and friends. I suggest the latter."

Rhiana touched Val's hand. "I'll be careful. You be, too."

The warrag gave a half-disgusted, half-amused snort.

Kate turned the headlights off half a block from the house and before she got there, shifted the van into neutral and turned off the engine. She coasted into the driveway, where everything was quiet except for the pounding of her heart and the raspy, nervous breathing of her colleagues. She turned to look at the shadowy shapes behind her and said, "We can do this. So let's go do it. Don't close the van doors when you get out. Tik, don't shoot unless you don't have any other choice. We're supposed to take Callion back alive." She took the gun from him, jacked a shell into the chamber, and said, "It slides forward and back. You slide the safety back until you see the red dot . . . you see it?" Tik nodded. "Then you aim and pull the trigger. It's loaded with shot instead of slugs, so it will cover a wide area. Don't shoot if anyone else is close to Callion, and don't carry it with the safety off." She stared into his gentle, oafish face, and said. "Be careful, okay?"

He nodded and tersely repeated her instructions back to her, including demonstrating clearing the chamber of the shell that was in it and jacking another one in. She reloaded the shell he ejected, and said, "You're fine. Put the safety back on and let's go. Everyone else stay behind Tik."

Val dropped out first and ran around to the back of the house.

Tik and Errga, following their agreed-upon plan, crept to the front door.

Kate stayed back with Rhiana, drawing up the magic that they were going to use to contain the Watchers. She kept seeing those bodies on the television, glowing and expanding and then, sucked dry, shriveling into nothing. She rubbed her hands over her fore-arms and swallowed; it was time to move in and do what she had to do.

Rhiana carried the little cooler. The handgun nestled against the small of Kate's back suddenly felt like ice. The two women walked forward together, behind the dagreth and the warrag, and though Kate tried to hear the normal night noises—the whir and shuss of traffic, the chirps and hums of insects, the breeze clacking and rattling through the palm trees—and though she knew those sounds had to be there, she could hear nothing but the beating of her own heart and the rush of air through her lungs.

Then she heard the warrag whisper, "Try it first."

"My way," Tik growled. The dagreth slammed his shoulder into Callion's front door. It went down with a tremendous crash. Tik charged in, the warrag right behind him.

Kate and Rhiana brought up the rear, Kate holding her magic at ready, Rhiana tensed to catch it and cast the spell that would pin down the Watchers. The downstairs lights came on as she stepped through the battered doorway, and she looked up in time to see a creature that looked like a large, upright badger come to the top of the stairway at the left of the door and stand there, rubbing his eyes with one clawed paw and swearing. In the other hand he clutched a fancy wine decanter. "What kind of morons are you, anyway?" he yelled.

The warrag rushed up the stairs at him, teeth bared and hackles raised. Tik pointed the shotgun and shouted, "Don't move, Callion, or I'll shoot."

Val came into sight along the back wall of the main hallway; he crouched and watched.

Kate had time to think, *No sign of the Watchers*, and then the shotgun exploded with a roar. Errga howled, Tik screamed, Callion toppled down the stairs clutching his arm, and Rhiana shrieked "Magic!" and scrabbled one of the baby food jars free of its wrap-ping; she threw it against the floor where it shattered

and all the world went white

searing

eyeball-burning

nuclear-explosion
standing-in-the-center-of-the-sun
white
noise deeper than the ocean
wider than the sky
the wordless scream of the infinite damned consigned to the
pits of Hell
and then silence

Kate's vision came back first, well before her hearing. Rhiana lay sprawled on the entryway tiles, red blood draining from her ears and her eyes onto the white of the tiles. To her left, Tik formed a mountain of unmoving flesh. Callion hung head-down along the last four stairs, an arm flung through the banister rails; Kate could see blood seeping from his eyes and ears, too. She could see the warrag at the top of the stairs, a gaping hole in his side and sticky red-black blood oozing from it across the white of bone.

Val stood against the back wall, looking back at her. His mouth moved, but no sound came out.

"I can't hear you," she said—or tried to say. No sound came from her mouth either.

He began to walk toward her.

She slipped her hand to the small of her back and pulled out the .9mm pistol. She switched the safety off, aimed it at him, and saw the surprise in his face.

Rhiana had thrown her magic bomb in his direction. In spite of how she'd felt about him, when everything went wrong she identified him as the source of the problem. Now he and Kate were alone. Everyone else was dead. She didn't know how she'd survived, but she knew that he'd survived because of his wizardry.

She motioned for him to lie on the floor. Slowly, his mouth moving soundlessly the whole time, he complied.

She wanted to kill him. She had come to like Rhiana a lot, and she'd liked both Errga and Tik better than she'd liked him. Now they were dead. Callion was dead. The Watchers were nowhere to be seen, and she didn't know what she was supposed to do with them anyway, but she did know that she couldn't do anything alone. Val was the wizard. She would make him help her find the Watchers, make him take the two of them into Glenraven, and she would see that the Rift was closed. She hadn't come so far only to lose.

" . . . not going to hurt you," Val whispered.

Sound. She heard a moan behind her. She risked a look back, and found Rhiana dragging herself upright. Tik stirred slightly— enough that she could see the huge bloody hole in his clothing over his right chest wall, and the way his right arm hung limp, and the seared and torn flesh dangling along the right side of his face.

Neither Errga nor Callion showed any signs of life.

Rhiana moved to Tik's side and began to stroke his hair. Kate could hear the crooning of her voice as if she were in another room of the house, behind a closed door.

"Crawl to her," Kate told Val. After she kicked him once in the side, he did as he was told.

He didn't look sorry. He didn't have the decency to show any remorse at all for what he'd done. Instead, he affected a look of blank puzzlement that got under Kate's skin and made her want to hurt him a lot. She restrained herself and managed to catch Rhiana's attention.

Rhiana turned and looked down at the prone traitor, and her face contorted into a mask of pure hatred. She spat on him. Then she got the binders out and slipped one over his wrists and one over his ankles.

Kate took the other pair and bound Callion hand and foot. His eyes opened as she bent over him, and he said, "Why aren't you hurt?"

"I don't know."

"I can't move my arms or my legs."

"I know."

"Why can't I?"

Kate left him where he was and headed up the stairs to check on Errga, the only one who hadn't yet moved.

Behind her, Callion shrieked, "Why can't I move my arms and *legs?*"

Errga wasn't going to move. Not ever. He was dead— killed, as far as Kate was able to determine, by the shell that had fired when the shotgun exploded in Tik's hands. It had been point-less, too. As far as Kate could tell, Callion hadn't made any attempt to fight them. He might have come with them peace-fully; perhaps he had wanted nothing more than an opportunity to go home and make amends for what he'd done. Even if that wasn't what he'd hoped for, Kate could see no reason why Errga had to die, or why Tik had to be so grievously wounded.

Val had a lot to answer for.

Rhiana stood at the bottom of the steps. "He's dead, isn't he?"

"Yes."

"I'm telling you, I didn't do anything!" Val lay facedown on the floor, his head twisted to one side so that he could look at Rhiana. "I can't do magic! I have no ability whatsoever to do magic. You should be able to look at me and see that."

"We have Callion and the traitor," Rhiana said. "We need to find the Watchers."

"Can't you close your eyes and feel them, the way you did before?"

Rhiana's mouth twisted into a bitter smile. "Thanks to my spell-jar, I am as blind to magic as you are. I imagine Callion and Val are both suffering from the same problem."

Kate brushed her hand against Errga's head, and told him, "I'll find a way to tell your mate and your cubs that you were brave," she said. "It won't be much comfort. It never is, but it will be better than nothing . . . and it's the best that I can do." She glanced down at Val and added, "And I'll do everything I can to make sure the wizard who killed you gets what he deserves."

She headed down the steps, crouched by Callion, and said, "My name is Kate. I've come to take you back to Glenraven, and to return the Watchers to the Rift. Where are they?"

"He isn't going to tell you anything," Rhiana said, and in almost the same breath, Callion said, "They're in the decanter I was bringing down the steps. I was holding them when her spell went off and everything exploded. I don't know where they are now—I can't see them or feel them or manage even the smallest spell to find them."

Kate stood. "If they fell down the steps, they can't have gone far."

"You aren't going to believe him, are you?" Rhiana asked.

"Why not? He's helpless right now. If he lies to me, I can hurt him until he tells the truth," Kate said. She wondered briefly at the woman she'd become, the woman who could casually threaten torture. She wondered if she would be capable of carrying it out, should she discover he was lying, decided that she wouldn't, and hoped neither Callion nor anyone else would call her bluff.

She started her search at the foot of the stairs, worked her way along the hall on the right—the same hall Val had come down—and found the decanter lying around the corner beneath a huge Boston fern. Evidently it had rolled there when it fell. She knelt and shoved the fern aside. She didn't intend to pick up the bottle with her bare hands. The images of those bodies in the mall glowing translucent ruby red and swelling until they popped wouldn't leave her. She wasn't going to become one of those bodies if she could do anything to prevent it.

The bottle lay on its side, its cork intact. A few little sparkles of light, like currents of static electricity, coursed over the surface of the bottle. The opaque ceramic surface hid whatever was contained inside. Still, watching those crawling lines of light sliding silently through the decorative grooves and over the false gemstones, she thought that she had most likely discovered the Watchers.

"As long as the bottle isn't cracked or the stopper loose, you'll be able to pick them up," Callion said.

Kate said, "Yes, I'm sure. But I think I won't."

She walked further back the hall. To the right she found a dark central room empty of all furnishings. Beyond that, she discovered a kitchen. In the pantry, she found forty or fifty jars of peanut butter of all brands and types, pounds of chocolates, an assortment of other high-fat, high-sugar foods, and a broom and dustpan.

She took those, located a brown paper grocery bag—Callion shopped at Publix, too—and went back to the bottle, which she carefully swept onto the dustpan and eased into the paper bag.

She didn't know if that would make carrying the damned thing safer, but it made it *seem* safer.

She picked up the bag by the top corners and carried it back down the hall to the foyer.

Tik had managed to sit himself up. A large part of the right side of his face, including his right eye, was gone. His right arm was mangled. "The bone is broken, too," Rhiana said. "If I could see the magic, I could heal him."

"You can't do it by memory?" Kate asked.

"I don't think so."

"We could try," Kate said. "At worst, you'll catch more power than you can handle and we'll blow another hole in the house."

Rhiana said, "I don't think magic can be done without sight."

"Maybe not, but I know that people who are blind in other ways manage to do things that would, on the face of it, seem to be impossible. I'm willing to at least try this. If you've done healing before, maybe you'll be able to carry out the steps by memory."

"Maybe." Rhiana said, "Tik, if you want, I'll try to heal you.

I can't promise anything, you know, and maybe you'll be worse off when I've finished than you were when I began, but I will do everything in my power to reverse the injuries Val caused you."

Tik nodded. "I trust you, Rhiana. Do what you can."

Rhiana looked up at Kate. "Can you get me the power to do this?"

"Why couldn't I? I could *never* see it." She closed her eyes and visualized the cold white light flowing to her from all around her, from deep in the earth and high in the sky, from things both living and nonliving, from flesh and stone, from leaf and water. She saw herself as a container, filling and filling until she was full to overflowing, and then she said, "Hold out your hand, Rhiana, and I'll let the power flow into you through your fingertips."

Rhiana held out her left hand and Kate touched the tips of her fingers to the tips of Rhiana's. She imagined the light flowing from her hand to Rhiana's, filling Rhiana, too, while she continued to draw more power in.

"I can't feel *anything*," Rhiana said. "Nothing."

"It doesn't matter. You are full of magic now. See yourself doing whatever you would have done if you could have felt the magic flowing through you."

Rhiana kept her left hand back, touching Kate's, but raised her right hand to Tik's face. She touched a hanging strip of flesh that lay open to expose teeth and bone beneath it and pressed her finger to the wound. For an instant, nothing happened. Then the skin began to draw together as if an invisible zipper were zipping closed, and angry pink seams of healing flesh replaced the bloody tatters and gaping holes.

Rhiana gasped. "It works."

Kate said nothing. She concentrated, instead, on keeping both of them full of light and magic.

"That feels better," Tik said.

"Don't move. I don't have much control of this," Rhiana told him. "If you move, the seams may not line up correctly, and you'll have scars worse than what you're going to have."

She let her hand move further up his face, across the broad planes of his cheek, back to a rag of skin that became once again a round, low-set ear, and then forward, to the socket where he had once had an eye. She slowed, closed her eyes in concentration, and rested her fingertip in the socket.

Tik whimpered, a pitiful mewling sound in a creature so large and strong.

"Just a moment longer," Rhiana told him. "Just one more."

She opened her eyes and saw the pink scar tissue filling the socket. No eye, though, blinked out at her. "Oh," she whispered. "No. That isn't right."

"It doesn't matter," Tik said. "I'm alive, and I can see from the other eye. If you could just set the bones in my arm and patch up the skin there . . ."

Rhiana turned to Kate, tears running down her cheeks. "If I could have seen what I was doing, I could have replaced his eye."

"He's right, Rhiana. You did the best you could do."

"It isn't good enough."

"It's going to have to be."

Rhiana turned back to Tik and rested her forehead against his broad, sloping shoulder for a moment. "I'm so sorry, Tik. I'm so sorry."

The dagreth patted her shoulder with his good arm. "We still have things to do, Lady Smeachwykke. I'll see as well with one eye as I did with two. I'm tough. But my arm truly hurts."

"I know." Rhiana straightened and said, "I'm still ready, aren't I, Kate?"

"You're ready."

Rhiana ran her finger along Tik's arm, and again the skin stitched itself shut. After a moment, Tik sighed. "Ah. That's better. I wish you could have gotten to Errga while there was still time to save him."

Rhiana looked over her shoulder, up the stairs to the place where Errga's dark form sprawled. "We will have payment for Errga's life," she said. "And we will have it in the coin that Errga paid." Kate heard in her voice an iron determination and a tone of command that she thought belonged much more to Lady Smeachwykke than it did to Rhiana. How hellish to discover love, and a day later discover that he whom she loved was a traitor and a murderer. Kate understood how she could slip into the fierce role of Lady Smeachwykke, who knew what she had to do and did it, and to temporarily smother Rhiana, who must want to curl up in a corner and weep for the loss of a love she so desired.

Thirty-seven

Kate asked, "What about the gate?"

She and Rhiana had finished wrapping the body of Errga for transport back to Glenraven. They had carried it down the stairs and placed it next to Val and Callion, who were propped against the hallway wall, still bound and helpless. Kate's backpack chafed, and she shrugged against the straps, trying to make the pack more comfortable. Kate wanted to feel terrible grief for the warrag's senseless death, but all she could find within herself was a vague, muzzy regret; Rocky's death had cut her deeper. She felt guilty for her feelings; the sentient warrag, who had been both husband and father, and whose death would cause pain to those who had loved him, had to mean more than the death of a dumb, if beloved, animal. But she could not change her heart, nor make herself feel the things she thought she ought to feel.

Tik sat with his back against the opposite wall watching them, sobbing, with the cooler full of Rhiana's spell-bombs resting

228

between his outspread legs. "He was my friend—my finest and truest friend—and now he's gone. Gone."

Kate moved to the window and stood staring out at the street, wondering when any of the neighbors were going to notice that something bizarre was going on. "We've done what we came here to do. We have the Watchers and Callion, we've found the traitor—"

"I am *not* a traitor," Val interrupted. "I didn't do *anything!*"

Rhiana, still in Lady Smeachwykke mode, said, "That will be all from you, or I will make you wish you had died instead of poor Errga."

"But I love you, Rhiana."

"Don't lie, damn you. Don't lie to me now, you murderer."

Kate picked up where she'd been interrupted by raising her voice. "*And* since we've done those things, now you should be able to go to Glenraven and force the closing of the Rift."

"Except the book is dead."

Both Rhiana and Kate glared at Val, who glared back, unrepentant.

"So I ask," Kate said, determined to make her point, "how do we create a gate?"

Callion looked up at them. "It would be more a question of finding it than of making it," he said. His voice was soft, with a burr that Kate found surprisingly pleasant. "There is one here."

"In the house?" Rhiana asked.

"I found it convenient to travel between places in the Machine World without being observed. It was pleasant to be able to get money from banks any time I needed it, for example, and I found being able to drop into grocery stores in the dark of night, once the stocking clerks had gone home, gave me . . ." he smiled, showing sharp, small teeth " . . . gave me an excellent selection at a remarkable price."

"I can see where it would," Kate said.

"The problem," Rhiana told him, "is that we don't just need any gate. We need a special gate, one that will take us through Glenraven's barrier."

"They're all the same, gates are," Callion said. "Any gate will take you anywhere, if only you know how to get there. The trick with getting to Glenraven from here is that you have to be able to picture the place you want to go perfectly in your mind. You won't be able to feel the place, as you would a location within this world, and you won't be able to lock on to an anchor. You'll have to hold the gate there on the strength of your vision alone—and that can be a tricky thing. The same holds true for going from Glenraven to here."

"Why are you telling us this?" Rhiana said.

"Because I am old and tired and I want to go home. And I've come to discover that the . . . Watchers . . . aren't as tame as I thought they were. They got away from me the other day in spite of everything I could do to contain them. I'm sure you're aware of the results."

"We noticed them, yes," Kate said.

He nodded. "Most people did. But you asked why I would help you. I assume, since you haven't already killed me, that I am to be tried when I am back home."

Rhiana said, "The Watchmistress herself will try you, and the Council of Glenraven with her."

He nodded. "That is as I expected. Well." He smiled a weary smile. "If it gets me home and lets me stay there, I will trust my life to the justice of the Watchmistress. I am weary of the Machine World and its smells and its noises and its constant hurrying bustle. I long for the dark quiet of the forests I knew as a child and the mountains and the sounds of bells from the villages. I long for people who do not count the time by seconds but by seasons."

Rhiana was nodding her head as she listened to him. "I understand this. I can't say what the sentence of the council will be," she told him. "I promise you it will be just."

"That's all I ask."

Kate said, "Then we need to find the gate, and we need to get you home. And then I need to get home so that I can take care of things." She glanced at her watch. The hands showed a quarter to ten. "In fact," she said, "it isn't too late to make a phone call. I could call Paul at home to let him know I'll be coming back tomorrow." She looked at Callion. "May I use your phone?"

"Of course." He managed a courtly nod.

"I thought you would go back with us," Rhiana said. "To Glenraven."

"Why?" Kate shook her head. "I would love to see this world of yours, but I need to take care of things back home. I need to let people know that I didn't run away. I need to stand up for myself and let them see that I didn't do anything wrong, and that the people who tried to hurt me weren't these wonderful pillars of the community; that they were scum. I can't do that from here, and I can't do it from Glenraven."

Rhiana nodded. "I suppose I will have to be grateful that you've helped us as long as you have."

Kate managed a small smile. "It turned into more than I bargained for." She hurried down the hall to the kitchen, where she'd seen a phone hanging on the wall.

"Paul," she said when he answered, "I just wanted to let you know I'll be driving home tonight—should be there tomorrow morning. I'll get things straightened out then, and when I do, I'd really like for you to stay on working for me—"

He cut her off. "I don't know that you want to come back right now," he said. "I don't know that you want to come back at all."

"Of course I do. Peters is my home. I have a house there, my work—"

"Kate . . . Peters evidently isn't as taken with you as you are with it." Kate heard strain in his voice, and something that sounded like fear.

"What's wrong? What's happened?"

"Sometime last night, arsonists burned your house down. And your barn. The horses died—they were fine when I went out to feed and water them and clean their stalls at seven, but some of your neighbors called the fire department when they saw flames sometime around nine. By then it was too late. I didn't know anything about this until the sheriff's department called me looking for you. They didn't find any notes, no crosses on the front lawn, nothing like that—they know it wasn't any of the men who were charged with assaulting you, because all three of them have independent alibis. They said the arson looked like a professional job. Nothing is there now but ashes, Kate. Nothing."

Kate stared at the phone, not breathing, not thinking, just numb. "No," she said at last. "That isn't true. You're joking."

"I'm not. I wouldn't joke about something like that. And when the sheriff came by to talk to me this morning, he was wondering if you owed a lot of money that you couldn't pay back, or if the store had been in trouble."

"No!" Kate felt the tears welling in her eyes. What little she had left from her past was in that house. The photographs of her dead brother, of the rest of her family, of herself as a child back before life got so complicated; the reminders of Craig, the pieces of her life since him that were promises she'd made to herself to get back on her feet, to keep on living, to keep on finding reasons to enjoy each day. Everything she owned had been inside of that house. None of it could be replaced. Her family was as far gone from her as if they were dead, her brother and Craig were dead, the child she'd been no longer existed. Now none of it remained.

Her past had ceased to exist in any place or form except her own mind. And they were going to try to say she'd destroyed it all herself?

"No," she whispered. "I want it all back."

"I'm sorry," Paul said. "I really am. I told the sheriff your business was doing fine and you didn't owe your suppliers or anything. I took him and a couple of police officers and the insurance adjuster into the shop and showed them your books for the last couple of years and your orders and your bank statements. I think they were convinced that you didn't pay someone to burn the place down. As they were leaving one of them asked the other if he thought you might have done it just so you wouldn't have to bother with selling the place before you moved away. But I don't think they believe that. You'll probably be able to get your insurance money."

"I wasn't going to move away," Kate said. "I was just down here helping out a friend. That's all."

"I think the way everyone here sees it, Kate, is that you have problems of your own that you should have been taking care of first. That the time to run away to Florida wasn't when you'd made complaints that got three men arrested."

"I didn't run away!" She glared at the phone, helpless and furious at the same time. "Though I suppose it looks like I did." Kate leaned against the wall, trying to picture her neat little house, into which she'd poured so much of herself, reduced to ashes and charcoal.

"If you're going to be here tomorrow morning," Paul said, "I suppose I could call around and line up a hotel room for you. I'd offer to let you use our guest room, but we're in the process of repainting right now—"

"Thanks anyway," Kate said. "I need to think about things. I think I'll stay here just a little longer."

"Well, yeah, I figured you probably would." Paul said, "Give me a number where I can reach you. I know the police and everyone will want to talk with you."

"There isn't going to be a number. When I get things figured out, I'll call them."

"Right. If you don't stay in touch, Kate, this is going to look a lot worse for you."

"Fuck that."

"Do what you want, of course. I've got the shop boarded up so that no one will break in. Your rent and utilities on the place are paid through the end of the month. You'll want to get your things out of there before that, though, so Mrs. Tabor can fix the place up to rent to someone else."

Kate closed her eyes. "I'll keep that in mind."

When she went back to the hallway, she couldn't look at Rhiana or Tik. She said, to no one in particular, "I guess I'll be going to Glenraven with you, just for a while."

Tik surprised her. He said, "I've been thinking. You were right to say you needed to stay here and fix your life. You're a good person, and even if the people in your town don't believe that now, they will. But only if you make them see it. And running to Glenraven won't make them see it, Kate."

"It doesn't matter." She managed to meet his eyes. "Someone burned my house down last night. The barn, too." She looked at Rhiana. "Your horses are dead, yours and his." She shrugged. "I lost everything that really mattered to me last night. I suppose I'll have to go back and get my leather tools and my books and my orders and customer list from the shop—assuming someone doesn't destroy those before I get back, too. But I'm not really in a hurry anymore. I don't have anyplace to go."

Tik studied her out of his one good eye, and she thought she saw tears welling up there. "That isn't right. You're a good person, Kate. I like you."

Rhiana came to her side and patted her on the back. "I'm so sorry, Kate. None of this would have happened if you hadn't been helping us."

"I don't know. Maybe it would have. Maybe they would have burned me inside of my house instead of burning it down while I was gone. Maybe I'm alive because I helped you."

"I'm still sorry." Rhiana gave her a quick squeeze. "Maybe in Glenraven you'll find something better than what you had. You'll find friends there who will stand beside you instead of running away at the first sign of trouble. I'm your friend. Tik is your friend. You already have more there than you have here."

"Maybe I do." She turned away. "But I was happy with what I had."

She stared at the wall for a moment. She could do nothing

to bring back what she'd lost. It was gone, and she didn't have the time to mourn it. She and Rhiana still had to find the gate that would take them to Glenraven; they still had to deal with Callion and Val and the Watchers. She couldn't say her personal problems were insignificant next to the problems she and Rhiana faced together, but they couldn't take priority.

"So how do we locate this gate?"

Callion said, "You're going to have to speak it into existence. It should manifest where you call it. Just see it in your head and touch your finger to the place where you want it to be."

Rhiana said, "I think I can do that. I know what a gate is supposed to look like—I should be able to bring one to me. And I've thought of the place I know most perfectly. I am almost sure I can take us there safely, even though I won't have an anchor and won't be able to see what I'm doing."

"The magic-blindness from the blast hasn't worn off yet?" Kate asked.

"No. I'm afraid perhaps it's permanent."

"You might be right. It hasn't worn off for me either," Callion said. "That was a fearsome blast you loosed."

Tik started to say something, then chuffed and shook his head.

"What, Tik?" Kate asked.

"I confess myself surprised that you would use a weapon that would hurt you as much as it hurt your enemy."

Kate said, "Think of it as leveling the playing field."

"Your method seems to have worked. Now everyone is blind."

"Is that right, Val?" Rhiana asked. "Are you magic-blind, too?"

Val said nothing.

Kate turned to Tik. "We'll still get you home," she said softly. "We'll make sure you don't have to suffer for their treachery."

Rhiana said, "Let's not wait any longer. I can picture the place now, Kate. I have it in my mind. If you can find your magic and pass it to me as you did when we healed Tik, I'll bring us that gate."

Kate dug deep inside herself and found the part of her that was still strong and determined, even after the latest disaster. She used that core to reach out and bring in the power Rhiana needed. When she made it as real to herself as she could, she took Rhiana's hand.

Rhiana stood like a marble statue, her chin lifted, her eyes closed, not even seeming to breathe. The air around her began to waver in a circle that grew large enough for the biggest of them to step through. The circle glowed, the light becoming brighter and stronger, and finally she opened her eyes and reached out a finger, and a dark circle appeared in the center of the brightness; it expanded outward until only a rim of brilliant white light glowed like a ring of fire around the fathomless black of the tunnel into *otherwhere.*

"You did it," Callion said. "You have some promise as a wizard, girl. Some real promise."

Rhiana looked grim. "Quickly, into the gate. Tik, you'll have to carry Val. I'll carry Callion—he's the lightest. Kate, you're going to have to get Errga's body."

"I can do it."

"Don't let go of your line to the magic," she added. "Or we'll lose my destination, and end up somewhere else or nowhere at all."

"I won't let go."

Tik, carrying Val, stepped in first. Rhiana struggled, but managed to drape the Aregen over her shoulder; she stepped into the blackness, too. Kate grabbed the cooler full of magical bombs and shoved those in, then took one end of the bloody sheet that covered Errga and dragged it behind her. She heard voices shouting "Hurry! Hurry!" though she could not see anyone inside of the tunnel.

Errga's body was heavy—much heavier than she'd expected. She braced her legs and leaned backward to get the sheet sliding across the tiles.

The corpse finally slid well, she was at the mouth of the tunnel, and then she saw the paper bag sitting against the wall, looking like nothing important. "Shit!" She jumped out of the way of the tunnel, got behind Errga, shoved his corpse into the mouth of the gate, and ran back for the bag. The circle of light began to waver as her hands clutched the rough brown paper. She turned again, ran back, still hearing the calls of "Hurry, hurry!" but fainter, and jumped into the darkness, wondering as she did if she would ever find the other side.

The walls around her billowed. She couldn't see anyone—the inside of the weird gate glowed with a crawling, pearlescent light that only emphasized the instability of her surroundings. She gripped the bag tighter. The sensation of forward motion mixed with an absence of gravity and the spinning walls around her to create in her the certainty that she was not moving forward at all, but was falling downward from a terrible height and at a hellish speed. She bit her lip to keep from crying out and tasted the hot metallic spurt of her own blood.

Then a circle of black raced toward her, and in it she could make out unevennesses in darkness that she hoped indicated Tik and Rhiana ahead of her. Without warning the blackness simultaneously enveloped her and spit her out, and she fell forward, disoriented, into the center of a room full of staring people.

Thirty-eight

"Rhiana!"

"Mother!"

"Lady Smeachwykke!"

"Oh, godsall, you're not dead nor tortured nor locked up in a prison!"

Rhiana sagged from Callion's weight; her seneschal rose from his place at table, rushed to her side, and relieved her of the burden of the Aregen.

"No," she said. "I'm not dead, but I've done much and seen much, and I bring us both friends and enemies."

Tik stood at her side with Val in a crumpled heap at his feet. The cooler full of bombs popped out of the gate, and an instant later, the body of the warrag, wrapped in its blood-smeared sheet but still unmistakably a corpse. A moment later, Kate appeared, stumbling, looking pale and sick in the glow of the firelight, hanging on to the paper bag with both hands.

Rhiana realized what she held and for a moment she felt

as sick as Kate looked. They'd almost left without the Watchers.

"I brought them," Kate said. Then she seemed to really see her surroundings for the first time. Her eyes grew round and her mouth dropped open as she looked upward at the corbelled vaults and stone pillars of the great hall. She turned slowly, her eyes glancing from the harlequin windows pierced by a thousand spears of the long light of early morning; to the long trestle tables at which the great and near-great of Ruddy Smeachwykke had been, until moments earlier, breaking bread; to the huge stone fireplaces at either end of the hall, in which fires burned brightly.

Rhiana, having seen Kate's world, understood how different her own looked. "This is the great hall of my castle, Smeachwykke, in the town of Ruddy Smeachwykke," Rhiana said. "This is my home."

Kate nodded, saying nothing. She'd begun studying the people; from time to time she looked down at her own plain clothes with an expression close to dismay.

Rhiana had no more time to worry about Kate, though. She turned to her seneschal, Cowen, and said, "The Aregen is Callion, who stole the Watchers and forced the Rift to stay open, and who tried to enslave the Watchmistress before she took oath. The Kin is Val Peloral, the son and heir of Lorus Peloral, with whom I was treating for land on the day we were forced by an attack of Rift-monsters to flee into the Machine World."

The murmur of amazement from the eighty or so assembled nobles, merchants, craftsmen, family members, and sundry entertainers drowned her out for a moment. She heard awed whispers about the Machine World, and about Callion.

She raised her voice, and the murmurs died. "Both the Aregen and the Kin are traitors. They must be held in the tower until they can be tried by the Watchmistress and the council. The dagreth needs a wizard with better skills than mine to tend to the eye he lost today. The noble warrag, whose name was Errga, had family, and someone must find them and tell them that he died in the taking of Callion. They must be permitted audience at the trial, so that they can ask for a sentence that will satisfy them. Kate Beacham is human, from the same town as our Watchmistress, though I gather they did not know each other well, and she has sacrificed everything she had to help us. Please give her a good room, find her some clothing, take her some food, and let her rest."

She turned to Kate to see if that would be acceptable to her. "You'll be all right alone for a while?"

"I'll be fine. I think being alone will be the best thing for me," Kate said. "This is . . . just a little too much."

"I know," Rhiana told her. "Then I will take care of the things that have gone undone in my absence, and I will see you in the morning."

Kate nodded.

Cowen waved over one of the serving girls to take Kate to a room, and got guards and the town's chief wizard, Harch, who almost always availed himself of the castle's table, and so was conveniently at hand, to take Val and Callion up to the tower.

Rhiana had said nothing about the Watchers. She left them in Kate's care, for she knew she could trust Kate not to open the decanter, and she didn't know for sure that anyone else would not be curious enough or stupid enough to do just that. When the Watchmistress and the members of the council arrived, Rhiana could have Kate hand the bottle over to them, and they could throw it through the Rift and be done with it.

Her son came to her side, already taller by half a hand than she was, and he had been that much shorter the last time she saw him. He hugged her and she wrapped her arms around his waist tightly. "Cowen came for me," he said. "He said you were missing and that we had to presume you were dead, and that I would be seated as Lord Smeachwykke until we found the truth . . . if we ever did."

"I'm sorry," Rhiana said. "I'm sorry I could not come to you sooner, but I had no choice. I was drawn into the Machine World by a spell and could not return until I fulfilled the conditions of the spell."

"I don't care how long you were gone," Tabin said. "I'm just glad you're alive. Every day when I got up, I told myself that would be the day you came home. And every night as I was falling asleep, I prayed that since you hadn't been able to come home that day, you would come home the next."

"And here I am," she said, hugging him. Thirteen years old, and he looked so much like Haddis. Pale-haired and gray-eyed, he had the look and carriage of a hunting hawk, except with her. She could see in him the gentleness and the compassion that he kept secret from everyone else. "So have you been invested yet?"

"Cowen wanted to wait. He kept saying he couldn't believe you were really dead, and that if we just waited a little longer, we might save ourselves the trouble."

Rhiana smiled. That was Cowen—as long as he didn't take the

final steps to any unpleasant thing, he could keep it from being real. He hadn't been avoiding nuisance or work—he'd been trying to make her alive instead of dead. This time, of course, he'd been right.

Two healers had been brought in from their cottage at the foot of the castle. They were still both panting a little from their run as Rhiana's messenger girl led them to Tik. One of them, a plump old biddy named Daes, clucked over Rhiana's clumsy work, the other, Oluen, skinnier and taller and ferretlike, elbowed Daes and murmured something under her breath that made Rhiana think she had reminded Daes the lady wasn't to be criticized for her ineptitude. Rhiana turned away so that they could work in private. She deserved criticism. The work she'd done on Tik had been hideous.

Another of the serving girls, this one the interned daughter of Lord Dirry, trotted up to her. Ladies didn't trot while in the great hall, but Rhiana was in no mood for teaching or correction. "What is it, Cathenn?"

"I've put out a day dress for you, Lady Smeachwykke," she said. And some slippers, and a good overdress."

Rhiana looked down at her sneakers and jeans and plain shirt of soft, alien cotton, and said, "I'll just wear this for a while. I don't really have time yet to bother with redressing. But thank you. I'll go to my chambers once I've done the few things that simply won't wait."

Cathenn ducked her head and bent a knee in the sloppiest curtsey Rhiana had seen in years. She winced and stalked off to find Harch, to see if he could summon the Watchmistress and the council to Ruddy Smeachwykke, to save her the trouble and danger of transporting her prisoners overland.

Thirty-nine

Callion, propped against a stone wall away from the blinding sunlight pouring through the barred tower window, looked at the Kin who curled up in the straw in the cell next to his.

"You're an idiot," he said. "You're a damned fool. I waited for you in my office chair, sleeping—at least pretending to sleep— and all you had to do was come in quietly and capture me. I left the doors unlocked, I trapped the Devourers inside of a bottle so that one of your people could safely and conveniently carry them. All you had to do was come through that door."

Val lay still, his eyes partly open, his face expressionless.

"But you had to make a huge scene. Had to let the dagreth and the warrag come through my front door like vice cops on a drug raid, had to put a spell on the shotgun so that it exploded and killed the warrag and tore up the dagreth and blew shrapnel into *me*. You and I could have walked in here—*walked* in—you unsuspected by anyone and me all humble and repentant and the fucking Watchmistress and all her cronies and those bitches that dragged us in

241

here would have been scraps of flesh and blood on the cobblestones before anyone realized anything. We could have overthrown Glenraven in two days, you and me and your friends."

The Kin lord rolled over, turning his back on the Aregen.

"Oh, yes. Just ignore me. But who is going to release the Devourers now, eh? Who is going to get the two of us out of these damned bindings before they burn us or behead us or kill us in whatever other manner they plan? Who is going to tell your friends to be ready, that we're here? Answer me that."

The Kin sighed.

"I thought you were clever. Cunning. I thought I could work with you. But you're a fool, and I'm a worse fool for not seeing it the first time you called me." Callion glared at the ridiculous loops of yellow nylon rope—loops that kept his arms and legs paralyzed and left him helpless to do anything.

Furious as he was, he aimed his anger at himself much more than at the Kin. He'd gotten the fate he deserved for being stupid enough to deal with a traitor.

Forty

Kate stood on the balcony outside of her room, listening to the midday noises of this world displaced in time. A blacksmith hammered metal at his forge; soldiers drilled with swords to the clash of steel and the bellowing voice of a sergeant; rich male voices sang an *a cappella* melody in complex counterpoint; a woman shouted imprecations and demands at a boy who hadn't completed a chore and who had evidently been distracted by something more amusing; wooden wheels rattled over cobblestones and shod hooves clanged and clattered; bells rang, water rushed.

In the cold air she could smell wood fires and horses and cattle, cooking meat and coming snow. Women in leather tunics and coarse homespun shirts and dark woven pants trudged by carrying bags, and men similarly dressed rode horses across a stone-paved courtyard just visible from her balcony. Every scent, every sound, every sight, told her how far she was from home.

Her home was not another country, reachable by ship or

horseback or car or plane; her home was another world, and it lay far behind her, and she didn't know if she would ever go back, or if she could.

Above the far wall of the castle she could see the peaks of mountains, white with snow, black stone showing through like night through a torn linen curtain. The sunshine, so brilliant earlier, had vanished beneath the leading edge of tight-packed gray clouds, and the workers below her had begun moving faster as they noticed the threat in the sky. She pulled the fur-lined velvet cloak more tightly around her shoulders, but a sharp-toothed rising wind bit through the cloth and fur and whistled its song of snow. At last the cold got to be too much, and Kate moved inside, shoved the mullioned glass doors closed, and put a few more logs on the fire.

The fire made the room less forbidding. The warm dancing light, gold and red, brought the huge canopy bed with its heavy damask draperies closer, made it seem smaller; the gray, stone walls shone ruddy and warm. She pulled a chair closer to the fire, lifted her full-length skirt a bit, and settled into it.

The girl had been in twice to bring her food, once to bring her clothes, once to see if she wished to have company or visit with anyone. Kate wanted no company but her own; she wanted only the silence, because only with silence could she reshape herself, settle into this world that wasn't hers. Only if left alone for a time could she sort out all the hard-edged differences in place and custom that shouted at her from the balcony; those voices of strangeness and change would be muted if mixed in with the voices of people, because people added an element of sameness, of comprehensibility, to any alien setting.

She wanted to know the differences first, so that she didn't crash through them unwittingly. She would discover the samenesses later, and appreciate them when she found them.

She turned at the sound of a knock at her door. Tik peered in, two-eyed again, his face still lightly scarred but without the raw red ridges and ugly mismatched creases it had borne the day before. He grinned at her, flashing huge eyeteeth and knife-edged molars, and said, "Now would be the perfect time for a beer, wouldn't it?"

She laughed. "It would, in fact."

"So I brought us some." He showed her a hogshead cask, wood-bunged, and two heavy wooden mugs. "May I come in."

"I have a place by the fire just for you."

She discovered, to her surprise, that she didn't crave solitude as much as she'd thought.

Tik pried the bung out with two claws, stuck a metal tap in, and tipped the keg on its side. He filled her glass first, then his. She couldn't judge the color of the beer once it was inside her mug, but the liquid that poured out of the cask, even backlit by the fire, looked as red-brown as walnut dye. She lifted the mug, sipped, and murmured, "Holy Pete!"

"Stronger than your beer, isn't it?"

"Strong enough to walk to the bar on its own—and pick a fight when it got there."

"It's Kirchmuen, harvest beer. I never had it until the start of the Peace. The Machnan brew it—do a good standup job of it, too."

Kate, longing for ripe hard cheese and crackers to cut the taste, nodded. "Standup, for sure."

Tik settled onto the floor across from her chair and leaned against the raised hearth. His red braid gleamed like burnished copper in the firelight and gold glimmered in the flowing folds of his robe, a full, heavy winter garment of glorious sapphire blue. "You've been kind to me," he said. "Truly kind and never condescending. I like you. You're a good woman, and brave, and you deserve better than you got in your world."

She didn't know what to say. She smiled at him, feeling foolish and awkward. "You're kind to say so."

"Bullshit, to borrow your phrase. I'm only stating facts. I'll state another fact, Kate. You don't want to be here. Glenraven isn't the Machine World and it can't ever be. For all your world's faults—and it had many of them—it was a better place than this. Safer. Saner. And you had a place in it."

"Trying to tell me I ought to go home, Tik?"

"In a way. I'm telling you that the life you'll have here will be dirty and hard and short, or else marked by privilege and the hatred of the people beneath you. You're a hero in this world. They'll give you a title and a castle and people to do what you tell them to, but there isn't a one of them who won't know you're magic-blind, crippled, nearly as helpless as the Watchmistress from your world who hasn't any magic at all."

"I was under the impression that everyone loved the Watchmistress."

"You were wrong. As many despise her as love her. She's an outsider, and Glenraven is not a world that welcomes outsiders with a cheer and a grand ball."

Kate nodded. "I know about being an outsider. I spent a lot of my life that way. Sometimes people will come to accept the outsiders among them."

"Sometimes they don't."

Kate took another sip of the bitter beer. It warmed her on its way down, but even after half a mug she found it overpowering. She said, "You don't like her much, do you?"

Tik's small dark eyes glittered, and his long muzzle dropped open in surprise. "Who?"

"The Watchmistress."

He laughed, his laughter a booming growl that rattled the tiny panes of glass. "I don't know her. I'm only Tik, the dagreth. I'm not someone who meets a Watchmistress or sits in court or leads a band of loyal followers. I'm not even of the Three Peoples— the Aregen, the Kin, and the Machnan. I'm Kin-hera, the Lesser People, sometimes not even people at all." His close-mouthed smile and the backward flicking of his ears showed a bitterness about his state that his words belied. "The warrags, the tesbits, the dagreths, the stone-eaters, the gorrins; in our lives we'll never be elevated enough to speak to a Watchmistress."

"But that didn't answer my question. You don't like her, do you?"

The dagreth shrugged. "I don't like what I hear of her, but my opinion is a thing of no importance. She changes established custom just to make change, and looks at this world as a defective version of the Machine World, one that won't be better—won't be good—until it mimics every excess and sin the Machine World claims." He chuffed. "And obviously I have my opinions, and just as obviously they matter not a whit to anyone but me."

"You don't think I'd like it here."

"Bluntly . . . no." He watched her over the rim of his mug, drew a long, loud swallow, and set the mug on the hearth beside him. "Because of what I am, I'm an outsider to all but my own sort of people. But hundreds of my own sort of people live near my hut, and I have dozens of eligible mates in my own stretch of forest. You'll be alone, more alone even than Jayjay Bennington, the Watchmistress, because she mated across species to some Alfkindir lordling so desperate for sex that he was willing to bear the shame of his cross-bred union for the rest of his life. You might think the Machnan are close enough to your sort that you could marry and be accepted, but they know you aren't Machnan and they will never forget that fact."

Kate looked at his earnest, kind face, and sighed. "I've thought about those things, Tik. I have. I don't want to be Lady anything or wear these long heavy dresses or live by candlelight or feel rich because I own a single book. I *like* electricity. I like being able to go to a bookstore and pick up ten paperbacks over the weekend and settle back on my couch and not do a damn thing from Friday night to Monday morning but read, and watch the New York Rangers hit a puck around on the ice."

"Then you know how hard it would be for you here."

"I do know. Of course I know. But I don't have anything left back there."

"You have more back there than you could ever have here, Rhiana's facile promises of friendships and futures notwithstanding."

"I'll probably go back."

"I have friends who can help you, Kate. Friends who could form a gate for you, if you could only picture the place you wanted to go."

She nodded. "Once the Watchmistress has tried Callion and Val and I've seen the Rift closed, I'm pretty sure I'll go back. When I came here I wasn't planning on staying. I just wanted to get away for a while from a place and people who would destroy everything I owned because I didn't see the world or religion the way they did."

"Once the trial is over?" Tik shook his head. "No."

"Yeah. I promised Rhiana I would stay for that, to give what little testimony I have to offer."

Tik still shook his head. He mumbled something, and Kate thought, but couldn't be certain, that he'd said, "That will be too late."

"What?" she asked.

"Merely thinking about the schedules of my friends, and how they will mesh with your plans. I'm not sure that they will if you don't act decisively."

"Decisively. Mmmm. Yes. I've spent a great deal of time lately acting decisively, and I can't say I like where it's gotten me. But never mind. My problems are just that—mine. Not something to whine to a friend about." Kate held out her mug. "Pour me another one, would you?"

The second mug was as bitter as the first. Dark and bitter. Much like her life. Kate thought if she drank the cask dry, the bitterness would never leave and never lessen.

Forty-one

R hiana dreamed of the walking dead, and woke in darkness
to the fact that the one love she had known in her life would
face death on her word. He'd killed the warrag, he'd nearly killed
the dagreth, and he'd intended the deaths of the Watchmistress,
the council, and her. Her guards had informed her of Callion's
one-sided rants against Val as they lay in their cells, and she saw
in their stories the anger of a man who had been caught and who
regretted only that he had been caught. She had no doubt that
Val Peloral, Lord Faldan, had intended evil against her and against
her world.

Which was not to say that she found his behavior entirely clear.
The evil he'd done—the evil he'd intended—those were clear
enough. But his gentleness to her, his kindness, his whispered
confession of love: those things she did not understand. He'd given
her reason to love him, and she had loved him. And as deeply
as she looked into the possible outcomes of his actions, and as
hard as she tried to find some material benefit he might hope

to gain by winning her love, she kept coming up against the fact that if his plan had been to destroy her, he gained nothing by having her love him first.

She slipped out of the bed and put on her bed shoes and a heavy robe—it had snowed between the time she went to bed and the time she woke, and from the sounds of the wind through the cracks between the windows and the frames, and the muffled closeness of the night sounds outside and a faint, gentle hissing that seemed to come from everywhere and nowhere, she thought it snowed still. The fire in her hearth had burned down to nothing; the air in the room beyond her closed bed drapes was ice, and the floor through the thin soles of her bed shoes was just as cold. She saw nothing but blackness and could hear no sounds of life above the blanketing quiet of the storm; she could as easily have been the only person in the universe as the just-returned lady of a busy, crowded castle. However, during her brief, restless sleep, her magic-sight had returned. With her eyes closed she could once again see the bright lines of magic that crisscrossed her world and the swirling, eddying currents through Ruddy Smeachwykke and the castle.

She opened her eyes to the darkness of the night, darkness that mirrored and amplified her bleakness of spirit. The soul suffered more in darkness and cold than in bright light and warmth, she thought. In bright daylight she would have felt no doubts about Val. She would have been able to see him as a traitor without also seeing him as the man she had briefly loved. In daylight she could have taken satisfaction in knowing she had brought him to justice. But she had no daylight to help her see reason, and no warm spring day to ease the hurt in her heart.

She tucked her robe more tightly about her and took her doubts and her rationalizations out her door and down the long corridor and through the passageways that led to the tower, and up the staircase that circled around the tower's wall, past the bursts of snow that blasted through the arrow slits and through the slick drifts on the stairs—worrying about the leather soles of her shoes and the dragging hem of her robe and how careful she would have to be not to fall—and stormed into the guards' chamber, where in the shocked expressions of the guards she got her first taste of what a sight she must be, with her hair disheveled and her eyes wild and her anger burning in her cheeks.

"Bring the Peloral to the audience chamber immediately," she said. Her voice came out harsh and angry and colder than the night. She saw the questions in the guards' eyes, but she gave no welcome to them. The guards nodded and called down to the marching guard below to send up a contingent to escort a prisoner to audience. Rhiana crept back down the stairs, wondering what possessed her, but neither her doubts nor her rationalizations were sufficient to prevent her from sending another servant to roust Harch out of his warm bed below his wizard's bell to attend her.

The impromptu inquest assembled—Val pale and crumpled, kneeling on the floor between six guards, his arms and legs unmoving, his clothing stained and soiled; Rhiana in bed gown and dressing gown and bed shoes and with her hair unbound, and in all of Glenraven no one but her husband had ever seen her so; Harch bleary-eyed and foul-tempered at being dragged through the yard and the snowstorm at the hour of the dead on some damn-fool errand; and the half-dozen guards themselves, straight-backed and blank-faced in their mail coats and red-and-gray surcoats, whose emotionless faces told Rhiana they thought they saw proof that their lady, recently returned from the exiles' hell of the Machine World, had brought madness with her. Rhiana glared at all of them. Her anger at herself, for acting on emotion in a moment when she knew she needed to be logical, spread to become anger toward the witnesses of her stupidity.

Rhiana told Harch, "Watch the Peloral with magic-sight, and if he makes any move to escape or to attack, kill him." Harch nodded. Rhiana told the guards, "Watch him with eyes and ears, and look for any sort of trick from him, and if he tries to escape or attack, kill him."

She stared down at Val. "You're doubly damned, and with even a single wrong move your heart will have a hole in it bigger than the one in mine." She saw him wince. "I just want to be sure you understand."

He nodded.

Then she knelt by Val's feet and rested her hands on the bindings around his ankles and murmured "K-Mart" so softly no one could hear her. The bindings fell away from his legs and he groaned. She released his hands and arms next, and picked up the loops of rope and dropped them in her audience chair.

She waited while he struggled to rub life back into his arms and legs, crawling and stumbling around. When he was finally able to stand, she said, "Face me, Val Peloral, Lord Faldan, son of Kinlord Faldan of the Faldan Wood."

He stood and looked down at her, and she saw anger in his

eyes. "You've already accused me of a crime I couldn't commit, and have left me without food or water and forced me to lie in my own filth, unable even to move myself to the chamberpot. Have you thought of some further humiliation to heap upon me, that makes you decide to drag me out of my snow-soaked, flea-infested, piss-drenched straw pile in the middle of stinking, bitter night?"

She ached with his ache. She hated herself for doing what she'd done to him, and she hated herself for being weak and doubting actions she knew were right, and she hated him for being someone other than the man she'd thought he was. She said, "The hour is for my convenience, not yours. This is an inquest. I want to know the facts, Val. I want to know why you did what you did. You conspired with Callion, you intended to kill the Watchmistress, the council . . . me . . ." For just an instant tears burned in her eyes and a lump in her throat kept her from speaking. But she blinked the tears away, swallowed, and forced herself to go on. "Maybe I can understand why you did those things—I know there are people who don't support Jayjay Bennington, who don't like the idea of a human as Watchmistress. I know politics; I'm a political creature, too." She frowned, stared into his eyes, nibbled at the corner of her lip. "We're on different sides of a political fence, and while you're going to end up dying for your cause, I can understand that you *have* a cause." She took a deep breath and moved a step closer to him before she realized that she'd done it. She stiffened, betrayed by the body that still longed for his touch, and said, "But why the rest, Val? Why the pretense of . . ." She realized the guards stood almost on tiptoe, leaning forward to hear what she was saying. She realized how much she could lose if they knew, if anyone found out, that she had once loved a Kin. "Of other things," she said. "Of friendship. Why did you pretend to be a friend?"

His expression softened for just an instant, and he murmured, "Pretend?" But that moment of tenderness passed, and his eyes narrowed and his lips thinned. "Are you finished?"

"Finished?"

"Finished with this charade. You've planned this very well, I confess. I've had time to think while I lay in my pile of straw, while I listened to your cohort spin his tale of blame to the listening guards. It was very clever. Callion blames me for his capture, you blame me for the death of Errga and the injury of Tik, and he confesses his intent to kill the Watchmistress and implicates me in the process, and there you are. You can get the Watchmistress here to try me on false charges and when she arrives you release Callion and the two of you set the Watchers on all of us. Everyone is dead who could blame you, Callion names you Watchmistress and as his puppet you remake this world to fit his vision of it."

Rhiana stepped back, staring in disbelief at the madman in front of her. "What? You accuse *me?*"

"You deny it?"

"Of course I deny it. *You* blew up the gun that Tik held. I felt the burst of magic as it exploded."

"If you felt it, it was because you created it, Lady Smeach-wykke." His voice was hard and coarse as broken stones. "*I have no magic!*"

"Then how did you make the gun explode?"

"I *didn't* make the gun explode."

"But you did. I saw it happen."

"I saw it happen, too, but I didn't *make* it happen. You must have."

"I didn't!"

"Lady Smeachwykke," Harch said, tapping her shoulder, "may I have a word with you in private?"

She turned and screeched at him, "Right *now?!*"

He backed up and blinked at her, eyes owlishly round with surprise. "Now would be best."

Rhiana turned back to the guards. "Watch him!" She stalked away from them to the far corner of the chamber, where the heavy drapes and tapestries would muffle the sound of their voices. "*What?*"

The wizard said, "I thought it best to tell you before this went any further. I have been watching him as you asked me to, with magical sight. Also, very carefully and on my own initiative I was doing more than just watching him, you know . . . sort of testing, I suppose you could say . . . though not taking any chances of course, because one doesn't want to get caught at that sort of thing . . . besides which I'm afraid it's highly unethical and under other circumstances I would never have even considered it, especially when you didn't expressly ask me to but I was considering Lord Faldan's importance to Ruddy Smeachw—"

"GET TO THE POINT!"

"Yes. Ah. He, ah, has no magic, Lady. None at all. The stones in your walls have more magic than he does."

"He's *tricked* you, you ass! Can't you see that? He's a wizard so powerful he can hide his magic!"

"Not from me, he can't." Harch crossed his arms over his chest and shook his head. I'm sorry, dear, but the wizard doesn't exist who can hide his magic from someone of my skill."

"Then maybe you aren't as skillful as you think."

Harch raised his eyebrows and tipped his head to one side. "Maybe you're wrong. Have you, ah, considered that?"

"Endlessly. And wished I were, too. But there isn't any other explanation for what happened." She pointed in the direction of the tower. "And don't forget Callion, who without torture, without bribery, without any provocation at all, freely names the lying bastard as his conspirator."

Harch said, "There are other explanations, Rhiana. Quite a lot of them, actually. And explanations that fit the facts better than this one."

"Are there? Many, you say? So give them to me."

"Well, ah . . . Lord Faldan's explanation would work. I couldn't believe it, of course—you in collaboration with Callion—though certainly you've shown enough ambition in the past that it wouldn't be entirely impossible—" He looked at her face, realized what he was saying and to whom he was saying it, cleared his throat, and moved on. "Or the human, Kate, could have been hiding from you the fact that she wasn't magic-blind. She could have been collaborating with the Aregen. Or, as another possibility, the Aregen could have acted alone. This would make more sense to me than any of the other explanations, though of course there are points in any of the three that don't sit well."

"*All* the facts fit the Peloral." She glared at Val.

"Except, lady, that he could not have done what you accuse him of doing. He has no magic at all. None." Harch's expression became thoughtful. "I could prove this to you."

"How?"

"I could kill him for you . . . slowly, with just a baby spell . . . in such a way that if he had the least magical ability, he could save himself."

"He'd rather die than prove me right."

"I beg to differ. At some point in the process, if he can, he will do whatever he is able to save himself. If he is what you say he is, he gains nothing by being a martyr."

"So show me."

"You seem unconcerned by the possibility that when we're finished you'll have an innocent dead man lying on your floor."

"Errga was innocent, and now he's dead. Tik was innocent, and
was maimed, and it's only through luck that he isn't dead. I *know*
I won't have an innocent dead man on my floor."

"Very well. We'll go find out right now."

Rhiana went back to face Val; this time she settled herself in
her audience chair. "Harch has proposed a little test to prove your
innocence. It seems that he believes you . . . rather, that he believes
you when you say you didn't cause the gun to explode. I'm willing to concede that if you didn't make the gun explode, the rest
of your claim of innocence is true, too."

He watched her, waiting.

"The test may be . . . unpleasant . . . but I see no other way
to determine the truth. I wouldn't want to do anything to you
without your permission, so you can refuse, and I'll tell the Watchmistress what I know now, and she can determine your guilt. Or
if you would rather confess, we can save a great deal of time.
For confession right now, I would be willing to offer you exile
to the Machine World rather than death."

"I can see in your eyes that you have your heart set on torture. So torture me. I'm innocent."

"Not torture at all," Harch said. "Simply a little test."

"Then test me." Val glared from Harch to Rhiana. "You're so
sure you're right, just do it."

"I've already begun."

Rhiana felt a flow of magic so tiny that it took her an instant
to realize it was the test Harch proposed. She closed her eyes.
With her magic-sight she could see a barrier of nothingness thinner
than the thinnest spider's silk beginning to cover Val's nose and
mouth, blocking them from the air beyond. The barrier was a
soap bubble, so ludicrously fragile a stray magical impulse would
destroy it. The merest nothing, a magical blink, would clear it
away.

She waited, eyes closed. The barrier remained. She opened her
eyes. Val clutched at his throat, clawing, trying to pull in air by
the simple mechanical processes of his lungs. He made a good
show of it. She waited. Her facts all fit, she knew what she had
seen and what she had felt, and she now realized that her wizard was right. No man, capable of clearing away that fragile
nothing that stood between him and death, would fail to save
his own life. A clever man, though, would hold out as long as

he dared, hoping for sympathy and a reprieve that would make him seem innocent.

She continued to wait, forcing herself to look calm while anxiety gnawed at her from inside. His acting seemed so real. Val's skin began to turn dusky, and his eyes bulged. She thought, *Breathe, damn you. Breathe. I don't want to watch you suffer. I just want the truth.* "Breathe. Just do it. Don't be so stubborn." She realized when her guards looked at her, startled, that she had spoken aloud.

His lips formed words, but airless, made no sounds.

She frowned. "What?"

Val repeated himself: *You . . . mock . . . me.*

I seek the truth, she thought. He dropped to one knee. His blue lips stretched back in an anguished, silent scream; his eyes pleaded, terrified; his hands clawed at his throat and tore at his clothes.

Stop it, she told him in her thoughts. *Gods' damn you, stop it. Save yourself.*

She turned to Harch, wanting to see in his face determination, purpose, a sense that he knew he worked to expose the truth, a sense that he'd felt Val's guilt. Instead she saw in Harch's eyes pain, and on his cheeks tears, and on his face anguish and terrible remorse.

She heard a thud, and turned to see Val lying at her feet, unconscious or dead.

She didn't think. She dropped to his side and broke Harch's bubble herself. She heard the ragged, strangling gasp of his first breath, and stared at him, wondering, bewildered. He didn't move, didn't wake up and smirk at her—he hadn't saved himself.

Instead, he'd lost consciousness, and magic was a thing utterly dependent on conscious intent. The moment that he dropped to the floor was the moment he could no longer have broken the bubble, no matter how mighty a wizard he might have been. No real wizard would have ever let himself reach that point.

Val would have died, and she would have killed him. The truth was as simple and plain as that. Magically, he wasn't capable of even a blink. He was innocent. He hadn't caused the gun to explode, he hadn't killed anyone, he hadn't schemed against the Watchmistress. No matter what the facts seemed to have been, Rhiana had been wrong.

She stroked his hair and whispered, "I'm so sorry. I was wrong. I'm so sorry," over and over. She was still saying it when he opened his eyes.

He looked up at her and shook his head slightly. "You didn't kill me," he murmured. "Why am I still alive?"

"I'm sorry," she told him again. "I was wrong."

"I know, but that isn't the point."

"The point? What do you mean, it isn't the point?"

"I know you were wrong. But you didn't kill me, and you seem to be truly sorry, and if I'm alive and you're sorry, then I must have been wrong as well." He sat up and rubbed his head. "And if we're both wrong, who killed Errga and wounded Tik? Kate? Callion?"

"One of the two must have. And Kate has the bottle with the Watchers in it."

"Kate. I can't see that. Callion must have acted on his own."

Rhiana said, "But he didn't. He couldn't have; and so Kate must have helped him. She isn't going anywhere, though. We could wait until morning, and take the Watchers from her before the trial starts." She shook her head. "But I don't want to leave this matter unresolved. I don't understand how Kate fits into this now, and I have to understand. Let's find her now."

"Lady Smeachwykke . . ." Val's expression was pained. "My apologies, but as long as the real culprit thinks you still hold me to blame, the plan, whatever it is, will remain unchanged. I could take the time needed to bathe and dress in other clothes than these."

She nodded. "The matter isn't life or death . . . yet. It will be come morning when the Watchmistress arrives. Very well, Lord Faldan. One of the guards will show you to the baths, and I'll have a girl bring you some clean clothing. Please hurry." She stared into his eyes, trying to see if the stiff, formal "Lady Smeachwykke" had been because people were listening or because he hated her. Probably because he hated her. She hated herself.

He rejoined her as she stood waiting in the servants' corridor with Harch and her captain of guards. Clean and dressed in a tunic and leather breeches loaned to him by one of the guards, he no longer looked beaten or lost. "I'm ready."

"Then let's find out what's going on."

Rhiana led them through the maze of passages and up two full flights of stairs to Kate's room, set off in a wing of the castle away from the noise and bustle common elsewhere. When Rhiana had first married Haddis, she had been young and lonely and burdened by obligations and duties and tremendous amounts of work, and she had lacked a quiet place or a quiet time from the moment the sun rose to the moment she pinched out the candles. But when she explored Smeachwykke, she'd discovered the far wing, used almost exclusively for visitors. And she had discovered the room she'd given Kate. She'd liked its prettiness and its comparative coziness. She'd liked the balcony and the view of the inner courtyard and the light that came through the windows and the intimate little fireplace and the tapestries that weren't more takes of blood and battles, but that showed women dancing in a meadow accompanied by minstrels, surrounded by children and birds and harts and flowers and beautiful trees and waterfalls and leaping fish. She didn't know who had once lived in the room, but whoever she'd been, she'd had a peaceful spirit.

Rhiana had thought Kate would appreciate the beauty of the room, and that perhaps its peacefulness would soothe away some of her hurt. Now she wondered if she had misplaced her kindness.

They reached the room at last. Harch's magical light illuminated Kate's door. Rhiana rapped on it. "Kate?" she called. "Wake up."

She waited a moment, expecting that after the time shift and everything else Kate had been through, she would need some time to wake. But when she'd waited and heard nothing, Rhiana rapped again, louder. "Kate! Wake up!"

Still nothing.

She frowned and tried the door. It was locked. She took the key ring from her waist and found the key that opened the doors in that hall, wondering at the same time how Kate had managed to lock it in the first place. After all, she'd had no key, and the door required one to lock as well as unlock it, from either side.

She opened the door and peeked inside. "Kate?"

The fire burned low. A tapped hogshead sat upright on the hearth, and two wooden mugs beside it. Two? Only one chair was pulled to the fireside. Harch's light moved into the room, illuminating all of it, and then Rhiana could see what she hadn't seen before. All of Kate's belongings from her backpack had been dumped in a pile on the floor. Someone had rummaged through them with little care. The wardrobe doors had been opened, too, and the clothes stored in it piled at the foot of the bed.

"What manner of madness is this?" Harch asked. Rhiana turned to see that he'd pulled back the heavy draperies on the canopy bed, and stood shaking his head at what he saw there.

Rhiana moved to his side as he summoned his wizard-light beneath the canopy. As she saw what he'd seen, the hairs on her arms stood up and her heart pounded and the air in the room seemed to become too thin.

Kate lay on the bed, sprawled atop the counterpane like a rag doll thrown by an angry child, her shirt ripped open and pulled inside out so that the sleeve cuffs, buttoned into place, kept it on her wrists. The twists of shirt fabric held both arms behind her back. She still wore her jeans and shoes, and the odd breast-binder favored in her world; her body faced the far wall.

"Is she dead?" Val stood behind Rhiana, looking over her into the bed.

"I don't know," Rhiana whispered.

Harch climbed onto the bed beside Kate and touched her shoulder, and Rhiana saw a current of magic run from his hand into her. "She isn't dead," he said after a moment, "but she's been deeply drugged. So deeply I could almost say she's been poisoned—and she's been spelled, too. A compulsion spell. . . ." He frowned and increased the amount of power he used, and Kate began to glow softly. "Extraordinary piece of work . . . truly extraordinary; certainly isn't the sort of thing I've seen before in that it doesn't seem to use the old forms; really a pretty spell, you know, as nicely done as a bit of good lace, all tight and twisted and knotted just so and patterned sweet as anything—I'm saying it's the work of a master even if it is just a little spell, because it's on so tight and hooked into so many—"

"What are you *talking* about?" Rhiana interrupted.

"Eh? Oh." Harch didn't look at Rhiana. "Just a minute, I almost have it . . . damn, it slipped . . . it's bound by a tie to the Rift, I *think* . . . and if . . . oh, yes, that will do it. . . ." He smiled up at Rhiana, triumphant. "There. No more spell. And I've undone as much of the drug effects as I could. She should wake now."

"Kate!" Rhiana yelled.

Kate jerked awake, tried to move her arms, thrashed with her shirt, rolled, saw the room full of strangers, shrieked and pulled her knees up toward her chest, and Rhiana grabbed Harch away before Kate could kick him into the middle of Holy Brodmert's Week, which she tried to do.

Rhiana heard fabric ripping and suddenly Kate's hands came free and she launched herself toward Harch, eyes focused on him; before she could grab and strangle him, which appeared to be her intent, Val jumped past Rhiana and grabbed her.

"Kate," he said, "wake up."

Kate growled. Not words but mad, crazed animal noises. Beast sounds.

Rhiana shouted, "Kate! Kate! It's us! Wake up!"

"Oh, dear," Harch said. "Lord Faldan, please hold her for me a moment. I didn't get it all."

"All?" Val said, but he hung on to Kate as she slammed her head back at his face and kicked his shins and jammed her heels into his insteps. "Ow!" His face twisted with pain and he grabbed her arms at the wrists, pulled them across her chest, and yanked her back against his chest. "Do it fast," he said, and grimaced again as she twisted her head around to try to bite him.

"Didn't get all the spell. One moment . . . just one moment . . ."

The back of Kate's head caught Val on the chin and Rhiana jumped in to try to help him steady her; Kate lifted both feet and kicked out at Rhiana, using Val as her brace. She caught Rhiana squarely in the middle of the chest, and Rhianna flew across the room and came up against the tapestry-covered wall with a thud. She lay stunned, trying to coax air back into her lungs, startled by the spinning white lights that suddenly filled the room. When her head cleared, she sat up; she realized had she flown only a bit further to the left, she would have crashed through the balcony doors and been slashed by shards of glass and perhaps thrown over the balcony to her death in the cobblestoned courtyard below.

Rhiana realized all sounds of struggle had died. She pulled herself to her feet and rejoined Val, Harch, and the guard. The guard had given his surcoat to Kate, who sat on the edge of the bed wrapped in the scarlet-and-gray, pale and wide-eyed with fright.

" . . . get you something to drink?" Harch was asking.

Kate shook her head vehemently. As Rhiana approached the bed, she looked up at her. "What happened to me?" she asked.

Rhiana shook her head. "I don't know. What do you remember?"

Kate frowned. "I don't . . . oh!" She clutched the sides of her head between her hands and began to rock back and forth. "Oh! It hurts."

Harch said, "Damn . . . still not all . . ." and touched Kate again.

When he pulled his hand from her shoulder, she put her hands down at her sides and said, "Better. Pain's gone. That was odd. That was . . . very odd . . ."

"What?"

"Oh. I was feeling so sorry for myself; terrible, really, and Tik came by with that barrel of beer, wanting to talk. It would have been great if we'd had a pizza to split between us—would have killed the taste of the beer. And he wanted me to leave here . . . to go home—not to Peters, you understand, but just to Earth . . . I mean the Machine World. He said he could arrange for one of his friends to make a gate for me, but I needed to do it before the Watch-mistress came . . ." She rubbed the sides of her head. "And I said, no, no, can't go back until after the trial and he said, 'but after the trial will be too late' and I said, 'I don't understand what you mean' or something like that, and he wouldn't tell me, but then something funny happened with the beer . . . Yes. The beer. I'd only had one and part of another, and he took my mug away from me and poured some more, and walked across the room to get some-thing to show me, and when he came back he handed me my mug, and showed me something so silly. So silly. Some sort of glowing stone. God, why can't I remember what he *showed* me?" She laughed.

"That's part of the spell," Harch said. "That amusement at what was happening . . . she's reliving the spell that was cast on her."

Kate's expression returned to its earlier seriousness. "And I drank my beer, and I changed my clothes so that I could go with Tik— I didn't want to go with Tik, but for a while there I felt that I had to, and I was fighting it pretty hard—but then I started getting so *sleepy* while I drank . . . I only had two beers . . . just two . . . and this is the really funny part. I remember as clear as anything that Tik said he could send me home another time after all, and he left, and as soon as he left a small, dark man with a scar across his face came in and ripped my shirt off and stole my gun—which I had tucked into the waistband of my jeans—and searched the room and stole the bottle with the Watchers in it."

"The bottle!" Rhiana gripped Val's arm.

"Her gun," Val said.

"And that's what's so funny," Kate said, not seeming to notice their reactions. "I remember it so clearly, but it didn't happen. The little man with the scar . . . I can see him but he wasn't really there. Tik did all of that. Took my gun. Took the bottle. And I can hear him saying, 'Even if you wouldn't go, at least now you'll be safe.' What did he mean by that? And why did he do that to me?"

Rhiana said, "Tik. It fits. It all fits, but how? And why? And . . ."

She looked from Val to Harch to the captain to Kate. "Tik had terrible injuries from that exploding shotgun. He lost an eye, his arm broke in several places. If he cast the spell that killed Errga, why was he so badly hurt?"

Val said, "Because he's brilliant, that's why."

"What?"

"Brilliant," Val insisted. "With his grievous injuries, you never once questioned his innocence. Neither did I. Neither did anyone. He killed Errga. He must have discovered that you knew there was a traitor, and by using a short, untraceable bolt of magic he exploded the gun he held, killing Errga and injuring himself. So he shifted the blame to me—I was the only person left who could be suspected. You locked me up with Callion, while he was left free to do what he needed to do: to whit, gather up Kate's gun and the Watchers in their bottle. And tomorrow Kate would have been up here, locked into the room and unable to get out because she didn't have the key. Maybe she would even have still been drugged into sleep, so that she couldn't attract any servants by pounding on the door or shouting from her balcony." He paused. "Meanwhile, Callion and I would be led to trial, Tik would appear as a spectator, holding the gun and the Watchers. He would . . . what . . . use the gun to force you to release Callion? Possibly. Then what? Give Callion the Watchers, Callion would release them, and everyone present would die."

Rhiana said, "He still has the Watchers. The Watchmistress will still be here by dawnbell with the council. The danger isn't behind us simply because we've found out the truth."

Kate had been listening. Now she said, "You can't allow him to be in the same place as the Watchmistress and the council. He was willing to lose an eye and suffer terrible pain to keep his plan alive. I think if he finds himself within reach of them with the Watchers in his possession, nothing will stop him from releasing them."

"But the full council will step through gates into our inner chamber at the sound of the dawnbell."

Kate shook her head. "You can't let that happen. But I think I know what you can do instead."

Forty-two

Dawn struggled to arrive, giving little notice of its presence beneath the bitter gray skies. More snow seemed imminent; the air was colder for being wet, and the clouds crowded close to the earth. In spite of Harch's intervention, Kate still felt compulsion clinging to her . . . a desperate desire to flee the castle, to flee Glenraven, to go back to her world and to fight anything that stood between her and home. Maybe, though, it was no longer the spell that filled her with such fear. Maybe at that moment the compulsion to flee came from inside of herself.

Dressed in the mail coat and cloth surcoat of Rhiana's guard, with a guard's cloak wrapped around her and with the deep hood pulled forward to hide her face, she stood in the snow with a few genuine guardsmen, waiting behind Rhiana while a dozen heavily armed soldiers brought out Callion and Val. Six of the soldiers carried Callion , still bound with Rhiana's spelled binders—between them. The other half dozen dragged Val.

Rhiana stood off to the side of the courtyard with her advisor and her wizard. Next to them stood a handful of grim-faced Kin, including the Kinlord, Val's father. Neither Rhiana's group nor the Kin group said anything; the silence felt both angry and dangerous, weighted with portents of an end to the tenuous peace Machnan and Kin had briefly enjoyed.

Tik burst out of a side door, saw Rhiana, and ran up to her. "What's going on?" he shouted. "I've been looking everywhere for you. Everything's going wrong—Kate told me last night that she wanted to go home and now I can't find her; I've been to the audience chamber looking for you and no one was there; now you're all outside in the cold when the Watchmistress and the council should be here any moment."

"The Watchmistress changed her plans," Rhiana said. "She and the council are meeting us at the Rift. She wants to see the Rift closed with her own eyes. Val's father has arrived to stand in Val's defense—he says he doesn't believe his son did the things we say he did. Kate found me earlier and told me she had to leave; she said it was urgent that she get back to her home. She seemed quite ill. Harch made a gate for her and now she's gone."

His eyes widened. "Kate gone? But you were going to have her testify."

"She said she couldn't. She seemed very confused—someone attacked her last night. An outsider."

"Ah. Then the search parties I passed were looking for her attacker?"

"More than an attacker. The man robbed Kate last night—stole her gun and the Watchers. She described the thief as a small man with a long, vivid scar across his face, with dark eyes and a twisted back that gives him a distinctive walk. I know no one in all of Ruddy Smeachwykke who matches his description, but I have every soldier I could spare searching for him."

"Won't that leave you shorthanded for the trials and sentencing?"

"Our main concern is with the Watchers, Tik," Rhiana said. "I have Callion and Val under control; if the thief releases the Watchers, however, that won't matter. The Watchers can devastate all of Glenraven."

"So you'll only have a light force at the Rift? That seems risky."

"I'm keeping my people where I need them." Rhiana glanced back at the castle. "If they can't find the thief within the building—and the guards report that no one arrived or left the castle last night, so I think he must still be in there—then they will widen their search to the village. We will find the man."

Tik nodded thoughtfully. "Of course. Where do you need me, my lady?"

"Since Kate is gone, you'll have to testify. You'll have to tell the Watchmistress about the injuries Val caused you, and about how he killed Errga, and you'll have to tell what you can about Callion. I would spare you facing off against Val's father, since I know he's your lord, but with Kate gone we have no one else."

Tik glanced at Val's father, and for an instant Kate could see hatred in his broad, friendly face. Then he said, "As you wish."

"I'm frightened, Tik." Rhiana looked up at the dagreth and rested one hand on his massive arm. "We have to find the Watchers. We can sentence Callion and Val, but without the Watchers, we merely trade one evil for another."

Rhiana lied well, Kate thought. As she presented her story to Tik, she made herself seem weak, poorly prepared to defend herself, and completely unsuspecting of Tik's role in the planned treason. In fact, she was nothing of the sort. Beneath her cloak she carried the spelled binders Val had worn, while a hundred armed troops waited by the Rift on the other side of the gate, ready to subdue Tik the instant he stepped out of the gate so that she could slip the binders on him. The search parties were a ruse created for two reasons: to make Tik think everyone believed the illusion he'd planted in Kate's mind, and to account for the hundred missing soldiers by making it look like they were searching the castle. Actually, the search parties consisted of nothing more than two separate groups of five soldiers each who crossed in front of Tik and behind him while the dagreth hurried through the castle.

Harch had a spell ready to throw around Tik just before they exited the gate so that the troops would be able to do their subduing without any bloodshed. No one underestimated the power of the dagreth—according to Rhiana they were deadlier than any twenty Machnan even without magical ability—but Kate thought the precautions they had taken to control him would be more than adequate. Even the Kin were in on the trick—they wanted to make Tik pay for using Val as his scapegoat.

The Watchmistress and the council, contacted with great difficulty in the middle of the night by messengers gated through to each of their homes, would not appear at the Rift until daybell.

By that time Tik and Callion would lie bound, helpless, and humbled; the Watchers would have vanished into the hell of the Rift; the spell that held the Rift open for the Watchers would have dissolved, and the Rift would slam shut.

Kate could claim the basic idea for the ruse; she, Rhiana, Harch, and the captain of the guard had worked out the actual details together. Kate had decided on a disguise because she didn't know why Tik had been trying so hard to get rid of her; she suspected her presence would somehow pose a significant threat to his plans, though she couldn't figure out how. So she wanted to be present, and if she weren't disguised, he would have to suspect something had gone wrong in his plans.

She still wished she had the pistol. She would have felt much more useful with that than what she did have. The magic bombs she wasn't sure would still work, and though the borrowed sword belted at her waist and the borrowed dagger sheathed at her hip looked impressive, she knew how to shoot a pistol. The only thing she knew about daggers was that underhand strikes were better than overhand ones; about swords she knew nothing.

It wouldn't matter. By preparing ahead, they had created a situation in which Tik would assume he had the advantage, both in weapons—because of the pistol, and in overall strength—with the Watchers. And by playing off his assumptions, they would strip all of his advantages from him.

From the castle and throughout the village, the bells began to ring. The castle carillon played a slow, mournful canon, the theme rung on the large bells and echoed with repetition and variation on the higher bells. Kate heard the bellringers in the village begin working their own variations on the music, so that for a few minutes, all the universe seemed steeped in the poignant, aching music.

"Canon for the Lost," Tik said.

Rhiana nodded. "It seemed appropriate for the day." She turned to Harch. "It's time."

Harch summoned the gate; it billowed out of nothingness and threw hard, cold shadows along the drifted snow.

The guards stepped quickly through, hauling Callion and Val with them. The Kin followed, their steps measured, deliberate, their bodies stiff with anger.

"Our turn," Rhiana said. She walked forward and the few guards who accompanied her took up places before her and behind. Kate stayed behind, keeping herself next to Harch, who because he'd created the gate and was holding it open, would step through it last.

This time Kate felt ready for the falling sensation, for the rippling walls, for the weird internal twisting that had accompanied her first trip along the path that she believed was nothing less than a road between dimensions. She and a guard stepped into the blazing circle of nothingness just behind Rhiana and Tik, and beside Harch.

Something slammed her down hard.

Harch screamed.

The walls wrapped around her and swallowed her up, and left her hanging for a no-time that could have been an instant or an infinity over an abyss as endless and empty as deep space, lacking stars or dust clouds or any light or shape or color; she found nothingness and in it found a silence so total it became an unendurable scream. She hung, helpless, lost . . .

And the world crystallized around her with the tinkling of breaking glass, and she could breathe again. But she could not move. Something tremendously heavy pinned her to soft, snow-covered ground. She heard whimpering to her right, and twisted to look up and behind her; Tik held Rhiana pinned against his chest with the pistol jammed up against her temple so hard the skin all around the muzzle blanched bone white. He also held Kate in place, his left foot pressing firmly on her back.

Harch, or what remained of him, made a frighteningly small pile of ragged, bloody meat a little distance from her. The old wizard's face remained recognizable, but that had to have been by Tik's design. It sat atop the pile, neat beard stained by blood, eyes glazed and half-open, mouth gaping. No one could question the identity of the remains, or the object lesson those remains presented.

Somehow, while still traversing the gate, Tik had killed Harch and grabbed Rhiana before the guards could react. Now he had more weapons than he'd had before.

The troops who had been waiting for Tik to come through the gate faced the three of them, and their faces spoke their outrage and frustration and fear more clearly than words ever could have. In spite of all the plans and all the precautions, Tik held their lady captive and they could do nothing about it. They stood in their ranks to either side of a writhing, pulsing rent in the fabric of reality that felt to Kate like a window into Hell; Kate realized she was looking into the Rift. She had never looked at something purely evil before, but in the Rift she sensed an enemy to all of life, and a vast, cold, awareness that looked back at her and hungered for her blood. If Callion and Tik were the lesser enemies, this hungering, hating void was the greater.

Tik told the troops, "You don't want to move. If you do, you'll be picking pieces of Lady Smeachwykke's head out of the snow until spring thaw."

None of the troops as much as twitched.

"Very good," Tik said to the soldiers. "I know what you planned, but as you can see, we're going to do things a little differently. I don't want to be captured, and I don't want to die. I intend to take Glenraven for the Kin-hera, and in order to do that, I have to live *and* win." He nodded to two of the closer soldiers. "You and you, go cut Callion's bindings. You're going to turn him loose."

The soldiers looked from Tik to Rhiana, and started forward.

"No," Rhiana said. "Attack him. If he kills me it doesn't matter. He intends to kill all of us when he's through anyway."

The soldiers stopped. Tik whipped the pistol around and shot the first one, and he toppled to the ground with a neat bloody hole between his eyes, dead before he could scream. Tik was better with the pistol than he had any business being. Or else he'd been lucky . . . but Kate didn't want to assume luck.

"If you want to be the next dead hero," Tik said to the second one, "by all means listen to Rhiana. If you do as I tell you, I'll let you live." He indicated another soldier. "You, now, go and help him."

The soldiers stood firm.

Tik shot the second one, and the second shot hit as perfectly as the first. As the second man died, the third one, eyes huge, began to move toward Callion.

"You with him," Tik said. The next man in the front row moved out, not listening to Rhiana's demand that he stand fast.

"They won't listen to you, lady. They're listening to the sounds of their own skins," Tik said. "Wise of them to do so."

Kate, flat on her stomach with the dagreth's foot planted in the middle of her back, wondered what she could do to turn the situation around. She thought perhaps she could draw up magic to pass to Rhiana—but then she thought, no, in this world, Rhiana would be able to find and control her own magic.

She considered the sword and the dagger—worthless if she couldn't stand. And the magic bomb . . . useless if Tik wasn't using magic, and maybe worse than useless because it would adversely affect not just him but every magic user in the area.

With his huge foot pressing her into the snow, she felt as helpless as the soldiers who stood watching. But she couldn't accept
helplessness. There had to be something she could do, if only she
could figure out what it might be.

She watched the two soldiers kneel beside Callion with their
knives drawn to cut away the bindings. When Callion was free,
Tik could release the Watchers. Callion would control them, and
she and everyone else would be dead. She had to find a way to
stop what was happening.

Tik's voice interrupted her frantic search for answers. "Kate,
I'm sorry about this."

"You're what?" Kate twisted up and around to look at him again.
He still held Rhiana with the gun against her head, but he was
looking at Kate.

"Sorry. I truly am sorry. I tried everything I could think of to
make sure that you would be safely away from the danger. I
intended to see you home before the purges began."

"Why?"

He shifted his weight a little; his foot no longer rested quite
so firmly on her back. "Because you liked me. And, honestly, I
liked you. Admired you, too. You have backbone. Courage. You
took some hard hits and you didn't roll over and quit on us."

Kate wasn't sure how to respond to this. "You like me so much
you're going to kill me, is that it?"

"Dammit, I didn't want to. I offered to send you home right
away; I drugged you; I spelled you; I locked you in your room.
What else could I do?" He sighed. "I'm afraid it's too late now.
I can't afford to let you go—you're as likely to try and save all
of these stinking sons of dogs as you are to fight with me. Like-
lier, I think."

Kate had to agree with him. She didn't get to tell him what
she thought, though, for he suddenly lost patience with the soldiers
he'd told to free Callion, both of whom still struggled to remove
the binders without noticeable success.

"Why isn't he free yet?"

One of the soldiers, gray-faced, looked up. "Our knives slide
away from the rope before they can touch it. We can't take hold
of it, either. And neither of us knows spells."

Tik said, "So you would have sat there all day, trying the same
things that didn't work over and over again. Bring him here."

Rhiana said, "Those binders won't come off, no matter what
you do, Tik."

"Perhaps not, but I'm betting you can do something to remove them."

Rhiana said nothing.

Tik was about to have to deal with one more variable. Kate forced herself to relax; she made no move, no sound, did nothing to divert Tik's attention from his problems with Callion, the soldiers, and Rhiana. She repeated over and over to herself, *I'm invisible. I'm invisible.*

The soldiers placed Callion on the ground well away from Kate, over to Tik's right side. That angle made it necessary for Tik to twist to see Callion, and when he twisted, his balance changed. Kate could tell he was having a difficult time keeping his foot on her back and holding on to Rhiana too. But he remained aware of her.

I'm invisible, she told herself. *Invisible.*

"Tell me how to remove them," Tik told Rhiana.

Rhiana laughed at him.

"Tell me."

"I won't."

Tik shot the soldier closest to him, once in the chest and once in the head. The man crumpled to the ground. The soldier beside him blanched and tears started from his eyes. Tik aimed the gun at him. "Tell me."

In response, Rhiana swung both arms up at his gun hand; her fingers interlocked as if she were hitting a volleyball. Arm and gun bounced up far enough that Tik shot but missed the man he aimed at. He didn't lose the gun, though. But he did shift, and his foot came all the way off of Kate. She was ready. She rolled, pulled her dagger, and sliced along the back of his heel, aiming for the place where the Achilles tendon would be on a human, and hoping that dagreths had something similar.

The knife ripped through soft tissue, and blood spurted across the snow and Kate's hand. Tik screamed and flung Rhiana across the clearing; her body crashed through the center of the soldiers, who, as soon as Tik released her, charged.

Tik shot the first wave of them. He hit every one of the first attackers, and the men behind them had to climb over the screaming injured and the silent dead.

But he quickly ran out of bullets. He threw the handgun down at his feet and drew his sword.

Kate scrambled to her feet and unsheathed her sword. She held it in her right hand, keeping the point of the blade up and aimed at Tik. She lunged, trying to run him through with the point. She didn't have the years of training or the strength of wrist she needed to make an effective strike, though. Even though he only had the use of one leg, Tik evaded the intended blow and neatly swiped her sword away from her with a little twist of his wrist. It flew across the clearing. He looked at her for just an instant, his eyebrows raised, a half-smile curling along his muzzle to the corners of his mouth. "You should have gone home."

The soldiers hit Tik like a tsunami. He flung them off, his sword whirling like a tornado, ripping faces and slashing through bones as he sent the soldiers flying—but he was outnumbered. He didn't have the time to pull together a spell; he couldn't run or even walk; and even with his back braced against a tree, the soldiers kept coming, attacking with swords and maces and daggers.

He no longer seemed to have much fight in him. He batted them away, but now their blades were finding targets; Tik's arms and hands bled, as did a long, shallow slash through his clothing to his belly. He would fall, Kate thought, but he'd killed a hellish number of men doing it, and maimed more.

He held up the bottle that contained the Watchers, and Kate screamed, "Tik! No!"

Tik looked at her, and in the fraction of an instant that he was distracted, one of the swordsmen got past his guard with a long thrust through the chest. Tik howled and ripped the man to ribbons with his claws, but he went down to both knees as he did.

He looked at Kate again.

"For you," he said, and pulled the stopper out of the bottle and flung it away from himself.

The air filled with a delicate stream of golden lights. Tik crashed facedown to the ground, ramming the sword the rest of the way through his chest and out his back.

The Kin, unarmed and magicless, had until that moment been observers. Now they were the center of the action, as the beautiful, deadly light cloud surrounded them and began to illuminate them.

The Watchers should have gone into the Rift, Kate thought. They should have returned home, but instead they were still hunting.

And Kate remembered what the Fodor's guide had said—that until Callion released them or died, they would never return to their own world, and the Rift would remain open.

Kate fought her way through the surviving troops, and the Kin, who were all fleeing. "Release them," she said to Callion.

He looked at her. Behind her, the screaming echoed through the snow-covered forest—the same screaming she'd heard from the reporter and the cameraman in that Florida mall. She gritted her teeth and waited.

"These people intend to try me and execute me," Callion said. "I won't help them. We can all die together."

"If you're dead, they're released," she said. She put her dagger to his throat.

"Quite right. But you can't kill me. I know people from your world." He grinned at her.

He was helpless, but they were dying. And free, alive, he could summon them again, reopen the Rift. She hesitated only a moment, gritted her teeth, and slashed the dagger across his throat. His eyes widened in surprise and disbelief; his blood poured down his belly.

Tears in her eyes, blood soaking her hands and forearms, Kate turned away from Callion to the forest behind her.

The Watchers were leaving. Leaving. Curling up from the fallen, some of whom still lived, spiraling into the air, spinning and twinkling in a thousand radiant colors. Floating toward the Rift, the hungry, angry, watching Rift. They floated into the void, and for a moment nothing changed.

Then within the void the feeling of awareness intensified— she felt the air around her shift, she felt the hatred and the rage die down, and suddenly she knew that from the other side of that raw wound in reality, something looked out at her. She didn't see a face. She didn't hear a voice. But the hair on the back of her neck and on her arms prickled, and she felt a pressure . . . a desire that she understand. Feelings flowed around her and enveloped her. Gratitude. Relief. Something that could almost have been a mother's rejoicing at the return of a kidnapped child. Sheer exultant joy.

And then the Rift began shrinking, smoothing out, until finally, without fanfare, it erased itself.

Kate stared at the blood on her hands, at the blood-smeared snow, at the bodies that littered the clearing. She looked at Tik, facedown with the tip of a soldier's sword protruding through his back. She stared at Callion, his binding still around his wrists and ankles, his throat cut by her hand.

She rose slowly and looked around. A few other people stood, hanging on to each other. Others crouched in the snow, attending to the wounded or the dead. Kate finally saw Val, kneeling in the snow next to a corpse. Rhiana knelt beside him, speaking softly. Kate realized the dead man had been Val's father. She didn't go to them. She didn't want to speak to anyone, to hear anyone speak to her, to answer questions or ask them. Not yet.

We do what we have to do, she told herself. *In war, when there are no right answers, no easy answers, we do the best we can.*

We do what we have to do.

A gate opened on the other side of the clearing, and a dozen men and women stepped out. The first woman through wore ski pants and a nylon parka. The Watchmistress, Kate thought. The other human.

The woman looked around her and said, "Jesus Christ. What went wrong?"

Forty-three

We could use you here," Jayjay Bennington said.

Kate sat in a comfortable chair next to a roaring fire, opposite the Watchmistress and her mate, Matthiall, a Kin with an easy smile and an infectious laugh. Matthiall laughed then. "Jay would love to have another human here with her. I think she gets lonely, even though she won't admit it."

Kate smiled, but it wasn't a smile she felt. "Glenraven is beautiful. And I'm sure I would make friends here, and . . ." She shrugged.

She wouldn't even pretend to consider the offer. She'd watched the hunting parties going out after the Rift closed, looking for stray monsters trapped in Glenraven. Kate thought of the thing she'd shot in her front yard and imagined running into another one. The parties went out on horseback, the hunters armed with longbows and magic. She listened to the rhythms of speech, to the easy talk of lords and ladies and oaths of fealty. She watched the people on the bottom of the system and realized that no matter how hard they worked, they couldn't rise above their state.

We've gone beyond all of that, she thought.

Jay said, "Yemus, the wizard who created that book you ended up with, took a trip back to our world. He figured out what Callion was doing—breeding half-Aregen children. He evidently intended to bring them back here and reestablish the Aregen race. But you wouldn't have to worry about that. Without him to bring them back, the kids will grow up never knowing what they are. They'll just be kids. Some of them might have real talent in magic, but so what? Other children have been born with the same talent on and off since the first outcasts arrived in our world. Maybe they'll do something good with their lives. Maybe they won't. But the world will keep on spinning."

"It always does that," Kate said.

Rhiana joined them, settling onto the hearth. "Val and I intend to take *eyran* vows after he buries his father," she said. "We'll claim ourselves to be bondmates before the Faldan Kin and the people of Ruddy Smeachwykke, and state that our marriage is political; we intend to unite Faldan and Ruddy Smeachwykke. The fact that we love each other can be for us to know."

"Your people will accept a political marriage but not a marriage for love?"

Rhiana shrugged. "Everyone will be able to see the benefits to themselves, so they'll swallow the distasteful fact that he's Kin and I'm Machnan. If they thought Val and I were the only ones to benefit from the union, they wouldn't accept it."

"It's an ancient world," Jay said. "It isn't perfect, any more than our world is perfect."

Kate stared into the fire, watching the tongues of flame dancing in sinuous arches between the blackened logs, watching sparks fly up the chimney and the soot on the stones in the back curl up and peel away, drawn upward with the sparks by the draft. She looked down at her hands, no longer bathed by blood, but reddened by the glow of the fire until they seemed to be.

We do what we have to do.

In spite of her fear, she had done exactly that. People lived because of her actions who would otherwise have died. Two worlds were safer. In Glenraven, she was a hero, with the promise of an income-producing estate of her own, title, and the knowledge that she was welcome. In her own world, no one would ever know what she had done, and even if she tried to tell, no one would ever believe her.

She had been a soldier chosen for her special skills, for her willingness to serve, and she had done what she had to do, frightening and difficult and ugly as it had been.

But the moment of dire need, of expediency, had passed. The moment when she had been needed, when she had been the only one who could do what she had to do . . . all of that was gone.

Now she had to get on with her life.

And her life belonged in her world.

Not in Peters, certainly. She had come to see that Peters was a fight she couldn't win, so she wouldn't stay and fight. Peters had no place for her. But Peters wasn't everything, or even very much of anything.

She'd lost a lot. She'd lost her family long ago, when they insisted that she be someone other than the person she was. She'd lost the people she'd thought were her friends, the ones she'd created as replacement family, and for much the same reason. She'd lost all of her things. Most of her past. The harsh events that brought her at last to Glenraven had stripped away everything she couldn't live without, and she'd discovered she could live without almost everything. Her desire to belong with other people and the pleasure she took in her possessions had hidden from her the truth; that she could depend on herself.

She knew who she was.

She'd tested herself in a crucible and discovered that she wasn't precisely who she'd always believed herself to be. She'd also found out she was tougher and more capable than she'd ever suspected and that she could trust herself in tight places and critical situations.

She knew what she wanted.

She wanted her world. She wanted her work. She wanted to create things that were beautiful for people who appreciated them, in a place where people let her be who she was.

Someday she would make friends again. Someday she might find love again. But she wouldn't waste her time looking for love, searching for friends, chasing after happiness. She would instead pursue the challenges of living her life in a way that mattered, doing the things she believed were important, taking the stands she felt she had to take in order to be true to herself.

Eventually, she thought, happiness would pursue her.

She glanced at the people who watched her, waiting to hear her decision. And she said something that surprised her. "Those kids could be more than just kids if they were pointed in the right direction. I'm going home, and I'm going to rebuild my life . . . but I'm going to find them, too. Maybe see if I can't do something to point them in the direction of honor. I don't think that bringing magic to my world would be a bad thing at all. The Machine World needs some magic."

Rhiana frowned. "You're blind to it, Kate. How can you teach anyone to use what you can't even see?"

Yemus laughed softly. Everyone turned to look at him. He turned to Jayjay Bennington and said, "I thought when I had the bookstore and when I recruited you and Sophie to come to our world, that my work there wasn't done. When I went back and found the wizard-children waiting, I became even more sure of that. But now I see where my path lies, too." He smiled at Kate. "I'm coming with you." His eyes were warm and kind. "You need a friend. You need a teacher. And you need someone to watch your back. Together, we'll go through Callion's records and track down his children. Together we'll figure out a way to turn what he intended as evil into something good."

Kate studied him. "You don't belong in my world, though."

The wizard shrugged. "I liked it when I was there. I could like it again." His words spoke of mere contentment, but his eyes, when they looked into hers, wondered at other possibilities. Private, personal questions . . . things that only long acquaintance and close proximity might answer.

Kate found herself smiling. Perhaps happiness began to pursue her already.